Lambert, A

GOLDEN LADS AND GIRLS

ANGELA LAMBERT

Golden Lads and Girls

F/450826

BANTAM PRESS

LONDON • NEW YORK • TORONTO • SYDNEY • AUCKLAND

TRANSWORLD PUBLISHERS LTD
61–63 Uxbridge Road, London W5 5SA

TRANSWORLD PUBLISHERS
c/o RANDOM HOUSE AUSTRALIA PTY LTD
20 Alfred Street, Milsons Point, NSW 2061, Australia

TRANSWORLD PUBLISHERS
c/o RANDOM HOUSE NEW ZEALAND
c/o Poland Road, Glenfield, Auckland, New Zealand

TRANSWORLD PUBLISHERS
c/o RANDOM HOUSE PTY LTD
Endulini, 5a Jubilee Road, Parktown 2193, South Africa

Published 1999 by Bantam Press
a division of Transworld Publishers Ltd

Copyright © Angela Lambert 1999

A catalogue record for this book is available
from the British Library.
ISBN 0593 041534

Typeset in Erhardt 12/14pt by Falcon Oast Graphic Art

Printed in England by Clays Ltd, St Ives plc

To my sister Minna,
who lives in and loves Dorset

ACKNOWLEDGEMENTS

In 1942–3 Mrs Priscilla Napier wrote a wonderful verse documentary entitled *Plymouth in War* (broadcast on Radio Four fifty years later). More than anything else, this vivid portrait of a city under attack helped me to understand and recreate the language and attitudes of the war years. Priscilla's clear, compassionate memory and her intelligence, stoicism and self-deprecating humour were an inspiration. After I had finished this book she died, aged ninety-three, in October 1998. I wish she could have read these words and known how great is my debt to her.

I am grateful to Stephen Chaplin, archivist at the Slade School of Fine Art, for his generosity and the care with which he supplied information about the Slade in the 1920s, later checking my typescript for errors, and for his scrupulous corrections.

Jenny Hartley eliminated hours of work by directing me straight to the relevant material on women during the last war. *Hearts Undefeated* (Virago, 1994), her anthology of women's writing during the Second World War, was essential reading. To her as well, my thanks. In the course of writing this book I read many novels and short stories set in the 1940s, too many to list, that helped me comprehend the war and women's part in it. For factual details I found Caroline Seebohm's *The Country House, A Wartime History, 1939–45* (Weidenfeld & Nicolson, 1989) and

Norman Longmate's *How We Lived Then* (Hutchinson 1971) particularly useful.

As always, Peter Scott leaped in to breach my ignorance with his omniscient military expertise. He knew exactly what sort of German gun would kill at two hundred yards, the status of conscientious objectors during the Second World War and how a fighter plane falls from the sky. Thanks to him, such details are accurate.

Dr S. Bhate from the University of Newcastle helped me on some early chapters with professional guidance on pre-adolescent sexuality. I am very grateful to him.

Dr Peter Jones, my learned fax friend, answered questions on all matters of language, slang and derivation. Another friend, John Morris, shared his entrepreneurial knowledge, thereby making the business dealings of the fictional Staunton Trading Company a good deal more convincing than they would otherwise have been. Jenny Towndrow corrected my pathetic efforts at Australian slang. My friend and neighbour, Mme Michèle Delpech, corrected my French. Sam Boyce's perceptive comments were invaluable.

My sister Monica willingly ferreted out books and information about Dorset, in particular the bit where she lives. To her and her father-in-law, Major Jack St Aubyn, whose knowledge of its wartime history was also helpful, many thanks!

And as always, Tony Price - my partner, researcher, first reader and last re-reader, builder, fixer and as often as not cook. Without his support and indulgence my last six books could not have been written, as he well knows. Thanks, my love.

Angela Lambert, Groléjac, September 1994–November 1998

'Golden lads and girls all must,
As chimney-sweepers, come to dust.'

Shakespeare, *Cymbeline*, Act IV, scene 2
from the song 'Fear No More the Heat o' th' Sun'

Relevant members of the
BLYTHGOWRIE FAMILY

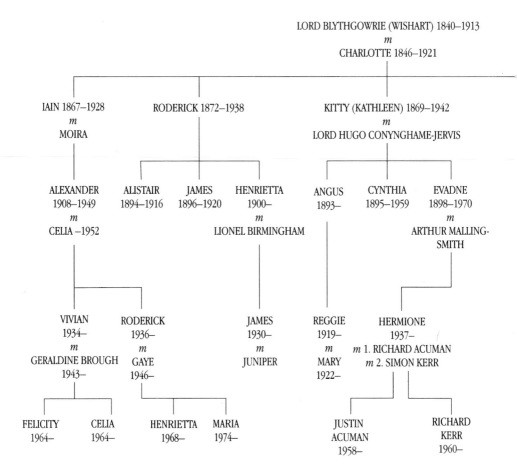

LORD BLYTHGOWRIE (WISHART) 1840–1913
m
CHARLOTTE 1846–1921

IAIN 1867–1928
m
MOIRA

RODERICK 1872–1938

KITTY (KATHLEEN) 1869–1942
m
LORD HUGO CONYNGHAME-JERVIS

ALEXANDER
1908–1949
m
CELIA –1952

ALISTAIR
1894–1916

JAMES
1896–1920

HENRIETTA
1900–
m
LIONEL BIRMINGHAM

ANGUS
1893–

CYNTHIA
1895–1959

EVADNE
1898–1970
m
ARTHUR MALLING-
SMITH

VIVIAN
1934–
m
GERALDINE BROUGH
1943–

RODERICK
1936–
m
GAYE
1946–

JAMES
1930–
m
JUNIPER

REGGIE
1919–
m
MARY
1922–

HERMIONE
1937–
m 1. RICHARD ACUMAN
m 2. SIMON KERR

FELICITY
1964–

CELIA
1964–

HENRIETTA
1968–

MARIA
1974–

JUSTIN
ACUMAN
1958–

RICHARD
KERR
1960–

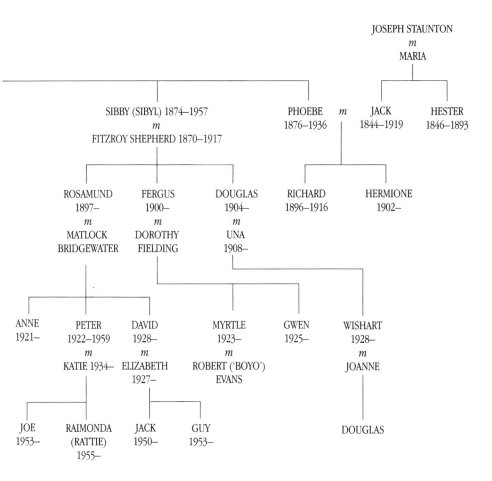

PART ONE

Golden Lads and Girls

May 1911 – spring 1920

CHAPTER ONE

HERMIONE STAUNTON WAS NINE WHEN SHE REALIZED SHE WAS IN love with Sandy Gordon-Lockhart, who was eleven, and although she wouldn't have used those exact words to describe the feeling, she never forgot the moment. Sandy was competing in the sack race. He was conspicuous among the stumbling village boys, his red hair bouncing up and down as he travelled over the grass in great leaps, hurtling ahead like a kangaroo, jaw set with determination, eyes on the finishing tape. He won by two yards before falling down entangled in his sack. Clambering out, he ran across to commiserate with the lad who had come second. Sandy seemed ringed in sunlight, a golden boy. Why did the leap from playmate to beloved occur at that precise moment? Because she hadn't known, till she saw him win everything, how godlike he was – because her father praised him – because they were children, ardent as the dawn – because his nature was trusting and cheerful, quite different from her own – or simply because at that moment, glowing and grinning and breathless, he was the image of sturdy boyhood? Was it because they shared a dog (his Labrador, Bobby) and Hours of Fun for Boys and Girls, as promised on the cardboard boxes containing their board games (Ludo, Peggotty, Nine

15

Men's Morris, L'Attaque)? Whatever the reason, all at once Hermione was in love. The grown-ups would have pooh-poohed any such idea. Love without consummation, without desire or even awareness of physical passion – impossible! Between children? What nonsense.

This was May 1911, the mythical Indian summer of the British Empire; the climax of the Edwardian era, soon to end with the death of the King, whose giant bulk and giant heart were fighting a losing battle. Meanwhile in the depths of Dorset the annual village fête was taking place on a green-striped lawn dividing the walled kitchen garden of the great house from its ornamental maze. The usual fête; the usual great house. Girls and young women from the village dipping and skipping round the maypole; people bobbing wet faces into barrels for sharp green apples pock-marked by birds; excited children queuing and squabbling. The occasion had been announced before Easter with a notice on the board in the church porch:

> By kind permission of Sir Jack and the Hon. Lady Staunton
> ... Grand Bazaar and Fête to be held at Chantry Manor ...
> maypole dancing ... stalls, competitions, raffles (prizes kindly
> donated by Sir Jack Staunton) – Entrance Free, contributions
> to the National Seamen's Fund welcome. Boys and girls, come
> and ride on the camel! Penny a go, 6d. for five!

The last announcement had been crossed out and amended in pencil, *5d. for six!* Beside that someone else had written, *Aint got it.*

Hermione drooped with boredom beside her parents. Mama said girls should stand still and keep a straight back, be seen and not heard. She wore a muslin dress with a sash round her waist and her thick brown hair was kept in place with a ribbon. Her feet were encased in long white socks and buttoned boots of tender white leather. Beneath her soft, pliant outer clothing she wore several undergarments: a vest, liberty bodice, bloomers and a petticoat. It was a very warm day.

Hermione's parents, Jack and Phoebe Staunton, inclined graciously towards their neighbours, Violet and Donald Gordon-

Lockhart. They were all pretending to watch the village boys competing for trophies. Phoebe Staunton – who would shortly present the prizes – was the youngest of the four; tiny, wasp-waisted, with shrewd, veiled eyes. For the moment she was directing shy smiles and little sighs at poor old Donald. She had not the slightest interest in her neighbour but flirting was her way of communicating with men. Donald slipped two fingers inside the rim of his collar to ease it and wiped the hand surreptitiously against his linen trousers.

'Ho'-uh-ho'-uh-*hot* weather for May!' he said. 'Those chaps ruhu-running about . . .' but the remark petered out, as Donald's remarks often did.

Jack Staunton was keen to talk, without upsetting the ladies, about the prospects of imminent war or – equally alarming – what would happen if the House of Lords stood firm against Lloyd George. The child beside them, impatient with the conversation, felt restless, mutinous, trapped, but she knew she must wait for a break in the talk, or for someone to ask, ''Mione, dear, what would *you* like to do?' knowing also that there was little hope of either. She heard the bang of the starter's gun and turned to watch the next race. That was when she fell in love.

Afterwards she stood like one of the marble statues in the maze, rooted, transfixed, as Sandy came racing across the lawn. His mother Violet moved towards him with a pretty mime of applause, her long skirt trailing like the wake of a ship, foaming bubbles of lace tripping over the sheared grass. She steered him over to the group and Sir Jack Staunton nodded towards the boy, saying in a strong northern accent, 'Your young fellow put on a good show.'

'Oh Jack . . . just village lads,' she murmured deprecatingly and, turning to his wife, 'Phoebe! So good of you both. These races must *ruin* the lawn . . .'

'Violet, congratulations, my dear – Alexander's a natural athlete! He's come first in practically everything, even against the older boys. *So* much vigour and go.'

Sandy, flushed and panting, looked modestly at his feet. His mother answered, 'One is going to have to tell him not to be so competitive. It isn't as though he needs the silver egg-cup; he simply can't stop going full pelt! Poor Hermione – life *is* tiresome for girls, always watching and hardly ever able to join in. *How* old are you, dear?' Not pausing for a reply, Violet turned to Phoebe. 'How I *envy* you. She can stay at home. In another year Sandy will be off to Eton. Gracious, I shall miss him . . . especially since he's the only one.'

Donald, her lanky, ginger-haired husband, was silent. He worshipped his son but it would be unmanly to say so, even if he could be sure the right words would emerge when he opened his mouth.

'It was my birthday last month,' Hermione answered in the pause. (You may speak when spoken to. Hold your head up. Look at the person you're addressing. Answer clearly.) 'I was nine on April the fourteenth.' When she was eight she had been only a little girl but at nine she knew the rivers of Europe, common British birds, the capital cities of the world, the tartans worn by each Scottish clan on ordinary and ceremonial occasions, the order of the Roman emperors and the movement of the planets round the sun. Now she also knew who she would marry when she was old enough.

'You look very grown-up for your age!' Violet meant tall.

'She's already taller than I am – how shall we ever manage to stop her growing?' Phoebe Staunton said with a little laugh. 'We shall have to put her in a box and nail it down.' Hermione looked at her mother in horror.

'Oh, I don't think we'll do *that* . . .' Jack Staunton said, pronouncing it '*thutt*'. He placed a reassuring hand on his daughter's shoulder, wondering why his wife was driven to torment her.

Phoebe glanced at her daughter's tense, anguished face and thought, I shall never understand her. Richard is clear and candid and I can tell by his face what he's thinking, but then he's a male and I can always handle them. *This* lanky, frowning child could be a changeling, except that mothers always know their own children.

While their parents stood talking Sandy gazed around, vital and curious. The two children had been neighbours in Dorset all their lives. Hermione's brother Richard was six years ahead of her, but six years yawn like a canyon between a girl of nine and a schoolboy of fifteen. Sandy was just two and a quarter years older – the perfect age gap – and he drew her after him like a magnet throughout

18

their childhood. Hermione thought, only another year and a bit before he is sent away! I vow to make the most of every day.

'I saw you win the sack race just now,' she told him. 'You went frightfully fast.'

'*Too* fast, Sandy dear,' his mother said. 'It's rather unsporting of you to bag all the prizes. You should give the others, the poor village fellows, a chance.' She bent over and whispered in his ear, 'One mustn't be swaggish, you know.'

'Very well, I'll sit the next two out. It's the egg and spoon race and the three-legged donkey. Can Hermione and me go and watch the maypole?'

Hermione flashed an instantaneous plea towards her father, who caught her look and said, before her mother could find a reason to refuse, 'That's very civil, young man. You may indeed, and then perhaps you'd bring her to the marquee for tea. Her mama will present the prizes for horticulture first.'

'Where's Nanny . . .?' said Lady Staunton, looking around, but her daughter had already set off, joyously nannyless.

Hermione reached a hand towards Sandy, for everyone always held her hand when taking her somewhere, but realizing that he would be embarrassed to be seen holding hands with her in public she altered the movement into an upward swing of curiosity.

'What did you win?' she asked.

'Nothing. A penny,' he answered carelessly.

'Mama gives me five shillings every Sunday, for the church collection and the poor children and the Church Mission to Africa,' she said.

Sandy was aghast. '*Five shillings!* I say, that's a great deal!'

'Is it? I don't know. I never get any of it. Nanny says one must learn to consider those less fortunate than oneself.'

Changing the subject he asked, 'Do you really want to see the maypole?'

'Not much. What shall we do instead?'

He was pleased that she didn't insist on the maypole, or ask ingratiatingly what *he* wanted to do, like most girls.

'Do you want to ride the camel?'

'There's already lots of people waiting.'

19

He looked across and saw a queue of sweaty children and a pot-bellied camel swaying reluctantly along the sand-strewn track.

'I daresay you're right. Come and see me toss hoops over pegs then. You get ten goes for a halfpenny.'

'Can I try, too?'

'I don't suppose you'll be much good at it.'

'I've got a very accurate eye, Papa says.'

They made their way past groups of servants – flushed and grinning, though they tried to straighten their faces as the children approached – and through knots of villagers, not noticing how they stood back to allow their passage since people always did and both children took it for granted. Under an awning in a booth they watched half a dozen youths playing hoop-la: squinting and aiming and throwing coloured rings at a set of wooden pegs hammered into a board propped up five paces away. One in particular was very skilled and the others teased him incomprehensibly.

'Look at 'im, gets 'is peg in 'ole every toime, does Jacko!'

'Aye, and Molly Dinsdale's proof on it!'

They laughed raucously. Sandy looked away, but before he could take Hermione away the stallholder, recognizing her (he was one of the estate foresters), asked, 'Why don't thee take a turn, miss?'

Hermione looked at Sandy, who held out his penny.

'A go for her, please, and one for me. She can start.'

Beginners' luck. Hermione's first hoop curled through the air in an adorable arc of perfect accuracy and dropped on to the projecting hoop. Over-excited by success, she missed with the second and third. Then she slowed down, calmed herself and curving her wrist inwards, steadied her hand so as to toss the hoop in the same shallow parabola as the first. It dropped over the peg.

'I say, jolly good throw!' Sandy murmured.

She ordered her muscles to repeat the movement exactly, and, in perfect imitation of the previous one, her fifth hoop fell neatly over the peg as though the two had never been apart.

'Your papa is right!' he said.

Trying too hard to impress him, Hermione answered in her clear, piping diction, 'Yes, and Molly Dinsdale proves it.'

The booth exploded in a shout of laughter. The watching youths behind her slapped their thighs and roared. They thumped their fists against one another's backs, stamped their feet and howled with glee.

'Clear off, you lot!' shouted the man in charge of the booth. 'You've had your turn – now clear off.'

A stocky, stunted child – daughter of one of the Chantry staff – caught Hermione's glance in a piercing bond of shame. The last five hoops went awry and she stood aside, her cheeks flaring.

'Your turn . . .' she muttered to Sandy.

Red-faced with laughter, the village youths shambled off, to bowl for the pig or watch little girls dressed up as flower fairies hopping about while the vicar's wife tinkled and nodded at the piano.

A few days later, Hermione and her mother drove over to tea with the Gordon-Lockharts. Brymer steered the newly acquired Lanchester through wet country lanes spilling with lush creamy blossom, past golden fields in which young corn and young weeds were shooting with equal abundance, described a slow sweep across the raked gravel circle and drew up in front of Otterbourne Court. Sandy must have been watching, for his first words as the butler showed them into the drawing room were, 'I say, what a spiffing motor car!'

'After your tea perhaps Lady Staunton would allow you a ride in it?' his mother said, arching interrogative eyebrows towards Phoebe. 'I'm afraid *we* aren't nearly so modern. Donald cannot bear to give up the carriage. One might almost think,' she simpered, 'he loved those horses more than his wife!'

'Let young Alexander take you up to the nursery now, Hermione dear,' said her mother, scenting a promising exchange about their respective husbands. 'Have Nanny bring you downstairs at five and Brymer will take you both for a spin.'

Hermione felt her heart light as a bubble in her chest. She and Sandy turned and left the room, then ran up the polished wooden staircase to the top floor where the nursery maid had laid out scones and sandwiches, Nice biscuits and a Victoria sponge. When they had made decent inroads into the food Sandy led

her to the schoolroom. Arrayed on an old billiard table was a magnificent panorama that he and his father had built, using a vast army of tin soldiers and showing the battle of Isandhlwana.

'Oh look!' said Hermione. 'Where's the Zulu leader? What's he called? – Cetewayo or something. I like him best.'

'You can't,' Sandy told her. 'He's a fuzzy-wuzzy. You're not allowed to like *him*.'

'Why not?' she asked. 'I feel sorry for him. He was frightfully brave and I'm sure he knew it would be the last Zulu battle.'

They argued fiercely, moving the soldiers behind tussocks of dried moss and knocking men over to show they had been killed. At the end Sandy said, 'You're pretty good, for a girl.'

'My brother Richard told me all about it. He's keen on soldiering. And Papa – he's *been* to Africa, you know – Papa gave me a topping book called *Jock of the Bushveld* – and I'm reading *She*, only Nanny doesn't know or she'd say it was a boys' book, about Leo Vincey and Ayesha, the mighty Queen who never dies. *And I've read Allan Quatermain.'*

'I've read that too – and *King Solomon's Mines* as well,' said Sandy.

Quits. They were equals in everything, even though she was younger and a girl. Hermione asked him what he thought her mother had meant by threatening to nail her down in a box to stop her growing. Sandy thought it was only a joke – the sort of joke grown-ups made about children, never about each other.

'It's not my fault that I'm tall,' she protested. 'Papa's not a bit tall, nor's Mama. It isn't as though I mean to grow. I just can't stop. *You* don't care, do you?'

They stood back to back, stretching their spines, and Sandy flattened his palm across the tops of their heads.

'We're the same,' he announced. Taking a deep breath, he added, 'This is awful cheek so you don't have to answer. Do you – I mean – well, do you *like* your mama?'

'I *love* her, though not *quite* as much as I love Papa, and she's awfully pretty, everyone says so.' She paused, holding the dark truth under her tongue like a piece of liquorice she wanted to spit out. Until now Hermione had denied it even to herself, but she had no secrets from Sandy. Though she took a deep breath, her voice was barely audible. 'All the same, do you know, I don't *really* like her – not like I like Papa or Dick or Nanny – even though she *is* my mama.' To show he must never tell anyone she uttered their code words, the sacred oath of loyalty from the Seeonee Wolf Pack, 'We be of one blood, Thou and I!'

Sandy nodded. 'Does she *know* how wretched she makes you?'

'I don't think so. Anyway she wouldn't care. Richard's her favourite.'

'She *should* care,' he said indignantly. 'I've seen her be beastly to you at times.'

'Nobody could *want* to be that horrid. She does it by mistake.'

'Maybe,' Sandy concluded. 'Everyone tries to be good, but grown-ups don't try as hard as they expect us to.'

Goodness, she thought, he doesn't mind. I have owned up to the worst thing in the world and he doesn't mind. He noticed how horrid Mama is to me. No one else really understands, not even Papa. She jumped up.

'Come on, the rain's stopped! Let's go out. Race you down the stairs!'

They could meet almost every day because Sandy was being educated at home by a tutor and a governess. An attack of diphtheria when he was six had weakened his heart and his mother insisted on keeping him under her own roof rather than subjecting him to the rigours of a prep school, with cold dormitories, cold showers and morning runs. This concession had been wrung from his father in return for the promise that she would not interfere when the time came for Sandy to be sent to Eton.

Sandy and Hermione made up secret games. Their favourite came from H. Rider Haggard's African tales with added bits from Kipling and the Mowgli stories. They both had a passion for adventure and danger, jungle or veldt but preferred to play outside, for in the nursery Nanny might come and shatter the mood by saying, 'Now, now, what's going on? More of your nonsense and malarkey!'

They often slipped away after lunch, creeping down the back stairs and out of the back door, then dashing for the cover of the woods. They followed old drovers' paths, almost invisible, to their favourite hideouts. At other times they would climb trees – oaks were good but cedars best of all – to dangle their legs from the branches, rapt in fantasies of Kipling's jungle, the prehistoric plateau of Conan Doyle's lost world, or the scorching plains of Africa. Hermione would always be Ayesha; Sandy was Leo Vincey. Bobby the dog could be wolf or tiger, wildebeest or lion, whatever they needed.

'*Whence comest thou, oh bold traveller, intruding upon my kingdom, yeah, even into my very temple?*' she would demand, chin held high.

'*To pay thee homage, oh great Queen, and learn thy timeless secrets!*' Sandy would answer humbly.

'*Come closer then, foolish mortal, but know that thy life is in great, in most great danger . . .*' and at the warning in her voice the lions and leopards that guarded her would take a step forward and growl deep in their golden throats.

'*He who would know the secrets of the universe must also brave its dangers, oh mightiest of women!*' Sandy would reply.

'*Thou speakest truly; thy words, I own, do please me. Approach. It is centuries since I looked upon one of the white race.*'

'*We are masters in all the world – save here, oh noble Ayesha, and here amid these endless plains thou art Queen of all thou surveyest!*'

At other times they would build a cave and he would kneel in homage before her and kiss her outstretched hand. This made the guardian beasts look aside jealously, flicking their tails.

'*Peace, curs!*' she would fling at them – so convincingly that Bobby cowered at her imperious tone. She would pause, for she could never resist the dog, and say, 'Here, Bobby – it's only *me*! There, there, poor old Bobby, did I scare you?'

'You've spoiled the game now . . .' Sandy would mutter sulkily.

'No I haven't – look, I'm back again: *Tell me, pale young foreigner with copper hair from distant lands, how cam'st thou here? Are all men in thy country as noble of countenance as thou?*'

Sandy marvelled at her ability to transform herself from tomboy into ancient ruler. Her regal bearing thrilled him; the long brown arm she held out to him, the grubby little hand he kissed, smelling warmly of earth and bracken – these were not the gestures of a little girl and nor, increasingly, were his the responses of a little boy. He had no idea, yet, that he loved her. They gave one another special names, to show that this part of their lives was different from their top-floor, nursery and schoolroom selves. They took an H as prefix, from H. Rider Haggard, adding Minor for her – because it sounded like Hermione and because she was younger – and Major for him. When they were alone they called each other H. Minor and H. Major, soon shortened to Major and Minor.

Sandy's father, if he noticed them at all, dismissed them as a pair of scallywags. Their mothers called them comical little creatures. The nursery maids, tutting over torn clothes and dirty shirts, said they were more trouble than a barrel-load of monkeys. Only the dwarf-child watched them enviously from her own hiding places, wondering what it must be like to be so close, so tall and so free.

Hermione's brother Richard, briefly home from the summer half at Eton before going to stay with a schoolmate, warned Sandy, 'Don't tell the fellows at school that you play with a *girl*. You'll get a frightful ragging!'

'Will I?'

'Why?' Hermione asked defensively. 'Girls are just as good as boys!'

'Oh no they aren't,' Richard said.

'They *are* – aren't I, Sandy?'

Treacherously, Sandy was silent.

Sometimes, when her mother had guests for a Saturday-to-Monday, Hermione would be presented to the company before dinner. Nanny would escort her downstairs in a clean frock and push her towards her mother, who smelled of scent and the sweet pomade she smoothed into her abundant hair. Her father smelled more strongly of cigar smoke, shoe polish and dogs. When he had been out walking or shooting his clothes smelled of sweat, but for the drawing room he would change into something less scratchy and pungent. Hermione ran into his arms whatever he was wearing.

Her mother recoiled from an attempted embrace, saying with an airy laugh, 'Careful, 'Mione, you'll bowl Mama over! You're such a big girl. You must learn to move more gracefully.' Yet at other times Mama might stretch a hand towards her saying, 'Come here, Hermione, and say how-do-you-do to *this* gentleman . . .'

She had to suffer the ordeal of a strange man's overwhelming smell, his facetious remarks, and sometimes his rough moustache or beard as he gave her a wet kiss while the ladies laughed. Then he would fish in his waistcoat pocket for a threepenny bit and she had to look very pleased and thank him, whereupon he might pinch her cheek or kiss her moistly again.

Once, in the drawing room before dinner, one of the strange ladies asked in a fluting voice, 'If a good fairy gave you one wish, what would you wish for, dear child, hmm?'

'A little brother,' Hermione said, 'or if I can't have one, then a baby sister. But Mama never finds any.'

They all laughed at that and one of the men chortled under his breath, 'Go to it, Jack!' Her mother had frowned and, after a moment, sat down at the piano to play and sing. One of the visiting gentlemen stood beside her turning the pages of her music. She smiled at him, but not at Hermione.

None of this troubled her as long as she and Sandy were left to their own devices. These were innocent, but their parents might not have thought so if they had seen Sandy lying worshipfully at Hermione's feet, or noted how intently she memorized his thickly tangled hair and the long muscles that bunched and relaxed along the back of his calves as he climbed the hillside ahead of her. Hermione often came home in the evenings covered with scratches and bruises. 'I slipped on a rock,' she told Nanny. Never reveal more than they need to know. Don't tell fibs if you can help it. Above all, tell nobody – *nobody* – about Sandy Gordon-Lockhart.

The summer heatwave rumbled on. The temperature stayed in the nineties day after day. Nanny in her thick belted uniform grumbled about prickly heat. She undid her belt and buttons and lay on her bed like a navy-blue seal, panting and fanning herself. The nursery maids were red-faced and listless. Sweat left half-moons under their arms. Even Hermione's mother wilted, her delicate lawn dresses wilting too in the relentless heat. Hermione was allowed to wear Aertex shirts and an old pair of knee-length linen shorts that had belonged to Richard. She was even spared her constricting cotton liberty bodices when Nanny remembered that Aertex against the skin was healthy because it let the pores breathe. In the long indolent hours when everyone else lay about becalmed no one bothered about Hermione and Sandy, each household assuming they must be with the other. Under a scorching sun the two dawdled through the heather, their skin gradually ripening like apricots. Bobby panted behind them, alert for the thump of a rabbit or the clatter of a rising bird.

One dozy afternoon, as bees zigzagged in the heather and grasshoppers ratcheted, Hermione, abandoned to the stillness, sprawled on a clump of grass. She picked a dandelion clock and blew on its feathery spikes, counting, 'One, two, three . . .' as the seeds drifted in the windless heat. She was thinking, this – *this* very moment – is what happiness feels like. Her eyes were closed. Sandy dropped to his knees beside her and looked into her sunburned face and the way her eyelashes lay in a shiny curve across her cheeks, like moths' antennae under his schoolroom microscope. Her mouth was relaxed and there were shadowy indentations in its upturned corners. She looked frightfully pretty all of a sudden, nearly as pretty as his mother. When he felt like this about his mother he put his arms round her and kissed her scented cheek. He leaned forward impulsively and kissed Hermione's warm skin. She sighed deeply without opening her eyes. After a moment he apologized.

'What for?'

'I daresay I ought not to have . . .'

'I liked it. I shan't tell anyone.'

'See? You thought it was wrong, too.'

'No I don't, not wrong in the least. But it's private and they wouldn't understand.'

She still lay back with her eyes closed. Suddenly she sat up and the tangled hair swung round her warm golden face.

'Shall I kiss *you* now?'

He was flustered. 'I don't know.'

'Don't you want me to?'

'I don't know. One doesn't kiss people, much.'

'I do. I kiss Papa and Mama and sometimes Nanny. Why shouldn't I kiss you?'

'I'll think about it.'

She knew, then, that he was serious. He could have said no and scrambled up and run off laughing; or he could have said yes, treating it as no more than a little girl's silly sentimental affection. But he had stopped to consider the significance of a kiss and that must mean it was important.

'Careful, Minor!' he said. 'There's a bee – just by your neck – don't let it – I'll . . .' He leaned close to blow the bee away and as it zoomed off, Hermione felt the breeze of his breath on her skin. Murmuring 'Thanks!' she turned and kissed his cheek where the line of his jaw ended under his right ear. Then she sat up and looked for another dandelion clock.

September was their last month before the rule of his tutor and her governess resumed. Richard, who was considered old enough at fifteen to stalk and shoot, had been sent to his grandparents at Gowrie Castle. Hermione's parents had sailed down the French coast and moored outside Biarritz. She had been afraid that Sandy's people might take him to Scotland for a fortnight's shooting but, alarmed by the rioting in August, they even had second thoughts about going themselves. In the end they decided to risk the train – nothing could happen to first-class passengers – but Sandy was left behind. Eleven *was* rather young to be handling a rifle. Left to themselves, Sandy and Hermione gorged from the laden bushes in the fruit cages before heading through fields dotted with stooks of corn towards the furthest boundaries of the Staunton estate. They returned hours later, overwhelmed by feelings more intense than those of the absent parents at their dinner-table flirtations. At the end of each day they had to part. Sandy would collect his pony from the stables and trot home under the eye of Billy the groom, or Brymer would be summoned to drive Hermione home. There she was undressed and given a brisk rub-down in the bathroom by Nanny, while the last rays of sunshine zigzagged between slats in the duckboard. For the rest of her life, whenever there was a heatwave, Hermione would be tormented by nostalgia for that lost and perfect summer.

CHAPTER TWO

HOLIDAYS ENDED, TO BE REPLACED BY THE SCHOOLROOM ROUTINE
– exercise books, blackboard and ruler, compass and protractor,
questions and answers. Hermione was far from stupid but she had
been educated at home by governesses, mademoiselles, fräuleins.
She spoke good French for her age and passable German, though
with quaint and outdated inflections, but she knew nothing whatsoever about physics, chemistry or anything remotely scientific or
mechanical. Her father, too, had been taught by amateurs: in his
case a Dame school mistress until he was twelve and in later years
by his own efforts, but any idea that his daughter might be sent
away to be properly educated was overruled by her mother.

'I won't hear of it, Jack. Girl doesn't need to be clever. Much
more important to have nice manners and a pretty face.'

Imprisoned in the schoolroom, Hermione and Sandy could
meet only once or twice a week. Hermione consoled herself by
trying to draw him. This was how she first discovered her gift. She
would focus unseeingly, conjure up Sandy's profile in her mind's
eye and transfer its outline to paper. She achieved an unerring likeness every time. She became more ambitious, catching the
moment when he swung his leg over a fence, sat astride the branch

of a tree or crouched beside his golden-haired dog. Bobby's tongue would loll from his mouth in the parody of a smile and Sandy's would be the grin of dog ownership.

Hermione's pencil could convey all this. She didn't show these drawings to Sandy – only some sketches of the dog – let alone to anyone else.

One evening, as her parents played a listless game of Bezique, their watching daughter sketched them both on the flyleaf of her book. Her mother's face was reduced to its essentials: the long-nosed, delicate profile, her neck elongated by shining dark hair drawn up from the nape and piled in a graceful sweep on the crown of her head. Below the shoulders a squiggly line indicated the ruffles of her fichu. Her father's profile, by contrast, jutted heavily from between his broad hunched shoulders, his con-centration conveyed by deep parallel frowning lines, his reddish goatee beard jutting too above a barrel chest.

When Hermione's head had ceased looking up and down from the drawing book her mother called out, 'Bring it over here, 'Mione! Show Mama!'

She shut the book protectively but her father turned, too.

'What? Show what?'

'Didn't you notice? The child has been drawing us while we played at cards.'

Reluctantly Hermione offered them the book.

Her mother frowned. 'So unkind: she's given me a double chin!'

But her father said, 'They're remarkably good! Wouldn't you say, Phoebe, she has real talent?'

Her mother dared not disagree or disparage the daughter who, along with Richard, was their only common interest.

'Talent, I don't know. She's certainly caught your likeness.'

'*You* try,' he said.

Phoebe Staunton took the pencil but after a few strokes she threw it down crossly. Beside Hermione's sketches her own attempt was hopelessly inadequate.

'It's harder than it looks,' she conceded.

From then on a drawing mistress called Miss Williams was engaged to teach Hermione twice a week. If anything she

30

constricted rather than encouraged their daughter's gift but she did convey the rudiments of technique: the use of watercolours (although prim Miss Williams modelled herself upon the tight little efforts of Queen Victoria rather than the joyful freedom of Turner), the different hardness of pencils with which to capture variations of light and shade, fine strokes and broad ones. Best of all, she brought faded brown portfolios containing reproductions and etchings purchased during one long-ago journey to Italy. These, when their fragile ribbons were untied for the first time in many years, formed Hermione's introduction to Giotto, Fra Angelico and the great Italian masters. They, and not her drawing teacher, opened her eyes.

But Miss Williams stole precious hours that might have been spent with Sandy. During the dark winter days and evenings she hardly saw him at all. Once or twice a month, perhaps, her mother might drive over to take tea with Violet Gordon-Lockhart; once a week Sandy might be allowed to ride his pony over to Chantry. It was thin gruel after the lavish expanses of solitary time they had been used to, but it taught Sandy how important Hermione had become in his life. That Christmas he gave her *Birds of Moor and Woodland* (chosen by his mother) and *Tom Brown's Schooldays* (which he chose himself). Reading it only made Hermione unhappier. He would leave her next September. Eight months remained.

Nanny kept her to the usual routine of rising, washing, dressing in front of the nursery fire, followed by porridge and toast for breakfast. By nine she was in the schoolroom, ready for Miss Protheroe to take her through that day's set lessons. The governess was not interested in her pupil's precocious questions – Hermione, in any case, soon stopped asking – but followed the book by rote. At eleven a kitchen maid brought barley water or lemonade and ginger biscuits on a tray. Miss Protheroe could sometimes be persuaded to let Hermione spend the rest of the morning in 'quiet study by herself', enabling the governess to occupy her usual armchair in the housekeeper's parlour. There she would read aloud from *Woman's Weekly* in her most expressive diction, following the progress of Captain Scott's expedition to the South Pole or tut-tutting over the suffragettes' antics. Once the week's news had

31

been delivered to an attentive audience, she would embroider initials entwined with forget-me-nots on to the corners of cambric handkerchiefs, following patterns printed in the magazine, while the other servants gossiped.

'The daddy's got the nicer nature,' they concluded. 'The mummy's very cold. A cold woman.'

'He may not be as . . . you get my drift . . . but he's one of nature's gentlemen, even if she *was* born a lady!' some daring spirit might remark before being silenced by a look from the butler.

When Hermione managed to escape from Nanny and Miss Protheroe she explored the long attics that wound round the eaves below the roof, following the meanderings of the house. They were stacked with previous owners' long-forgotten possessions . . . rotting chairs, their embroidered covers faded and split, or upright ones carved from solid oak, blackened with age and gritty with bird- or mouse-droppings; desks and tables whose drawers burst with brown and yellow documents. She glanced at these, dusted down her hands and crept further. Her best find was an old crystal chandelier that spilled across the attic floor, its faceted drops grey with dust. They came alive when arrows of sunshine slipped through the roof tiles or milky parallelograms slanted through dormer windows to shed a powdery light. The chandelier had been brought from Venice in the eighteenth century. It had been intended for the Great Chamber but, suspended from the ornate plaster ceiling, it hung too low for the room's narrow English proportions and dark oak panelling and was relegated to the attic. Someone must originally have wrapped it in a calico sheet, but in the course of 150 years the fabric had rotted to shreds.

Hermione fetched water in the jug from her nursery bathroom. Using a pair of huckaback hand towels – one to dampen and clean, the other to dry – she polished the facets until the chandelier sparkled like crystallized geometry. Triangles and rectangles, trapeziums and rhomboids lay scattered over the attic floor. They must once have been crowned by a many-sided glass globe designed to sparkle and fizz, its rainbow facets mirroring the points of light from a hundred flickering candles. She could not wait to bring Sandy to admire it, hidden from grown-ups in their private world.

That February they were separated again. Hermione and her nanny accompanied her parents to Madeira, to escape the interminable chill and darkness of an English winter. Phoebe hated the cold. As their yacht (the *Phoebe*) sailed through dark blue seas, rolling and chopping round Biscay and steadying as it neared its destination, the high bright sun sharpened every colour and outline. Every morning two or three members of the crew in white duck uniform and bare feet would scrub down the teak deck and railings, which dried and sparkled in the sunlight. An awning was stretched over the rear deck and her mother lay under its shelter protecting her pearl-pale skin while Hermione and her father marched round *Phoebe*'s deck together, clocking up the half miles and looking out to sea for dolphins. It would be years before they were so close again.

Nine-year-old girls remember everything and Hermione's lifelong memory of her father was formed during these weeks. He on his side noticed that her mind was becoming as sharp as her pencil; she observed everything going on around them and her assessments of the crew were acute; remarkably so for a little girl. It began to dawn upon Sir Jack that his daughter, as well as his beloved son, might inherit the running of his world-wide business interests. In that case the sooner he talked to her about the Staunton Trading Company the better.

'Do you know what Papa does when he is at work?' he began.

She looked ill at ease. 'Yes, Papa. You are in *trade*,' she answered reluctantly, and he knew her mother had been disparaging the source of their wealth.

'My company is at the heart of what made Britain *Great*,' he told her. 'Why do you think we have the biggest navy in the world? To protect the trade routes and activities of companies like mine! They form the cornerstone of the empire. Britannia rules the waves – remember? If it weren't for great trading houses like Staunton we would not *have* an empire: in fact it was a company just like it that first brought India to the empire.'

'Yes, Papa,' she interrupted eagerly, 'I know its name – the East India Company!'

'Good lass. Staunton is as honourable a name as Curzon or

Balfour, believe ye me! Why should you or your mama be ashamed that I am, as she puts it, "in trade"?'

The question was too complicated for Hermione to answer. She jutted her lower lip and muttered, 'I don't know.'

Her father smiled, lifted her chin and said, 'Look at me. It *is* trade, rather than a profession, certainly, and I inherited no money whatsoever, not a shilling' (*shillink* echoed in her ears, *mooney, coomp'ny*) 'though when I die, you and yer brother Richard will inherit a fortune, one that *I* have worked for. See that ye make good use of it. It'll be a heavy burden.'

'Will we be rich then, Papa?' She could not quite keep the echo of her mother's distaste out of the word 'rich'.

'Ye're rich *now*, my darling girl, and so is yer mother – richer than the rest of her family put together, and don't think she doesn't know it! We're sailing over the sea taking the sunshine in February because I *made* myself rich, while her lot are shivering in that raw Scottish castle of theirs, trading their pride for a cold in th' ead. Where would ye rather be, eh?'

'With you,' she said, and he patted her cheek because he knew it was the truth.

'Listen to yer papa, my pet, and don't ever forget what I'm telling you now. I trade with the whole British Empire. I sell to Australia, India, Africa, Canada . . . whatever their peoples need, and I buy from 'em whatever they're best at producing. My ships – much bigger ships than this one – sail all over the world. I have the largest English fleet in private ownership. Did your mama tell you that, too?'

She noticed how, as always, his accent grew blunter, his words more emphatic, when he was filled with energy and zeal. Alone in her berth at night, she would hear in her ears the ring of his rollicking voice when he talked to her and try to copy it, inventing conversations and muttering to herself in the darkness. ' *'Ere, pet, tell oos now: d'ye loov yer mama or yer papa best, eh?*'; answering in an emphatic whisper: '*I loov thee best, Papa!*'

'No,' Hermione admitted. 'Mama never told me that.'

He didn't let her see his disappointment, reflecting that there was plenty of time to counter her mother's snobbery. She would soon be ten. He must rid his daughter of contempt for money *earned* as opposed to money handed down. Plenty of time for all that. He had yet to see seventy and was in excellent health. Even his hair was still thick although now it was more grey than russet. He'd let a few years go by before talking to Hermione again. Already he lay awake at night, planning how best to transfer the Staunton Trading Company's huge assets to his children in due course. He didn't want them surrounded by predators and opportunists. The money should be tied up in trusts, but if he did that, the damned lawyers and accountants would rob them of hundreds of pounds a year in so-called fees.

The best way to protect their legacy would be to put the ownership of the works of art, the properties (three since last year, when he'd bought a villa on the Riviera) and Phoebe's extravagant hoard of jewellery into a discretionary family trust, enshrining that as part of his bequest. But greater by far than all those put together was the value of the company itself. This would best be safeguarded by creating two classes of shares, ordinary ones distinct from special voting shares, so that the capital of the business was controlled separately. All this the law allowed. But who could be trusted to guard and oversee it? Not his wife, for sure.

Who else could he have faith in, but his own children? He would make lavish provision for their mother so that she had no excuse for battening on her grown-up children and their families, and leave them jointly in charge of the rest. His thoughts circled endlessly around the advantages and disadvantages. Finally he decided to will Richard control on reaching his majority, should he himself have died by then, but not to burden Hermione with too great an awareness of her responsibilities. Money distorted people's reactions – let her think she would be scarcely richer than the Gordon-Lockharts. Full control over her share could wait until she was thirty, protected from any husband she might acquire. He knew the havoc a fortune-hunter could wreak. It was already obvious that his lanky daughter would not be a beauty; she took after his side of the family in everything except her extreme height. Phoebe's father and brothers were tall; her sisters elongated, gawky creatures. No matter: height would give the girl authority, as long as her mother did not destroy her confidence.

When they reached Madeira the *Phoebe* moored in the sheltered harbour. She was the largest vessel in port, except for commercial liners carrying more than a thousand passengers. The Stauntons disembarked and, accompanied by Phoebe's personal maid and Jack's valet, moved into Reid's Hotel. Phoebe hired two young women as companions for her daughter; one to take personal charge of her clothes and meals, the other to act as guide and tutor on the island. They were both young English girls, marooned there by their parents' job or misfortunes, and they pressed her eagerly for news from 'home', as they called England. Hermione had no news to give. Instead, she told them stories about the Dorset countryside, spicing them with the African adventures she re-enacted with Sandy. The two were left with a wealth of misinformation about the lives of the rural gentry.

Hermione wrote postcards to her brother and her Scottish grandmother. 'May I send one to Sandy Gordon-Lockhart as well?' she asked, as casually as possible.

'How thoughtful of you, darling . . .' said her mother abstractedly.

Hermione chose a hand-tinted postcard showing the old town of Funchal perched on its rock overlooking an unnaturally cerulean sea. She wrote, with a restraint she hoped he would interpret correctly, *It is nice here and it would be nice if you came too. There are lots of torpical flowers.* Tropical, corrected her mother. *Please remember me to your people, yours Hermione.* She did not add 'H. Minor', knowing he would understand that, too, and deduce that her card had been written under supervision.

'You should have written "ever, H",' her mother pointed out. 'Anybody can read one's postcards.'

Gross, highly coloured blooms flourished everywhere around Funchal, threatening to overwhelm the short, swarthy people who could never pick enough to make inroads on their feverish profusion. By the time the Stauntons had sailed back to England, winter had turned to spring in Dorset; a cooler, altogether paler spring. Hermione found the daffodils and tulips in their gardens, above all the subtle mist of the bluebell woods, far lovelier than Madeira's jungle foliage. She was overjoyed to be home.

'I got your postcard,' Sandy said laconically when they met again. She seemed strange to him. She had grown taller by another inch and her complexion, despite Phoebe's instructions that she must not take a step without her parasol, had been bleached dark gold by weeks of sunshine. He could not tell her he had missed her. 'Thanks awfully.'

'How's Bobby?' she asked.

'Oh, old Bobby's in fine fettle.' His voice was about to break. It had acquired a fuzzy, unfamiliar edge. He seemed strange to her.

'Did you ride a lot?' she asked.

'Not much. Foul weather, you see. Not fair on the ponies.'

'Sun's coming out now,' she said, adding in the grown-up manner she had observed in her parents, 'Care for a walk?'

'I don't mind.' He sounded indifferent.

'Where's Bobby?'

He whistled, and Bobby came bounding towards them. He greeted Hermione rapturously, jumping up and then grovelling foolishly, whining with pleasure, embarrassed by his own sentimentality. Sandy grinned at him, then at Hermione.

'Soppy old dog,' he said, bending down to ruffle Bobby's furry cheeks. 'Shall we go walkies, then? *Soppy* dog! Come on, Minor!'

Their separation and reunion were the prelude to a spring and summer filled with discovery. In April Hermione celebrated her tenth birthday.

'What have you been given by your dear mama and papa, my poppet?' Nanny asked as she came upstairs from her annual treat: birthday breakfast alone with her parents.

'From Papa, a telescope to look at the night sky and another pearl for my necklace,' she said. 'And Mama gave me a parasol because she says I mustn't let my skin get sunburned again, *now that I'm ten*. She says it's unladylike. Richard gave me some polished stones and some fossils. Miss Protheroe kindly gave me a book of dolls to cut out and historical costumes to dress them in. Look, you cut round the ladies' shapes and then you cut out their outfits very carefully, minding the lace and frills, and when you've done that you can choose what they are to wear.' So dull, she thought.

'They're ever so pretty, Miss 'Mione!' said the young nursery maid enviously.

'And *Sandy*?' asked Nanny significantly. 'Did Sandy Gordon-Lockhart give you anything?' She leaned across the table with a meaningful grin and winked. Hermione felt the heat rise from her throat to her cheeks, and then subside.

'No,' she tried to say carelessly. 'Course not, why should he? His mama gave me a trowel and fork for my own garden. I shall write a letter in my best handwriting to thank her.'

'Oh dear, that must be a disappointment,' Nanny said. Poor lamb! she thought; it's plain as plain can be that she dotes on him. 'Never mind. Brymer can carry the letter round to Otterbourne Court and perhaps he'll take you, too. Look: *Nanny*'s got something for you. A surprise. Give Nanny a hug, my precious. There! Good girl! Now, you open it.'

A crocheted cardigan, in cream wool. It had taken hours of patient, eye-straining effort.

'It's truly lovely!' Hermione said generously. 'Dearest Nana, you are kind! Thank you, thank you most awfully. I'll wear it this afternoon when I take tea with Mama.'

Now Nanny blushed. 'There's my treasured girlie.'

Her brother Richard was the only person who ever asked where she and Sandy went or what they did and even he – preoccupied with his horses, preparing for next season's hunting, schooling them both to be good enough for the cavalry regiment he'd set his heart on – after a while even Richard took little notice. Within a range of ten miles, the estate was their world. Their legs and arms grew tough and sinewy with exercise as they became more confident and more reckless. Hermione would watch Sandy shin up a tree, noting how the muscles in his narrow back strained as he pulled himself up from branch to branch or tried to bridge impossible gaps, letting himself fall forward the last six inches, finding a handhold in the nick of time. She got to know his limitations, and her own. How high he dared climb; how far up a tree she would let him go before tipping her head back and cupping her hands to call, 'Look out, Major! They won't bear your weight much longer!' Then she would join him twenty feet up until they straddled branches as high as birds, peering down through the leaves to where Bobby, his forepaws propped against the trunk of the tree, whined uneasily.

They would scale the walls of deserted buildings and pick their way round the topmost line of stones, watching pebbles and infill dislodged by their sandalled feet roll and bounce to the ground. He dared her to sit astride the keystone of a crumbling arch and, shaking with fear, she did so.

'I dare you to jump down!' she called up to him, after feeling her way gingerly back to comparative safety on top of the wall.

'It's nearly fifteen feet – and there are *thickets* of brambles . . .'

She was instantly remorseful. 'I didn't say you must. I said I dare you. Dares are silly anyhow.'

He bridled. 'You'll have to carry me home if I break my leg.'

'I'll give you a fireman's lift, like Papa used to do me.'

'What's that?'

'Jump and you'll find out, oh ye of little faith!'

He jumped, and rolled, and stood up laughing with triumph and relief. Along his legs a tracery of scratches oozed blood.

'I'm not scared of brambles,' he boasted. 'Now you come down! You don't have to jump. Can you leap over those stinging nettles – look, those there?'

The clump of nettles was nearly four feet high, and even wider. She hesitated.

Because he loved her, though he had never said so and did not even know it, he relented. 'I withdraw the dare.'

A moment ago she had made him take a risk for her sake. She in turn would do anything for him. She jumped, and lurched, and tripped, and crashed down on the far side a foot short of the safety of the cool grass. Standing up, she arched her body backwards, eyes shut, thumbs locked in the crook of her waist, moaning, 'Ho, oh, ooh, uh . . .' Her calves were aflame. He was instantly contrite.

'Minor! You *idiot*! I never meant you to . . .'

Hermione clenched her lips so as not to cry. 'Never mind. It's nothing. No blood.'

Sandy hunted for dock leaves, crushing their stalks to get at the healing juice. 'Stay still,' he said tenderly. 'Don't move. This'll make it better.'

He pressed the broken dock leaves back and forth along her legs, their tawny surface now peppered with angry purple spots.

'Ow,' Hermione wailed, unable to suppress it. 'Ow, Major, it really does hurt. Sorry.'

'Do you want to go back now? Should they be properly bandaged?'

'I'll be all right. Just give me a minute. Worse things happen at sea!' she said, remembering Nanny.

'Press gangs . . .' Sandy agreed.

'Keel-hauling . . .'

'Flogging . . .'

'*Eating the cabin boy!*'

There was nothing to top that. He let her have the last word.

They rolled down shorn fields, tumbling over and over until the breath was knocked out of them. They ran races along drovers' paths barely wide enough for a cart but ample for two wiry children. Her legs were longer but his stamina gave him a final burst with which he sometimes beat her. She was physically his equal despite the age gap of more than two years. Her mind was as good as his, though much less well schooled, and her imagination far superior. Their fantasy games became an obsession.

'*Diamonds thou canst not give me, for I have so many that they are no more to me than little pebbles. Gold, too, is nothing to me, for my mines carry rich seams of it, so that mine eyes have come to prefer the dull gleam of baser metals. How, then, wilt thou please me, my Leo?*'

'*For all thy wealth, there is something thou dost lack. Here, deep in my heart, lie the true mines of Queen Ayesha.*'

The golden child she was then, barely ten years old, had no inkling of the future, confident that they would spend a lifetime together.

'*Thy words are very bold, Englishman! What secret treasure can thy heart hold for me?*'

'But one thing: my love, oh Queen. Not all thy treasure is worth a fraction of its value.' Bobby had dropped a stick beside them and stood with pleading eyes braced for flight. *'Not my heart only; my body is thine to command. My arms to serve thee, mine eyes to worship thy beauty, my legs to race at thy bidding. This lion is fleet of foot, my Queen. Let us see if I can outrun him . . .'*

Hermione hurled the stick and Sandy and his dog chased after it together. She picked dandelions for Nanny, crushing their stems in her hot hand as she carried the wilting bunch home, releasing their white milk and leaving a bitter smell and taste on her palm.

On rainy days (and there were many, for the August of 1912 was as wet and cool as the previous one had been hot and dry) they stayed indoors. In Sandy's day-nursery or Hermione's the toy chest would be opened up to reveal neatly stacked board games: Nine Men's Morris, Lotto, Snakes and Ladders, Mah-jong. They would sit opposite each other, heads bent forward, focused on winning. If Richard was home he occasionally joined in, half-mocking their seriousness.

'Up the Stauntons!' he'd cry when Hermione made a good move; or sportingly, 'I say, bad luck,' if Sandy lost a game. At sixteen and a half her brother was too close to adulthood to be an equal companion. Besides, Hermione was torn between loyalty to Richard and her desire to be alone with Sandy. The presence of both at once confused her. She would lose concentration, Sandy would pounce and she would be defeated. The two boys sometimes joined forces and teased her for being 'only a girl'. Then Nanny might prepare a tray for Kim's Game, giving them two minutes to memorize the items before taking it away. They had to scribble down as many as they could remember. Richard invariably scored lowest with a mere twelve or thirteen objects. Sandy usually got more than fifteen. But Hermione, being the youngest and exceptionally observant, would score eighteen or nineteen. One object always eluded her. 'Cotton reel, ink bottle, hair ribbon, doll's shoe,' she would recite steadily, reading them out in the order in which they had been placed on the tray from left to right; 'tin soldier, water tumbler, draughts counter, bookmark . . .'

'The draughts counter! That's what I forgot!' Richard would exclaim.

Rain lashed sideways against the window, darkening the nursery like dusk.

One sunny afternoon at Chantry she took Sandy up to the attic to show him her chandelier. It had already acquired a film of dirt that dulled its bright angles. He picked up one teardrop, polished it against his shorts and put it to the pulse in her neck so that the heavy crystal seemed to hang suspended from her ear. She looked unsmilingly back at him. He reached for a second drop, and the two framed her face like flashes of lightning.

'*How thy beauty shineth amid the stars,*' he said. '*Oh eternal Queen!*'

'*But* thy *beauty, my Leo, needs no adornment,*' she answered. '*For thine eyes are bluer than the turquoises deep in the heart of my sacred mountain; thy hair is bright as gold from my distant mines, and thy arms are stronger than all my slaves who quarry these treasures and bring them to me.*'

He shook his head. 'H. Minor, don't be silly,' he told her. 'It's rude to make personal remarks.'

The spell was broken.

Not content with the spilled profusion of the chandelier, Sandy was eager to explore the rest of the attic. He stood on tiptoe trying to reach the dormer windows before clambering on top of old cases to peer through their smoky glass. They had been fastened down for so long that the frames had rusted in place, but finally one gave way to his shoulder's impatient heave. It swung outwards and sweet fresh air coursed along the hot tunnel. They were at the back of the house, the side that looked over the stable, the court-yard and two wings of outbuildings. Muted sounds from outside now rang clearly in their ears. They heard Elias Brymer shouting to his son, Billy.

'Easy with her, Billy, she's but young. Easy does it with high-steppin' young mare like this'n!'

'Time she larned manners!' Billy retorted and the sullenness in his voice reached Hermione, crouched at Sandy's feet, longing to grasp hold of them lest he fall. Her hand hovered beside his ankles.

'Hold on to my ankle, Minor!' he ordered suddenly, as though he had read her mind. 'Not both, just one – the left' – and he shook that foot as though a horsefly had stung it – 'I'm going to climb out.'

'Major, no!' she said, horrified. 'You might fall and hurt yourself!' She meant, kill yourself.

'Not me. I'm as sure-footed as a mountain goat. Hold on. Don't let go till I say.'

With both hands she clamped his foot to the top of the cabin trunk and shut her eyes against the sudden fall of dust that his emerging body scraped off the blackened window-frame.

'Now – let go!' he whispered urgently. She did, and his sandalled foot arched upwards, escaping like a bird into the hot blue sky. Hermione rose from her crouching position and pushed her head, neck and shoulders through the gap left by the open window to watch.

Sandy crawled along the tiled roof several feet above the guttering, below him a forty-foot drop to the ground. At first he moved cautiously, but after a few yards he gave up his handholds and rose unsteadily to his feet. He peered back at the window from which he had just emerged and called to Hermione, 'It's easy! Easy as pie! Don't you come though, Minor, this is boys' work.'

Inaudibly she begged him to be careful. She dared not speak, as if the breath of her words might dislodge his precarious balance. Now that he knew she was watching he grew bolder. He stood up straight, his feet clinging like limpets to the roof-tiles. *What if one is loose?* she thought. Swaying like a tightrope walker, arms outstretched for balance, he began to traverse the length of the roof. Sometimes he leaned forward, ready to grab the ridge tiles if he slipped. The brilliance of the sun transformed him into a burning silhouette, black against blinding whiteness. She shut her eyes.

Minutes passed. Hermione's heart thudded against her ribs, anticipating the slither and slide of his body down the sloping roof, the shout, the pause while he scrabbled for a handhold; then a cry, an interminable silence, and a broken thud as he hit the ground.

Her hands, forehead, face were sweating; her mouth dry.

From the cobbled yard below came a shout: 'Oi! You up there! Whatcher think you're doin'?'

Don't distract him, Hermione prayed under her breath.

Sandy called back defiantly, 'Walking along the roof, silly ass. What does it look like?'

'Come down at once!'

'Don't give me orders. It's none of your business,' shouted Sandy, and she heard the tremor of excitement in his voice. 'I'll do as I want.'

'I'll get me dad . . . *He*'ll tell on you!' came the distant shout and Hermione heard Billy Brymer's steel-tipped boots striking sparks as he strode across the yard. At the same time she could hear above her head the scrape of Sandy's feet and hands as he hurried back across the open window. A moment later his body blotted out the sunlight. She ducked aside as he squeezed through the narrow gap and dropped beside her.

'Told you I could!' he panted triumphantly. His knees and the palms of his hands were black with dirt. 'You can see for miles! Nearly as far as my house!'

'And *be* seen,' she said, furious with relief. 'Major, you'll be gated if they find out.'

'I don't care. It was worth it. Anyhow, who'll believe Billy? He's only a stable-lad. He wouldn't dare give me away.'

But now he has us in his power, she thought. He knows that if he tells, Sandy will be in trouble. *They won't let us play alone.*

Heads bent, they scuttled along the attic corridor, climbing backwards down the stepladder to the top floor. Following her, Sandy paused to swing the trapdoor shut and slide the bolt into place. Hermione kept cave outside a little-used guest bathroom while he washed his hands and knees, emerging clean and grinning all over his face.

Hermione wondered whether to tell Sandy what Billy said next day when, giving her a leg up into the saddle, he was out of earshot of Miss Protheroe for a moment.

'I saw 'im!' he hissed malevolently. 'Your sweetheart, up on the roof! Be the devil to pay if 'is father finds out. Yours too. And *that*'s only the 'alf of it . . .'

'How dare you!' she muttered.

'Hermione? Did you say something dear?' her governess asked, and Hermione was forced to move away.

As she did so she just heard Billy say gloatingly, '*She* don't know what you get up to but *I* do, so! You'd better watch yerselves!'

Hermione spotted the dwarf emerging from the milking shed with a large enamel jug in her hand, and grasped eagerly at the diversion supplied by this oddly small, stocky girl.

'Here! You!' she called out. 'You shouldn't be carrying that, it's much too heavy. Give it to Billy. He'll take it.'

'I can manage it, miss, thanks all the same,' the dwarf said. 'I'm older'n I look. And stronger.'

'And uglier,' Billy hissed as he strode off scowling. Better not tell Major, Hermione decided in the end, but from then on they explored more distant territories.

Two weeks later Sandy sat the entrance for Eton. It was a formality, since his father and grandfather had gone there and his name was down for their house, but all the same he was bucked to learn that he had put up a thoroughly creditable performance. Hermione counted off the days to his going. They had been measured in months; then weeks; finally thirty days, twenty days; and at last, as the end of August came, ten days – nine, eight, seven . . .

'*What shall I do during the time of thy absence, oh my Leo?*' she mourned.

'*Oh Queen, thou who livest for thousands of years – three months will pass in a flash. Thou wilt scarcely notice the moons wax and wane.*'

'*Assuredly I shall notice!*' she said.

'*I shall send thee word, borne in a cleft stick by swift runners . . .*'

'No you won't,' she said. 'You know how you hate writing letters.'

He grinned in recognition. 'I know,' he said. 'Never mind: you can write to me!'

One of their final days shimmered with heat, a throwback to the previous summer. Both wore short-sleeved shirts and belted linen shorts and looked alike except for the length of Hermione's hair. They had agreed to meet after lunch, and she found Sandy waiting in the stables. Billy Brymer and his father were in the tack room, sorting through saddles and bridles with Richard, deep in a discussion about whether the new cavalry saddle imported from France was any better than the tried and tested English version. Billy glanced up and winked knowingly at Sandy, who ignored him.

'Where are you two scamps off to?' Richard asked.

'Nowhere much,' said Hermione.

They climbed the hill that rose up from the arboretum behind the house and after a mile or so, turned up a path into a field where placid black and white cows lay ruminating in the torrid heat. The field was dotted with cow-pats, as whorled and shiny as chocolate pudding in the mixing bowl. Sandy, shading his eyes to gaze up at a circling buzzard, stepped in one by accident. Black splashes covered his leg from the knee down.

'Ugh, poor Major, how horrid!' said Hermione.

But Sandy laughed and running ahead, deliberately jumped into another cow-pat with both feet. More splashes mottled his legs.

'You do it,' he said. 'It's a lovely feeling, not horrid at all. I dare you, Minor!'

She searched until she found a crusted, dried one. Gingerly she lowered one foot into it. The crust broke, covering her highly polished sandal and clean white sock with rich-smelling ordure. A cloud of tiny flies rose into the air.

'Cheat!' he called out. 'Look – like *this* –' and he ran and jumped again. This time the splashes reached the hem of his shorts. The cows turned wondering dark eyes as they followed his progress from one dark circle of manure to another.

Encouraged by Sandy's whoops, Hermione joined in, racing between cow-pats, landing on their sticky centres in an ecstasy of the forbidden. She had never done anything so wicked in her life. The sensation was thrilling as well as repellent. Her feet were black and a miasma of stench clogged her nostrils. Just as her reckless excitement reached a pitch of wild abandon she slipped, falling full-length, hands outstretched, into a fresh puddle. She clambered slowly to her feet and looked round for Sandy. He ran towards her, stopped short a few yards away and burst out laughing. Her legs, both hands and the front of the white Aertex shirt were black with liquid cow-dung. Her white socks were black. The yellow hair ribbon lay in the middle of the pool.

'Oh Minor! *Minor!* You *can't* go home like that! *Whatever* will *Nanny* say?'

'I can wash in the stable yard.'

'No you can't – the rainwater butt is for the horses. You'll muddy it and Brymer will be furious. We shall have to clean ourselves up before we go back. I know – the stream in the valley. Let's head downhill.'

The muck was drying on their legs by the time they reached the stream that ran through a fold in the valley, shaded from view by overhanging trees on both banks.

Sandy remembered *Scouting for Boys*. 'We'd better beat our clothes against flat stones and then paddle about till they've dried in the sun.'

'What about me?' she asked, suddenly shy. They had never seen each other naked.

'I'll go round that corner, there, to wash mine. You stay here. I won't look.'

He disappeared and she heard the startled twitter of birds a dozen yards away.

'Minor? You're quite safe! I can't see anything! Take off your clothes and sort of splash them vigorously about.' A stream of dirty bubbles eddied downstream, indicating that Sandy was doing so.

She pulled off her socks and banged them against a tree root until the dark stains were a bit paler; then unpeeled her shirt and pulled it cautiously forward over her head. Some of the filth had gone through on to her chest and, suddenly disgusted by the sight and smell of her skin, Hermione took off her cotton vest followed by her shorts and knickers. Now she was naked. It was cool under the trees and by the time she had washed herself and her clothes – which took several minutes – she was shivering.

'Major?' she called.

His voice came from the bank behind her, out of sight yet re-assuringly close. 'What?'

'I'm cold.'

'So was I, but now I'm lying on the grass in the sun. The flies are jolly tiresome but it's lovely and warm. I'm bone dry already. My things'll take a bit longer.'

'What if somebody comes?'

'We can always go back under the trees again. But there's no one about. You're perfectly safe. What have you got on?'

'Nothing.'

A pause. 'Nothing at all?'

'Everything I'd got on was covered in muck. Now my clothes are all wet but they don't smell beastly any longer. Now it just looks like ordinary dirt.'

Another pause.

'I told you,' he called out, 'I won't look.'

'Major, if I lie down near you, will you *promise* to keep your eyes shut?'

'I promise. Cross my heart and hope to die.'

'Shut them now, then. I'm coming.'

She tiptoed across the damp stones and, parting the tall grasses at the edge of the stream, stooped under the overhanging branches and emerged into a glade of shining warm grass. The sunlight was brilliant after the gloom under the trees. She spread out her clothes to dry. Over to the left, about ten yards away, Sandy lay with one hand flung across his eyes. His body looked very white beside the brown of his limbs, face and neck. His torso was elongated and there was a little flap of flesh at the top of his legs. At that moment he turned on his side away from her, tucking up his legs. A row of protruding knobs emphasized the arc of his spine.

'I'm coming now . . .' she said.

In the heat and silence of the sunny afternoon they soon dozed. Once she opened her eyes to watch a ladybird climbing a grass stem. It quivered and bent under the tiny weight. Sandy was breathing deeply, in and out, constant as a ticking clock. One outflung hand twitched spasmodically. She stared at his back and shoulders, then let her gaze travel down to his buttocks. They were oval and slightly concave. Between his legs, just where they began to fold forwards, she could see a wrinkled, darker bobble. Quickly, she turned on her side away from him. They lay on the green slope a few feet apart, alone in a burning Eden. The sun concentrated its golden focus on them as though the whole earth had contracted to this grassy hillock. Hermione drowsed, and her heavy eyelids shut out the brilliant light.

While they slept, Billy Brymer – escaping the stuffiness of the stable yard to fish for an hour in the shade of the trees overhanging the stream – suddenly found himself looking through a curtain of twinkling leaves at the naked body of his employer's daughter. Her shape was entirely that of a child; her chest as flat, her hips as narrow as those of a boy the same age. Her legs and arms were tanned dark gold by the sun. Sandy lay a few feet away from her. Billy was transfixed. Well I'm darned, he thought, dirty little buggers! He crouched in the moss beside the stream, the fishing rod slack in his grasp, gazing at the motionless figure of Hermione Staunton. A fish swam lazily round his bait, ignored by Billy. His eyes wandered over her body, trying to probe the shadowy arrow where her legs and torso met. The rod quivered and jerked upwards, startling Billy. He dropped it with a tiny splash and fled over the soft verges of the stream to higher ground. Hermione rubbed her eyes but did not wake.

Half an hour later – more, perhaps – a large cloud obscured the sun. The brilliant light dimmed and the air cooled. The changes woke them both. Sandy, forgetting, sat up and turned towards her just as Hermione opened her eyes, too. He closed his quickly.
 'Sorry,' he said, 'I forgot. I didn't see anything.'
 'Doesn't matter.'
 They both spoke at once:
 'Are your clothes . . .?' asked Sandy.
 'Do you know the . . .?' began Hermione.
 'No, you.'

'What time is it?'

He opened his eyes and looked up at the sun, still high in the sky but beginning its decline.

'Must be teatime.'

'Are our clothes dry by now, do you suppose?' she asked.

'I don't know. Shall I go and look?'

'No, I will,' she said, and began to stand up. He closed his eyes. 'No . . . doesn't matter. I don't mind.'

'I've never—' he said.

Hermione got to her feet and Sandy deliberately raised his head and looked full at her. For a few seconds he gazed at the pale cloven mound that disappeared between her legs. She looked so pretty that he would have liked to touch her, to stroke the tender skin of her belly or her long golden thighs, but he thought, no, better not.

'Do *you* want to, now?' he asked.

Hermione said, 'I have already.'

'Of course, I forgot. Your brother.'

'No, actually, not him. Never Richard. You. Just now. When you were asleep.'

'Oh.'

He glanced down at his small pointed penis and saw to his embarrassment that it was beginning to thicken. Soon it would be rigid. He felt awkward.

'That's enough, H. Minor. I think we'd better not look any more.'

She turned and ran towards her clothes, ducking out of the trees a few moments later fully dressed. Meanwhile Sandy climbed into his own, only slightly damp garments.

In a quite different voice she called over to him, 'Are your things dry?'

'More or less. What about yours?'

'Not too bad. They're not awfully clean, though. Hope Mama doesn't catch me. She'd throw a frightful bate.'

'Minor – you won't, you'd better not, *tell* anyone that we . . .?'

'*We be of one blood, Thou and I*. Now you swear.'

'*We be of one blood, Thou and I*,' he answered.

They walked back to Chantry through the radiant light of dusk and went their separate ways with no more than a casual wave of the hand and a muttered 'Bye,' on parting. Hermione ran up the wide main staircase. It smelled of beeswax polish and old wood and creaked under her sandalled footsteps. At the sound, Nanny emerged from the nursery and, leaning over the topmost balustrade, broke into a string of reproaches. For the first time in her life, Hermione felt herself blushing.

'*And* you've caught the sun,' Nanny added crossly. 'What will your mama say? You've gone all golden and there are freckles on your nose. Oh deary-me!'

That, it turned out, was to be their last day together. As a punishment for having come home in such a disgusting condition, Lady Staunton refused to let her daughter see Sandy again before he left for school, three days later. Hermione bribed Billy – for who else could she ask? – to deliver a note, sealed against his curiosity with a red blob of sealing-wax. It said, *Dear Major, I got a pi-jaw from my mama and have been gated since Thursday. I hope school is topping. If you get hungry I'll send you a cake. I will think of you sometimes and when I can I'll write. Roll on Christmas and the hols! Love, H. Minor.*

Billy broke the sealing-wax, opened the letter, read it, laughed, crushed it into a ball and threw it away. Serve her right! She wasn't half forward, for her age.

CHAPTER THREE

A FEW WEEKS LATER SANDY'S SCOTTISH GRANDFATHER DIED suddenly. He had been sitting in the smoking room with a cigar, swirling brandy round a balloon glass and reading the *Times* leader about the Turks invading Serbia – infernal scoundrels! James Alexander MacAlistair Gordon-Lockhart of the Clan Lockhart was sixty-four when a heart attack brought his indignation to an abrupt end. Donald, his only son, a most un-Scottish figure, inherited Ellismuir Castle, the square, gloomy house in the Lowlands, along with all its furniture, paintings, armour, linen, silver, glass and china; not to mention dogs, horses, carriages, land, cottages, tenants, fifteen household servants, eight outdoor staff and a good many debts that no one had warned him about. He was, poor Donald, hopelessly unsuited to the task.

But duty is duty, the Clan awaited, his mother expected it of him and Donald acquiesced. They travelled north for the funeral, to bagpipes keening a lament in the minor key and the old chief's coffin athwart a rowing boat, two pairs of oars dipping and rising in slow, slow unison, floating across the loch to its resting place on a pine-topped island. It was followed by a week when relatives gathered to pay their respects; then servants, tenants, farmers, crofters and the poor. All this Donald endured with stoic dignity, thankful that Scots are a laconic tribe and he seldom had to speak. Sandy, summoned from Eton for the first two days of the funeral rites, realized for the first time the nature and extent of his future responsibilities. He emerged from the obsequies ten years older than the white-faced, tearless boy who had followed his grandfather's body into the dark granite church. In those two days he left his childhood behind; no longer a Dorset lad but a young Scots clansman.

The Gordon-Lockharts decided to take up residence at Ellismuir in November. Before they left, the Stauntons and the Daubenys, along with the Master of Hounds, the vicar and a dozen other local gentry, were invited for a valedictory dinner at Otterbourne. When the ladies withdrew, Violet lamented having to leave Dorset, its kinder climate and familiar neighbours.

'Donald considers it my duty to keep his widowed mama company and take charge of the servants and household retainers and of course he is right. But we can hardly be expected to maintain two households for the three of us – four, including my mother-in-law.'

They sympathized, reminded her of Donald's ancestral obligations, enquired how Sandy was enjoying school life.

Violet wondered what on earth one was supposed to do about Alexander's nanny, who had been with him since he was born. 'He's far too old for her now but he'd make no end of a fuss if she left.'

The ladies simpered in unison:

'*Such* a warm-hearted boy!'

'Nannies can be quite a *bind*.'

One said, 'We kept ours and let her do the household mending.'

Phoebe thought, I'm damned if *I* would.

The ladies prattled knowledgeably about husbands, fashions, alliances. Phoebe smiled and nodded but her own thoughts ran on. It was most remiss of Hermione's nanny to have let her wander off with Violet's boy all summer. Gracious only knows what those two young creatures would have got up to if left to their own devices for very much longer. Just as well they're moving away. If she gives me letters to post I'll tear them up. Let us hope the new people at Otterbourne turn out to have daughters. High time 'Mione found suitable playmates. She's supposed to grow into a young lady, though God knows how, since she bears every mark of her father's vulgar stock. Every day she shows more outward and visible signs of the sort of man I married. Fool that I was!

Phoebe would have been riven by contradictory emotions had she known that there was another reason for the Gordon-Lockharts' move, concerning the despised husband with whom she no longer had carnal relations. Jack Staunton and Violet had conducted an intermittent affair for almost two decades, each having married someone who, for different reasons, had little or no physical interest in them. Edwardian society recognized and tolerated grand passions or practical solutions. Jack and Violet pleased each other in bed and out. It was a discreet arrangement that suited them and harmed no one since apart from Bernadette, her lady's maid and confidante, no one knew. They had taken care to keep the liaison secret from their respective spouses, Jack taking particular care. Phoebe's jealousy was not to be contemplated.

Jack had observed his daughter's growing attachment to Sandy and so had Violet. They privately agreed that, while Sandy was much too young to *love* the tomboyish Hermione, that might change as they grew older. Better to separate them now, before the whole business became tiresome and difficult to forbid. The children of parents who have had a secret affair should not be allowed to marry, in case the weight of that old passion sours and overshadows their own. Occasionally Violet Gordon-Lockhart would try to work out whether there was a possibility that Sandy could be Jack's son; but this, if true, would be so humiliating to Donald – happy and proud to have produced a son and heir after eight childless years – that she dismissed the idea. A wife who continues to sleep with her husband can allow herself the consolation of ambivalence. Sandy's looks offered no clue since both men – conveniently – had red hair, though Donald's was pale ginger and Jack's a deep russet colour that, when he was a boy, might have been darker or lighter. Her son's hair was gold, the glinting reddish gold of her wedding ring. Sandy seemed to share Jack's zip and zest and to have a mental energy that her husband lacked, but twelve-year-old boys do tend to be livelier than men of Donald's age. If suspicion were ever to become certainty, Donald must never know. Should Jack be told? Time enough to decide when Sandy was older. Meanwhile it was best not to let the children write to each other. They'd soon find new playmates and forget.

Violet helped her husband to shoulder his responsibilities and take over rather than sell the Lockhart house and estate. She would support him in this new task and before long Sandy would be growing up. As for her own needs, accommodating neighbours were doubtless also to be found in the Lowlands. And if not . . . being past forty now, the lack of physical satisfaction would not be as hard to bear as it had been in her twenties. *Then*, as a young wife, she had felt parched for want of something she could not name because she had never had it. The arrival of Jack Staunton had been as welcome as rain after drought.

Soberly, Violet arranged a final tryst. She told Jack that she had loved him (*love* was not a word that had often passed between them) and would miss him.

'We both loved each other,' he replied. 'And no harm done, eh, my flower?'

He would have liked to bring her a parting gift – a pretty tiara from Garrard, perhaps, or a good brooch – but how would she explain it away? Instead, he told her, he had deposited a sum of money in her name in a private bank account so that she could look after herself and her son if the need ever arose. He gave her the address of his lawyers, through whom, he said, she could always find him. Violet had one last favour to ask.

'Anything,' he said.

'May I take your photograph? That's why I brought a camera. Don't worry – I shall keep it secret. And you might like to have a matching one of me.'

Jack trusted her absolutely; he had been trusting her for twenty years. Deep in a copse of rhododendrons, their usual meeting place, he sat down on the garden bench, crossed his legs and smiled broadly at Violet as she bent over the camera. She fiddled and twiddled, determined to get it right, until in the end he grew impatient and extended his hand, inviting her to forget the camera and sit beside him. At that moment she released the shutter. They changed places and he took her photograph, hardly giving her time to arrange the folds of her skirt (still crushed from having been pulled up to her waist, her back cushioned on his jacket, as she leaned against a tree for him).

'How will you develop the pictures?' he asked.

'Bernadette will take care of it.'

There, with affection and sorrow, they had said goodbye.

Several weeks later, Phoebe sat in the blue drawing room planning her imminent visit to India for the Coronation Durbar of George V. A package had arrived from Paris. Inside was a shagreen box containing designs for ball-gowns and costumes. She undid its velvet ribbon, folded back the ivory tissue paper and turned over the elegant sketches, choosing the most fashionable and flattering. Each bore her name: *Dessiné pour Lady Staunton, Worth de Paris, 1912.* Her husband had been tiresomely difficult about leaving Hermione for nearly three months but Phoebe had persuaded him that with Nanny Rideout, Miss Protheroe, Molly, Agatha and two nursery maids to take care of her, as well as a houseful of servants, the child would be perfectly content. In the end Jack Staunton had acquiesced, not because he agreed but because he hoped the Indian adventure would amuse his wife. Without the solace of Violet, it was more important than ever to keep her good-humoured. Even if the trip failed to divert Phoebe, it gave him an opportunity to visit the Staunton Trading Company's offices, newly transferred from Calcutta to Delhi, and those in Surat and Bombay on the way back.

When Hermione first learned that her parents were going on a long sea voyage, leaving at the beginning of December, she had asked Nanny to intercede with her mother and arrange for her to be invited to Gowrie Castle. She dared not say, 'or with Sandy, wherever he may be', not least because she did not know where he was. Nanny, who understood Hermione's real reason, did her best.

'Poor lamb, she'll be ever so bored, all alone in the house with no one for company but the maids and me! Perhaps milady her grandmama would have her to stay in Scotland? Then she could enjoy the festive season with her cousins, madam? It would be very suitable.'

Phoebe received Nanny's request in silence. The sleeves of her afternoon gown dragged across the plump armrest as she raised a porcelain cup to her lips. When she had paused for long enough to give the impression that she was considering it, she frowned and said, 'I think not. The child will be happiest here, amid her own familiar things. She's a trifle young for such a long railway journey. And she hardly knows her cousins. No.'

Hermione had sometimes said to her mother, 'Tell me about you when *you* were a little girl!'

The reply was always: 'You ask too many questions. You should know by now there are certain things I don't care to discuss. My family is one of the oldest and noblest in Scotland and that is all you need to know.'

Phoebe kept up a desultory correspondence with her two sisters, and envelopes might arrive several weeks later addressed in flowing handwriting that Hermione learned to recognize, although she could not have recognized her cousins. They seemed familiar yet at the same time remote, not real boys and girls at all. She often ran through their names in her mind to make sure she hadn't forgotten anyone. There were cousins Rosamund, Cynthia, Evadne and Hetty, and boys known as the three Guses: Angus, Fergus, and Douglas. Last of all was somebody's baby called Alexander. But they never invited her to stay and nor did they ever come to Dorset, although Chantry, with more than thirty bedrooms, could have accommodated every Campbell-Leith in the clan, along with all their maids and nannies.

When the time came to set off for Southampton where Sir Jack and Lady Staunton were to join the royal party sailing for India, Hermione's father said a heavy goodbye to his daughter, conscious that it was wrong to leave the child alone. They walked to the front door, she holding on to his hand so tightly that in order to get into the car he was forced to wrench it from her grasp.

''Mione!' her mother hissed. 'You are making a disgraceful exhibition of yourself! Kindly show more self-control.' Staring ahead she said into the speaking tube, 'Brymer, why are you loitering? We shall be late! Start the motor car at once!'

The Eton half ended. Hermione – counting the days in case a miracle happened and Sandy ran into the hall shouting, 'Minor! Where are you? Goodness, you didn't think I'd forget you? Bobby, Bobby, go find!' – saw the dates come and go and march on towards Christmas. She guessed he must have gone to Scotland – he had often told her what fun he had there. Her brother Richard made a brief appearance but he was impatient and preoccupied and when she asked if he had seen Sandy, retorted that he couldn't be expected to look out for a new-bug. He selected clothes for Nanny to pack and disappeared to stay with a school friend, leaving Hermione once again the only member of the family at Chantry.

The old year died. Hermione waited stoically and in silence for Sandy's return. Otterbourne Court remained empty and was eventually sold. Still he did not write. Hermione learned about the sale from Cook, who had been offered a situation by the new owners. It was five pounds a year more and she took it. '*She was a good cook, as cooks go;*' quoted Nanny philosophically, '*and as cooks go she went.*'

The afternoons, when the servants dawdled or gossiped, were for Hermione the times of greatest freedom. Nanny would go 'to rest my weary bones', the new cook to 'take the weight off my feet' and while the nursemaids chattered and giggled, Hermione was left to her own devices. She discovered that the best way to summon up her father was to tiptoe into the dressing room lead-ing off her parents' bedroom, open his mahogany wardrobe and bury her face in one of his rough jackets, or shroud herself in the folds of a sleek dark suit. Their distinctive smell – the smell of meerschaum pipe and male sweat mixed with traces of pomade and soap and even the dry, tickly smell of his beard – made her feel almost as if she were held in his arms.

The long winter weeks taught Hermione the pleasures as well as the tedium of enforced solitude. For the rest of her life she would be content with her own company and not rely on others for amusement. Nevertheless, each morning during her monotonous lessons she gazed at the calendar pinned up in the schoolroom, willing the time to go more quickly. She spent many afternoons curled up behind the faded red velvet curtains in the library, reading to herself. Nanny and governess patrolled the nursery floor hunting for her with birdlike chirrups of exasperation but Hermione was too absorbed to hear. *Slowly and in the midst of this most solemn silence the minutes sped away*, she read, *and while they sped the full moon passed deeper and deeper into the shadow of the earth, as the inky segment of its circle slid in awful majesty across the lunar craters.* Time stopped; she was transported to the arid plains of Africa. *Driven mad with fear of the gathering darkness and of the unholy shadow which, they believed, was swallowing the moon, the companies of girls broke up in wild confusion and ran screeching for the gateways.* Suddenly the heavy curtains were yanked aside.

'*There* you are!' said Miss Protheroe's voice, sharp with anger. Having searched both the attic and the cellar in vain, they had begun to think Hermione might have been kidnapped. 'Such a bad, *wicked* girl! Oh, whatever will Lady Staunton say?'

'Nothing, unless you tell her,' Hermione answered.

'Now dear, that's not very polite,' Nanny rebuked. 'And you'll ruin your eyes if you read in the dark.' Dusk had fallen without Hermione noticing. 'Now tell Miss Protheroe you're sorry and come upstairs for nursery tea. Cook has made crumpets for a treat.'

After this she was permitted books only at set times: for an hour after her morning cocoa and another half hour after the bath before Nanny put her to bed. When it became a duty imposed by her governess, the pleasure of reading was quite spoiled.

One afternoon she decided to practise L'Attaque so that when they met again, Sandy would find her more of a challenge. She had never yet managed to beat him. She fetched the box from her games chest, set up the soldiers and sappers on their tin stands and positioned the mines. But it was no good with just one player. However hard she tried, she couldn't split her brain in two or forget where his Commander-in-Chief stood. Perhaps somewhere up in Scotland he was imagining playing L'Attaque with her. No, that wouldn't be like Sandy! He wouldn't dream and brood and pine, as she was doing, he'd walk off any ill-humour. Hermione sighed and gazed out of the window. The bare trees looked cold against the waning light.

'I wish I had a *dog*,' she said.

Nanny started and jumped and asked, 'What did you say, my precious?'

Hermione realized that Nanny was growing old. Her whiskery face was sagging and her hair had nearly gone white. They'll make Nanny disappear soon, she thought. Mama has made her whole family disappear. Sandy disappeared. They can make anyone disappear if they want to.

'Would you like a nice game of Snakes and Ladders, dear?' Miss Protheroe asked. She had not quite finished preparing Hermione's geography lesson, having mastered only half the Balkans, with the aid of maps accompanying reports in the newspapers headlined *Balkan Unrest*. It was hard to keep pace with all the changes. 'We can pretend the snakes are the rivers of Europe and you can tell me their names.'

'Starting from the Mediterranean and going north towards the Baltic Sea: Rhone, Rhine, Seine,' Hermione rattled off, 'Danube, Elbe, Volga.'

'You've forgotten the Tiber, dear, haven't you? In Italy,' and Miss Protheroe murmured to herself, '*Oh, Tiber! father Tiber / To whom the Romans pray . . .*'

Hermione thought, she always quotes the same poems. I know them by heart, better than she does.

One cold January afternoon she was invited to take tea with Rose Daubeny and, if they condescended to join two little girls in the nursery, Rose's three older brothers. Hermione and her governess were sitting side by side in the back of the car as it made its leisurely way down the mile-long drive towards the village. Miss Protheroe had made several improving remarks and could not think of anything else to say. She did not know how to talk to her disconcerting pupil, so old for her age in many respects, not like a child at all but not yet a young lady, either. Hermione knew she was much cleverer than Miss Protheroe and although she was never rude or patronizing she was tired of pretending to be interested. She would rather sit and look out of the window.

Elias Brymer steered a stately pace through eddies of leaves whipped up by the January winds and round the puddles left by last night's storm. Hermione watched through the glass panel between them. The back of his neck was deeply creased into three plump rolls, scored with short hairs. Brymer kept passing his gloved hand across the back of his neck as though the stubble irritated him. He twitched his shoulders, twisted his head from side to side and settled his neck into the grey collar of his uniform without slackening pace.

Beside the road, Hermione caught sight of a stunted figure whom she had noticed before. She was staggering under the weight of a pile of kindling slung across her shoulders like a yoke. Her arms were hooked over each end and her dangling, stubby hands were purple with cold.

'Oh look, Miss Protheroe: that poor little girl!' Hermione said, pointing.

'It is impolite to point, Hermione. And it isn't a little girl. People like that are known as "dwarfs" or "midgets". So what do we call her, dear?'

'A dwarf.'

'Or you could say, "a midget". Good. She is the daughter of one of the estate workers. Her mother cleans the stable block. We must always remember to count our blessings and be kind to those less fortunate than ourselves.'

'I've seen the girl there sometimes. Do you know her name?'

'I do not, Hermione, and I wouldn't think of asking. She isn't your class, you know.'

Hermione had assumed that the child was about eight years old. Now that she looked more closely, she saw that she was a good deal older than her height – barely four feet – suggested. Her square face was compressed as though the features had been crushed, giving her a low forehead and heavy glowering eyebrows. The hem of her shabby coat had been shortened by some twelve inches and the extra material was wrapped round her neck to form a muffler. Her cheeks were buffed red by the wind but there was utter

61

dejection in her mouth and unfocused eyes.

'Can we stop?' Hermione asked. 'I want to talk to her.'

'Of course you can't *talk* to her, Hermione dear, she's a dwarf, as I said.'

'But Miss Protheroe, you also said just now that we must be kind to those less fortunate than ourselves. The poor dwarf is much less fortunate than I am.'

'Nearly every child is less fortunate than you are, Hermione,' Miss Protheroe retorted sharply. 'Now turn round and face forwards. It is unkind to stare.'

Hermione put one gloved hand on her governess's arm and looked directly into her eyes. 'Please . . .?' she implored. '*Please* let me.'

Miss Protheroe, staring ahead, knocked on the partition and ordered emphatically, 'Make haste, Brymer, or we shall be late!'

Hermione brooded on the small, struggling figure. She understood how it might feel to be freakishly short, being herself so very tall. Rose Daubeny, towards whom they were now speeding, was a whole year older, yet several inches shorter. Hermione told herself firmly that she was definitely not a freak, but it would be a relief when she stopped growing. At this rate she would soon equal Richard's height.

Miss Protheroe greeted Rose's nanny and they propelled their charges towards each other.

'Here's your *friend*!' said Rose's nanny.

'Dear Hermione has looked forward to this treat *all week*!' said Miss Protheroe.

The two girls scowled.

'*I*'ve got a new *doll*,' said Rose.

'I've been reading *Coral Island*,' said Hermione.

'Cook's made a chocolate sponge for tea,' said Nanny Daubeny.

'Hermione's brought Rose a *present*,' said Miss Protheroe.

'Can you play L'Attaque?' asked Hermione.

'Course not, it's a boys' game. But my brothers can,' Rose said.

'So can I and *I*'m not a boy.'

'They'd beat you easily.'

'*Rose!*' said Rose's nanny.

'Call them and we'll have a game and see,' said Hermione.

'They've gone out,' said Rose. '*Just this minute.*'

'Ah, grand, you've arrived,' said Laetitia Daubeny, Rose's mother, sweeping past on her way to the drawing room. 'How is your mama, dear? In *India*? Good gracious, whatever for? Well then, up you go to the nursery, have a jolly time!'

Hermione did her best but she failed to have a jolly time. It only made her long all the more for Sandy. She did not see the dwarf on the drive home.

The next day Hermione was sullen and uncooperative. Finally Miss Protheroe closed the book and said, 'Teach yourself then, miss, for I'm tired of your sulks!' They stared at each other until the governess dropped her eyes. Miss Protheroe left the schoolroom, was reported 'indisposed' at lunch, and Nanny told Hermione she was 'a wicked child and in disgrace for being haughty'. Then even Nanny turned her face away. They ate in silence.

Hermione never used tears as the easy way out of trouble. Sandy despised cry-babies. She was ashamed of having provoked her governess and upset by Nanny's ill-humour, but she finished her meal and said politely, 'Please may I get down?' Standing correctly beside her chair she muttered grace and left the room straight-backed. Once she reached her own room she slipped off her clattery shoes and ran silently downstairs, meaning to comfort herself by inhaling her father's aroma. She went into her parents' bedroom and, seeing a female figure seated at the dressing table, shrieked as if it had been a ghost. The figure turned. It was her governess, festooned with Mama's second-best jewellery. On her head she wore a tiara of garnets and pearls; long pearl and diamond earrings swung merrily with the speed of her movement; and her throat was encircled with an eight-stranded seed pearl and turquoise choker. Amid this bejewelled splendour, Miss Protheroe's pinched grey face stared aghast.

'How dare you!' said Hermione. 'How *dare* you open Mama's jewellery case, how dare you wear her things, how dare you sit at *her* dressing table . . .!'

'I shall be dismissed,' Miss Protheroe said bleakly. 'If you tell your mama I shall be asked to leave my post.'

Raising her hands to her ears, the governess began to unscrew the long pendants.

Hermione went over to the dressing table and undid the tiny gold hooks that fastened each strand of the choker. She lifted the sparkling mass – it resembled a miniature chandelier, she thought, and like a chandelier it tinkled delicately as the facets tapped against one another – laid it down carefully on the polished walnut surface and walked away.

Hermione saw the dwarf again a few days later, waddling along the village street, a tattered shawl draped over her big square head. Her stunted shape and rolling gait were unmistakable. Hermione had thought about her in the last few days. This time she turned to her governess and said decisively, 'I am going to talk to that person.'

Miss Protheroe did not reply.

Through the speaking tube Hermione instructed, 'Stop the car here, please, Brymer.'

The Daimler glided to a halt. Hermione threw aside the heavy rug covering her lap and stood up. Brymer alighted and opened the car door with a questioning glance at Miss Protheroe but the governess said nothing. Hermione levered herself out of the car and crossed over to the dwarf. She said, 'My name is Hermione Staunton. I live at Chantry Manor. I'm lonely and I need someone to keep me company. Would you like to come and live there with me?'

If the dwarf had stared dully back, incomprehension or hostility on her face, that would have been the end of it. But her protruding eyes fastened on Hermione with brilliant intensity and she said, 'Yes, miss, I know who you are. Everyone knows you. Fancy your being lonesome! I'm lonesome too.'

Hermione reached out and took the dwarf's cold hand.

'How old are you?' she asked urgently, sensing across the street the stolid bulk of Miss Protheroe stepping laboriously from the running board of the car.

'Fourteen.'

'You're older than me. I'm ten and a half. What's your name?'

'Florabelle. I chose it myself. I was christened Nora.'

'It's a nice name. Would you like to come with me, Florabelle? *She* can't stop you. She's not in charge. I'll talk to my papa when he comes back. He mostly gives me what I want.'

Miss Protheroe caught up with them as Florabelle clutched Hermione's hand in a desperate grip. 'Make him give you me!'

When Florabelle climbed into the back of the Daimler, the governess ordered Brymer to wind her window down, although sleet came slicing in and exposed her to its stinging damp. Hermione ignored Miss Protheroe and turned to Florabelle.

'Where do you live?'

'Downabouts the end of main street, left by church, through the trees, down to where the lane runs out,' the dwarf answered.

'How did you know who I was?'

'Mother helps out the head stableman, Mr Brymer I think he's called . . .'

'Him? This one, driving us? Brymer the chauffeur?'

Brymer turned for an instant and smiled at Hermione. He pulled his end of the speaking tube to his lips and said, 'That's right, Miss 'Mione. Her mother's Mrs Pinchbeck. She helps muck out the stables and hens and rabbit hutches. Her father does kitchen garden when work's heavy. Not like proper estate staff; they're casual helpers. Outsiders.'

'I see. Thank you, Brymer.'

Addressing herself directly to the dwarf again, Hermione said, 'Can you tell Brymer how to find your house?'

Florabelle sat bolt upright to enable her to see out of the windows and gave confident directions.

When the heavy car stalled in the muddy ridges of a cart track, Hermione got out and, holding Florabelle's starfish hand, walked with her up to the front door and banged on it. There was a shout from inside and the door was opened by a woman with bedraggled hair and a baby on her hip.

'Nora! Where you bin? Your pa'll strap you when he gets back. And who's – beg *pardon*, miss, I didn't see you properly – Miss Staunton, innit? What she done, then, my Nora? Bin stealin' has she? I'll make her give it back!'

'No,' said Hermione, speaking slowly to conceal her bewilderment at the clogged smell that emanated from the house and the gruff voice of Florabelle's mother. 'She hasn't stolen anything. We've come because I would like to borrow her – I mean, your daughter – for a while. My parents have gone a long way away, and I sometimes get lonely. Could Florabelle stay with me for a bit – a few weeks? I could give her back to you when they return. If you like,' she added.

'What for? What you want 'er for? She's a dwarf. Strong though. And who'll fetch me wood and dig fer me taters if you 'ave 'er?'

'*Mr* Pinchbeck?' Hermione said.

The baby had been staring round-eyed. Now it broke into a thin wail. Florabelle reached up for it. The baby held out its arms and Hermione realized that the baby, not the mother, was the magnet from whom Florabelle must be detached.

'I'll send a man down to bring you wood and – coal – and – here's some money,' she said hurriedly. She reached inside her cape and rummaged in a lace pouch that hung from her belt. 'It's only a few shillings – I haven't got my golden guinea with me – come, Florabelle, Miss Protheroe will be getting anxious. Don't worry,' she added as Florabelle handed back the crying child, 'I promise I'll be kind to her. We'll be friends. She can pay you visits and bring you nice things for Baby. Very soon. Goodbye.'

They climbed into the car, leaving wet marks on the upholstery and mud between the slats of the floorboards. Brymer spread the rug over her lap and Hermione pulled it towards Florabelle. They held hands under its warm folds, not needing to talk. *I've done it!* Hermione thought. Goodness, how she smells!

When they arrived, Hermione led the dwarf up three flights of stairs towards Nanny's room and knocked on the door. She heard the bed creak as Nanny levered herself off it, then her shoes creak as she laced her feet into them. She heard her stays creak as Nanny straightened up, and then the summons: 'Come in, my poppet!'

'*Wait a minute*,' Hermione whispered to Florabelle before entering the room by herself. 'Nanny,' she said, 'I've brought a friend to meet you. I want her to stay. Her name is Florabelle and—' she took a deep breath – 'Miss Protheroe says she's a *dwarf*.'

'A *dwarf*, dear? But why not a normal friend? I'm sure your mama wouldn't mind if Rose Daubeny came to stay for a few days. Well, show me this dwarf.' Patting Hermione's hand she added, 'Mightn't it be best to send her back home? Somehow I don't think your mama would like the idea at *all*.'

'Mama isn't here,' Hermione said. 'If she didn't mean me to be lonely she should have invited my cousins, or told Richard to stay and keep me company, not go gallivanting all over the country-side.' (This was a phrase she had heard the nursemaids use and she liked its fine indignant sound.) Nanny sighed. 'Just till they get back,' Hermione urged, calling out, 'Florabelle! Come in!'

'All right . . .' Nanny conceded; then, seeing the stocky, appre-hensive little figure: 'Well look at her, poor soul! Come here, ducky, let Nanny brush your hair.'

The crucial acceptance secured, Hermione and Florabelle headed down the corridor.

'There's where the nursery maids sleep – Molly and Agatha – and after Nanny's room comes mine and after that a sewing room and an ironing room and here's the schoolroom, and a room for doing experiments and painting in, then some more bedrooms, first of all my brother Richard's . . .'

Florabelle said, 'Where do *we* sleep?'

'You can sleep anywhere you like. Agatha or Molly will take the room next to you, so you'd have someone to call out to in the night.'

'I'll sleep with you,' Florabelle said firmly.

'You can't sleep in my bed with me!' Hermione protested.

'Then I'll sleep on the floor beside you, or ghoulies and ghosties'll come for me.'

'Not on the floor, dear,' Nanny said kindly. 'We'll look out Miss 'Mione's previous little bed. You can go in her bedroom if she wants you to. But young ladies don't share beds.'

'Now I must use the box,' Florabelle said firmly.

*

'Feed you, that's what we got to do,' the new cook promised once she had got over her surprise. 'Regular nourishing meals and you'll shoot up!' If Miss Hermione was the one in charge then Miss Hermione had better be obeyed. Rather her than that mother of hers, any day. Never trust a thin woman.

'Bread an' milk before breakfast; bread an' milk at night and eat up your greens in between. Good red meat an' lots of it. And 'arf a pint of porter when no one's looking!'

Florabelle knew better. She would always be a dwarf. Nothing would add an inch to her stature. What mattered was that in this household, under Miss Staunton's protection, she would no longer be despised and neglected.

Thanks to Hermione's fierce protective friendship and Florabelle's skill in adapting to the transition, she was quickly accepted as Hermione's companion. They were linked by acute intelligence. Florabelle had learned to read in Sunday school by the time she was eight. Miss Protheroe made the best of the situation and set herself to teach the girl to write a beautiful script, spending hours in the schoolroom with a handwriting book. On one line an anonymous calligrapher had inscribed *dog, good, gone, gold* with firm upright strokes and curvaceous loops below the line, like the reflections of a row of trees along a canal bank. The next line was empty for the pupil to copy these perfect words. Florabelle soon progressed to *The dog leaps high to catch the yellow ball* and in no time at all had mastered *Saint George slew the writhing dragon*. Soon words and sentences were marching steadily down the page, easy to read and a joy to the eye.

'*All work and no play / Makes Jack a dull boy!*' said Nanny when they had finished lunch. 'What are you going to do with yourselves this afternoon?'

Miss Protheroe smirked. 'My plan is that we all go for a drive to the Saxon church at Mapperton where I will teach these young *ladies* the difference between Saxon, Norman and Gothic.'

'Rounded, pointed and pierced . . .' said Hermione wearily.

Nanny frowned. 'Now now, dear, don't be impertinent.'

'It's raining. Can't we stay indoors?' Florabelle asked.

'Capital! We could play hide-and-seek!'

'You know all the best places already,' Florabelle objected. 'Let me have Betty to help me.'

'You can't play games with a *housemaid*!' said Miss Protheroe, scandalized.

'Why not?'

'Yes we can, if I say so!' said Hermione. 'I think it's a splendid idea.'

Betty was a broad-shouldered, rosy-cheeked girl of fourteen filled with energy and good humour. She had strong forearms, big hands and a bosom that already overflowed like a brimming fruit bowl. She and Florabelle had attended the same Sunday school class and both had been confirmed by the visiting Bishop of Salisbury. He had seized the opportunity to preach a sermon afterwards on the subject of those 'despised and rejected by men', the unfortunate outcasts of our society. Florabelle had never been to church since.

Crouched behind the library door, Hermione could hear them coming down the corridor. Their shoes squeaked on the polished oak floor and they were giggling.

'Which one do you like best?' Betty asked.

Florabelle replied, in a voice more strongly Dorset, 'The youngest footman – what's his name – Edward?'

'Milady calls him Edward but his real name's Joseph. We all have different names for milady.'

'Why?'

'It's 'cos she's Madam-nose-in-air. Thinks *Edward* and *Mildred* sound more *genteel* than Joe and Betty.'

They stopped and Florabelle lowered her voice so that Hermione could only just hear. 'What's she like?'

'She's a wicked monster, for all that she's got the loveliest little face you ever saw. She even looks down on Sir Jack. Master Richard's her darling. Look, she walks like this . . .' Betty's foot-steps became dainty as she minced up and down the corridor and Florabelle tittered her appreciation.

'Which one's *your* sweetheart?' she asked.

'Billy,' said Betty, adding in a dreamy voice, 'I'm going to marry him when I grow up. We'll suit each other. Think of it: Billy and Betty Brymer. Hasn't it a fine ring to it?'

'He's ever so handsome . . .' Florabelle said doubtfully.

'Ever so *bold*,' Betty said, and they tittered again.

Hermione felt as though she had been caught eavesdropping. The servants never discussed her parents in her hearing and she was shocked by Betty's frank criticism. Before they could resume she called out, 'Getting *warmer* . . .' and the footsteps speeded up. Hermione pushed the polished brass door handle so that the door swung outwards and jumping to her feet exclaimed, 'I won! Now we two will hide and Betty can seek.'

She did not like the way they had exchanged secrets behind her back. Florabelle is *my* friend, she thought, but she didn't tell *me* about Edward. But then, I never mention Sandy, either. Sandy was private; he lived at the heart of her, hidden from everyone. Hermione took the dwarf's hand and told Betty, 'Shut your eyes and start counting to a hundred.'

Betty thought, I don't know all the numbers up to a hundred. I'll go as far as twenty lots of times. '*One, two, three* . . .' she chanted firmly.

Within two months Florabelle had been transformed. Hermione's discarded clothes were let out to fit her. Dresses were shortened by nearly eighteen inches and triangles of material inserted in the bodice to accommodate her disproportionate bosom. The brow-beaten, scowling figure in a torn coat was well on the way to becoming an educated and refined dwarf; but no matter how much she changed or how much Hermione had grown to love her, Hermione knew her mother would never tolerate Florabelle. She must win over her father.

It was mid-March when her parents returned and the daffodils were in full bloom, the forsythia a glory. Their big black motor car swept round the gravel and halted with a flourish precisely in front of Chantry's stone archway where the staff waited in a semicircle, indoor to the right, outdoor to the left. Lady Staunton descended, followed by Sir Jack, an unfamiliar figure with a deep tan. At the sight of him Hermione broke loose from Miss Protheroe and without a glance at her mother, launched herself at her father.

'Papa!' she cried. 'Oh dearest Papa, how I've missed you! I have *languished* without you!'

He folded his arms round her (he had to reach up slightly to embrace her) and inhaled his daughter's sweet smell. Good Lord, how I love her! he thought. Now that Violet has gone, she and my son are the only people in the world I care for.

Phoebe's clear tones cut through father and daughter's embrace. 'And *what*, may I ask, is *this?*' she demanded.

Hermione stood back. 'Mama . . . Papa . . .' she said, and her voice trembled slightly, 'this is my friend Florabelle. We would like her to come and live here – with your consent, naturally.'

Florabelle dropped a perfectly judged curtsey – one that demonstrated both respect and dignity – before stepping forward. It was obvious that she expected to shake hands and Phoebe, taken by surprise, automatically extended her own; then snatched it away as though contact with that stubby paw would contaminate her.

'I was lonely while you were gone,' Hermione pleaded. 'Dick was away with his chums and I needed a friend.'

'Friend!' said Phoebe. 'Friend? *This?*'

Sir Jack did not share his wife's disdain for people of lower class or caste, or her dismissal of anyone who did not possess beauty, power or (as a last resort) wealth. Of course Hermione had needed a playmate. Alone in this huge stone house, surrounded by servants but with no one of her own age to amuse her – no wonder she had looked for a companion!

'Let us go inside,' he suggested.

The scene that followed quite spoiled their homecoming. Phoebe swept towards the drawing room saying curtly, 'Jack, we must *speak*.' When Hermione tried to follow the butler was ordered to close the door. The two girls were left sitting on a chest in the hall, half hearing the quarrel that raged inside. Eventually Sir Jack summoned his daughter.

'Your mama,' he told Hermione, 'absolutely refuses to admit that young lady . . .'

'*Dwarf!*' spat his wife.

'. . . to the household. I hoped I might persuade her, but she is adamant.'

Lady Staunton sat on a sofa opening her post with a silver paper-knife. Hermione addressed herself to her father.

'Dearest Papa,' she said softly. 'I know she is a dwarf. But she is a dear, good, clever dwarf, and my friend. You surely cannot send her away now!'

'I do not care for the word *cannot* . . .' her mother interjected silkily, without looking up. She scanned her letter with apparent amusement.

'Florabelle has become used to living here with me. Her life was utterly wretched before. I would . . .' Hermione searched for an adult phrase – 'I would *never forgive myself* if she were sent away!'

Her father shrugged his shoulders imperceptibly, the corners of his lips compressed. His ships sailed the globe and thousands of people all over it owed him their livelihood, but he could not compel his wife to do anything she did not want to do. Hermione turned.

'Mama, I beg of you! I *beg*!' In desperation she pitched herself at her mother's feet. Lady Staunton drew her skirt fastidiously away from her daughter, who remained sprawled on the carpet.

'This is not a Spanish court,' she said, 'and we do not need a jester. Jack, you may summon one of the maids to pack up the creature's belongings. She may keep the dress she is wearing. Brymer can drive her to – wherever she came from. No doubt her family will be more than willing to take her back in return for five pounds. Hermione, you are about to become hysterical. Go to your room and ask Nanny to give you some medicine to make you sleep.'

'*Mama!* Mama Mama Mama – *no!*' Hermione screamed. '*No!*'

Florabelle heard her from the hall and knew the good days were over. The cruelty of other people had been stronger than their kindness. It always was.

Hermione's face contracted, became scarlet, her eyes closed and clenched. Her father reached out, took her hands and drew her to her feet. He wrapped his arms round her. She buried her face in his linen jacket and wept for Florabelle, for the loss of Sandy, and because although she was not quite eleven years old she already knew with absolute certainty that her mother did not love her.

CHAPTER FOUR

BY 5 NOVEMBER 1914, THE LAST GUY FAWKES CELEBRATION FOR six years, Richard Staunton had already been in France for more than two months. Aged eighteen and fresh from the OTC at Harrow, he had joined the British Expeditionary Force as soon as war was declared; keen as mustard to show off his bravery and horsemanship and send the Germans packing, tails between their legs. 'You'll be home by Christmas,' everyone said, waving their boys goodbye. They had all been innocents then, seized with glorious optimism. They welcomed the war with open arms, thrilled and patriotic, certain of victory. 'A walkover,' everyone gloated. 'Send the Hun back where he belongs!' 'Teach the Kaiser a lesson.' Hermione had been innocent too, secure in the love of her father and Nanny. Only the absence of Richard darkened her happiness. That, and the fact that Sandy had not written. Since the sunlit afternoon in the meadow and the stream more than two years ago she had neither seen nor heard from him. Her own letters had petered out in the face of that implacable silence.

Richard survived the battle of the Aisne and his parents were confident that he would cover himself with glory before coming back to finish his academic career. Even Sir Jack, more realistic than most, viewed the war as a temporary, if tiresome, interruption to his long-cherished plans. It might be good for the boy to see action for a few months. Test his mettle; give him practical experience of leadership. A brilliant First was predicted after that (Oxford, Greats) and then – since his father was already seventy – his son would gradually step into his shoes at the Staunton Trading Company.

Richard Staunton had inherited his father's energy, generosity and decisiveness. From his mother's side of the family, thank God, he seemed to have taken only height and his dark good looks; so far he showed none of their capacity for idleness, arrogance or cruelty. Jack Staunton knew very well that he was exploited and despised by his wife. When the time came to die, his chief regret would be leaving Hermione to the mercy of her mother. Otherwise he would go willingly enough, knowing he had made his mark.

The estate workers in 1914 had shown their defiance of the Boche by building a higher bonfire than usual, topping it off with a Guy wearing an old tin saucepan at a rakish angle, in mockery of a German helmet. The fire was surrounded by a ring of charred potatoes that people tipped from one hand to the other until they were cool enough to hold. They warmed the palms and tasted of the bonfire, black and smoky on the outside, crumbly in the centre. A couple of tins of Saxa salt were passed round the circle.

Hermione stood beside Nanny watching red and yellow reflections sparkle in her mother's eyes.

'Isn't this *grand*?' Phoebe Staunton said, becoming aware of her daughter's gaze. 'I wonder if Richard's men have built a bonfire, too!'

'Unlikely,' her husband responded.

He lowered his heavy eyebrows and his forebodings created hellish pictures in the fire. Bomb or grenade explosions hurled earth and rocks skywards. The bodies of men and horses sprawled and groaned as burning fragments rained down. Jack Staunton had begun to realize that this war might not be straightforward. Winter was coming, trenches had been dug, but they were grim places from which to fight. He did not articulate the thought, for in November 1914 only protestations of patriotism were called for.

Just as long as Richard came out of it alive . . .

Their celebrations were interrupted by an elderly police constable, bumping his push-bike laboriously across the field to remind him that 'the ignition of bonfires and fireworks within defended harbours and proclaimed areas was forbidden after 8 p.m., as per the Order in Council proclaimed on 15 October 1914'. Jack Staunton clapped the uniformed figure on the back: 'Quite right! Very remiss of me! Douse the fire, lads – out with the flames . . . don't want to offer a target to the Hun!'

They all went indoors to drink to Victory.

The following year when Hermione was thirteen, her brother came home for a few days' leave. She asked him what the fighting was like. Richard scowled. 'Nobody who hasn't been out there can possibly imagine how dreadful it is. Not even Father. Mother must never be told and I'm certainly not going to tell *you*! No, don't sulk. You'll never know how lucky you are to be a girl.' The set fury behind his words, far more than the little he said, made her realize what horrors he had endured. For the first time she feared for him.

Richard survived the first two years of the war and emerged unscathed from the carnage of the Somme, only to die two months later, in September 1916, his fine profile quartered in the telescopic sights of a German sniper's Scharfschutzen-Gewehr 98. His death had been instantaneous; the padre's letter and the one from his superior officer assured them of that. He was twenty years and six months old. After this Phoebe Staunton disliked, even hated, her daughter for many reasons but above all for *not being Richard*. She would gladly have seen Hermione dead if that would have saved her son.

Now he lay in a war cemetery in northern France, a random collection of hastily gathered bones under a wooden cross like tens of thousands of other crosses; the carved letters spelling out his name: LIEUT. THE HON. RICHARD JOHN STAUNTON – KILLED IN ACTION 31-9-16. IN PROUD MEMORY. The black letters were rimed with frost in the cold dawns. The weight of grief at her brother's death propelled Hermione out of childhood. A great silence fell

75

between her parents. They spoke only to discuss details of the marble effigy and memorial that would stand for all eternity in the local church.

Often, during the next two years, Hermione sat with her father in the library after dinner, stroking his hand; but although a book or newspaper usually lay open on his lap, he seldom turned the pages. His fingers would tighten in response to hers but their former easy conversations were replaced by long silences. Occasionally he would talk to her half-heartedly about the responsibilities she would now inherit alone. He tried to pass on his guiding principles for Staunton Trading, but without conviction. Hermione knew that in time she would accept the finality of Richard's death and be young enough to get over it. Her father never would. It was impossible for him to acknowledge that his son, so young and brilliant, lay in a graveyard in northern France; that even after the war, when things returned to normal, he would still not come back. Richard was the last in the male line of the Stauntons of Oldham, shrewd hard-working men who for generations had stood with their legs braced and heads cocked, watching, listening and making up their own minds. Richard had represented the future of the business and the opportunity for a better shot at life than he himself had managed, despite the money. Without Richard, misery and old age descended, slackening his will, limbs, features, finally even his mind. Grief doesn't end; it hardly even recedes. People just lose interest.

Hermione knew that her father had not long to live. He was the only person who could tell her Sandy's fate. She did not trust her mother to give a truthful answer; she had to ask her father before he died. One evening, after they had been reminiscing together about Richard, she dared to ask, 'Papa, you remember the people at Otterbourne, the Gordon-Lockharts . . .'

'What about them?' he responded with a frown.

'Their son. Alexander. Sandy.'

He shook his head. Hermione put her hand on her father's arm.

'Papa, you *must* remember! You couldn't confuse him with anyone else – he was their only child!'

'If you say I must, I must.'

76

'Did you ever hear more about him? He must have joined up as soon as he was old enough. Whether he was wounded, for example, or . . . missing, or . . .'

'Why should you care? It must be seven years since you set eyes on him.'

'We were playmates when we were young.'

'Running wild all summer – I'm surprised yer mother permitted it.'

'She didn't know,' Hermione said simply.

'I daresay not.'

'Papa? *Did* you ever hear what became of him?'

'Not a word. And ye're not to go chasing around or finding out either.'

'Why not?'

'It wouldn't be suitable.'

'But *why* not?'

'Because I say so. There are certain things I'm not prepared to discuss. I'd know if he were dead and he's not. Now oof ye go and tidy yeself up. Yer mother'll be in any minute.'

'Don't tell her I asked,' Hermione pleaded.

'Why should I do that?' Sir Jack gave his daughter a rare smile.

At the end, watching the flesh fall away from his bones, his arms sag, his eyes collapse into craggy sockets from which only his eyebrows shot sparks, she did not want her father to live longer. Richard's death had taken all the fight out of him and Hermione knew he would surrender with relief to the first good reason for dying. Already hollow, he had neither resistance nor the will to resist. Sir Jack's death certificate in November 1919 gave the cause as pernicious flu. He was seventy-five. His body lay in the local church near the cold marble likeness of his son, under a plain grey memorial slab of granite that – on his specific instructions – said only: JACK STAUNTON 1844–1919 'FOR THIS RELIEF MUCH THANKS'. Now all three – the only three – people Hermione loved were gone, leaving her alone with her mother.

Old Nanny Rideout was dismissed with a pension of fifteen pounds a year. 'I've no idea where she'll go,' Lady Staunton said in response to Hermione's distress. 'She's a doddery old thing, no earthly use to anyone. You should have outgrown her long ago. Besides,' she added, 'I can't abide the way she shuffles up and down the corridors *looking for Master Richard*! It gives me the heebie-jeebies! There must be places that take people like her. She isn't my responsibility. Or *yours*, my girl, so I don't want any sentimental nonsense.'

Lady Staunton re-entered society after barely a month of formal mourning. The observance had been a pretence. Her main feeling on being widowed was one of relief, to which were soon added curiosity and greed. Leaving Hermione behind, she fled the dripping trees of Dorset as soon as possible – once she had ascertained the contents of his will and made sure her husband had kept to his stated intention of making her Hermione's main trustee. Having verified this, Lady Staunton celebrated her widowhood by cruising for five months aboard the *Phoebe* in the balmy Caribbean. She sent a Christmas greetings cable, directing it 'To All at Chantry'. 'All' meant Hermione and the servants. This time there was no Florabelle to keep her company.

Hermione preferred to grapple with her sorrow alone. For a time after the death of her father she had wanted to die as well. Who was there to live for? She visited the sick, hoping to be infected with flu, but her strong, well-nourished body had too much resistance to let her succumb. One afternoon, accompanying the district nurse on her rounds, she found herself in the lane where Florabelle lived. The two girls had glimpsed each other occasionally but her mother had forbidden them to speak and Miss Protheroe had self-righteously made sure that they did not. Now, ordering Brymer to stop the car, Hermione picked her way through mud and puddles to the end of the lane. She knocked. The door was opened eventually and a bedraggled woman, Florabelle's mother, glowered at her.

'You're too late, miss. She's gone.'

'Gone where?' Hermione asked. 'Away?'

'Where should she go? Her grave. Nobody wanted her – stunt and useless thing.'

'I wanted her,' Hermione said. 'I am sorry.'

'Too late,' the woman said again. She stared at the visitor's thick coat and scarf, her warm hat and high-sided boots speckled with mud. Hermione understood that she expected to be given money. She fished around in her purse and extracted two pound notes.

'Five pun' alive and two pun' dead then, is that it?' the woman said bitterly.

'It'll pay for a perfectly good tombstone,' Hermione said, in a flash of answering hostility. 'Put Florabelle on it, not Nora. She hated Nora.'

'Pinchbeck. Nora Pinchbeck,' the woman said stubbornly. 'She were my child, all right. *And* his.'

'She liked to be called Florabelle,' Hermione insisted. Turning away from the woman's closed expression, she trudged back to the waiting car.

'Dead then?' said Nurse Flowers, seeing the expression on her face.

'Dead,' Hermione confirmed.

'What was her full name? I ought to make a note of it.'

'Nora Pinchbeck. A very angular name for such a tender person. She was also sometimes known as Florabelle. She must have been twenty or twenty-one when she died.'

How odd, thought Hermione, that I have lost the use of tears.

They had hardly known her in the village before, except as the tall plain Staunton girl who sat stiffly in the car or the front pew in church. They must have thought her as cold as her mother, of whom it was rumoured that she gave the remnants of Chantry's Christmas dinner to the poor as an act of charity, having first ordered that everything – turkey, potatoes, soup and plum pudding – should all be scraped into one bowl and ladled into the waiting plates as grey, inedible slop. Such charity was despised, but by the time the flu epidemic had receded, Hermione's practical kindness and generosity had made her popular and even, in some households, loved. The district nurse told her, as they slogged wearily round the last of that day's visits, that she had an intelligent heart. Hermione could imagine no higher praise. From then on she was rooted in Chantry. Whatever her mother might say, she would never let the house be sold.

By the time Phoebe returned to England in the spring of 1920 her skin was translucently pale, the shade and texture of a delicate rose. A New York beautician had performed the first of many peelings; this one, she was assured, merely to remedy the coarsening effects of the sun. 'I assume you must soon celebrate your fortieth birthday, madam, but the smoothness and fine texture of your complexion is remarkable. You will be taken by everyone for thirty-four!' Phoebe, who was in fact a decade older, gave a small, sphinx-like smile. One expected adulation from minions. One did not respond. However, she did select a young woman, French, as it turned out, whose hands were notably swift and skilled, to act as her personal maid. Agnès – needless to say, she was downgraded to plain ordinary English *Agnes* at once, losing the fluid French pronunciation of her name – was to be Phoebe Staunton's lady's maid and closest companion from then until her death.

There were few celebrations when Hermione reached her eighteenth birthday that April. It was the age at which she might have been presented, had the Court resumed, but her mother returned to England only briefly to deal with the remaining formalities of her husband's will and to assure herself that the war had not depleted his fortune. In the end the girl would inherit everything but meanwhile, as his widow, she enjoyed the income from his millions. The interest alone would have financed six Chantrys and ten yachts. Phoebe Staunton had waited twenty-five years for this and felt she had earned every penny. She spent that summer in the sunny, spacious villa in the south of France, attracting a growing retinue of friends, some of them male, some of them young.

On Saturday 5 November 1920 the villagers gathered in the grounds for the first Bonfire Night in six years. The estate workers had made a special effort and the night sky crackled with shooting sparks. The huge pile of logs popped with little explosions that made the veterans flinch. More than one covered his face with his hands and melted into the night, racked with uncontrollable tremors. People murmured, 'Gun shy,' or perhaps, 'Shell-shock,' their tone sympathetic or contemptuous, depending on where they had spent the war.

Hermione stood by herself, a little apart, watching the bonfire blaze. She was thinking about Joan of Arc, trying not to think of Richard as well. Her imagination cast him as a wildly leaping figure encircled by a ring of flame, like the devils or witches from books of martyrdom. To change the subject in her mind's eye, Hermione wondered how she would paint flames. Not with water-colours – too wishy-washy – and although oils would whip up a storm they were too obvious. Ink would be interesting – a Samuel Palmer effect of radiance and sparks in the night. She stared mes-merized into the golden core of the fire. Her mother glanced sideways through the rich haze of an upturned sable collar and thought, the girl looks half-witted. Mouth open, eyes locked on nothing. What a blessing I didn't invite Rose and the youngest Daubeny boy – she corrected herself: the *only* Daubeny boy – and their parents to join us. Not the sort of impression one would wish one's daughter to create.

Hermione's newly appointed lady's maid Phyllis, straight from the employ of Lady Fitzmaurice in London, stood on the far side of the bonfire with the other servants, their faces lit up like roast meat by the crackling flames. Young Billy Brymer had spent the last two years of the war well behind the lines, looking after horses in readiness for the cavalry charges that never happened. His courage had not been tested. He had manoeuvred himself beside Phyllis and Hermione had seen the coy glance she gave him, and his answering wink. Billy, now an arrogant 26-year-old, had risen in the servants' hierarchy. He was no longer just a groom but in overall charge of the stables, while his father looked after Lady Staunton's growing fleet of automobiles. Secretly, Hermione was still afraid of Billy. Five years ago, at the servants' Christmas party, he had made a surreptitious grab and kissed her clumsily under the mistletoe when Nanny wasn't looking. 'There!' he had hissed triumphantly. 'Never forget that Bill Brymer gave ye yer first smacker!' She thought to herself, no you didn't, it was Sandy Gordon-Lockhart! – but of course she hadn't said so. She would marry Sandy; she had always known that as surely as she knew the capitals of Europe. He had been gone eight years now but that changed nothing. He would be back. '*Ah my Queen,*' he would say, '*thou hast not doubted me? I needs must prepare and make myself worthy for thee . . .*'

Hermione felt a touch on her shoulder and turned.

'Yes, Billy, what is it?' she asked coolly.

'It's the horses, Miss 'Mione,' he said. 'They're restless. The fireworks is fretting them. I can't see my dad nowhere.'

'You call me Miss Staunton now, Billy. I'm eighteen, not a child any more.' To demonstrate her adult authority she would show him her power over the horses. 'Very well, I'll come with you and calm them down. Mystery will be soothed by my voice. I'll just go and tell Mother—'

'Don't do that or my dad'll be in trouble,' he pleaded. 'Won't take more'n a few minutes. You'll be back before she notices you're gone.'

Hermione glanced at her mother and seeing her absorbed in her thoughts, left the warmth of the firelight and followed Billy's lantern across the springy meadow through the darkness until they reached the stable block.

The stable doors were double-bolted to shut out the noise and flashes of light. Unbolting the top half, Hermione could hear no sound from the six horses inside. She hardly had time to form an apprehensive thought before Billy's hand reached rudely past her to unlatch the lower half of the door. Pushing it open, he shoved her violently inside. The warm peaty smell of hay and horse manure filled her nostrils as she pitched forwards. She stumbled and would have collapsed but he grabbed her from behind. His right arm locked across her shoulders, his left hand covered her mouth. The skin of his hand was rough and his fingers, pressed hard under her nostrils, smelled of smoke. Against the back of her thighs she felt a hard protuberance that reminded her of the thickening of an over-excited horse. Each sensation was stupefyingly rough. Nobody had ever touched her so brutally before; not even her mother when, in a rage, she hurled a stinging slap at her daughter's cheek. Hermione's face would redden for a few minutes but it was never bruised afterwards.

Billy's grip would leave bruises. Her heart thundered in her chest.

'I'm goin'ter take my 'and away and yer not goin'ter cry out,' Billy said hoarsely into her ear. 'Nobody kin hear yer anyway. They're all watching bonfire.'

Hermione nodded her head once and he took his hand away.

'Nor yer not goin'ter tell no one,' he went on. 'I bin watchin' yer a long time, you an' that Sandy fellow. You was ever so fond of him, as I recall. Did dirty things together, didn' you? Billy Brymer can't be fooled. Billy was watching. Now yer ready fer this. Yer want it. Ever since I gave yer first kiss. Five years I bin waitin'.'

Hermione shook her head emphatically and the arm round her shoulders tightened abruptly so that her head jerked back against his chest.

'I bin waitin' an' so 'ave *you*,' he insisted. 'Now do as I tell yer an' there'll be no 'arm done. More likely do yer good. But never a word. Or –' he pointed to the thin, mean riding crops hanging beside a row of gleaming saddles – 'I'll thrash yer afore I go. An' I'm goin' where nobody'll find me.'

'I've never done you any harm,' she said, to delay him, 'and I've never given you any encouragement. You know that. So why, Billy?'

His voice hardened. The mocking banter disappeared from his tone. She heard him grind his teeth. 'Because of Betty.'

Hermione said nothing. She had forgotten who Betty was. All the female staff were unsettled by Billy's seething masculinity. He would stride through the stables carrying buckets or bales of hay, transmitting the stink of unwashed young manhood around himself like a shock wave.

'Betty, her name was, though your arse-nosed mama called her *Mildred* because "that's always the third housemaid's name". Saved her the bother of sortin' one from t'other. My Betty, my blessed Betty. The day she were thrown out I promised meself I'd make you pay.'

Betty, Hermione thought. She played hide-and-seek once, with me and Florabelle, and she had talked about Billy then. He was her sweetheart. She realized she had not even noticed Betty had gone. So that was why he was full of anger and revenge.

Dribble and mucus began to stream uncontrollably from Hermione's slack mouth. Her face wrenched into a grimace of terror. Billy, still behind her, could not see it but he shook her again so that her teeth rattled. Pushing from behind with his knee, he urged her forward.

'Git on up!' he ordered. 'Up them steps!'

He put the lantern down on the stone floor of the stable and its thin light illuminated the grains of corn and strands of hay that had been swept into the gully. A stream of urine gleamed iridescently. His knee jerked forward again.

'*Up!*' he ordered.

Hermione drew the back of her hand against her nose, spreading slime over her face. She turned round to confront Billy.

'You're wrong, Billy,' she said as slowly and distinctly as she could. When the housemaids had broken something, this was the voice her mother used to calm their hysteria and assert her authority; the voice his father, old Elias Brymer, used when soothing a nervous horse. She tried to maintain the same steady, toneless note. 'It's not my fault that Betty was dismissed. And whatever you do now it won't bring her back.'

He laughed into her face, a choking cough. His breath was hot and floury.

Hermione attempted a smile. 'Let's make a pact, shall we? Let's both turn round now and go back to the bonfire and as long as you don't lay one finger on me again – now or ever – I'll say no more about it. I give you my word of—'

Before she could finish the sentence he had pushed her hard in the chest and this time he did not catch her. Hermione fell, striking the back of her head against the stone floor. Her ears rang with the impact. Billy dropped to his knees and sneered into her face: 'Your word of *what*? Honour? I dun' know no honour, *Miss Staunton*. I'm good for nothin' but cleanin' tack an' scrubbin' horse-shit an' holding your mare's head! *Ain't I?*'

Her mouth dried up; she could not speak, her heart was beating so hard she felt sick. She realized he was angry enough to kill her, years of pent-up rage spilling out in bile and sputum. He pulled hard at her arm, swung her upright, and began shouting into her face, his eyes and mouth large and wet, his coarse brown complexion with its pockmarks magnified like the craters of the moon.

'I'm not good enough to pick a girl an' get married! I'm not livin' breathin' flesh 'n' blood – oh no, not like *you*, not like your mother, Lady Muck herself, all turned-up nose and "stand aside from me, you dirty under-groom".' (He mimicked her mother's high supercilious voice and her way of saying 'grum'.) 'But there's one thing I be good enough for and yer goin'ter find out what.'

He swung her round and propelled her ahead of him to the wooden ladder leading to the stable loft. With one hand under her buttocks he shoved her upwards while with the other he fumbled at the fly-buttons on his leggings. At the top of the steps she collapsed into a layer of hay, its sweet country smell entering her nostrils as her weight crushed the stems. Billy Brymer pitched on top of her.

Later that night Billy disappeared. His father Elias seemed as baffled as everyone else. Lady Staunton remarked casually that it was really most inconvenient but she did not pursue the matter. Head grooms were easily found. Hermione never told her mother about the rape. She might have told her nanny, but Nanny had been dismissed and Phyllis was too recent for such an intimate confidence. Shame, ignorance, rage and a deep internal pain made Hermione desperate to talk to someone, while fear of pregnancy made her crave information. Her knowledge about how her own biology functioned was minimal. She had been terrified when her first period started, convinced that these cramping abdominal pains must mean she was bleeding to death. Nanny told her they meant she could now become a mother and it was more important than ever that she allowed young men no liberties. 'Best not to go near them, my pet. Never know what a kiss might lead to . . .' Hermione would not dream of confiding in her mother. Since there was no one she could ask about the unseemly and – as she now knew – repellent details of human sexuality, she searched for a book to enlighten her.

There were several puzzling passages in the Bible and Shakespeare, too vague to be much help. 'Big with child' – that she already knew; she had seen plenty of pregnant women – and 'spilled his seed upon the ground' – had Billy done that? She didn't think so. Hamlet said to Ophelia, 'Lady, will you lie with your head in my lap?' but Billy hadn't asked her to do that. She sat in the dusky library, freighted with leather-bound tomes, her head bent over their brown and wrinkled pages. Finally she pieced together sufficient information from a volume on veterinary care for horses that set out the process between mare and stallion in straightforward terms with helpful illustrations. Billy had done to her just what the stallion seemed to be doing to the mare, without a groom holding her head. She consulted a dictionary and an encyclopaedia to find inexact definitions of words such as 'womb' and 'gestation' and 'vulva' that she had encountered in the horse manual. Putting two and two together she worked out that Billy had copulated with her and that if gestation occurred its duration would be approximately forty weeks. She could find no information about the early signs of pregnancy and horses were not necessarily a reliable guide as to when *her* womb could be expected to start swelling. Hermione spent six months in a state of fearful apprehension but when at the end of this time her stomach remained flat, she decided it was probably safe to assume that she was not carrying Billy Brymer's child. By then she was just nineteen.

She possessed two secrets, now and for the rest of her life. She had given her heart entirely to a boy of twelve. Nearly ten years later, she had been violated by a groom. His slime had been smeared across her face, her mouth and her thighs. The shame was so appalling that she could only bury the memory and be thankful that the theft of her innocence had not been compounded by the humiliation of giving birth to a bastard.

PART TWO

The Tyrant's Stroke

1894–1926

CHAPTER FIVE

ONLY THOSE BORN TO GREAT WEALTH CAN IGNORE MONEY, treating it as just another of nature's gifts like sun, air or water. Hermione had no taste for luxury – or so she believed, never having known austerity. She would sometimes wonder why, since her mother already owned all the jewellery, clothes, furniture and paintings she could possibly need, she seemed driven to acquire more and yet more, until their houses in London and Dorset overflowed with the new, the useless, the modish, the expensive, the glittering, the hand-made, hand-painted, hand-fitted. Phoebe's brothers and sisters and her 77-year-old mother could have told her the reason but they seldom saw Hermione and were hardly likely to admit that a member of their august family had been – there was no other word for it – *sold*.

At the age of seven or eight the Honourable Phoebe Campbell-Leith had already been awesomely beautiful. Charlotte, Lady Blythgowrie – her mama – sometimes escorted the ladies to the top-floor nursery after dinner, leaving the men round the dining-table with the port. They would enter a darkened bedroom where the only sound was the soft breathing of three sleeping children. Bending over by candlelight to gaze at the flawless little girl, they would draw back and say to her mother, 'With such astonishing looks, one almost fears for her!'

'And you haven't yet seen her with her eyes open!' Lady Blythgowrie would murmur, smoothing the counterpane as she whispered, 'Ssh, Phoebe, my pretty pet, it's all right. Mama has come to give you a kiss.'

The other two girls were sometimes awake and might murmur, 'Mama, Mama . . .' yet the sweetly scented ladies seldom came to bend over them, for the Honourable Katharine (Kitty) and the Honourable Sibyl (Sibby) Campbell-Leith were big bony girls with square jaws who took after their father. They complained that it was not fair; Phibby had *all* the looks.

As the ladies processed down the stairs again in a flotilla of creamy bosoms and silk trains, their hostess would point out a portrait high above the great hall, adding, 'I have never seen eyes such as Phoebe's, except in this painting, here, by Ramsay. That is one of Wishart's ancestors, a young woman rumoured to have been a common laundress. She lived with the third son, a marriage by habit and repute not sanctioned by the church. When both the elder sons were killed – in the Peninsular War, I believe – she became countess, whereupon she finally agreed to marriage so that her son could inherit the title. Look: she has the very same eyes.'

The ladies could hear the men shouting raucously at some off-colour joke and knew that this smooth-skinned child would one day be a wife, outwardly gracious, privately submissive to her marital duty. Her beauty should ensure her the grandest of husbands – and it is some consolation for brutishness if the brute is also a duke.

Born in 1876, Phoebe was the latest child in an ancient and noble Scottish family. As well as her two sisters she had an older and a younger brother. The Blythgowries had been impoverished within a single generation by the agricultural slump and, though the scandal was never discussed in front of her, by gambling debts. Iain, the heir, so weak-willed as to be almost feeble-minded, was easy prey for any bounder who challenged him to a game of cards or bet him he could not hit three targets in a row. Her parents believed gambling debts were debts of honour, so when Iain had squandered his allowance his father paid them to maintain the family's good name; something he could not afford. Everyone and everything suffered as a result. The roof of the tower suffered, when its heavy stone tiles slipped off in the winter storms and were not replaced. The curtains in the drawing room hung practically in shreds, but were not replaced. Lady Blythgowrie sold her grandmother's diamonds, secretly and at a bad price, having first had them copied in paste. The rotting joists below the bathrooms were not replaced with good pine, though they had forests full of it. Phoebe never wore a dress that had not been handed down from one of her sisters.

By the time she was seventeen, Phoebe embodied the looks most admired in the 1890s. Her hair sprang from her head in shining abundance, her eyes were as large and velvety as pansies. Although she hardly reached five feet in height she was perfectly proportioned, her narrow ribcage and waist emphasizing a generous bosom and shapely hips. Her parents were impatient to present her at Court, after which a great marriage was bound to follow. Once the grand alliance was concluded, Phoebe's husband would take care of the cracks in the structure of the castle and her brother's debts.

Wishart Blythgowrie and his wife Charlotte mulled over possible alliances in bed at the end of the day, the only time they were alone together. All their hopes were pinned on Phoebe.

'Wishart, I have been through our visitors' books and *Debrett* and there is no one in Scotland under forty who possesses what we need.'

'Why so young? Phibby will marry where she's told. A widower, fifty, sixty . . .'

'A widower will have children of his own; they will have first claim on his wealth.'

'You are right. And *The Times*? Anyone suitable there?'

'One or two English dukes are sickening,' Charlotte said thoughtfully. 'The Marquis of Rothesay has just died. Then there's a new premier baron of England. He's only thirty but his house is as ancient as his name. No doubt it has the same problems as ours.'

'Whom shall I invite for the shooting?'

'Young Rothesay. This premier baron – won't hurt to look him over. The usual neighbours. Some moneyed fellow.'

'We don't know anyone with money. Not enough.'

'Who was that tradesman who wanted to buy five thousand acres of forest? Buys cheap, sells dear, beads for the natives, the usual exchange.'

'Staunton,' said Wishart, after a pause, as the name struggled to the surface of his brain past several malt whiskies and two glasses of port. 'Staunton of Staunton Trading. Came here with Gordon-Lockhart. Not *old* Gordon-Lockhart – his son, young Donald. The stu-stu-stu-stutterer . . . *you* know.' They smirked at the recollection of poor Donald and his vulgarly rich friend.

'Sounds unspeakable,' said Charlotte comfortably. 'Ask *him*, if he hasn't already got a wife. And ask that amusing friend of Iain's – what was his name? – yes, Harry! He'll have some sport with Staunton.'

Wishart yawned. 'You are a clever woman, my dear. And now I am going to sleep.'

They pushed their mouths together, turned away and slept heavily in their four-poster, impervious to the woodworm tunnelling through its frame.

Their plans crumbled into dust because within a month the Honourable Phoebe had fallen in love. Her sheltered Scottish upbringing had never exposed her to worldly wit and charm, let alone to sensations that made the blood thunder so hard in her veins that her hands tingled and her head swam. The same girl who, a few weeks earlier, had recoiled in disgust from a pregnant housemaid now found herself enthralled by a languid, fascinating bounder. His invitation to stay at the castle had come from her brother Iain – who owed him more than he could afford – in the hope that it would gain him extra time to pay. The bounder's name was Harry. He was more than twice Phibby's age and quite without scruples.

On the first day of his stay he threw himself upon her mercy. ('I know scarcely anyone here – I am quite overwhelmed by all these brilliant people. *You* must know someone who will take pity on me . . .?')

On the second day she offered to show him the best hide-out for stalking when the wind was blowing from the north-east.

On the fourth day she undid six bone buttons on the front of her jacket for him.

On the sixth day she raised her skirt as far as her knees and parted her legs a little for him.

On the seventh day he told her she must go to church to think and perhaps pray about what she was doing.

On the ninth day she pulled her blouse up to her chin, tugging impatiently when it got stuck in her belt buckle. After that he told her (whispering the words into her small cold ear) to slip her fingers into her soft cleft that night in bed and wiggle them about a bit to see what she found and whether she liked it.

On the tenth day she came to his room of her own accord at one o'clock in the morning, barefoot, wearing an old sprigged dressing gown.

'My precious pearl, I have something to tell you that will prevent your surrender. Ardently as you offer yourself . . .' (He kissed her small moist lips fervently, here and at every endearment, each pause between sentences.) 'Yet I cannot take you.'

'Nothing! Nothing can stop me! If Mama walked in now, this minute, I would tell her that we love each other!'

'*I am married.*'

'I don't care! Do you love her? No? Then I don't care one bit!'

'My angel, my treasure . . . oh my flawless little Phoebe . . . Now you must be very quiet.'

'We *are* whispering.'

'I know, my pearl, but you mustn't shriek, whatever happens.'

'I promise. Oh *Harry* . . .'

He didn't force her, not at any stage. It is easy to seduce a virgin if you have awakened her sexual responses. She yielded willingly to his whispered words, smoky fingers and teasing moustachioed lips. They had two weeks of trysts in the heather and four nights of love in the small hours before he had to go back to Lincolnshire, where for the last twelve years he had been living in the dower house, waiting for his titled bachelor uncle to die.

*

93

Phoebe Campbell-Leith, lissom, shining and only just eighteen, shimmered like a water-nymph. Her skin seemed rosily phosphorescent and every movement of her slender arms and legs had the effortless spring of youth. She was the most desirable creature Jack Staunton had ever seen. He could not know that her intoxication with the bounder was such that her laughter bubbled and spilled over everyone, even himself. At the end of two weeks, Harry borrowed fifty guineas from the man he despised for being 'in trade' and caught the train back to Lincolnshire. Once the bounder had departed, Phoebe's melancholy shadowed eyes seemed to hint at greater depths to her nature than girlish frivolity, or so Jack thought, having no clue as to the real reason. He proposed and was loftily rejected.

A few weeks later, the unfortunate consequence of Phoebe's seduction could no longer be denied. Her parents told her that she had disgraced both herself and her family's good name and had no choice but to marry Staunton. There were, after all, advantages to be gained from the transaction. He was hugely rich and childless.

Jack Staunton was a northerner of humble origins, the only son of an Oldham undertaker who had fallen on hard times when his wife died giving birth to their second child – a daughter, Hester. Until then his father Joseph Staunton had been a craftsman joiner, a man who worked in wood, who built and knew and loved furniture and might have risen to be a cabinet-maker if Maria had been spared. Jack was a brilliant lad; always gifted with figures, he began doing his father's accounts when he was nine years old. He started his working life at the age of thirteen as a clerk in a clapboard office with windowed doors, through whose panes he was watched as he added up columns of figures, trying to make their totals correspond to what his dishonest employer told him the amounts should be. He learned a good deal about how numbers can be made to lie and gave notice after eight months, just a week before the police arrested his employer for swindling. Honesty is the best policy was the lesson that fourteen-year-old Jack learned from his first job.

Thirty-five years later the Staunton Trading Company Limited had its head office in a granite ocean liner of a building in the City of London, and a secondary branch in Liverpool, backed by others on Wall Street and two more in Chicago and Buenos Aires. Jack Staunton employed agents all over the world: sweating in the moist heat of Bombay; wrapped in furs against the Arctic winter in Canada (wolverine for wear, sable for beauty); and grappling in Australia with illiterate sheep farmers offering tens of thousands of carcasses. Wherever goods could be bought, processed, refrigerated and shipped at a profit, Jack Staunton's entrepreneurial genius was there.

By the time he was in his late forties he worked in mahogany linenfold-panelled offices with green-shaded brass lights that illuminated his papers for the equally steady beam of his concentration. He lived in a world of men. Several hundred male clerks toiled over bought ledgers keeping them up to date; male secretaries saw to the minutiae of his life, freeing his mind to occupy itself with tides and interest rates, harvests and weather forecasts. A valet, a cook and a butler waited on him and his unmarried sister Hester, in an apartment occupying three floors on the north side of Eaton Square. (Staunton rented out the ground floor and basement. He had no use for them; why leave prime residential space to waste?) The servants padded around on velvet feet, adjusting the temperature of his food, drink, bedding and bathwater. Jack Staunton had had a frugal upbringing and he preferred his drinks cold, his food tepid and his bedroom icy.

As long as Hester lived he could tell himself that he had a family. Hester, poor lass, was plain, with a long nose and chin like Mr Punch and red hair like his own, but she had a sweet and playful nature whose innocence had never been coarsened by the need to scrape a pittance or find a husband. Jack looked after her. He had no other relations; no close friends, few acquaintances. He trusted no one, loved no one except his sister. Nobody touched him, except to shake his hand or slake his sexual appetite. When his penis burned with frustration he cooled it, just as he would thrust a red-hot hammer into a bucket of water. Jack Staunton never visited the same whore twice, which kept the transaction simple and free of awkward consequences.

Two years before his marriage, Staunton had bought a country

95

property: a fifteenth-century house hidden at the end of an overgrown drive guarded by fine wrought-iron gates. It had stood empty for five years; the buildings had been neglected, the gardens run to seed, but as soon as he clapped eyes on it Jack knew Chantry Manor possessed everything a man could possibly want from a house. He believed the same of Phoebe for a few months – that she personified everything his heart desired – but although wrong about the girl, he was right about the house. He bought it in a probate auction for four and a half thousand pounds, which made the locals snigger and say the man must be a fool, it'd cost him that much again – nay, Bob, reckon *twice* that – before it'd be fit for him to spend a night under its roof!

Chantry was composed of three or four separate houses connected to one another at angles, not one of them an architecturally correct right-angle, facing wide swards of tender Dorset green and the traces of a once-splendid garden. Its high timbered roof was like the hull of a great ship turned upside down; it had heraldic stained glass set in tall oriel windows, and fireplaces wide enough to accommodate a blaze that could heat the stone hall, seventy feet long and forty feet wide, and warm the paws of hunting dogs as well as ladies' cold feet. It had flagged stone floors downstairs and golden oak floors upstairs. It was as venerable as any Scottish castle and by the time Jack had finished it would be much more comfortable. Even the neighbours were congenial.

One in particular, Violet Gordon-Lockhart, went out of her way to be welcoming. She would order the carriage and bring a hamper of cold lunch for him. She watched as he strode around in shirtsleeves, checking progress, issuing orders, overseeing the masons, carpenters and glaziers who swarmed over the old house. His thick-set, muscular body and purposeful manner intrigued her. Ardent glances led to an ardent embrace and for the first time in his life, Jack found himself making love to a woman of the upper class. She told him that she was devoted to her husband but marriage, alas, left much to be desired. So, he said, did the bachelor life. They sighed, caught each other's eye, and laughed. Jack had never before experienced a physical relationship in which the pleasure was mutual. He and Violet suited one another very well. Love was never mentioned.

When half the craftsmen in Dorset had laboured for more than a year to complete the rehabilitation of Chantry, Jack Staunton and his sister installed themselves. The house was the cause of Hester's death. The year was 1893 and she was not yet fifty. Two or three times her brother had brought her down to Dorset to view progress and on one of these occasions she poured herself a glass of water that had flowed through a foetid pipe. 'Ugh, that tasted funny!' she said after she had drained it. 'Don't you drink it, Jack.' Within days she began to develop a fever. By the time modern plumbing had been installed the damage was done, and poor Hester lived barely six weeks in the great house. She sickened, rallied, sickened again and died. Jack had counted on her companionship for the rest of his life. In the months after burying her he found himself longing for intimacy; for a domestic life lived in harmony beside another human being. Violet was tender and consoling but even as he mourned Hester, he knew the time had come for him to marry. He resolved to find a woman like his sister but younger (so that she could bear him children) and prettier, so that he could play his marital role with ardour. Ironically, it was Violet's Scottish husband Donald who first introduced him to the Blythgowries.

Within two months of setting eyes on his host's daughter, Jack had appointed Lord Blythgowrie to a well-paid non-executive director-ship on the main board of Staunton Trading. Shortly after that he made Phoebe's father a conditional offer of shares in his companies and government bonds worth almost three-quarters of a million pounds. In 1894 Staunton's gift was sufficient to restore Gowrie Castle, pay Iain's debts and usher the Blythgowries into a secure old age, as befitted people of such ancient standing. In return her parents promised him the hand of their silent – he thought modest, pure and understandably apprehensive – daughter. Phoebe accepted his pro-posal (what difference did it make, she thought, since her heart and body were pledged to Harry for ever?). Jack did not know that his bride was pregnant and nobody stopped to wonder if he loved her, not even Phoebe. A week later, in the castle's private chapel, the

Honourable Phoebe Campbell-Leith, of the eleventh generation of Blythgowries, became the Hon. Mrs Staunton. If the bounder felt a pang of remorse on hearing the news, he hid it well. 'Deflowered his bride *and* took money off the fellow!' he would boast. He pronounced it 'orf', as was usual among men of his class; the lender would have said 'ooff', as Oldham people do. Harry would add, 'That'll teach him not to mix with gentlemen above his station!'

Phoebe's new husband had spent thirty years surrounded by people who obeyed his instructions to the letter because their wages and families stood or fell by his favour. He was tired of the loneliness of authority, the weight of decisions, the great responsibility that enormous wealth imposed. He envisaged a new side to his life in which intimacy, tenderness and loving glances would replace the male formality of orders. He saw his young wife as a shy creature to be tamed very gradually, not forced but coaxed to accept his touch.

He took her to Bordighera, on the Italian Riviera, for their honeymoon. He had the self-control not to hasten into her bed but bided his time. Each morning he heard her vomiting in the bathroom adjoining his dressing room in the villa he had rented for two months. He took this as a sign of nerves or homesickness but when, after four days, she was no better he began to worry. Food poisoning could kill with devastating speed.

They shared a silent breakfast of coffee and rolls on a marble-floored terrace. A white tablecloth sparkled in the winter sunshine and the dark blue sea danced and glittered all the way to the horizon. Phoebe crumbled the fresh dough listlessly, sniffed the milk and turned away.

'You are not well, my dear. I should like the local physician to examine you. Perhaps the food here, or the water, disagrees with you?'

'No!' she said. 'Nothing is wrong! Leave me alone! I do not need a physician!'

'Would you prefer to cut short our stay? Perhaps you are missing your mother?'

'No!' she said vehemently. It was not her mother she missed.

After two more weeks he thought perhaps shyness and modesty

rather than nerves prevented her surrender. That night he knocked on her bedroom door.

'What do you want?' she called, her voice as rapid and febrile as his heartbeat. 'What are you waiting for? You are my husband. You have conjugal rights. Why do you act as though I had any choice?'

'You have every choice.'

'I am your wife, aren't I? I am your chattel – your possession. Anything is better than this suspense.'

Feeling ashamed of himself, he opened the door, entered and took her.

Phoebe had believed her parents when they said no man of good reputation would marry her and in Scotland, with its puritan distrust of pleasure, they might have been right. As it happened the reason for her marriage, floating blindly in darkness, eyes closed, fists clenched, weighing less than a pound, was miscarried at the end of the fourteenth week. By then Jack Staunton had noticed her swelling abdomen and knew he was not its cause. When she began to bleed one night he called the local physician; an Italian who treated the young mother with the utmost tenderness, laying firm competent hands on her heaving body and thrashing forehead. After disposing of the small corpse and bloody placenta, he soothed the weeping girl with a mild dose of laudanum. He withdrew to the study where her husband waited by the light of a gas lamp as dawn crept over the headland. He assured him that there was no reason why *la signora Stonton* should not bear him many healthy children.

'You must be patient with her. Every mother has special feelings of love for her first-born. I will pray for the soul of the dead child and for the future happiness of you and *la vostra moglie*, signore.'

When the honeymoon was over Jack brought his wife home, not to Eaton Square, but to Dorset. With the house he had also bought the Chantry furniture, much of which had been there for so many hundreds of years that the feet of chairs and tables, linen chests and dressing chests, had almost grown into the floor. The first thing Phoebe did when she took possession was to have this furniture stored away in attics, barns and outbuildings so that she could commandeer her own. She ordered heavy carved baronial pieces specially made by Waring and Gillow. These overwhelmed the soft stone and panelled rooms but they reminded her of the dark gloomy spaces in which she had grown up. Now she was mistress of her own grand establishment, and still hardly out of childhood.

Phoebe had married Staunton convinced that she would never take pleasure in his attentions, but a young woman with a powerful sex drive that has been awakened with the utmost skill and a husband who is neither cruel nor repulsive, finds her own biology hard to deny. Acquiescing in his love-making once or twice a week made her moan hectically and throb to her own rhythm, but afterwards she was filled with self-disgust. Phoebe thought her husband's working-class origins made him coarse, mistook his restraint for stupidity and spent the rest of her life exploiting the bottomless well of his genius for making money. Jack Staunton had begun by being deeply in love with his wife, although he soon stopped telling her so and after a while stopped hoping she would learn to love him back. Love – giving and getting it – was an experience he craved, having been without it for most of his life. But Phoebe only ever loved two people: Harry, her seducer, and Richard, the second child she conceived – Jack's son – who was born in March 1896 when she was still a few months short of twenty.

Laughing once – decades ago it seemed – languid and replete with love, Phoebe had asked Harry to tell her his other names.

'I'll test your history, minx. Let's see if you have been a good girl and paid attention to your governess. I am called after Plantagenet.'

'Richard!' she said immediately.

'Richard. You shall be kissed for paying attention in class.'

'What else are you called?'

'John.'

'Harry Richard John. And what else?'

'Ah! That is my secret.'

'Cuthbert? Aloysius? Ethelred? Inigo?'

'NO! I am Rumpelstiltskin and you shall be my bride!'

By some strange alchemy Phoebe's baby, named Richard John, grew up to look like Harry, almost as if shreds of the infant miscarried at fourteen weeks had clung to the walls of the womb, there to be transmuted into its half-brother. This likeness was not lost on her family, who indulged in a good deal of waspish speculation. They were wrong. After that momentous August in the heather, Phoebe never saw the bounder again. Dorset is a long way from Lincolnshire, and in any case he still owed Jack fifty guineas.

Phoebe's two plain sisters had married morose Scotsmen, men of their own class and kind. Kitty, poor Kitty, was now Lady Hugo Conynghame-Jervis, having married the third son of a marquis – a runt of a man with the bad smell expression of hauteur on his face. Sibby's husband, Fitzroy Shepherd, was so stupid that it took him several seconds to work out what a joke meant, and he sat in company with his Adam's apple gobbling convulsively. When Jack received his baronetcy in 1897 (a fervent believer in free trade, he had given thousands of pounds to the Liberals) they all laughed behind his back. To his face they asked to borrow money. 'I say, that's awfully good of you. I wonder, could you make it three? Just for the time being?' No question of paying interest. Not much hope of paying it back, either. After all, the fellow had money to burn, what?

In 1920, a quarter of a century after the marriage in which she had sacrificed her happiness for them, Lady Staunton's family continued to disapprove of her, even the dissolute heir she had bailed out. Her sisters wrote letters of condolence on the deaths of her son and her husband – not because they cared about either or about Phoebe herself, but because it would have been bad form not to. The upper classes, however monstrous, set great store by good manners. In a secret vision of the future she saw herself as a shrivelled, quavering old crone whom nobody desired and nobody touched, forced to rely on unreliable servants; unadmired, unwanted, alone.

Long afterwards, when her mother was dead and Hermione reconstructed her own youth, it made her sad to realize how great a gap would have had to be bridged if her own extended hand were ever to grasp her mother's small, limp one. They shared no nicknames, no secret language, no private jokes, no made-up words. Although they both craved comfort, they had no vocabulary for affection and had never been in the habit of tenderness. If she had told her mother that Billy Brymer had raped her, Phoebe would probably have laughed.

CHAPTER SIX

WHEN SHE WAS JUST TWENTY, IN 1922 – THE YEAR WHEN FORMAL presentations were resumed after the war – Hermione Staunton, one of the richest young women in England, was presented at Court. She inclined her large, triple-feathered head and curtsied to the King and Queen, a pair of stout marionettes who hardly bothered to hide their indifference. This signalled official acceptance by society and allowed her to attend the dances held nightly in Belgravia and Mayfair.

Each evening before setting out, Hermione's face was dusted with pink powder, her highly coloured cheeks were rouged, her mouth dabbed with more rouge to make it shine. Strands of jewellery – pearls or diamonds – were draped limply about her person, their long loops emphasizing her height. When this ordeal was over Hermione stared into the mirror knowing that she looked grotesque. A reassuring word from her mother would have brought life to her expression, but Lady Staunton only tightened her lips in speechless despair before preceding her down the stair-case in a delicious slipstream of Mitsouko. They emerged through the porticoed front door, and Brymer handed them into the waiting Rolls.

Once, exasperated by her daughter's silence, Phoebe leaned forward and enquired languidly through the speaking tube, 'Didn't you have a *son* once? What happened to him? Is he dead?'

'He found another situation, madam,' the chauffeur answered without turning his head.

'Oh. Not the war, then?'

'No, madam. He left your service two years ago in November.'

Lady Staunton had no further interest in the matter. Had she turned to look at her daughter she might have been startled by the brilliant rush of blood that suffused Hermione's face; but instead she closed her eyes with a small sigh of boredom.

Hermione's debut attracted little attention. Charm, even a puppyish eagerness to please, might have helped but she was painfully shy. Her large features drooped with an unhappiness easily mistaken for disdain. The Blythgowrie tendency towards height had been exaggerated by a childhood of good food, vigorous exercise and fresh air, and Hermione had shot up like a foxglove – not a delicate and cultivated plant. Billowing white organza and tulle sprinkled with diamanté stars only accentuated her size and the plump white mink stole round her shoulders made her look larger still. Had a man shown any interest, perhaps her heart might have lifted and with it her eyebrows and her glowering expression, transforming her into someone quite different. But even if she had been one of the restless, effervescent debs whose behaviour earned them the nickname Bright Young Things, she would still have been overshadowed by her mother – for who, presented with Phoebe's sparkle, praise and pretty feminine artifice, would look twice at Hermione?

Phoebe glittered like a tiny brilliant bird in this jungle of matchmaking. Her shingled dark hair would have shown off one of her diamond tiaras, but unless royalty was present she preferred to wear a satin band set low across her forehead, into which jewels had been sewn in artless profusion. The band covered some of the lines that, at forty-six, faintly indented her brow. Her pliant form swayed in dresses from Madame Grès in Paris, every movement seeming to undulate along her body down to her narrow feet.

The men who had survived the war despised the empty ritual of the Season. How could they be happy and frivolous among people who had never known their dead friends or lived through the trenches? If they did attend a dance it was to get raucously drunk, in defiance of pre-war decorum. Those too young to have fought were boys newly hatched from public school, their world bounded by Greek verse and house cricket. In spite of this, the small band of debs' delights : . the salons and ballrooms of London were the object of intense competition. None could live up to the image Hermione carried in her mind's eye of an eleven-year-old boy, half Peter Pan, half Mowgli. Her gaze was always a little distant as she searched the faces of the crowd from under her pale eyelashes, with little hope of finding Sandy – for what would that wild and golden boy be doing in *this* prancing company?

Now and again she danced with someone who had been to the same school and might have known him.

'Sandy Gordon-Lockhart and his family used to be neighbours of ours,' Hermione would say non-committally lest her tone betray too much interest.

'Oh, really?' her partner might say. ''Fraid I've completely lost touch with him. Had rather a good war, I believe.' More often the response was, 'We were in different houses . . .' or regiments, or colleges, or counties. She searched like Bobby for his elusive trail but never caught his scent: the smell of muddy boots, tweed jacket, tousled hair and white mice.

Right at the end of July, at one of the Season's last dances, a sturdy young Scotsman said in answer to her tentative question, 'Gordon-Lockhart? Comin' to shoot in a few weeks' time. Ken Sandy, do you? Fine chap. One of the best.'

Hermione stumbled and lost her rhythm. She halted on the floor of the crowded ballroom and looked into her partner's eyes.

'You know *Sandy*?' she said. 'You'll be *seeing* him soon?'

'Aye. Your people shoot?'

She lowered her head and muttered, 'My father's dead. And my brother . . .' her voice trailed away, '. . . was killed.'

Something about her snagged at his interest. 'What did ye say your name was?'

'Miss Staunton. Hermione Staunton.'

'He had a good war, as they say. Decorated, twice I think. Now? I seem to remember something aboot Sandy an' Oxford . . .' (He rolled the 'r's like a cat purring.) 'But dinna take my worrd furrit. I've a memory fule o' holes.' He grinned, then asked abruptly, 'Are ye all right? Ye look, I don't knoo, peely-wally all of a sudden.'

Hermione laughed (thinking, that's the first time I've laughed all evening . . . all *week*) and said, 'What does *peely-wally* mean?'

'It means, och, like –' he cast his eyes around the room – 'like that old woman over there. Washed out and poorly-looking. It's no' very complimentary.'

'Oh, you mean pale and willowy! That woman there is my mother and she wouldn't thank you for calling her *old*.'

'You lost all yer colour for a moment. Aye, that's better now.'

The music stopped.

'Ye'll no want to dance again?'

'No.'

'That's a relief,' he said, leading her to the conservatory. They subsided on to a creaky wicker sofa and looked at each other properly for the first time. She thought, finally I've met someone who doesn't talk nonsense. Who is he?

'I'm sorry, I didn't catch your name.'

'It's Buchanan. Hamish Buchanan . . .'

'How do you do, Mr Buchanan?'

Courtesy was second nature, however heathery his accent. So as not to embarrass his partner, Lord Hamish Buchanan said, 'I'm no' so formal. Ye could call me Jamie.'

'Thank you. Is it all right . . . sitting out? I expect you'd rather dance with someone else?'

'No, I would not. I can kick up Scottish reels all night but this kind o' *nothing* dancing tires me out.'

'Then why are you here?' she couldn't resist asking.

'It's my sister's dance.'

'Your *sister* is Lady Elspeth Buchanan?' Oh glory, she thought: he must be the son of the Earl of Dunglaister! I should have known.

'Aye. Tell me about your mother,' he said. Hermione's

shoulders slumped and he added quickly, 'Ye dinna have to. I must say, she doesnae *look* like yer mother! She looks, though I shouldna say it, a mean woman. Not like you.'

'I look like my father. I don't take after her side of the family except that I'm what Mama calls *strapping*. Her family is Blythgowrie and they're much older than his. He was plain Staunton from Oldham.'

'The Blythgowries of Peebles?'

'Yes: do you know them?'

'I do not. Old they may be, but thieves and vagabonds they are too. Though it's said their women can be lovely. Ye've a bonny smile, when ye care to show it. Better'n paint.'

She wanted to say, *please tell Sandy Gordon-Lockhart! And give him my . . . regards and ask him to get in touch with me. Tell him, H. Minor said so . . . please* but Hamish was cupping a hand under her elbow to indicate that he wanted to stand up. He smiled to show he was sorry to leave her and said, 'Ye'll forgive me, Miss Staunton . . .'

'Oh, please, won't you call me Hermione?'

'If ye wish – *Hermione* – but my mother will be after me for neglecting oor guests! It's been a breath of fresh air to talk to ye. A real pairson is a rare thing, down south. An' ye're nae strapping, ye're bonny!'

'Jamie . . . thank you . . . yes . . . goodbye,' she said.

He bowed and left with a swirl of his kilt.

Returning home with her mother well after midnight, Hermione would go up to her bedroom, where Phyllis helped her to undress and prepare for bed. She often regaled the maid with an account of her evening, although she could hardly hide its stupefying and repetitive dullness.

'You have to *smile* all the time,' she sighed. 'You're supposed to smile at the other girls to show that you are friendly and not stand-offish; you're supposed to smile at their mothers to show you're enjoying yourself; you're supposed to smile at the men to show you're good fun. Smile, smile, smile. I've given up smiling. I just let them have my ordinary face.

'And then,' she would continue, as Phyllis brushed her hair dreamily, 'you must always, always be polite. Not that I want to be rude, but nobody ever says anything *real*. Such as, I'm hot, or I'm tired, or, isn't this just exactly like all the other dances? You have to say, aren't the strawberries delicious or, don't you just adore champagne or, doesn't our hostess look charming? You might just as well say "Remark number four" or "Remark number sixteen". You could have them all printed on the back of your dance card and just point. It would save your breath for dancing.'

'Do the men have to do it too?'

'Not nearly as much. They're allowed to boast about how many runs they scored or what high fences their horses can jump. Then you're meant to smile again and say, "Oh how *clever* of you! It must have been wonderful! Did everyone applaud?" That's all they expect. The dullest, ugliest, clumsiest man is better than you are.'

'*No*, Miss Hermione, he's *not*!' Phyllis assured her loyally. 'What do the young ladies say?'

'They talk about the best way to get a husband. When they're sitting out the girls talk about nothing but love, and when they're in the ladies' room having their hems mended, if there are no mamas about, they sometimes whisper they were kissed behind a curtain. But none of them ever says anything interesting.'

'It sounds interesting enough to *me*!' Phyllis would murmur.

CHAPTER SEVEN

THE SEASON BEGAN, THE SEASON ENDED. NOTHING CHANGED. Then, one day in late autumn, having returned from a languid month in the south of France, Lady Staunton found her daughter's sketchbooks. Idly she flipped through their pages.

'Good gracious!' she exclaimed. 'These are really not bad. How very surprising. What is your drawing teacher called again? Williams, yes, that's right. If you want her to come twice a week I daresay it could be arranged.'

'Miss Williams stopped instructing me more than a year ago, Mama. But I *should* like to attend art school. Chelsea, the Royal Academy – if they accept women students – St Martin's, the Slade . . . If you haven't time to look into it I will.'

'Enough!' Her mother covered her ears. 'Not Chelsea – far too Bohemian. I can't have you running wild all over London. What was the last place you mentioned?'

'The Slade.'

'I've heard of it. Send them a letter and say you wish to apply. You will have to live here with me, naturally; no *question* of some hall of residence – but Brymer could drive you there and back, always supposing I don't need him. Write a letter, address it to the

Principal, and see what happens. It's most unlikely that they'll accept you in any case.'

'Yes, Mama.'

Hermione learned that the Slade School of Art had no entrance examinations and no requirements apart from basic ability and a burning desire to paint. Four months later, in January 1923, she enrolled. Her drawing teacher was a crusty fellow called Tonks, Professor Henry Tonks, a teacher of genius. In class he often reduced untalented female pupils to tears – 'Do you *knit*, Miss Parker?' – but to anyone with a spark of inspiration he was mellow, caressing, encouraging, inspiring. Hermione was one of his favourites. She learned fast, perched amid a semicircle of attentive young women, all sitting on short benches with an easel at one end called 'donkeys'. Her life at the Slade was all stimulus.

Each morning on arrival she grabbed a calico smock from a row of pegs. They had deep pockets for chalk, paint rags and erasers and reminded Hermione of the starched, pleated cotton smocks that Nanny had dressed her in, ten summers ago. Several of the female students wore long loose dresses in imitation of Dorelia, the statuesque beauty who had borne several – though by no means all – of Augustus John's children. Dorelia epitomized the artist's muse; silent, patient, self-effacing; content to serve his genius and his offspring, immortalized by his art. Nobody tried to look like his sister Gwen, though Hermione thought her the better painter.

Hermione wore hand-tailored tweed suits ordered by her mother in winter and dull, expensive silk or crêpe de Chine frocks in summer. Her hair was parted in the centre, looped back from her forehead in two wings and held on top of her head by a narrow ribbon. Her blouses had wide floppy collars bound with more ribbons and she wore trailing scarves ('to try and disguise your *bust*,' her mother said). It was not a style she would have chosen for herself but it wasn't worth the hysteria and insults that followed any disagreement. Her hand-made pigskin shoes, moulded to her big feet and fastened with ivory buttons or silver buckles, betrayed her wealth to anyone with half an eye, but if people commented she would pretend they had been handed down by a rich cousin. Above all she wanted to be ordinary. She had not earned her fortune, struggled for it or done anything to deserve it. Not long after the spring term had started, she instructed Brymer to drop her at the corner of Euston Road. She preferred to walk the two hundred yards up Gower Street to the Slade, hoping to hide both the Rolls and the fact that she was richer than anyone else in her motley, chattering crowd.

Hermione spent hours with her trustees, assenting to decisions taken on her behalf. Jack Staunton had known his wife too well to give her control. Phoebe could turn on the taps and money would gush forth but the reservoir belonged to her daughter. Each Monday morning, extending a white arm from her pillowy double bed, her mother would say, 'Here is your allowance . . .' Then she would hand Hermione three new one-pound notes. A meal cost sixpence and a shilling bought a feast, so three pounds was wealth. It meant that after class, Hermione could pay for coffee and cakes in the cafés along Fitzroy Street, offer cigarettes all round (she did not smoke herself), or lend money to needy students. She shared her drawing materials – great blocks of Ingres paper and tomato-red chalks – when they copied classical casts of the Venus de Milo and Discobolus in the Antiques Room. She never minded whether paper, chalk, coffee, cigarettes or money were repaid and she never felt exploited. Art was the passion that made them all equal.

Hermione found friends at the Slade, in particular three other girls: Pixie, Dolly and Victoria. The four called themselves 'the clique'. Dolly Simpson said 'click'. They were the first friends – apart from Florabelle – she had ever chosen for herself and she valued them far too much to bring them home. Pixie might have gasped and spun round and said, 'Oh my word, Hermione, isn't all this just the *greatest* fun? I mean, it's too ridiculous for words!' but the other two would have been intimidated by the vast Eaton Square mansion and she had no desire to emphasize the gulf between them. Occasionally she caught glimpses of their home lives. Victoria might say, 'Four o'clock – Daddy'll be back soon – my mother will be putting the kettle on to boil,' or Dolly would sigh, 'Laundry Monday . . . and I'm not helping Mum to mangle the sheets! Can't believe my luck.' Pixie laughed, 'What *would* my mama say if she knew I had walked down the street beside a man who was not a relative? She'd have the vapours.'

'She'd have you verified *virgo intacta*,' said Victoria.

'Might not be easy . . .' Pixie answered daringly.

Pixie Renfrew – she had discarded her baptismal name, Penelope – was gay and capricious, defied every rule and cared not a fig for convention. Hermione would have given anything to be like her: reckless, untidy and wayward; a true Bohemian. Pixie wore marvellous colour combinations – lime green and oxblood red, deep ultramarine blue and pale cadmium yellow – cribbed from the colour wheel. Her loose frocks were topped off by bright red lipstick and embellished with ropes of beads that swung as she gestured. She was the only female student to consort openly with men, for her parents lived in Yorkshire, too far away to know that she had rented a tiny studio flat in Chelsea to which – she told Hermione – she invited friends of both sexes in the evenings.

Dolly Simpson was the oldest in their group. The daughter of a seamstress and a clerk, her dazzlingly original talent had won her a full scholarship, without which she would not have been able to attend the Slade. She was the darling of the tutors and the apple of Tonks's eye. But she had half a dozen younger brothers and sisters and the moment classes ended she would dash for the 244 bus to go home and help her mother. Her father had suffered shell-shock in the war and could not hold down a job.

Victoria Waterman, the fourth member of the clique, travelled up by train every day from Herne Hill, where her father taught in a boys' private school. Her older sister was married and had a handicapped child, so Victoria had to hurry home to share the responsibilities of domesticity and motherhood. She was at the Slade because her mother was determined that her daughter should avoid her own fate: a life of dreary self-sacrifice to her family. Victoria herself was more realistic. The Slade years, she suspected, would be a brief emergence from the chrysalis of suburbia but when they were over she would earn – if she were lucky – a few extra shillings a week doing sketches for fashion magazines.

Male students at the Slade – scarred and caustic war veterans or clumsy young puppies straight from school – were greatly out-numbered by the women, as they had been during the Season. Pixie regretted this but Hermione did not. No flesh-and-blood man could compete with Sandy's intoxicating, imaginary praise.

'*I say, old thing, that's pretty good!*' he might comment admiringly.

'*Which – the Laocöon or this torso of a dying warrior from the Parthenon?*'

'*I don't know about the Laocöon . . . I'd have to count its arms and legs. But that fallen figure – marvellous. You've really captured his beaten look.*'

She would demur. '*Sandy, you praise me far too much.*'

'*Don't be silly, Minor. You're really good. Good as – who was that lady artist whose exhibition you took me to?*'

'*Gwen John?*'

'*That's the one! Every bit as good as Gwen John.*'

These fantasies were some consolation for the absence of male company, or of Sandy in person.

As the end of the first year approached the clique could usually be found working side by side. On a warm summer's day when classes were over, Hermione and Pixie would stroll, arms linked, through the streets of Bloomsbury. At weekends they ventured into the Modernistic galleries of Bond Street or peered through the windows of narrow, noisy cafés in the grimy back streets of Soho where the artists gathered. Hermione mistrusted the brutal aggression of contemporary painting and sculpture. Pixie listened to her judgements and said, 'I know where several of them meet. I could introduce you. Be grand to argue with them face to face.'

'How? Where?'

'Well, we could try the Café Royal first. That's full of noisy, exotic types. Or we could gatecrash Bellotti's. It's a dinner club in Soho. Only we'd have to disguise ourselves as men. Easier for you than me. What a lark! What do you say? Are you up for it?'

Not yet, she thought. 'I'm not as adventurous as you. Give me time.'

Pixie looked at her. 'I say, old thing, you aren't by any chance nurturing a secret sorrow?'

'No,' Hermione said.

Sandy wasn't a sorrow. Since meeting Jamie Buchanan she had a fresh aspect of him – a soldier's courage – from which to create new fantasies. She knew war was not glorious and this made Sandy's bravery seem all the greater. She pictured him crawling through mud as the two of them had once crawled through bracken, only this time it was not a pretence. Like a magician, he had stepped through a black curtain that day in September 1912 and vanished. She was obsessed by the image of a tousled small boy silhouetted against the sky.

'*Buck up, Minor!*' he was shouting. '*Do come on! It's simply topping up here!*'

And she always called out, '*I'm coming.*'

One day during a life class Professor Tonks paused beside her donkey and gazed for so long at her drawing that Hermione feared a torrent of criticism. Used to her mother's sarcasm, Hermione doubted if she would be easily disconcerted but as his silence lengthened she began to tremble. Abruptly he asked, 'Planning to marry, Miss Staunton? Hm? Are you? See yourself as a wife one day?'

'I hope to be an *artist* one day, Professor,' she replied. 'If I am good enough.'

'Stick to it. Trouble with you young ladies, after twenty-one the genius that I, *I*, have nurtured, wobbles and wavers' – he shivered like a jelly and his hands trembled derisively – 'and you begin to think marriage is more important. Genius in women must be chaste as a nun. If you seek fulfilment, concentrate on art. If you want babies, take a situation as a nursery-nurse. Or be wife to some dull stick in the City.'

'I do not seek marriage,' Hermione assured him.

Tonks softened. Poor brute, he reflected, she's not likely to find it. He said kindly, 'Marriage may seek *you*. Steel yourself to withstand its blandishments.' He laid a stern finger on her arm. 'Don't let me catch you talking to a man, not even on the staircase, not even to excuse yourself for brushing by him in passing. *Chaste as a nun*, Miss Staunton! Now, this drawing. That shoulder there – look. Use your *eyes*! What is the artist's most valuable tool? Hm? Hm? Brush? Hand? Colour? Scale?'

'Eyes,' she said.

'*Eyes*, Miss Staunton. *Eyes*. Look at that shoulder – let your eyes absorb it – *then* let the hand reproduce it . . . good, good!'

He moved on, leaving her shaken with exhilaration.

For her degree show Hermione painted a canvas in which a scene of carnage from the war and a shooting party in Scotland were inextricably mingled. The bodies of men, who might have been dead or merely asleep, surrounded by dogs, pheasants and stags lay on the ground like toys whose mechanism had run down or been stamped on by a malicious child. The colours – green, purple and steel grey – could have been those of a battlefield or a moor. The sky above was the colour of a rotten mildewed grape, threatening a storm. The sun, its rays splintered like the facets of a chandelier, threw an uncertain light upon the scene. The picture seemed filled with menace but if you looked closely, in the top right-hand corner the figure of a small boy surveyed the scene with interest. In grubby shorts and an Aertex shirt he sat with his chin propped on his fists, elbows on knees, as though admiring his handiwork. The picture was called 'cynical' by many and cited as proof that the horrors of the war already seemed no more than a nursery game to the present generation.

Only Professor Tonks raised his bushy eyebrows as he peered at it, then turned to his waiting pupil and said, 'You do me credit, Miss Staunton! You can draw and you can feel! You've a great future, if you choose to grasp it. But have you the hunger? Eh? Eh?'

CHAPTER EIGHT

HERMIONE WAS TWENTY-FOUR BY THE TIME SHE LEFT THE SLADE. She had – not a degree; they were not awarded in 1926 – but a diploma that entitled her to teach. She had a clutch of friends, all female. But she still lived at home, entirely subject to her mother's whims, not even free to choose how to spend her money or the next day, let alone her future.

Phoebe resented her daughter's talent, especially since she herself had no gifts, small intelligence (though great guile) and at the age of fifty her beauty was fading fast. She disliked living with Hermione yet would not let her go. Rather than allow the trustees to buy her a house with a studio – which Hermione could have shared, quite respectably, with one or two friends from the clique – Phoebe chose to keep her daughter under her own roof. She could not have explained why. Because Hermione gave her a pretext for remaining in London? But she needed no pretext; she could do as she liked. Because she might bring young men to the house in Eaton Square whom Lady Staunton could amuse herself by fascinating? Phoebe could still attract men, though nowadays it was her riches rather than her flower-like face that attracted them. Or was it simply that, like any mother and daughter, they were caught on the barbed wire of shared birth, blood and memory?

'There's no question of your *working*,' she told her daughter. 'Asking people to pay for your little pictures would mean depriving others, who need the money and have far more talent, of the chance to earn a living. It would be wrong.'

'Perhaps I could go to Paris for a year,' Hermione said, trying to keep the request and her voice casual. 'It would be good for my French.'

'Paris? I don't want to spend a year there!' her mother objected. 'I am prepared to go for a week or two. You know how I hate the boat train, though for your sake I would endure it – but a *year*? Put that notion right out of your mind.'

Hermione looked at her mother's face dispassionately, the alabaster skin stretched over bones as neat and elegantly pointed as a cat's, the highlights on cheek and chin, the petulant crease in her forehead and the lines round her large dark eyes that could no longer be disguised. She itched to draw the languid gesture with which Phoebe stroked her brow, conscious of the indentations. The curve of her hand was like that of Japanese ladies in the drawings of court life by Utamaro – the same vanity and world-weariness. She turned to look out of the window as a delivery van from Whiteleys clattered past. It was a rainy July day, the streets sluiced and gleaming with iridescent blues and blacks, the shattered puddles reassembling to mirror the greenery in the square and the fastidious galoshed feet of passers-by. Those umbrellas – what could she do in paint with umbrellas that the Impressionists hadn't done already? Paint the feet instead! she thought. Put the feet at the top of the canvas and paint the puddles and an upside-down world reflected in them . . . the pavement your horizon, the sky in the gutter.

'What do you want me to do all day then?' she asked.

Her mother laughed, a sound like a lapdog's bark. 'Do? Do what I do. Make your toilette, write letters—'

'To whom?' her daughter murmured, and was ignored.

'—be fitted for costumes for the autumn, have your friends to tea, or dinner – I have never refused to entertain your friends . . .'

'I have never asked anyone to dine.'

'Perhaps you should begin! You have a responsibility to marry. It takes a man to run the business, administer the trusts, supervise our investments. How do you expect to find a husband in Paris? Or do you propose to marry a Frenchman?'

'I don't propose to marry anyone.'

'Well then you *should*. Think of me! Think of the burden of responsibility I carry on your behalf . . .'

I cannot bear this petulant tirade again, Hermione thought; I have heard it so often already. Mama can't accept her age – woe betide anyone who remembers her birthday! – and longs to have her youth and beauty back. She would love to talk to me for hours about how to fascinate men. I am the wrong daughter for her. Yet I have to live with her for another twenty or even thirty years. I must be pleasant, control myself, try to find excuses for her and look for the best in her nature.

'Mama,' she interrupted. 'Please don't let yourself become agitated. Let me ring for champagne. That will lift you up, the Boy always does. Are you expecting a guest to luncheon?'

'Champagne, yes,' said Phoebe. 'Luncheon? I have no appetite. Go away. Leave me in peace. I'll try and think of some suitable artistic venture, since you are evidently bored to tears by *my* company . . .'

Hermione's sole concern was to dispel Phoebe's perpetual boredom – and her own, if possible. One day she persuaded her mother to come with her to the Wallace Collection. Hermione admired the rosy frivolous French nudes and met the tenderly appraising gaze of Madame de Pompadour. Her mother wanted to know what eighteenth-century ladies did to preserve their looks.

'Nothing,' Hermione said. 'Most of them would have been dead at fifty. *She* was' (pointing to the gaily-beribboned Pompadour). 'They died in childbirth or caught a fever or a cold. Painters flatter them. I don't suppose they preserved their looks at all. Their skin was pitted with scars from the pox or ruined by lead poisoning, their hair fell out because they wore wigs every day, and they smelled bad.'

'*Smelled?*'

'Everyone smelled. But candlelight softened the imperfections. In the corners of ballrooms and salons it must have been almost dark. Only the very important or the very young stood in the centre, under the full glare of chandeliers.' She would have liked to talk about Gainsborough or suggest going to the National Gallery but Phoebe merely said, 'Candles! *What* a good idea.'

From time to time Hermione managed to escape her mother's stifling company. Victoria Waterman might telephone, or Pixie, and together they would visit the Tate or the Omega galleries; or spend an hour browsing through the Cooling Galleries in Bond Street, where the London Artists' Association exhibited. Hermione studied the work of her contemporaries, trying to assess whether her own was as good. Her friends showed their portfolios and sometimes a gallery owner would display some interest, but she had not yet dared to do so.

One afternoon while her mother was resting with a sick headache, Brymer drove her and Pixie to Heal's Mansard Gallery, to an exhibition of French artists such as Matisse, Derain, Picasso, Cocteau and Braque. Their colours and shapes excited her – Matisse with his palette of stinging primary and secondary colours, his ability to catch the essence of something without being distracted by shading or detail. She was staring fixedly at one of Picasso's seaside paintings, saturated with blue and grey like a sky after rain, when Pixie tugged at her sleeve.

'Look!' she whispered. 'Over there! Wasn't he one of Tonks's favourites – what *was* his name?'

'I don't think we were ever introduced,' said Hermione, thinking: *I* was one of Tonks's favourites and what good has it done me? At that moment the young man became aware of their covert glances and looked up. His face broke into a tentative smile and he raised an eyebrow. Pixie crossed the floor towards him and held out her gloved hand.

'Dr Livingstone, I presume?'

'Gerald Shebeare, actually,' he replied with a broader smile.

'I'm Penelope Renfrew – but you can call me Pixie – and this is my friend Hermione Staunton. How do you do? We recognize you from the Slade, don't we?'

Gerald shook hands with each of them. '*That*'s where it was! Yes. How do you do, Miss Staunton . . . how do you do, Miss Renfrew? What do you think of the show?'

Pixie said, 'It's marvellous, all this new, fresh work. I can't *wait* to get back to my studio and try out the same effects!'

He smiled at her enthusiasm, which seemed to make her curly hair and bright blue eyes sparkle with energy.

'Oh, absolutely! Frightfully thrilling – what do you say, Miss Staunton?'

'They're *grand*,' Hermione agreed. 'I was just examining the brushwork on that Picasso . . .' and she launched unself-consciously into a technical discussion, forgetting to be modest or deferential or, as her mother so often told her, to let the *man* do the talking.

' "Let the hand guide the brush, but let the brush do the work",' Gerald quoted.

' "Thick or thin, light or heavy, transparent as water or clotted as cream . . ." '

'Yes, that's right – and do you remember how Professor Brown always drummed into us "the beauties of the accidental and the spontaneous"?' Hermione went on. 'He made us give up all our lazy preconceived ideas and never paint generalizations. An apple had to be as individual as a face. Picasso does that too. If you look at this rock here – it isn't just *a* rock; it's *the* rock; *that* rock; one *particular* rock . . .'

'How do you know?' Pixie asked. 'Maybe he invented it.'

'Oh no! He *couldn't* have done! That's what makes his paintings so truthful.'

'May I invite you ladies to join me for some refreshment, so that we can continue this delightful encounter over coffee and perhaps a slice of treacle tart?' Gerald interrupted. 'I believe Heal's has a cafeteria . . .'

Hermione hesitated, unused to being paid for, but Pixie beamed.

'Goodness, you are kind! That would be *topping*!' she said, tucking her hand through his arm. 'There, now that's quite enough "Miss Renfrewing" . . . you must call me *Pixie*. Come on, 'Mione, you take his other side and Shebeare will escort us to this cafeteria.'

Travelling back to Eaton Square by cab after seeing Pixie into the Underground station at Goodge Street, Hermione thought, this has been the most thrilling afternoon of my grown-up life. Not since Sandy have I talked to a young man as an equal, wanted to hear his opinions and win his approval. *Gerald Shebeare*. To think we worked in the same rooms, drew the same classical models, for three years and I never knew his name!

As she crossed the hall her mother called out querulously from the drawing room, 'Hermione! Come here! Where have you been? Come here at once!'

The butler helped her out of her jacket, opened the door to the drawing room and stood back as she entered.

'Where have you *been*?' her mother repeated, puckering her lips to expel an irritable V of cigarette smoke.

'I went to see a new exhibition with a friend.'

'One of those Bohemian, "artistic" young women, I suppose, with modern ideas and hideous frocks.'

'Yes, Mama, one of those,' Hermione said.

'A perfect waste of time. It gets my goat, the way you *will* go on meeting those arty types. Now sit down and listen. No, Ridley, no tea, nor for Miss Hermione either – Hermione, sit down. I have had a brilliant idea. It will give you something to do and get you out of the house and has the further advantage of enabling you to meet all sorts of *suitable* people. Young *men*, even. I am going to write to some of my friends and suggest you might paint their *dogs*. What do you think of that? Isn't it beany?'

'Thank you, Mama,' said Hermione and the joyous enthusiasm she had felt with Gerald and Pixie ebbed. Have you the *hunger*, Tonks had asked. She should have replied, have you met my *mother*?

From then on Hermione lived a double life. To please Phoebe, they travelled to the houses of her friends – sometimes in the country, more often in London – where Hermione would do an anodyne sketch of some bad-tempered pet dog, a King Charles spaniel, perhaps, or a pug, which she would later work up into a 'charming' oil. This would be placed within an elaborate gilt frame. Visiting the framer to order and collect it was the only interesting part of the process, for stacked up in his workshop (visible in the background through an open door) or leaning against the wall behind the counter, Hermione would see other works brought in for framing. She scrutinized them hungrily in the short time it took for her own picture to be parcelled up. Most were studio scenes, a row of apples on a windowsill with triangles of grimy roofs beyond, or floral studies, or landscapes – the banal stuff of the Royal Academy's annual summer exhibition – but occasionally she glimpsed work that showed real originality. There were other artists out there, seeing what she saw, working as she burned to work.

Her mother would telephone the friend.

'Hermione has a little surprise for you, darling! Yes – yes – it's ready. Well, we hope you'll be pleased. Shall we bring it over? Or would you care to take tea with us this afternoon?'

Hermione's portrait of this canine child never failed to delight the new owner. Many of these women had lost a son in the war and their frustrated maternal love was poured out upon their pets. They would exclaim over the picture, the likeness, the vivacity of expression in the dog's eyes and then often remarked with surprise, 'But Hermione dear, you haven't signed it! *Oh* yes you must. Every original painting has the artist's signature.' And, with a twinkling glance at her mother, her patron might add: 'How else will I prove it's genuine, later on when you're famous?'

Heaven forbid, Hermione thought, when I have done my utmost to make it anonymous.

''Mione's so modest,' Phoebe would sigh. 'She has no idea of her own worth.'

At this the friend would pretend to become serious.

'Yes of course . . . what do I owe you, my dear? You must tell me! No, I insist.'

'Hooey!' her mother would protest in a little drama of repudiation. 'We wouldn't dream of it! No, not a penny. She loved painting Flossie. It gave her something to *do.*'

Then the picture would be shown to its subject; a favourable place to hang it would be discussed, the handyman summoned to knock a nail into the wall – followed by another pantomime of standing back, admiring, comparing with the original. After every such visit Phoebe expected her daughter to express fervent gratitude. If the intention had been to bring her into contact with the sons of her friends, however, it failed. Hermione met a few of their daughters – listless girls pining for something to do – but no young men.

Hermione tried to arrange a meeting with Dolly Simpson, keen to know what she was doing with her blazing talent, but Dolly was already obliged to give art classes in the mornings at a girls' school and spend her afternoons at home, helping her mother with the younger children. Once so bold and brilliant, she was reduced to sketching during quiet moments in the staffroom between lessons, or drawing rows of hats for newspaper advertisements at sixpence per hat. To supplement her wages, on which her mother and her younger siblings depended heavily, she also worked secretly two or three evenings a week as an artist's model, earning one shilling and sixpence per hour clothed, two and sixpence nude. Dolly had no time to meet Hermione and the clique in the cafés clustered near the Bond Street galleries. Instead, she sent postcards, each with a drawing full of vivacity and observation executed on the reverse and a few scribbled words: 'Love to meet – not a hope – ever so sorry! D.' These served to remind Hermione that there were worse fates than her mother's petty tyranny.

Hermione's circle of friends shrank to two – Pixie and Victoria Waterman. Victoria lived in a hostel – 'digs', she called it – in De Vere Gardens, which prided itself on its respectability. Prayers were held at quarter to nine every morning in the large communal drawing room. The girls were allowed out twice a week till midnight, if they gave notice of where and with whom they were going, and if the Principal, Miss Roseveare, approved. Anyone expecting a male caller could commandeer the drawing room by hanging a notice on the door announcing 'Reserved for Miss Blank'. (Miss Roseveare understood the problems of getting to know young men and was prepared to make certain concessions to help her young ladies towards that vital destination: marriage.) If the caller stayed after 10 p.m., however, the Principal herself would come and eject him. Hermione visited Victoria once or twice but found the female atmosphere of her digs oppressive. Victoria seemed to be losing the ability – or the desire – to paint or even visit galleries. Within six months, Hermione guessed, she would be teaching at some girls' boarding school, set for a life of spinsterhood.

Pixie's studio flat was Hermione's window on the real world. Her mother had peered at it suspiciously through the back window of the motor car when dropping her off but fortunately she had assumed that Pixie's parents owned the whole building, a tall red-brick house in a street near the Chelsea Physic Garden.

'It's a very curious address!' she told Hermione. 'It must be most unhealthy living so close to the river. I'm surprised they don't move somewhere less damp. Nevertheless I think it would be fitting if I were to come in and meet her people.'

'The Renfrews are in Yorkshire,' Hermione said hastily. If her mother saw the assortment of small studios that filled the house, the paint-stained basins on the landings and the door marked WC behind which stood a grimy lavatory serving two floors and half a dozen people, she would never be allowed to visit Pixie again. 'Perhaps when they return we might invite them for tea . . .'

She waited by the front door until the car had disappeared into the wintry fog of late afternoon before ringing the bell marked 8: RENFREW.

Footsteps clattered noisily on the encaustic tiles and Pixie appeared, wearing a shapeless blue dress with a deep square-cut neckline over which dangled two long strings of brightly coloured beads. Bright red lipstick emphasized her pale skin and her short, black hair was parted in the middle and gleamed like a gramophone record. She had recently adopted a fringe in the style of Louise Brooks and looked dashing and modern.

'You couldn't possibly guess who's here!' Pixie announced breathlessly. '*Gerald Shebeare!*' Her eyes shone.

'*No!*' Hermione closed the door and followed her friend up to the third floor as Pixie chattered excitedly, turning to watch Hermione's reaction.

'Do you remember Randall *Finch*? – no? – you would if you saw him – tall, red-haired, perfectly *splendid* chap – well, one afternoon I was just bringing him a pot of tea – I forgot to say that *he* has a studio here *too* – and *Shebeare* was with him! They're *friends*; they were at the Slade together, like us.' She lowered her voice as they reached the narrower steps leading to the upper floors. 'I left them alone but *afterwards* I persuaded Finch to ask him *again* so we could all have a conflab . . .'

The door directly ahead of them swung open.

'. . . *and here they are!*' she concluded triumphantly.

'Who?' asked Gerald Shebeare.

'Well, as a matter of fact, *you*,' said Pixie.

They sat in front of the fire toasting bread and crumpets, talking as Hermione had not talked for months. Randall Finch was very tall and thin with long limbs and bony fingers and he held forth with such intensity that sometimes he would fall to his knees in front of one of them and grasp their hands between his, as though compelling his opponent to hear him out. Shebeare was more self-contained; a better listener than talker. He watched his friend with amusement and occasionally he and Hermione would exchange a glance as Finch and Pixie became more and more animated in support of an artist or a theory. They moved on from painting to poetry. Pixie defended Marinetti the Futurist – a daringly incomprehensible poet.

'I've never read his work,' said Hermione.

'You don't *read* it, ''Mione,' said Pixie. 'You have to hear him declaim it. It's frightfully thrilling! His *voice*!'

'Where does he . . . declaim?' Gerald asked and Finch said, 'Crabtree's. It's a nightclub with wooden tables and benches and a platform where musicians or modern poets perform their latest stuff. You have to be a member to get in, or the police would raid it. Well, sometimes they do anyway.' He turned to Hermione. 'Would you be interested?'

'I shall have to ask.' Hermione hesitated. Mama would never allow her to visit such an eccentric new-fangled establishment. Gerald, watching her, thought, poor old girl – completely under her parents' thumb.

'Why don't I accompany you home this evening – where do you live? Is it far? – then you could introduce me to your mother and *I'*ll ask her. She might find me an acceptable escort.'

Hermione's face lit up and Gerald thought, she may be plain as a pikestaff but she's got hidden depths. Wonder what her work's like?

'Oh, *would* you?' she said gratefully. 'Yes *please* – that would be simply grand!'

The cab rattled along the Embankment, the dark river lifting and lulling on their right, the lights of tugs and houseboats shimmering. Hermione sat stiffly, conscious of the silence, wondering whether she ought to make some bright remark, dreading Gerald's discovery of her home, her mother, her wealth.

'Where do *you* live?' she asked. 'I'm not taking you miles out of your way?'

'No, I rent a studio near here, right at the top of a house off the King's Road. It faces north so the light's ideal. And there's something about being near the river . . . Shades of Turner and Monet, you know.'

Everyone has a studio except me, she thought enviously. Yet Tonks had said she had a great future, if she chose to grasp it. The *hunger*, that was the point: was her hunger to paint sufficient?

The cab drew up outside the porticoed building in Eaton Square and Hermione stepped out and waited while Gerald paid. The front door was opened by Ridley who murmured, as he ushered them in, 'Lady Staunton has been anxious . . .' She looked up to see her mother sweeping down the marble stairs in a dinner dress.

'Mama,' said Hermione, 'may I introduce Mr Shebeare? A friend from the Slade.'

He negotiated Lady Staunton's astonishment, her suspicion, her flirtatiousness, changing tack to follow her every whim. He cajoled her by saying that Hermione was a highly promising artist and begged Phoebe to encourage her daughter to continue painting. He mollified her by subtle flattery.

'This Ramsay you have hanging here – an ancestor, surely? – is exquisite; but no one paints like that today. Allow me to suggest that a person of your very great sensitivity would find it rewarding to patronize *contemporary* artists.'

'*Not* that dreadful *modern* rubbish?' Phoebe said with a little shudder.

'Perhaps I might accompany you and your daughter to the Leicester Gallery or Arthur Tooth. Such a visit would allow you, Lady Staunton, to see the work currently on show and, if it wouldn't bore you too much, I will try to explain why not all of it is *dreadful*. It would also enable the dealers to examine Miss Staunton's current work.'

''Mione dear,' Phoebe said, 'fetch that thing you've just done for Mrs Madingley – *wait* till you see *this*, Mr Shebeare . . .'

Hermione, stricken at the idea of showing Gerald the latest pug or peke, said, 'Mama, not just now. Let Mr Shebeare go on explaining . . .'

He smiled at Phoebe. 'I can see you're immensely proud of her. Today's artists desperately need discriminating patrons. Do you know that the New Chenil Galleries, not a mile from here, have just been forced to close for lack of public support? Regular purchases by cultivated people like yourself could have prevented that.'

'Really?' Phoebe breathed. 'How *fascinating*!'

By the time Gerald Shebeare left he had persuaded Lady Staunton that she had an exceptional eye for quality and innovation, that her daughter's artistic talent was inherited from her mother, and that they both owed it to posterity to take their place in the front rank of enlightened collectors. From this it was a small step to obtaining permission for Hermione to accompany him to the Crabtree Club. So entranced was Phoebe by this vision of herself as a lover of all that was new that he had some difficulty in preventing her from coming too. Only the information that the club did not serve champagne finally convinced her.

The Crabtree Club was in Soho. Its entrance was inconspicuous – a shabby door; a narrow corridor, a grimy flight of stairs that plunged down to a basement room so wreathed in smoke that it was practically impossible to see and so filled with jazz that it was impossible to hear anything else. It was lit by red lightbulbs that, at ceiling level, barely pierced the cigarette fumes. Finch led them past crowded tables, skirting a sprung wooden platform serving as dance floor and performance arena, to a table ringed with the stains left by a thousand beer glasses. They settled themselves on long benches, Hermione and Pixie facing outwards into the rose-tinted gloom, the men opposite. Finch waved his cigarette in the air making red-tipped figures of eight and bellowed, 'Waiter!'

Hermione had never been in such a place. It seemed the epitome of everything decadent and dangerous. The jazz played at the more daring debutantes' dances was a timid echo of this trumpeter's swooping screams; the catchy ballroom rhythms to which they had jiggled were a pale imitation of the blatantly suggestive crescendos this drummer was pounding out. Hermione stared at the five black musicians, whose faces shone with sweat and exposed every nuance of emotion and desire.

Pixie drew her close and said into her ear, 'Isn't it *thrilling*?'

'*Thrilling*,' she responded fervently.

The musicians launched into a blues number and Hermione found herself suffused with melancholy and yearning. She was afraid she would weep – for her father, her brother, for Sandy, but above all for herself. She dared not look at the other three but stared fixedly ahead. A hand stretched across the table to cover hers.

'Are you all right?' asked Gerald Shebeare.

Hermione nodded, almost submerged by a wave of sorrow, anger, regret but above all, understanding. For the first time she understood what she had missed. Brought up to think herself more fortunate than others, she suddenly saw the irony of money – that it was not a servant but a tyrant, a huge golden statue of

Baal, enslaving her with its demands. Money had to be secured, guarded, tended and multiplied. Her fortune was a mad, foaming despot (the trombone moaned and shivered) increasing her isolation, piling up possessions, inciting pride, greed, envy, covetousness, suspicion, deceit. Her life had been spent in luxury and she suddenly realized how stultifying that comfort was. It denied spontaneity, cut her off from ordinary pleasures – and from people, too, unless she managed to hide her wealth. Nobody had embraced her with real affection since the death of her father six years ago. She looked at Shebeare's large hand spread hotly over her own and raised her eyes.

'I was thinking how much I hate money!' she exclaimed, as the trombone solo shuddered to an end.

Gerald grinned. 'You can afford to!' he said.

The musicians began another number, catchier than the previous ones, and several people started to dance. Pixie and Finch left the table and joined in. The sound of stamping feet added to the racket in the stifling room.

'You ought to *paint* more, you know . . .' Gerald said above the din.

Hermione spread her hands in a helpless gesture. 'I know!' she said. 'But my mother won't let me.'

He made a face and shrugged. 'Too noisy to talk in here! Some other time!' He came round to sit at Hermione's side, leaned close and said, 'I want to find out more about your *mother*.'

Even *him*, Hermione thought.

'Mama has always been beautiful,' she began wearily. 'She's used to homage. She wants to be . . .' her voice rose to a staccato shout, 'amused – entertained – praised. She hates to be alone. Nothing much goes on *inside* her head, so she gets bored very quickly.'

'I expect all beauties are like that,' he said. 'I daresay it's our fault – us men – for pandering to them.'

The hot bulk of his body seemed very close. In Hermione's previous experience most young men had been stiff and awkward, holding themselves away from her as though contact would burn. Shebeare, in his rumpled trousers and open-necked shirt, reminded her of Sandy. She shut off that thought. Nobody was like Sandy.

'Would you care to dance?' he was saying. His face was red and perspiration was gathering at his temples. Soon the drops would run down his cheek to the angle of his jaw. His hands would be hot. Moisture, heat, sweat, smell . . . these were danger signs. Furthermore the idea of joining the press of bodies on the dance floor was not appealing. She was as tall as he was; they would be conspicuous. She doubted whether she could do these shaking, juddering steps.

'No thank you!' she said, smiling in an attempt to show there was nothing personal in the rejection. She liked Shebeare, even found him attractive in the abstract, yet still the imps and goblins of her childhood stalked up and down, baring their teeth at intruders.

Finch and Pixie returned to the table, hands clasped, excited by the dance rhythms. Pixie's lipstick was smudged and her face shone with a dew of perspiration.

'What are you two jawing about?' Finch asked, as chatter filled the sudden silence the band had left behind.

Gerald said, 'Beautiful women and why they behave so badly . . .'

'*Especially* to their daughters,' put in Hermione.

Gerald answered his own question. 'They're spoiled. Men find them all too easy to love.'

'Can't blame us!' Randall Finch said, glancing at Pixie. 'It's the way we're made.'

Shebeare stood up.

'Come on then,' he said, 'my turn now!' and Pixie wheeled back on to the floor as the players struck a harsh minor chord and began a slow number.

Randall Finch sat down opposite Hermione, took a red hand-kerchief from his pocket and wiped his gleaming forehead, mouthing, 'Hot work, dancing!' She nodded. The smell reminded her of something – another wave as he lifted his arm to summon a waiter – yes! Billy Brymer had smelt like that. The feral smell of the male in rut. She felt trapped. At deb dances the ladies' room had been a refuge at times like this. She stood up. 'Excuse me,' she said, and threaded her way through the steaming press of dancers to a red neon sign that said LADIES.

There were three cubicles, two of them noisily occupied. Hermione locked the door of the third. She leaned against it, eyes closed, until the thudding of her heart slowed down. Billy Brymer. Because of Billy she was dirty, damaged, afraid. Sandy had disappeared from her life. Beyond the door the music approached a crescendo of agony, throbbing and shuddering. Richard, her darling brother Richard, had been killed in some unknown place by some anonymous Hun. Her father had died, leaving her alone with her mother. Now Phoebe tormented her and would go on doing so until she died. Hermione sat down on the closed lavatory seat and sank her head into her hands.

Ten minutes later when Pixie came into the ladies', Hermione had just finished splashing her face with cold water and was drying it with a handkerchief. Her eyes glittered but otherwise she looked normal.

'Are you all right?' Pixie asked. 'I was worried about you.'

'Thank you, yes, I'm all right. Isn't this an amusing place?'

''Mione, are you *sure* you're all right?' Pixie said, looking at her more closely.

Hermione heard herself say, with a ferocity that astonished her, '*I hate my mother!*'

The bedlam had stopped; the musicians were taking a break. Finch and Shebeare had ordered champagne.

'Real pain for your sham friends; champagne for your real friends!' Shebeare said. The atmosphere of the nightclub had infected him with its exhilaration. 'What's up?' he asked, seeing her expression. 'Is anything the matter?'

Hermione smiled recklessly. 'Yes,' she said. 'I've only just realized that I hate my mother.'

He tilted his glass towards her. His eyes shone.

'I'm not at all surprised,' he said.

PART THREE

Nothing Ill Come Near Thee

1927 – 1945

CHAPTER NINE

FOR A FEW MONTHS PHOEBE BOUGHT EVERYTHING GERALD
Shebeare suggested. As he began to grasp the extent of the
Staunton wealth the cost of the paintings he selected ran into
hundreds, even thousands of pounds. He chose with a young
man's taste, picking the work of his own time. He went for a
young man's subject-matter, too – big-breasted, unembarrassed
nudes who almost rolled out of the frames under the weight of
their own sensuality. Thanks to his family connections, he was able
to introduce her to private owners and dealers in London – where
he favoured the Omega or Cooling Galleries – and, thanks to
friends from the Slade, some in Paris. They both enjoyed these
visits, although Phoebe enjoyed the attention of dealers more than
the pictures she was shown on these privileged, private expeditions. Once, as she was strolling with Gerald through the
Louvre, it happened that the Third Secretary at the British
Embassy was whiling away a rainy Sunday afternoon in the same
gallery until it was time to collect his new fiancée. Phoebe, who
had last seen him when he was a boy of twelve, did not recognize
Sandy Gordon-Lockhart. His attention was caught, however;
initially by her expression of petulant boredom. It reminded him

of someone from the distant past. Moving closer, he heard her escort say, 'This line of light, Phoebe – isn't it wonderful?' 'Mmm, darling,' she murmured, 'wonderful!' and at once he remembered who she was: Minor's mother! Must be! No doubt about it! But if that young and beautiful mama were now this faded creature, what could have become of H. Minor? Suffused by a complicated blend of emotions – curiosity, nostalgia, guilt – Sandy Gordon-Lockhart strode out of the long windowed gallery a good deal sooner than he had planned, his mind full of crashing discordant thoughts that would not have amused his young and pretty Chloë in the least.

Phoebe told Bobo Madingley about her visit to Paris with Gerald:
'Such an *angel* – and what is so *sweet* is that he thinks he's teaching *me*!'
'How do you *do* it?' Bobo said with silken malice, aware that Phoebe was well over fifty. 'The *energy*! He must be *half* your age, darling.'
Phoebe laughed. 'Sweetie, *no*: though he must be half yours . . . hmm?'
Bobo nuzzled the dog's face. '*Who* loves his mummy then?' she said with a sly glance at her friend.

Gerald steered Lady Staunton towards Cubist still life and per-suaded her to buy works by Braque and Cézanne. All by herself she picked a dappled Bonnard breakfast scene. These hung in the Eaton Square dining room and although at first Phoebe pretended to be thrilled with her newly acquired pictures, she quickly got bored with them, especially when her friends dismissed them as uncouth. She was soon bored by Gerald as well. He was very young and serious and terribly shy about sex. She had seduced him mainly to spite Hermione. Her interest in becoming a significant collector of modern art waned and her own taste reasserted itself. She complained to her daughter.
'I'd rather have our original hares and stags or even those slimy fish and lemon ones. At least you can imagine *eating* those. But plates of sour green apples . . . why bother to paint them? They're not even *round*!'

134

'They're not meant to be, Mama. They're apple-shaped. Look!' Hermione held up an apple from the brimming fruit bowl on the table.

'Hooey!' Phoebe had said dismissively. 'I'm tired of them. Have them removed. Sell them – even if it's at a loss. I don't care. Pass me my cigarettes.'

Hermione had no intention of selling the paintings and was reasonably confident that her mother would never ask what price they had fetched. *She* did not value them, therefore they must be valueless. Brymer conspired to hide the still lifes under a rug in the boot of the Rolls and spirited them down to Dorset one or two at a time, to be hung unseen in minor guest-bedrooms.

Soon Phoebe declined to take Gerald's calls. In due course all his recommendations were taken down from the walls, although Hermione persuaded her mother not to get rid of the nudes.

'I think they're quite fun,' she said insincerely, knowing that her mother could never resist the idea of *fun*.

'As long as they're out of my sight,' Phoebe conceded. 'Big fat blowzy girls . . . I can see why they appealed to Gerald but I can't *imagine* what *you* see in them.'

'I'll see to it that they are taken down today,' Hermione soothed. 'You won't ever need to look at them again.'

She had the nudes hung in her bedroom and from then on, every day for the rest of her life, Hermione woke and retired to bed under the serene, heavy-lidded gaze of three monumental Picassos and two Matisse odalisques. 'They're better than a night-cap,' Phyllis used to say. 'Makes you want to yawn just looking at them.' Phoebe had ordered the rest of the collection to be disposed of except for two Dufys depicting the curve of the bay at Nice which she said cheered her up in winter. 'London is so gloomy, one *pines* for light and colour!' (The Dufys were the only pictures Hermione sold after her mother's death; the rest emerged safely from their hiding places.)

For a year or two after Gerald had receded from her life Phoebe continued to attend gallery openings (they offered a rich seam of young male company) and even went on buying half-heartedly – the odd picture by Marie Laurencin; a few lightweight Picassos: beach pictures, plump adoring children, enfolding mothers. Large oils gradually became small oils, then watercolours, then drawings, until finally she lost interest altogether. By then she had bought enough pictures to found the Staunton Collection, later to be regarded as the finest group of Twenties art in private hands.

If Hermione had cherished the brief hope that she might be attracted to Gerald Shebeare and he to her, his involvement with her mother dispelled that idea. He had the decency to look sheepish whenever he crossed her path and he avoided the Chelsea house where Pixie lived. The blossoming love between Pixie and Randall Finch was an altogether different matter. Hermione envied their absorption in each other, their shared passion for everything experimental and new, their willingness to attempt other ways of seeing and hearing. Two years after leaving the Slade they married and moved into a modern flat in Hampstead, drawn by the artistic community there. Once again, Hermione found herself alone. She tried to contact Dolly and Victoria but Dolly sent back one of her postcards saying, 'Topping to hear from you – must meet some time – ever so busy just now – long live the click – Love D.' Victoria's mother said her daughter had a teaching job. Yes, at a girls' school. Yes, in the country. Sussex. Yes, *so* nice for her. Yes, she'd pass the message on. After that she heard nothing more from either.

Once her debutante season ended, Hermione had never again considered the possibility of marriage. She failed to see the announcement of Sandy's engagement to Chloë Jourdain, 'younger daughter of HE Sir Hector and Lady Jourdain, of Paris and Broadway, Worcestershire', since it appeared in *The Times* during the week when Phoebe and Gerald were in Paris, and Hermione always cancelled *The Times* when her mother was away. The episode with Gerald ensured that she brought no more young men to Eaton Square and in any case, the few to whom she was introduced by match-making friends of her mother – keen to embrace the Staunton wealth – were of little interest.

Phoebe drew on a gold-tipped cocktail cigarette and said petu-lantly, 'I don't know *why* you don't care for the yacht. Most girls would give their eye-teeth for a winter cruise. One meets *such* amusing people. You're missing valuable opportunities. Time's passing, you know . . . you won't be young much longer.'

Hermione had seen enough of her mother's cocktail party friends to know that none could possibly appeal to her, nor she to them, but she merely said, 'I am twenty-seven, Mama, and I am trying to become an artist. I need something of my *own* to occupy me, besides the business of the company.'

'The *company* is just humouring you. If you weren't the founder's daughter no one would think twice about you. And twenty-seven is dangerously close to thirty.'

'Yes, I do realize that.'

'*Marriage* ought to occupy you. A husband, a household, your children. If you want something of your own, have a baby. That is how any *normal* woman occupies herself. Besides, you owe it to *me*. Good Lord, am I to be closeted alone with my spinster daughter to the end of my days?'

'I hope not, Mama,' Hermione said fervently.

For a short time, Phoebe persuaded herself that she had an affinity with India. She had reminisced so often and so colourfully about the Last Durbar that she began to believe her own tales. India was fashionable – the Prince of Wales had been there, too – and Phoebe always liked to keep up with the modish, the current, the very latest thing. She boarded the yacht at Southampton with a party of friends and was gone for months, travelling via Port Said *en route* to Bombay.

Her departure, whether to the tropics or the south of France, would be preceded by a week of increasingly frenetic choosing and packing of clothes to wear on board ('cruisewear') on land ('beach-wear') and in the evenings ('cocktailwear'). Agnes, her maid, would iron, fold, wrap in tissue, and place the chosen garments in a cabin trunk that looked like a chest of drawers. Phoebe's lingerie was folded around tiny sachets of perfume and slipped inside individual cambric bags. Telegrams would be sent to people met on previous trips: 'LONDON IMPOSSIBLE STOP DEPARTING END THIS WEEK HEADING FOR YOUR NECK OF THE WOODS STOP DYING TO SEE YOU STOP HANG OUT THE FLAGS EXCLAMATION LOVE PHOEBE.' There would be expeditions to Simpson's for deck shoes or tennis-wear, to Debenham and Freebody for sun hats, to Innoxa's Bond Street salon to buy soothing lotions for Phoebe's delicate skin. A flurry of irritable last-minute instructions ('I forgot to cancel the Wynne-Osmond do next week ... *make sure* you go to the Symington wedding ... Which *hat* will you wear? No, *not* that one – the navy blue') and at last she would be gone, leaving a diminuendo of Sobranie and Mitsouko like a snake's coils on dry sand.

Why do I put up with it? Hermione always wondered in the calm that followed. She would cancel *The Times* and the frivolous magazines that supplied her mother with society news and gossip. She preferred the *Financial Times*, from whose pages she was learning about the City and the stock market. In the ten years since her father died, Hermione had become an active participant in Staunton Trading. She visited its City headquarters every Monday afternoon to be brought up to date on last week's movements and told about current projections and problems. She listened, watched, evaluated. The men instructing her with grave, deferential faces were never quite sure if these sessions were a mere formality, like meetings with her mother. In fact, Hermione absorbed, learned and began to trust her own judgement. Before the New York stock market crash she had already been recommending caution. After it, she suggested that Staunton Trading should switch most of its resources to shipbuilding for a few years. Prices of raw materials were comparatively low; men needed work. Philanthropy and good business came together. The men in the boardroom began to listen to her with real instead of feigned respect. Yet she remained quite unable to handle her mother, except with the mute obedience of the child she had been when she first grasped the extent of Phoebe's indifference. That had dealt a blow to her self-esteem from which she still recoiled. It was safest never to oppose her again.

*

By the time Hermione reached thirty she was no longer ashamed of her spinsterhood but welcomed the freedom it gave her to please herself. After a lifetime of conforming to other people's expectations – nanny, governess, tutors at the Slade, above all, her capricious and domineering mother – there was nothing Hermione liked more than the chance to do what *she* wanted.

'Phyllis, nothing smart today . . . just one of my painting frocks. Push a couple of rags into the pocket as well, would you?'

'Yes, Miss Staunton.'

'Ridley, I shall be out all day! Ask Cook to have a light supper ready at eight.'

'Very good, Miss Staunton.'

'Brymer – I want to be at the British Museum by nine. I don't know how long I'll stay but I can make my own way home.'

'Yes, Miss Hermione. You won't attempt the omnibus?'

She laughed. 'I don't know why not – but if it puts your mind at rest, I'll take a taxi cab.'

She prowled through galleries and museums copying Old Masters and new ones. She trained her pencil and her brush, refined her eye, developed her style. She used to feel herself at the apex of a double V: one line of energy streaming from the picture to her eyes; the other travelling down her arm on to the canvas. She loved the absorption and anonymity of painting and didn't care if people thought her eccentric. Hours would pass like moments, until the realization that she was thirsty or needed the ladies' persuaded her to wipe her brushes, cover her canvas with an old cloth and hurry down to the basement canteen, the problems of creating light, air and space on a flat plane still occupying her mind. Occasionally someone would stop beside her stool and fall into conversation, or offer to buy the picture when it was finished. She would sell it for the sum they suggested – or not, depending on whether she liked the look of the buyer – and if anyone gave her a pound or two, she would treat herself to a Bath bun with her cup of tea, and a taxi home.

She had some curious encounters with London's other eccentrics. There was an old man who haunted Soho Square. He spoke in a voice of Edwardian refinement but wore a suit so shabby that it was held together with safety pins and belted with string. He told Hermione his name was William Benson but he had been known as 'Magic' Benson before gambling ruined him.

'What did you put your money on?'

'Racehorses, my dear. I had a system. It was madly complicated. I used to spend hours every day working out which horse was on top of its form, which jockey was riding well, matching the weather and the going to the trainer and the stables. I had to balance twenty-seven different factors. With my ability to calculate odds I should have been in the insurance game. But I lost it all.'

'Why?'

'Bookmakers became greedy and started fixing the races. Jockeys started taking bribes. Flat racing used to be a gentleman's sport. Not any more. Mind you, it hasn't stopped me betting.'

'Can I perhaps advance you something?'

'Dear girl, how very kind. I should need more than something, however. I am looking for everything.'

'So am I,' said Hermione.

Her life was marked by alternating periods of light and gloom; activity and inertia; painting and *ennui*. The colourless times co-incided with her mother's presence in London or at Chantry. One evening, after Phoebe had had too many dry Martinis, she lashed out at her daughter with a more than usually vicious tongue. Afterwards Hermione lay awake planning how to tell her mother that it was time they lived apart. She rehearsed the words in her head until they sounded simple, even sensible. She persuaded herself that Phoebe would think so too.

Next morning at breakfast she said, 'Mama, I am thirty-three years old and I do not care for scenes like last night's.'

Her mother smiled vivaciously. 'What scene? Oh look, a note from Hughie! He's *such* an angel.'

'*You* may forget, but I don't. You said some cruel, dreadful things.'

'I don't care for your tone. It makes my head ache.' Phoebe lit a cigarette and inhaled with a frown, her face a concentrated knot of dry lines.

'Mama, I have made up my mind. You may pretend to yourself but you can't pretend to me. It is high time we lived separately. You would be better off without the constant irritation of my presence. I am going to ask the trustees to let me buy a house, quite near, in Chelsea or Kensington. You will stay here, that goes without saying. Nothing will change for you. You will continue to enjoy every comfort. I hope we can share Chantry – and in any case I shall see you often, of course. But I *must* live by myself.'

'Gracious, what a long speech! Have you finished? Are you sure? Then go and fetch me an aspirin.'

'Mama, I'm not a child any more. I suggest you ring for Agnes.'

'*Get* me an *aspirin*, Hermione. And a glass of water.'

Furious, Hermione rose to her feet, went into the hall, found Ridley, asked him to bring some aspirin for her mother, and returned to the small dining room. Phoebe smiled radiantly at her.

'*Good* girl. Now let's hear no more of your bile and nonsense. Ah, Ridley, at last!'

Foiled in the attempt to speak, Hermione wrote her mother a letter, sending a copy to her trustees. She made no criticism or complaint, on the contrary, she said that she hoped relations with her mother would remain 'exactly as hitherto', and that they would continue to see each other frequently. However, she stated her wish and intention, now that she was fully adult, to live on her own with the minimum complement of servants. Phyllis would come with her; she would engage a cook-housekeeper and a man for all other duties. She intended to play a greater part in Staunton Trading and would begin to involve herself in charitable work. To help her in this she would need the services of a secretary three or four times a week. At thirty-three she was no longer (her heart contracted at the word) 'a minor' and wished to live an independent life. Her mother ignored the letter. A week later she received formal notification from the trustees that they were unable to accede to her request without her mother's permission. 'This permission Lady Staunton, as your guardian and protector, is entitled under the terms of the late Sir Jack Staunton's will to withhold until you have attained the age of thirty-five.'

Two more years. She prepared to sit them out.

Life went on exactly as though Hermione had never spoken, the letter never been sent, except that her mother's drinking became more blatant. Once, after an evening at a nightclub, Phyllis, who had been keeping Phoebe's maid Agnes company while she waited up for her mistress's return, reported that milady had come home with a bruised face and a black eye. Hermione was shocked, but when she tried to enter her mother's locked bedroom she was rebuffed with incoherent shouts. Next morning at noon, when Agnes eventually opened the door, Hermione could see that both her mother's eyes were swollen and the scarf swathed round her head did not conceal livid striations at her throat.

'Mama, who did this to you? Was there an accident?'

'I fell,' her mother said sharply, and refused to say more.

It was just possible that she was telling the truth, her daughter thought. Her legs, once so shapely, were now as narrow as sticks and the bones had become brittle. Alcohol made her unsteady on her feet, but Phoebe refused to admit that she was drinking too much. She would say nothing more about the incident but demanded to have the telephone placed on her bed. She lit another cigarette, picked up the receiver and started dialling. Hermione left the room.

She went to the mews behind the square in search of Brymer. He was burnishing the car's acorn-shaped chrome headlamps with metal polish.

'Brymer, I am concerned about my mother,' she began gently, to show that she did not hold him responsible. 'Do you know how last night's accident happened? Did you see anything?'

'No, Miss Hermione,' he said, ill at ease, his gaze averted.

'Who was with her?'

'Lady Staunton went to the club . . .'

'Which one?'

'It's called the Green Parrot, miss. In Mayfair. Behind the Connaught Hotel.'

'I don't know it,' said Hermione and they smiled at each other for an instant.

'Her ladyship often meets her friends there.'

'What friends? Have *I* met them?'

'I doubt it, miss . . .' he answered, and his voice trailed away. She knew he disapproved, and knew too that he would not criticize her mother openly.

'Did someone escort her from the club? One of these "friends"?'

'The doorman, Miss Hermione. And two Negro gentlemen.'

'Thank you, Brymer.'

She could not ask if her mother had been drunk. Besides, she knew the answer.

Next time Phoebe came home intoxicated, Hermione called their personal doctor. He was closeted with her mother for half an hour, towards the end of which Hermione heard a storm of hysterical sobbing. When she heard his footsteps descending the marble staircase into the entrance hall, Hermione beckoned him into the small drawing room.

'Will you have some tea or coffee, Dr Cathcart?' she asked.

'No, thank you. Miss Staunton, I wish there were a more pleasant way to say this. Your mother is drinking too much. If she does not stop it will kill her. Already there is great strain on her heart and liver. I have tried to make her understand, but she denies absolutely that she takes excess alcohol. I can give her advice but I cannot force her to stop.'

'Nor can I,' said Hermione bleakly.

'Lady Staunton tells me she is fifty-one . . .'

'Mama has never found it easy to acknowledge her age. She will be sixty in July.'

'Perhaps she no longer has the will to live.'

'Perhaps.'

Dr Cathcart looked searchingly into the heavy, serious face of his patient's only child. 'And you, Miss Staunton?' he enquired. 'I hope *your* will to live is unimpaired?'

'My health is good and I have much to live for,' she assured him.

'Good. I have given your mother a sedative; she will sleep for the rest of the afternoon. You are not your mother's keeper, as I hope you realize, and if people are set on self-destruction, little can be done to divert them. Love is what they need. Love is the only effective medicine. Forgive me if I intrude.'

His bill for fifty guineas arrived at the end of the month. Her mother continued to drink.

Phoebe spent the early summer of 1936 in London – in order, she said, to be there for the Season. She received few invitations. She drank all day, calling for a Bloody Mary or a pink gin by mid-morning although Hermione guessed that she kept a secret supply in her bedroom as well. The effects of drink accelerated her decline. She walked with a stick-insect's jerky elegance. Her manner had become erratic and her conversation merciless. Painfully thin, with veined hands and neck, she was no longer a beauty; not even a faded one. Hermione could not love her mother but she pitied her for being exposed to the disdain of men who would once have been proud to escort her. Phoebe no longer had anything to recommend her except the wealth displayed on her bejewelled fingers. It was sad to watch her – once the epitome of arrogant beauty – trying to conceal her stumbling movements, trying not to fall; trying to be witty or make malicious gossip to prevent people drifting away. Her mother had always dreaded being alone.

Hermione contacted various members of the Blythgowrie family – now comfortably off, thanks to her parents' generosity. Phoebe's sisters replied that alas, they seldom came to London . . . 'And Phibby would hate it *here*, after the luxury she's used to!' Her older brother Iain was dead and had been succeeded by his only son Alexander, now 13th Lord Blythgowrie. He wrote back civilly enough announcing the birth of a son, Vivian, and ending his letter with a request for a large sum of money – 'desperately needed for the roof, which hasn't been repaired for forty years!' Since he did not invite his aunt Phoebe, or his cousin Hermione, to inspect the state of Gowrie Castle for themselves, no money was sent. Hermione said nothing to her mother.

In the end Phoebe was compelled to buy companionship. There were always people willing to cruise the Caribbean or stay in a lavish villa in the South of France, if food and drink were freely available and most of their expenses paid. At the end of July she set off – without her daughter, as usual – from Croydon Aerodrome to fly to Nice, where the *Phoebe* was moored awaiting her arrival and that of various friends. She planned to cruise for two or three weeks before spending a fortnight at the villa. Phoebe was probably happy for the next week or so. It is quite hard to be miserable on board a pennanted yacht sailing across a transparent sea beneath a sapphire blue sky. It is hard to be miserable when people prance up to you, laughing, to say, *oh*, isn't this *divine?* as you drift past bays and inlets reclining under a white awning, a glass of chilled champagne in your hand, a bowl of olives warming in the sun beside you. It is hard to be miserable when you feel yourself the object of envy at every mooring; when restaurant owners clamour for your custom and small boys run down the quay after you, shouting and trying to sell shells, kittens, pastries, scarves, postcards, cigarettes – anything, really. These things are quite a plausible substitute for happiness.

'Isn't this *heaven?*' Phoebe said a dozen times a day in her smoky voice, and each time answering voices assured her, 'Bliss!'

'Blissy-*blissy*,' she would smile, leaning her coiffed head against a plump cushion, and the chorus would flute, 'Divine!'

She watched them bobbing round the boat in the evenings, raising her glass of champagne in response to their shouts.

'You should come in too, Phoeb' – the water's like *toast!*'

'I'll swim later,' she would call. 'Bottoms up!' and like dolphins they would up-end and swim underwater to amuse her. They were all younger than she was, some very much younger, and she did not care to expose her emaciated body to their scrutiny. She preferred to wait until the last gleaming bathing-costumed figure had climbed on deck and disappeared to the cabins to shower and change before dinner. Only then did she hand her enveloping beach wrap to Agnes, who came with her everywhere, and lower herself unsteadily down the ladder into the clear water. Her white limbs became turquoise and warm ripples shimmered round her in the thick evening light. Her guests, clustered round the cocktail bar at the far end of the boat, would be playing gramophone records and the latest polished, catchy tunes drifted over the water. Phoebe swam by herself, listening to the music and their shrieks and laughter, watching the occasional couple detach itself from the rest to embrace out of sight or retreat to one of the cabins. After ten minutes she would signal to Agnes, laying out her clothes for the evening and from time to time checking the porthole for the summons, to help her up the ladder. Swathed in a towel, clutching the handrail, Phoebe would make her way across the still-warm teak deck to her cabin to dress for another starlit dinner.

Swimming thus, one July evening at dusk, she developed cramp in her left leg. The leg became rigid; the muscles clenched; the pain was excruciating.

'Help!' she called out. 'Help! *Help!*'

She was at the far end of the boat. One young creature leaned over the distant rail and waved at her.

'Hell*oo* – oh!'

'*Help!*' Phoebe cried, with all her strength. The effort seemed to make her lungs contract and a searing flash shot through her ribcage. She waved her arms feebly, called inaudibly, swallowed a mouthful of water, tried to spit it out, and the pain stabbed again, hotly, as though she were inhaling fire. Another head leaned over the distant rail to peer at her. A hand raised its glass towards her, merrily, before head, arm and glass disappeared. Phoebe felt, more intensely than she had felt anything in her life, panic, terror and the certainty that she was dying. She screamed with all her might and a cracked squeak escaped from her gaping mouth as more water poured in. Her heart – never a powerful organ – gave up the struggle at the same moment as her maid raised the alarm. By the time they fished her out her carmine lips had turned blue and only her eyes were bloodshot.

Hermione was at Chantry when the news came of her mother's death and her first reaction was that of any prisoner unexpectedly freed ten months early. She felt overwhelming relief. Next came anger. How could her mother, surrounded by friends and a crew of more than a dozen, have drowned? Was no one looking out for her? *Was* it an accident? Anger was followed by guilt – should she have been there, instead of abandoning her mother to her dubious friends? The guilt did not last long. They had been more like prisoners shackled unwillingly together than mother and daughter. Neither had looked after the other. Hermione had not loved her mother since she was ten years old; nor, probably, had Phoebe ever loved her. She would not hide behind sentimental illusions but deal with practical matters. She had to fly to Nice, attend the inquest, see to the formalities, bring her mother's body back to England, arrange the funeral. Here, or in London? Chantry had always belonged to Hermione, her father and her brother. London was Phoebe's domain.

The most senior of her trustees made a ponderous, formal telephone call offering to accompany her 'on your mother's last sad journey'. Hermione declined the offer. It was followed by a letter: 'As you have not yet arrived at the full maturity at which your father wished all responsibility to devolve to you . . .' Hermione, conscious that in ten months' time she would be thirty-five and her own person at last, ignored it. She chose Ridley, who had been butler at Chantry and Eaton Square for the past twenty-one years, and Cowley, the head gardener, to fly with her to Nice. Brymer – now almost seventy – drove them out of London. Cowley, uncomfortable in a suit, sat stiffly in the front, Ridley ill at ease beside her in the back. Brymer would meet them on their return and lead the undertakers' procession from Croydon back to Eaton Square. The last thing she did before boarding the aeroplane for her first-ever flight was to post a letter to her trustees, informing them of these arrangements.

In the end about thirty mourners attended the funeral. Phoebe might have been disappointed but Hermione felt it was quite a good showing. The raffish young people among whom her mother had spent the last few years stayed away. Hermione would have liked to talk to someone from the cruise about the circumstances of her mother's death, but nobody admitted to having been there and in the end most of her information was derived from the coroner's report (death by drowning and asphyxiation brought on by coronary thrombosis) and a highly coloured report in the local newspaper. (*'Inéxorablement, Lady Staunton, la belle veuve de notre ami bien-connu, Sir Jack Staunton, était saisie de sa vie au silence éternel de la mort!*')

The mourners came back to Eaton Square after the funeral for champagne – 'Always dear Phoebe's favourite tipple!' someone said, not unkindly. A handful of Blythgowrie relatives went through the motions of concern but Hermione could see that most of them were really only concerned to know whether Phoebe had left them anything.

'Dear lovely Phibby . . . we thought of her so often! I do hope she thought of *us*?'

Hermione had no idea what her mother's will said but she was able to assure them sincerely that her mother had, indeed, often thought of them. Phoebe's favourite brother Roderick – a tall, austere man in his mid-sixties – turned up for the funeral, as did the head of the family, young Alexander Blythgowrie, with his wife and their toddler son, Vivian. So did a cocky, good-looking boy called Reggie, who informed her with some panache that he was her first cousin once removed.

'Have we ever *met* before?' Hermione asked him.

'Doubt it!' he said breezily. 'I'm Kitty's grandson. Just left Fettes. Thoroughly browned off. Foul place. Brutal incarceration. Now, thank God, life can begin. You know Kitty? Must do. Your mother's sister? No? I *say*, old bean, you *are* out of touch!'

'My mother's sisters did not keep in contact with *us* much,' she said, meaning to snub him.

'Never mind – *I* will, *rather*! Now I know you've got this topping great house. Jolly good show, that. Always looking for a London berth. Trouble with living in Scotland.'

'I *trust* you'll telephone in advance,' she said and he grinned and answered, 'Don't bank on it, Cousin Hermione!'

Secretly, she liked his honesty. The only other person she liked was her uncle Roderick's daughter, a woman of her own age called Henrietta who brought with her a quiet, rather insignificant-looking husband and an attractive small boy called James who reminded her of Sandy.

'Are you going to be all *right*, my dear?' Henrietta enquired, looking hard into her cousin's eyes. 'Will you cope, do you think?

Yes, of course you will – what I mean is, can I *help* in any way?'

'Thank you for offering. To tell you the truth I haven't the foggiest where to start, but I daresay I shall manage and the trustees are only too eager to help.'

'Don't let them bully you. Besides, they charge an absolute fortune. People like lawyers and bankers always do. I suppose you'll miss your mother dreadfully?'

'I don't know, I suppose so, yes. Thank you. You must keep in touch. When all this is over perhaps you would come down and stay at Chantry? It's a heavenly place for children. Your little boy would love it.'

Well, she consoled herself, Henrietta was a find. But the rest were greedy and hypocritical behind the veneer of good manners. A man of about her own age called something or other Shepherd buttonholed her, claiming to be related, and a couple called Bridgewater with two or three children. Who on earth were *they*?

Placing a tenderly sympathetic hand on her arm, people would say, 'We saw the notice in *The Times*. So *sad*! *Darling* Phoebe! We were so *touched* that she always remembered us at Christmas!'

They could hardly hold back the real question: has she remembered us in her *will*?

Hermione was astonished. *Had* her mother remembered her uncaring relatives at Christmas and if so, how?

The only people she had hoped for did not arrive. Hermione thought Sandy Gordon-Lockhart and his parents might have come to say their goodbyes to a former neighbour, remembering her from the days when she was young and beautiful. But although Donald and Violet were both still alive and, sitting opposite each other over a Scottish breakfast, had seen the announcement of Phoebe's death, circumstances prevented them from attending. Violet did not think it necessary to send a message of condolence to someone whom she had last seen as a child of ten. Had darling old Jack been alive that would have been very different, but his spendthrift widow had survived poor Jack by nearly twenty years. As for Sandy and his wife, they were on their third foreign posting by now, this time stationed in Egypt. No question of them coming.

Sandy had not told Chloë about Hermione and his wife would have been most surprised if he had gone home for the funeral of an unknown widow who had been a neighbour a very long time ago when he was only a small boy. It might have been different had he been in London; then he might have slipped along covertly, ignoring his mother's strictures, to catch a glimpse of Hermione. But from Alexandria? – impossible. As it was he had missed the notice of Phoebe's death in *The Times*, being of an age to read the Hatches and Matches but not yet the Despatches.

When the last mourner had gone, Hermione turned to the staff who stood in the hall with folded hands and downcast eyes. She knew they did not grieve for her mother but they must be concerned about their own future. She ought to tell them her plans.

'I am shutting down this house for the time being,' she ended. 'I prefer to live at Chantry. Those of you who would like to come with me are welcome but if anyone would rather stay in London, they may consider this their home for the next six months while they look for another place. Once again, *thank* you all for everything you did for my mother.'

They all chose to stay, except Agnes. When in due course Hermione saw the will it revealed that Phoebe had made only the most derisory provision for the stoical little Frenchwoman who had been privy to her secrets for twenty-five years. Shocked again by her mother's cold-heartedness, she increased the legacy by a factor of ten, giving Agnes a pension of £75 a year.

Finally, she was on her own! Waking up on the first morning in Chantry in the late autumn of 1936, she walked barefoot round her bedroom smiling at each of the nudes in turn, feeling light as a feather, as though her nightdress floated, Botticelli-like, in her wake. She leaned on the windowsill and gazed across the lawns, radiant in the fresh morning light, listening to the wood-pigeons in the top branches of the cedars. The copper beech had grown higher and wider since her childhood. She would have liked to grab a sketch pad and pencil and start drawing there and then, to make up for all the indolent, squandered years. But there was so much to do, a dozen people awaited her orders, and an architect was motoring down from London in time for lunch. She clung to the certainty that her spirit was not crushed, she had survived, she was her own person. It was twenty-four years since she had seen Sandy, twenty years since Richard had been killed, nearly seventeen since she had lost her father and now she was coming into her own.

CHAPTER TEN

IN THE COURSE OF THE FOLLOWING YEAR OR SO SHE FOUND IT WAS more complicated than that. Hermione began to realize the extent of the damage inflicted by her mother. She had always imagined she would write immediately to her friends from the Slade, invite them down to Chantry, arrange painting parties – yet somehow her spirit shrank from these intrusions. She had dreamed of patronizing young artists, making over a wing of Chantry to a painting colony, but now that she had the freedom and the money to do so, she hesitated. Would they merely exploit her, as her mother had been exploited? Would they laugh at her, find her archaic, her work outdated, ludicrous? Best, perhaps, to deal with the house first. She estimated that about fifteen people were needed, indoors and out, to run Chantry. The present total was thirty. Some would have to be dismissed – and that she would find hard, considering how many had lived in the house for most of their adult lives. But could she justify keeping such a retinue for herself alone? Her mother had justified it by pretending that she still gave house-parties, though in truth the house had seen hardly any guests for several years.

Hermione craved time to herself, but this was not easy.

Paradoxically, she was also lonely. With her mother she had had intimacy of a sort – a nightmarish intimacy, but one built up over time, relying on shared memories, family and acquaintances. Even if they were locked in battle, even if her mother had not scrupled to resort to bullying, sulking, deceit, manipulativeness, derision and in the end, rage and drunkenness, still they had had a kind of partnership. What had seethed below the surface to make Phoebe into a monster?

One morning in the spring of 1939, Hermione's eye was caught by an advertisement on the front page of *The Times* – one of many such placed every day. *Clever, willing, cultured daughters of good family seek sponsors or employment in kind English household. Rachel (17) and Hannah (14), together if possible. Jewish hosts preferred. All papers in order, could travel immediately. Write Rosenbaum, Maria-Theresienstr., Berlin.* Why did this, rather than any other, attract her attention? It did not state that they could cook or sew, which must mean that they could not. Not servants, then. Perhaps, being longer than most, it offered more clues. Perhaps it simply spoke, that particular morning, to her need for company and conversation. Perhaps because she was about to have her thirty-seventh birthday and although the prospect of bearing a child was receding into the mists of improbability, she yearned for a daughter – two daughters, even. Hermione went up to her old schoolroom and took down the German dictionary, untouched since the days of Fräulein, who had been dismissed in 1914 when the war broke out. She opened it at random. *Hoch* – high. *Hoffentlich* – let us hope. *Höflich* – polite. *Hübsch* – beautiful. She didn't want beauty or high birth; she hoped for politeness and decorum. If the girls really were cultured and clever, they would more than suit her. She spent an hour studying the dictionary before composing a letter in English, to which she attached a schoolgirl's German translation. A week later the telephone rang. 'Sherborne 314,' she answered.

The voice of the local operator said, with an undertone of disapproval, 'There is a *German* lady on the line, Miss Staunton. Shall I connect you?'

'Yes,' said Hermione. She waited a moment, and then heard a far-away voice asking doubtfully, 'Miss Staunton, is it, please?'

'*Guten Morgen,*' she ventured, but to her relief the woman continued in English.

'I telephone about my daughters, Rachel and Hannah Rosenbaum. My classified advertisement in the London *Times* appeared. You are writing – *wrote* – me a letter . . .'

Ten minutes later, Hermione had agreed to travel to London and collect two unknown Jewish girls from the boat-train arriving at Waterloo in six days' time – on 14 April, which as it happened was her birthday. She would hold an envelope bearing their names, so that they could recognize her.

Twenty-one years – exactly a generation – after the end of the last war, another loomed. People forget what wars are like; the random, pointless deaths and the fact that the dead are gone, not just for the duration of the war, but for ever, and forever missed. A new generation of young men had grown up with no experience or recollection of war beyond a sepia photograph of Grandad on the mantelpiece. They'd do their duty and defend the King. Hitler threatened the honour of Britain; Hitler must be humiliated. As for the women, they hadn't the least idea. Ignorant, unprepared but blindly patriotic, they knew Hitler and the 'Narzies' were pushing the Poles about or kicking the Czechs to bits and it was time to put a stop to it. Besides, men in uniform looked so dashing; glamour-boys one and all.

On 3 September 1939, Britain declared war on Germany.

Hermione's first reaction was to give Hannah and Rachel two hours of English lessons daily. If the countryside were teeming with soldiers, Jewish girls with obvious German accents would fare badly. Until now she had concentrated on being kind and welcoming and getting them used to the food served up from the Chantry kitchen, different and much more plentiful than they were used to. The girls were no longer strangers, but whatever she might have hoped when she answered their mother's advertisement, they were not daughters, either. After some indecision over what to call her they had settled for *Tante* – Aunt – Hermione,

154

which they soon shortened to *Tante Meini* – 'Mione: a name she had not heard since childhood. Every morning she sat with them in the old schoolroom for two hours' practice in spoken English and dictation. At eleven they had a break for Ovaltine and ginger biscuits, after which they took it in turns to read aloud passages from H. Rider Haggard, a dictionary beside them. Every afternoon she set them lists of vocabulary to learn.

The girls began to emerge as two separate individuals and Hermione grasped the extent of the anguish they suffered at being away from their parents. Hannah, at fourteen, was especially vulnerable. She clung to Rachel, feared even five minutes' separation from her, and cried herself to sleep at night. Her older sister on the other hand was resourceful and mature; a naturally strong character with a bright, curious mind, a passion for the violin and the survivor's knack of making the best of any situation. They knew that, in theory, they were extremely lucky to have escaped from Germany and the increasing restrictions placed upon Jews. This did not stop them feeling utterly miserable. They lived for the regulation one letter a month from their parents and spent hours poring over their reply, limited to two sides of a single sheet. For the time being, the letters continued to arrive.

One afternoon, during that becalmed, breath-holding autumn, the unreal months of the phoney war, Hermione was overseeing the storage of Chantry's household linen. It had been folded between sheets of tissue paper to preserve its whiteness and placed inside cabin trunks. The men heaved these up the attic steps and ladders, manoeuvring them along the dusty corridors under the roof. Hermione went ahead, marking on her inventory where sheets, pillowcases, bolsters, towels, tablecloths and napkins were stored. The sheets would be needed again after the war ended – people would always want to sleep between linen sheets and eat off damask and these had been woven to last a century or two. Directing her torch beam into a distant corner, Hermione saw something wrapped in heavy calico. The chandelier!

'*How thy beauty shineth amid the stars,*' Sandy had said all those years ago, '*oh eternal Queen!*' Piercingly she longed for him, her only love, who had loved her in return. Had anyone praised her appearance since then? Her father, perhaps, once or twice, as she negotiated the awkward transitions through girlhood, but who else, since his death? Hamish somebody at a deb dance long ago had called her 'bonny'. Stooping low, she crossed the wide gaps between the roof-beams and poked with her foot at the yellowing parcel. Behind her, a woman's voice warned tremulously, 'Madam, it doesn't look very safe! Sorry, I spoke out of turn, madam.'

'No, you're quite right, Rawlinson,' Hermione said and she made her way back.

It took three weeks, with everyone working at full throttle, to organize and protect Chantry and its contents for an unforeseeable length of time and an unguessable future. Drawers and cupboards were emptied, their contents sorted, labelled and wrapped in protective canvas bundles. (Hermione had learned this trick when her mother's passion for the Near East and India was at its height. Phoebe would buy things in bazaars that turned up months later – long after she had forgotten what they were – wrapped in exotic-smelling canvas and stuck down with sealing-wax. Sometimes she had hardly bothered to open them.)

Papers from her father's study, mostly untouched since his death, were put in rough order and locked away in filing cabinets. Leather folders marked TELEGRAMS, IMMEDIATE, CORRESPONDENCE, and SHIPS were neatly arranged on the polished surface of his desk. Apart from some unused telegram forms and sheets of embossed cream paper headed Chantry Manor, near Sherborne, Dorset, telephone Sherborne 314, station: Sherborne, the folders were empty. Hermione glanced into the top drawer of her mother's desk but she was not up to the ordeal of sorting through that correspondence, with its freight of unwanted secrets. She emptied the lot into two large canvas sacks, fastened them securely and ordered them to be added to the bonfire. Everyone looked to her for decisions, never questioning her authority, as she issued dozens, *hundreds* of logical, sensible, necessary orders.

A harassed young man from Sotheby's catalogued the paintings.

They were protected with layers of felted wool, wrapped in brown paper and string, labelled and sent to Wales for safe keeping. Hermione watched with regret as the Matisses and Picassos were lifted down from her bedroom walls, packed and sent away 'for the duration', as everyone put it.

The best of the silver was wrapped in special tissue paper, wedged into tin trunks and buried secretly under a certain oak that grew to one side of the hill behind the house, where she had played as a child. Her mother's jewellery went to Mappin and Webb for safe keeping. Hermione wondered if she would ever bother to retrieve it. Unless by some miracle she were to have a daughter . . . don't be so ridiculous, she told herself, banishing the old dream. She was becoming very fond of Rachel and Hannah but she could not look on them as daughters while the girls still pined desperately for their real mother, longing to be back with her 'when it's all over'.

Albert Grange the carpenter, helped by one of the gardeners, tacked wooden battens diagonally across the shelves in the library to form a lattice enclosing the leather-backed books. The oak panelling presented a greater problem. In the end she had a brainwave. The Oriental carpets that lay across the floors of the grand rooms were taken up and suspended from butcher's hooks over the shelves. Only the invisible topmost line of panelling was defaced and both carpets and panels were safe from all except the most determined wreckers. Furthermore it had been done in a way that did not look offensive to people who might, if they ever arrived, turn out to be meek, harmless, civilized invaders.

Most of the furniture was stored under the roof. Valuable china and glass – a Meissen baby, one of hardly a dozen that survived intact; a pair of porcelain vases designed for Madame de Pompadour – was locked in the vaults of the bank in Sherborne, since London would be too dangerous, once the threatened air raids began. For the rest, there was always Messrs Chapman's Depository at Taunton, but why bother, when the abandoned ice cave in the kitchen garden would do just as well, *and* it was nearer and cheaper. (This was a wise decision. Chapman's was burned down at the end of the war and all its stored treasures were lost in the fire.) Furniture that couldn't be moved was dust-sheeted. Last of all, the great oriel window had to be blacked out, with the help of Ridley, two housemaids, three ladders, and a thirty-yard roll of heavy duty funeral crêpe.

The letter requisitioning Chantry for war use arrived in the next morning's post. More of a form than a letter, and more of an order than a form, it began: *To the owner and occupier of the land and buildings described in the schedule hereto annexed, known as Chantry Manor with its surrounding demesnes, I, Colonel Ernest Williams, on behalf of the Secretary of State, take possession of the land and all buildings attached, not excluding the house known as Chantry Manor.*

'Take possession' was a bit much, Hermione thought. She would have expected it to say 'do hereby requisition' or 'claim temporary rights over' or even 'declare the intention of this office, on behalf of the nation, to borrow', but no: Colonel Williams was *taking possession* of her home. Did he mean to move in personally, and if so, would he let her stay? What about the staff, some of whom had lived and worked here since she was born? Mrs Brookes the housekeeper would be most upset if she had to vacate the room she'd slept in for nearly forty years. What would happen to the furniture, to say nothing of the housemaids, some of whom were very well-developed girls?

Hermione ate her breakfast with a stoicism she did not feel. Did one have the right to object? Apparently not. Besides, on what grounds could she object? 'Upsetting Brookes' wouldn't cut much ice with the War Office. The best course of action, she decided, would be to contact Colonel Williams in person. Better to be prepared than taken by surprise. She would inform him that her home and its – what was the correct term? – *civilian personnel* were at his disposal.

At the end of the day she walked alone through the dark green gardens in the cooling evening light, along wide turf alleys, past the rhododendrons whose waxy leaves shone like oil in the dusk, past urns on pedestals stippled with lichen and age, past Italian statues and the latticed summer-house where she and Sandy used to play, thirty years ago. It was overgrown with ivy now, its octagonal seat splintered and green with mould. The whole ordered landscape seemed to quiver with imminent destruction.

Next morning, Hermione assembled everyone in the empty stone-flagged hall. Since her mother's death the staff of nearly thirty indoor and outdoor servants had been drastically trimmed. In addition, the first wave of enlistment had already taken some of the male servants, leaving just twelve people – fourteen if you included Hannah and Rachel, though as they spent most of the time closeted in their room and had never done housework in their lives, they didn't really count. Nor did Mrs Brookes, whose increasing infirmity meant that for the last couple of years her role as housekeeper had been performed by the butler and Rawlinson, the senior housemaid. Now they stood in a semicircle before her, the women's hands clasped across their aprons, the men's behind their backs, everyone curious and submissive.

Above their heads soared the fifteenth-century hammerbeam roof copied from Westminster Hall; behind them the Minstrels' Gallery. There was a pile of logs in the fireplace and two massive iron firedogs; otherwise the great hall had been emptied of furniture. Oh help, thought Hermione, what would my mother say at a moment like this? She corrected herself: what would my *father* have said? No, what matters is what shall *I* say? She drew a deep breath, looked into their anxious faces and smiled.

'We have all lived here together and loved this great house,' she began, 'some of us for ten, twenty' – she caught the housekeeper's eye – 'even forty years. Mrs Brookes could tell you some stories – I daresay she does – about the times my brother Richard and I used to invade her domain to watch Cook and the kitchen maids at work. So could Rawlinson, who has been here since I was a little girl. The years we have all shared, these stones that we have crossed so often, have woven our lives together.' She was getting muddled but it didn't seem to matter since every attentive face radiated nostalgia and goodwill.

'In the same way we are united by love for our country. A great link binds us from Chantry to Dorset, Dorset to England, England to Great Britain and onwards, right across the empire.' One of the housemaids began to snivel and fished in her pocket for a hand-kerchief. Ethel Goodbody was engaged to young Joshua Rideout, who had already been called up and was thought to have been sent abroad. Hermione smiled encouragingly at Ethel. If she started it would set off Hannah and Rachel, and she was having a tricky time choosing her words so as not to upset them.

'Very soon, this building, these gardens, and the land that surrounds Chantry will be requisitioned for war use. I expect official notification from the War Office any day now as to exactly what they have in mind. Difficult times lie ahead. We have already made a start by preparing ourselves and the house for whatever purpose it may be needed.' Ouch, she thought. I'm being pompous and what they need are simple words. 'I want to thank you all for your loyalty and hard work, your support when first my beloved brother Richard and then my father died; and your practical help after my mother's recent death.' She glanced at Ridley and Cowley, her two chief supporters.

She heard a suppressed sniff and, looking up, was surprised to see tears in people's eyes. Were they weeping for her *mother*? It did not occur to Hermione that their sympathy was for her. I had better finish, she thought; mustn't upset people. She formally released the remaining men for war work, assured them that their jobs would be waiting when it was all over, and wished them a safe return. She ended, 'Has anyone any questions to ask? No. Then, from the bottom of my heart, God bless you all, God bless Chantry, God bless England, and God save the King!'

'Hear hear!' they responded raggedly.

She dismissed the staff, promising Rachel and Hannah that they could join her later for elevenses. Back in her father's study, Hermione looked through the tall leaded windows towards the late autumn trees, now almost bare. Cowley had forecast a bitterly cold winter. She turned back to the house and its future. Chantry might shelter an evacuated school. Next best would be a hospital or perhaps some sort of assessment or training centre. The worst of all possible fates would be to have it requisitioned by the Army. She had seen country houses taken over during the First World War, their ancient stonework and panelling clumsily incised with initials and slogans. Soldiers made a terrible mess of things. She squared her shoulders, read out the War Office number to the local telephone operator and when she was put through, asked to speak to Colonel Williams.

He came to the telephone eventually sounding harassed and short-tempered.

'Ah, Miss – it *is* Miss, is it? – Staunton, yes.' She heard him snap his fingers and call out, 'Get me the Staunton file!' There was a pause before he resumed.

'Righty-ho. You're just in time. One more day and your month would be up.'

'It has taken me a month to prepare the house, Colonel Williams. Subject to a number of questions, Chantry and its grounds are now ready.'

'What sort of questions, Miss Staunton? The form you were sent does not allow you to make *conditions*.'

She ignored him and ploughed on, aware that at the first sign of uncertainty or deference his irritable courtesy could turn to bullying.

'I wish to remain in the house. I will naturally contribute in any way I can: though I am afraid I have no professional skills to offer my country.' (Except as an artist, she added to herself, and a fat lot of use that is to the war effort.) 'This whole business makes one's blood boil. Chantry has always been my home and I do not wish to leave it unless absolutely necessary.'

'Absolutely, Miss Staunton,' he echoed sarcastically. 'Rest assured, we have no intention of turning you into an evacuee. Anything else?'

'Yes. I wish my former housekeeper to remain in residence. At her age she cannot do much towards the war effort except knit.' (Hardly even knit nowadays, with her twisted fingers and bad eyesight.) 'The house has about thirty bedrooms and if necessary she could sleep in my dressing-room.'

The colonel, who had an ancient and beloved nanny and a sneaking sympathy for old retainers, laughed – a harsh snort down the telephone.

'I will see what I can do. You will hear soon what has been decided.'

*

She scanned each morning's post and when a month had gone by she could hardly stop herself from telephoning Colonel Williams again. Only the rumour that some houses had been requisitioned and then nothing more had been heard – as though the orders were buried and forgotten in the labyrinthine files of the War Office – made her restrain the impulse. But she did receive a visit of inspection from a man designated the Dorset County Representative. He claimed to remember both her parents and, since he was in his seventies, this seemed likely. Until he added, 'Dear, *dear* Lady Staunton . . .' which made it seem unlikely.

'Under the Emergency Hospital Scheme,' he informed her, 'your house may be requisitioned at any time for use as a hospital. Alternatively, it may be needed as a school for pupils evacuated from vulnerable areas, or an army billet: not necessarily the *British* Army. We expect large numbers of our imperial allies, all of whom will have to be housed somewhere. If your property is re-quisitioned you have no choice in the matter but must simply make the best of it. There is a County Equipment Store from which you may request essential supplies but if they have not got what you need you will have to use your own ingenuity and find it else-where.' Finally he smiled. 'Think of this house, as Shakespeare put it, *as a fortress built by Nature for herself, Against infection and the hand of war.*'

Not having done *Richard II* with Miss Protheroe, Hermione missed the reference.

In the interval of calm before the storm she intensified lessons for the Rosenbaum girls. They had a good grasp of basic grammar but still found English word order a struggle; they needed up-to-date idioms and, above all, better accents.

'Man,' Hermione would enunciate clearly. 'Woman.'

'Mun,' Rachel would repeat. 'Voomun.'

'You sound like my father – that's a northern "a", just like his. *Man.*'

'*Mun.*'

'All right . . .'

'Ull hight.'

Both girls had a good ear and although their pronunciation remained unmistakably German, the heavy accents were gradually modified. They brooded about where and how the family would be reunited. Rachel asked Hermione what she thought was happening to the people the Nazis had taken from their homes. Hermione tried to reassure her.

'The Red Cross will bring people together again. There will be lists showing where everybody was moved to. Try not to worry.'

'Vee must vorry.'

'*Wu*rry,' she corrected. 'Does your mother mention our food parcels? Are they getting through?'

'Last month, yes. This month, vee – sorry, *we* – do not know.'

At the beginning of 1940, after two months of suspense, Hermione received an official letter informing her that Chantry Manor was to be requisitioned with immediate effect for use as a convalescent hospital. Female staff could be retained as ward orderlies. She herself would assume the role of Commandant. Hermione stared at the letter. Commandant! What did it mean? It sounded autocratic and military. What were her duties? Who would tell her what to do? When did she start? Didn't they realize she had no one to advise or guide her, and had never done a serious job in her life?

CHAPTER ELEVEN

THE ONLY SOLUTION WAS TO RUN THE HOUSE IN HER OWN WAY, whatever that might be. Hermione sat down at her father's desk and worked out how many convalescent patients and how many nurses and other helpers Chantry could house. The figures came to 45 and 30 respectively. This meant she needed at least 70 beds. Where, in the bitterly cold midwinter of 1940, could she hope to find 70 beds, 70 mattresses, 70 or more pillows and 70 sets of warm blankets, even if she supplied the sheets? To say nothing of bedside tables, chests of drawers, wheelchairs, bedside lights, crockery . . . oh help!

She drew up a plan of the house, assigning a suitable purpose to each room and listing what she thought she would need. She telephoned the County Equipment Store. A harassed operator put her through to the superintendent.

'Margaret Kellaway here, Super of the Dorset CES,' said a brisk and breezy voice. 'What are you after?'

'How do you do? This is Hermione Staunton . . .' she began.

'Ah, yes, good morning, Commandant! The brig has told me about Chantry and I've been wondering how soon I should hear from you. Everything under control? When are your chaps arriving? How many can you take?'

'I thought perhaps forty-five . . . ?'

'Forty-five! Good gracious no, you're going to have to pack in more than that! I've got you down provisionally for seventy patients, twenty nursing staff, five doctors, two therapists – physios, you know; we let someone else worry about their heads – and as many cooks and cleaners as the house and village can supply.'

Hermione thought rapidly. That added up to ninety-seven incomers. Some doctors and therapists could live in neighbouring houses . . . 'Right,' she said, 'call it ninety people in all. Have you got ninety beds, mattresses, blankets, all that?'

'Good-oh!' said the superintendent. 'I thought we might have to bargain you up.'

Hermione registered her first lesson: you don't *have* to accept what they say. You can negotiate. I'm to be treated as an equal. It's not like dealing with my mother.

'Some of the medical staff may have to be billeted on neighbours,' she said firmly. 'Better that way. It means their days off will be a proper break for them.'

'I'll see what I can do,' Margaret Kellaway conceded.

They ran through Hermione's list, the super adding other items that hadn't occurred to her. She was instructed to make three carbon copies of the final tally, sending the top copy and a carbon to the Ministry of Health as soon as possible, keeping a copy for herself and posting the third to the CES. Finally Margaret Kellaway said, 'Can I give you a piece of advice?'

'Oh, do, *please*!' said Hermione gratefully.

'Don't live in the house yourself. If you do you'll never be off duty. Can't have *you* cracking up after six months.'

(I am *needed*, she registered.)

'Install yourself in one of the houses nearby – dower house, gatehouse, gardener's cottage, doesn't matter. Ask to have a telephone line put in – I'll do what I can to speed that up – and tell no one its number except your nearest and dearest. Only way you'll ever get any peace. Hold on a sec while I make a note to remind myself.'

'Right-ho,' said Hermione.

*

In the pause that followed she wondered who would count as her nearest and dearest. Madeleine Finch, her nine-year-old god-daughter? A nice child and a great joy to her. Or maybe Henrietta Birmingham, the redoubtable cousin with whom she had felt a rapport ever since Henrietta had come to her mother's funeral, or even the dashing young man on the flying trapeze – as she always thought of him – Reggie Conynghame-Jervis, Aunt Kitty's grand-son, now in the RAF flying Spitfires. He was a great charmer. If he survived the war and if Chantry did as well, perhaps *he* . . . no; plenty of time in years to come for those sort of thoughts. Then there were the people among whom she had always lived: Phyllis, her personal maid for almost twenty years, Brymer, Mrs Brookes, Ridley, and Ada Rawlinson, who had come to Chantry as a plump giggly young child, almost. Hannah and Rachel were dear, clever, tender girls of whom she had great hopes – but they were not her blood or even her nationality and once the war ended they would hurry home to be reunited with their parents. In the end, Sandy would always be her nearest and dearest, in spite of the fact that she might pass him in the street without knowing it. Sandy would be forty now – at least he wouldn't be fighting in the front line or risking his life flying Spitfires. The idea of Sandy as a middle-aged man was hard to grasp. He would always be a ginger-haired small boy, burnt golden by the summer heatwave, shouting from the top of a tree or behind a clump of bracken as she shaded her eyes against the sun and Bobby came bounding back to fetch her . . .

The superintendent's voice came down the line again.

'No peace for the wicked,' she said. 'Sorry to have kept you hanging on. By the way your telephone bill counts for expenses from now on. If you like.'

'Thanks for the tip,' said Hermione. 'But don't worry about that. I can cover it. I'll wait to hear when I can expect the equip-ment to arrive.'

'I haven't the foggiest. It'll just turn up one day. I'll mark the order form urgent, not that it makes any difference: everyone always does. Give me a tinkle when it's installed – we're desperate for the extra beds. Goodbye, Commandant.'

'Goodbye, Superintendent.'

Hermione put the telephone down and felt her heart racing. She looked out of the study windows across the icy landscape and murmured out loud, 'I *say*! Oh I *jolly* well *say*!'

Then she summoned Ridley and Brymer.

One Tuesday morning, two weeks after her conversation with Margaret Kellaway, a convoy of three lorries turned into the wrought-iron gateway of Chantry Manor and rattled along its frozen drive, stopping at the entrance to the stables. Elias Brymer emerged just as a young woman jumped down from the driving seat of the first lorry and strode towards him.

'Beds,' she said crisply. 'Convalescent patients, for the use of. Where shall we put them?'

'Lord, miss, I dunno,' said Brymer, flustered by her confident manner. At that moment Hermione appeared.

'Ah, good, the beds,' she said. 'At last!'

'Good morning. You must be the Commandant. We're from the Ministry of Health. Ninety beds, ordered and checked. Where do you want them unloaded?'

Hermione looked at the three young women.

'Have you got anyone besides yourselves?' She meant, strong young men to carry all these iron bedsteads into the house.

'Nope. Where shall we unload?'

'As near as possible to the front door.'

'Righty-ho then! Lead on, MacDuff!'

It took the rest of the morning to unload the bedsteads from the lorries, along with their sprung iron bases and mattresses, and all afternoon to carry them into the house and put them in the designated rooms. Everyone joined in ... men, women, the two German girls, peeling off layers of clothing one by one until they were in dresses or shirtsleeves despite the bitter cold. Mrs Brookes supplied tea to the sweating workers, tottering from kitchen to hall on her old arthritic legs. When everyone was exhausted and darkness was closing in fast, Hermione gave up directing operations, wound a scarf turban-fashion round her head and lugged beds and mattresses with the rest of them. At six o'clock she rang Margaret Kellaway.

'Superintendent? Hermione Staunton from Chantry. Those beds have arrived and been installed.'

'Jolly good. I'm hoping to get the rest of the gubbins to you by the end of the week. Ready to receive your first patients from next Monday onwards?'

'It might be a bit of a muddle along and bungle at first but we'll cope. Yes, Monday'd be grand.'

'Good show! Mind you get some sleep over the weekend . . . it never rains but it pours and you'll be up to your eyebrows once they start arriving. Goodbye for now, Commandant!'

'Goodbye, Superintendent.'

Every limb ached, her hands were blistered, her feet sore and – she suddenly realized – she smelled of perspiration. It was the first time in her life she had exuded sweat like one of the servants. That's the smell of hard work and I can do it, thought Hermione exultantly. *I can do it!*

She had a few days left before the first patients arrived. It was not time to be frittered. First thing next morning she rang the president of Dorset Red Cross, a woman a few years older than herself who lived in one of the country's great old houses just outside Wimborne Minster. Lady Avenell was quick and kind.

'My dear Miss Staunton, I'm so glad you telephoned! Margaret Kellaway has already spoken to me about your splendid work. How can I help?'

Hermione explained that she and her staff, all perfect amateurs in medical matters, needed guidance in the care of badly wounded patients.

'Excellent idea. A little forethought saves so much distress. Let me send a couple of my girls over. They're trained in first aid, of course, but better than that: they'll give your people some idea of what to expect, otherwise it can come as a bit of a shock. And what about you, my dear? You've got a good right-hand girl, I hope?'

Hermione confessed that the need for such a person hadn't occurred to her.

'Oh but you must! Have you got a friend who could help? No? Let me think for a moment . . . do you know, I can't think of anyone suitable just now. How tiresome! Nothing for it: you'll have to advertise in *The Times*. I'm sure you'll get a very good response. Don't take on anyone married, would be my advice, nor a mother. Their minds are bound to be elsewhere and you need someone absolutely dedicated.'

'A man, perhaps,' Hermione ventured.

'A man! Oh my dear, there aren't many of *those* around any more. Unless you mean a conscientious objector.'

It hadn't occurred to Hermione that she might take on a conscientious objector.

'It seems rather a good idea,' she said thoughtfully.

Lady Avenell demurred. 'Some of them can be splendid chaps with genuinely high principles – but you'll get a lot of flak from the patients. Serving men in the forces, especially wounded ones, haven't much time for conchies. No, better not. Now then, when shall I send Maud and Edith over?'

Maud and Edith appeared on their bicycles sharp at nine o'clock two days later. They wore dungarees under moth-eaten fur coats and their hair was hidden by bandeau-style headscarves, which had the further merit of keeping their ears warm. Their arrival coincided with that of a consignment of medical supplies from the Ministry of Health. They set to at once, helping to unload, commandeering a former linen cupboard next to Hermione's old bathroom as the perfect place to store bottles and bandages, labelling shelves with practised efficiency. At the end of a busy morning Hermione suggested they might like to lunch with her in the small dining room.

After a moment of surprise they grinned at one another and said, 'Oh, we're not stuck-up! We'll eat with the workers!'

I'm not a worker, Hermione registered; or if I am, we should all eat together. Well, it's been the way it is for too long. Nearly thirty-eight years. I can't change now.

After lunch the pair gave a two–hour–long demonstration of emergency first aid techniques – 'just in case you're wheeling some chap round the rose garden and he decides to peg it!' They showed everyone how to sterilize instruments on a primus stove ('for when the electricity fails') and the right way to take temperatures, pulses and blood pressure ('you'll find everyone gets roped in to do everything'), making their audience practise on one another. They showed how to offer and remove a bedpan inconspicuously, doing as little damage as possible to the dignity of desperately injured men, and instructed their listeners always to stay with a patient while he took his pills. 'If you're in any doubt afterwards, tell him to open up,' Edith instructed firmly, 'and have a good old peer around. Above all, remember to laugh. If he tells a joke, laugh, even though you've heard it a hundred times before. If someone else tells a joke, laugh. When all's said and done, laughter's the cheapest medicine you've got. Never mind how you may be feeling inside, *you* don't matter – just keep laughing.'

The lecture ended with sobering words about the anger, grief, frustration and terror these men would have experienced; about nightmares; about the ease with which some of them – yearning for gentleness and female company – could fall in love, and the unscrupulousness others might display towards a naive or idealistic young woman. They wished everyone good luck and pedalled off into the thickening dusk.

Soon the sick and their medical attendants will be here, Hermione thought. Already the house has been transformed. I should make the most of these last few days, for hullabaloo and mayhem are about to descend and – in spite of everything – I feel utterly inadequate and unprepared. She went in search of Rachel and Hannah, to comfort them and let them thereby comfort her.

She knew the two Jewish girls felt guilty about enjoying good meals, when their parents might be going hungry. Through the telescope of their yearning for the distant, beloved Mutti and Vati, Hermione glimpsed a cameo of family life unrecognizable to her. Their mother, they had told her wistfully, used to read poetry to them in the evenings – not an image that Hermione could reconcile with memories of her own childhood. Their father would take them for long walks on Sundays through the parks of Berlin, talking about the city's history and pointing out where great men had lived. Remembering how her own father had talked to her about his pride in trade, she found this easier to imagine. She had shown them his panelled study, one wall lined with books, and described her own memory of leaning against him as he sat at this very desk before an open atlas of the world, tracking his ships through its oceans, teaching her the names of the ports they visited. Hannah listened with her thumb in her mouth, leaning against Rachel. On an impulse – for she was not a physically demonstrative woman – Hermione asked, 'Hannah? May I give you a hug?'

The girl gazed through large, dark-ringed eyes, hesitated, then came shyly to the desk. Hermione held out her arms and Hannah climbed awkwardly on to her lap and rested her head against Hermione's shoulder. Rachel watched, trying to smile.

Hermione received nearly forty answers to her classified advertisement seeking an administrative assistant, mostly from women with no obvious qualifications for the job. She had phrased the insertion as neutrally as possible but mention of the countryside acted like a magnet. Nearly half the replies were from young mothers desperate to find safety in the country along with children from whom – as one said – 'I simply can't bear to be separated!' Hannah and Rachel were daily proof that this was literally true. Loving families *cannot bear* to be parted. Such letters gave Hermione further insight into the devotion possible between mothers and their children but she steeled herself to reject the pleas. The seventy men who would soon be in her charge must remain her first priority.

She had nearly finished reading through the applications, none of which seemed ideal, when she came to one written in a small, clever hand. This was the only letter from a man. He explained that he had trained as a priest and been ordained; that he had served five years in a Manchester parish before having a crisis of faith. His bishop had released him from pastoral work but suggested that, rather than renouncing the Church altogether, he might spend a few years pursuing a different vocation and then perhaps return to the priesthood. The writer had accordingly spent the last two years training as a medical student. Hermione read the letter with mounting excitement – here was the perfect candidate!

The letter finished, *As to my personal situation, I am thirty-five, unmarried, and in good mental and physical health. You will doubtless have worked out by now that I am a conscientious objector, although I am not an absolutist and therefore willing to work with serving men. I appeared before a tribunal which concluded that I was insufficiently qualified for the RAMC but recommended some form of administrative work, preferably in a medical setting. I therefore apply for the post you advertise, which fulfils these criteria.* The letter was signed *Nicholas Hobson*. He gave an address in Islington (where the heck is Islington, Hermione wondered) and a telephone number. She picked up the phone on her desk and asked the operator to connect her.

CHAPTER TWELVE

MID–FEBRUARY 1940 WAS CRUELLY COLD. IN THE EMPTY STONE fireplace a double-handled basalt vase bloomed with sprigs of early forsythia and white blackthorn. Someone had put a posy of early sweet violets on Hermione's desk and their heart-shaped leaves and faint perfume were a poignant reminder that beyond the unimaginable bustle and responsibility that had overtaken her, the old calendar rolled on. The snowdrops and celandines will be out soon, she thought, and after them the furry catkins Nanny used to call 'lambs' tails'. This bitter winter can't last for ever!

Nicholas Hobson, her new assistant, knocked on the study door and came in. He had been with her a week but although they worked side by side all day, they had not yet begun to feel at ease with each other. Awkwardness made him abrupt.

'Ration books,' he said. 'I've checked what "residents" is supposed to mean, and it only covers people who have been living here for eighteen months or more. Medical staff and patients get an automatic allocation; you don't have to obtain books for them unless they will be staying longer than six months.'

'But I don't *know*,' said Hermione. 'I can't tell how long they'll be here.'

'In the case of the patients, in six months' time they'll either be better or dead,' he told her briskly. 'That excludes all of *them*. As for the medics: half and half, at a guess.'

'Half *dead*?' she asked in horror.

He laughed. 'Let's hope not. No – half still here and half moved on. Best to obtain ration books for them all, registered under their home addresses.'

'How many should I apply for?'

'Fifteen, isn't it? Five doctors, eight nurses, two physios. Yes, fifteen. Then there's the household staff, your two refugees – if we're lucky; they may not qualify – and you and me. How many more is that?'

'Fourteen, maybe sixteen. Oh, help! Seems funny to think that *I* need a ration book when the hens are laying, the cows are producing, and we'll soon have a kitchen garden full of vegetables.'

'Commandant,' he said patiently, '*everyone* needs a ration book. And who is going to plant the kitchen garden?'

'The . . . gardeners?' she replied, but her voice trailed away. Of course. There were no gardeners left apart from Cowley.

'If we want fresh vegetables – and we do – you'd better ask to be allocated two or three Land Girls. Can you find space for them, as well as everyone else?'

'There's the under-gardener's cottage,' she said. 'I don't think I've ever been inside but it must have at least four or five bedrooms.'

Nicholas Hobson thought, not for the first time, how astonishingly unworldly she was. 'Not necessarily that many,' he suggested. 'I'll check it out myself later.'

A letter arrived for Rachel Rosenbaum, postmarked Berlin, addressed – as Hermione had predicted – to the Red Cross in London and forwarded, by some miracle, to Chantry. The two girls scrutinized it for several moments before taking it up to their room to read privately. Half an hour later they came down in search of Hermione. Both had been crying; Hannah was still trembling and shuddering.

'Oh Tante 'Mione, they have *gone*! Mutti and Vati! They had to leave our home and now . . .'

'Steady on,' Hermione said. She drew them into one of the small sitting rooms and sat them on a high Knole sofa, one on either side of her.

'Now then, tell me first of all who is the letter *from?*'

'It is from my old schoolmate Lidy,' said Rachel. 'We were best friends when we were small, even though she was not Jewish. It did not matter, *then*. But when . . . *things* . . . began, it was better we did not talk. When Hannah and I left Berlin I sent to her a letter. I said she must write me through the Rote Kreuz.'

'And she *has*, you see . . .' Hermione said soothingly.

Tears sprang to Rachel's eyes. 'But such a letter! Mutti and Vati have gone away and Lidy does not know where and now shall we find them ever again? How can I picture them if I do not know where they *are*, what *doing*? Can they to us still write?'

Impulsively, Hermione put an arm round each girl's shoulders and drew them towards her. Hannah's head nestled into the soft hollow below her neck and Hermione could feel her body reverberating. She thought, such *pain*! She smoothed the hot hair from their foreheads and kissed them both, amazed at the immediacy of contact, her lips against their skin. She never kissed people. The two shuddering girls drew closer until all three formed a pyramid of sorrow and comfort.

The phoney war was over. The cold, dark winter months were over too and with the coming of spring, people's spirits began to lift. Suddenly the news got much worse. Germany had invaded Holland and Belgium; France was bound to be next.

'We are fighting for survival now,' the men said, listening to the solemn voice of the announcer on the nine o'clock news. 'You wait. Everything else will seem like a rehearsal compared to what's coming.' They were not being melodramatic: Mr Churchill said the same thing in May when he took over as Prime Minister.

Yes, Hermione thought, blood, toil, tears and sweat just about sums it up. Chantry's old ways had vanished so utterly that it was hard to imagine 'normal' life ever being resumed. The kitchen garden now extended right up to the walls of the house and cabbages had been planted out amid the Italian statuary. Wood nymphs and piping shepherds, hunters and fleeing maidens struck poses between tidy rows of onion spikes, feathery carrot tops and baby lettuces. The herbaceous borders had been uprooted and replaced with potatoes, Brussels sprouts, beetroots. The cold frames and greenhouses that had once supplied Chantry with fresh flowers now sheltered hundreds of tomato plants, and radish and lettuce seedlings. Bulging bags of lime and Growmore lay underneath slatted tables in the potting sheds. Bean plants marched on stilts beside gravelled paths.

She had changed, too. At first she had felt like someone play-acting authority. Day by day, the pretence was becoming real. Ten years of meeting the directors of Staunton Trading had given her a better grasp than she realized of how to run an organization efficiently – any organization. Think clearly and realistically. Issue orders directly. Make sure they are understood. Follow them up. Praise where praise is due. One thing she still dreaded: the necessary, daily tour of the patients. A knock on the door, and Nicholas entered.

'Brace yourself, Com – it's that time again!'

Hermione stood up and tidied her hair nervously. He knew that the twice-daily tour of the rooms where the patients lay terrified her, but she hoped no one else did. Some of the men had been horribly wounded and, although they were recovering now, most were still in pain and one or two sometimes became delirious or even abusive.

'Come with me, won't you?' she asked. 'Bring your pad to make a note if anything's needed.'

'Roger, willco, chocks away!'

Hermione stood looking down on a patient whose head was almost entirely swathed in bandages, leaving two sinister gaps for his nose and mouth. The bandages moved stiffly.

'That you, Commandant?' asked a muffled voice.

'Clever you!' she said cheerfully. 'I don't know how you can tell under that blind man's buff disguise!'

'The smell,' he said, adding hurriedly, 'no offence meant. Nice smell. Posh soap.'

'You're sounding better today,' she said. 'Anything you need? Any complaints?'

'Yes – a letter from my girl. No letter for weeks. Only medicine I need.'

'I bet she hasn't the foggiest where you are. But I'll see what I can do. Mr Hobson, make a note to ask about Lieutenant Mottiford's forwarding arrangements.'

As she moved away Hermione thought, how can they do it? Here's a man who, two months ago, was almost burned to death, whose hands may never function properly again, whose face – well, it's too early to know about his face – and some wretched, selfish young woman can't be bothered to write him a loving letter. Heaven preserve him from a 'Dear John'. That's the last thing he needs.

One by one she passed seven beds in what had once been her own bedroom, noting who smiled, who gave her the thumbs up and whose head turned wearily away. She stopped at the seventh and final bed, in which lay a chap younger than Richard would have been when she saw him for the last time, returning to another war. That was nearly twenty-five years ago; now she could only remember Richard's face as it looked in his last photograph, set in an uncharacteristically resolute expression. The laughing, teasing boy had gone for ever.

'Commandant?' said a young voice. 'When will I be out of here?'

'Goodness, is it *that* bad?' she asked with a smile.

The young man blushed. 'I don't mean that. I feel a rotten fraud, lying here in the lap of luxury when there's men much worse off than me.'

'That's for the doctors to decide. But I'll have a word – if you'd make a note, Mr Hobson – and try and find out something definite. How's your appetite?'

'Not too bad.'

His face was gaunt with what might have been hunger but by now Hermione could read the signs and knew that it was pain that tightened his jaw, narrowed his pale lips and hollowed his eye-sockets.

'Try and make the most of this chance to rest,' she advised him. 'Got enough to read? There's a schoolroom upstairs full of my brother's and my books . . .'

'I used to love reading,' he said wistfully.

'Good-oh! I'll dig out some of my old favourites. Sherlock Holmes, Father Brown?'

'I say, Com, that'd be topping!' he said boyishly. She leaned over to pat his arm and saw him wince.

'Sorry,' she said hastily.

In the corridor the doctors were waiting for her. She turned to check that Nicholas was there. 'I'm right behind you,' he murmured. Hermione squared her shoulders and followed the medics into the office and dispensary they had set up along one wall of her old bathroom.

She ate dinner these days in the small dining room with Nicholas and any of the medical staff who happened to be off duty. Afterwards she would go into the blue parlour, whose walls were covered in silk that had once been azure blue but in the course of the last two hundred years had faded to palest eau-de-Nil. Darker squares marked the gaps where some of the pictures had been removed into safe keeping. She always left the door open invitingly for anyone who might want to chat, listen to the wireless, or put classical music on the gramophone. The first time this happened one of the doctors had said wistfully, 'What I'd give now for a glass of port or a decent brandy!'

'I'm sure the cellar's full of it,' said Hermione. She was about to ring for Ridley from sheer force of habit, but stopped herself in time. Beckoning the doctor to follow, she led the way to the butler's pantry where she found the cellar keys hanging on a board behind the door.

'Come and choose for yourself!' she said. Unlocking the door and switching on a light at the foot of a flight of worn steps, she revealed to his astonished gaze a series of arched stone recesses in whose racks lay bottle after bottle of vintage port, brandy, and rows of wine that shone deep red beneath a layer of dust.

'Holy Moses!' he said involuntarily. 'This lot must be worth a fortune!'

'Do you really think so?' she asked. 'I don't think anyone's been in here since my mother died. I daresay it could do with being drunk. Does wine go off? Why don't you choose a nice bottle of port – or brandy, if you'd prefer that?'

From then on Hermione found herself, most evenings, at the centre of a gregarious group. They would talk 'shop', discuss the progress of the war, speculate about the rumours of an imminent cross-Channel invasion, gradually releasing the tensions of a day spent looking after too many patients with too few staff in less than ideal conditions. Everything stopped at nine o'clock while they listened to the familiar voice of a newsreader – Freddie Grisewood or John Snagge – reading the main news bulletin on the wireless, after which most people would disperse, exhausted, to bed.

Before making her way by the light of a torch down the drive to the Dower House where she had installed herself with only Phyllis for company, Hermione would occasionally have a more private chat with just one person ... sometimes one of the doctors, or perhaps Rachel and Hannah would seek her out, but more often than not it was Nicholas. She looked forward to these gentle half hours filled with warmth, companionship and trust. At other times, before turning in, she might wander alone through the familiar upstairs bedrooms that now housed seventy strangers for whom she felt profoundly responsible. There was something theatrical about the converted wards during these quiet late-night walks: the shaded lights, rows of identical iron beds filled with young men who tossed and turned, groaning in their sleep, sometimes crying out, sitting up, shouting grotesquely before subsiding meekly, apologetically, as an attendant nurse hurried forward. Others would be fast asleep in a world of their own, peacefully unconcerned with the anguish of their fellows. All this was new in Hermione's experience – never having been to boarding school or in hospital – and she felt humbly grateful for the chance to observe the devotion of those who ministered to the suffering men through the long, restless nights. She told herself that one day, when the war was over, she would work up these stark monochrome visions into a series of paintings. She even made a few preliminary sketches, but the focus of her mind was elsewhere. Drawing seemed a luxury. Later, when she saw Henry Moore's studies of the sleepers sheltering in the London Underground, she knew he had seen what she had only half observed and that his eye and hand had done the work of recording it.

Nicholas had been her assistant for six months. Everyone said what a good team they made: she the instigator, he the administrator. It worked like clockwork.

One late summer evening when they were alone together, he began tentatively, 'You know, I still find it hard to believe that all this belongs to you . . .' He waved an encircling arm to indicate the shadowy room, the house with its attendant buildings – wash-house, bakehouse, hothouses, stable block – the kitchen garden, rose garden and maze, the rhododendron walks, and beyond all these the gently sloping fields that stretched to the very limits of her property. '*All this*. So *much*. How did you come by it? I mean, most families can dig up a male heir from *somewhere*. I don't want to sound rude – I'm just curious.'

'There *was* a male heir – my brother Richard – but he was killed.'

'In the last war?' She nodded. 'Poor old you.'

'Poor young him,' Hermione corrected. 'He was only twenty.'

'And you?'

'Fourteen at the time. Seventeen when my father died.'

'You were seventeen when you inherited all this?'

'Nearly eighteen, yes.'

'No uncles in the background – no cousins, long-lost, sheep-farmers in Australia?'

'No, no one like that. In any case,' she said defensively, 'my father had already begun to teach me how the company worked. He used to spend a good deal of time explaining the geography, the to and fro of it, showing me bills of lading and accounts. Weather, ships. My mother hated it. People like her despised all that.'

'Why on earth?'

'It was trade. My father was *in trade*.'

Nicholas looked around the room. A pair of minor Dutch

landscapes hung on one shadowy wall, a Turkey rug lay sleekly over the polished oak floor. At the opposite side stood a massive Venetian table, too heavy to lift up to the attic and therefore too heavy to loot, its marble top inlaid with multi-coloured arabesques like a floral still life. Above it hung a gilded baroque mirror, bolted to the wall.

Hermione caught his appraising eye and laughed. 'I know what you're thinking, but to my mother's people it was a comedown. In her family, everything was inherited. She married a *parvenu* . . . a man who'd had to *buy* other people's furniture! At auctions! In fact most of it came with the house but it made no difference since he'd also bought that. They never really forgave her.'

'What was she – a duke's daughter?'

Hermione laughed again and he thought, for all her wealth she's absolutely straightforward, far too trusting of others, far too unsure of herself.

She went on, 'Gracious no, nothing half so grand. Her father was just an ordinary Scottish baronet. But quite an *old* one, if you see what I mean. They'd lived in the same place for generations. Still do. She had heaps of brothers and sisters but after she married my father, they were on non-speakers. She became *poor Phibby* – Phibby was her nickname as a little girl. Not many of them even bothered to turn up for her funeral, though I found out later that she'd been sending them money for years.'

'Rotters!' he said, with real contempt. 'When did she die – your mother?'

'Um, let me see – gosh, nearly four and a half years ago! In a boating accident in the south of France. We had a villa on the Riviera – still do, I suppose, God knows what's happening to it now. I ought to find out. Sorry, where was I? Yes – Mama often cruised there in the summer.'

'On board the yacht, I suppose, with a crew of twenty?' he asked, with a sarcasm she failed to notice.

'Yes, that's right. Actually not quite as many as twenty. A dozen or thereabouts.'

'Were *you* there when she died?'

'Oh no – Mama didn't like me coming with her. I'm, you know, *too big*. And it gave her age away, having a grown-up daughter. No, she had taken a party of her friends.'

He wanted to ask exactly what had happened to her mother; how it was possible for a woman surrounded by an experienced crew and a party of friends to suffer a fatal accident. How, for that matter, was it possible for a mother to exclude her own daughter for being too tall? But that question had better wait. Instead he said, 'You must have been shattered.'

'Well it *was* ghastly, of course, but do you know, it was also – I shouldn't own up to this – it was also a great *relief*.'

That's done it! Hermione thought. Now he'll despise me – this dear, good man on whom I so depend. But instead of being shocked, Nicholas leaned across the low table between them and held out his hands. After a pause, Hermione extended hers. People had so seldom touched her and suddenly it was happening all the time.

His warm hands enfolded hers and he said, 'Do you want to tell me about it? I'm pretty good at keeping secrets. Had a lot of practice.'

Hermione glanced at the long-case clock in the corner: ten fifteen. She ought to go to bed – they had ten new patients arriving tomorrow, eight being discharged back to their units, a great deal of paperwork . . .

'Yes,' she said and leaned back in her chair, releasing his hands. 'Yes, I *would* like to. Oh crumbs, where on earth do I start?

'The first thing you need to know about my mother is that she was a beauty. A real dazzling *beauty*. So you can imagine what a disappointment *I* must have been. I look like the men in her family – so she said; I never met them, except once at her funeral. I just knew their names.

'Anyway – I really don't know why she married my father. I *hope* because she loved him. He was a good deal older – let me work it out, yes, heavens, more than thirty years older – and he must have been simply glorious to look at when they met. She was only about eighteen and I expect he fell head over heels, you know?'

'Yes, I know,' Nicholas confirmed.

'He was a very lovable man, my father. His manners were sort of abrupt; he was very direct, didn't suffer fools gladly; but he was full of energy and kindness. He loved *her*, I'm sure, he must have done.

'Unfortunately the marriage didn't turn out very happily. It got worse when my brother Richard was killed in 1916 – that was, oh, the most dreadful blow you can imagine. It more or less finished my father. He went grey and quiet, lost all his oomph and died three years later. From then on it was just Mama and me. I *wanted* to please her, I knew I was an unsatisfactory daughter for her but what could I do? One can't *shrink*. I daresay she's given me a life-long inferiority complex, as the trick-cyclists call it. Luckily people don't expect that from someone who's six feet tall. She probably hoped I'd get married but she didn't make it easy for me and there weren't many men of my age about. If ever I *did* bring someone home she couldn't resist charming him. She had to prove she was more sort of alluring to men than me. Silly, really – it was perfectly obvious. So I never actually had a proper beau. Not surprising with a phiz like mine . . .' She gave a disparaging laugh.

'Dear Com, stop it. Don't run yourself down. Not to me. You're an extremely handsome woman.'

'Crikey, do you really *think* so? Handsome? Gosh!'

'I do, yes,' he said. She blushed with pleasure at the backhanded compliment. I must be careful not to give her the wrong idea, Nicholas thought. It would be dangerously easy to start her off. She does so crave affection. He said, 'Go on about your mother.'

'As she got older, like, I daresay, a lot of beauties she tried to *stop time*. She spent a fortune on beauty treatments and charlatan women who come to your house and give you massages and lotions and potions and I don't know what, pretending they can preserve your looks. Towards the end of her life she had a lot of young men friends and I'm afraid some of them were a bit of a menace . . . *not* awfully nice people. I tried to tell her, but she accused me of being jealous. "Just because *you* lack admirers, my girl," she used to say . . .'

Hermione let the rest of the sentence trail away. Nicholas sat in silence, waiting for her to continue.

'She was ashamed of having married beneath her, as she saw it, and she thought her people were *right* to have rejected her. She used to try and buy their approval. I had no idea how much money she gave her family until after she died, when these letters started coming in. *Your dear mama was so good to us . . . could always rely on her for £500 a year* – sometimes it was more, a thousand or two – *do so hope that you* (meaning me) *will feel able to continue in the same generous way – vital to preserve the good standing of the family* – that sort of thing. Phooey! Not much good about *their* behaviour!'

'And did you?' Nicholas couldn't help asking.

'I know this is going to sound awful but I couldn't help feeling it was *my* money she'd been giving away. It wasn't until after she died that I saw my father's will for the first time and discovered that for years I'd been entitled to the income from various trust funds he'd set up for me. Mama had never told me and wouldn't let the lawyers tell me, either. I seem to remember when I was twenty-one some old boy reading the will out to me but he gabbled so fast I couldn't follow and I didn't like to ask him to explain in case he thought I was being greedy. Well, these relatives who had been – sorry but it's the only word – *sponging* off us, I decided it wouldn't be fair to cut them off just like that. So I wrote to the ones who hadn't come to her funeral and told them the amount would be reduced by ten per cent per annum over the next ten years. That way seemed less brutal. The few who did turn up, I let them carry on as before.'

Nicholas thought: I bet she's a sharp businesswoman!

'Good for you!' he said. 'Serve them right.'

'Well, to go on about my mother . . . sure you're not bored?'

'Bored? *Fascinated!*'

'She was always angry, all her life – above all with me. She could be fearfully charming on the surface but underneath she had a frightful temper. It could make her tricky to live with. And then, not long before she died, she started to, oh well, *drink* too much, I mean, *alcohol* – which made everything ten times worse. She may have been drunk when she drowned . . . Poor her. Not a very happy life.'

Nicholas said, '*How* you must have hated her!'

She met his gaze. 'Mmm–hmm,' she concurred, as though the word *yes* were too extreme to be spoken out loud.

There was a series of rapid, delicate chimes from the clock in one corner of the room and Hermione said, 'Oh glory, listen to that! Eleven o'clock! I'm keeping you up! You've been frightfully patient, letting me ramble on . . .'

'Stop it, Com,' he said firmly. 'Your mother's is an extraordinary story. However it *is* bedtime – for both of us. Will you promise to tell me more some other evening?'

'Don't you think after all these confidences you might now call me Hermione?'

'Honoured . . .'

'There's not much more to tell, really – but, yes: some other time. Thank you for listening. Good night, Nicholas.'

'Good night, Hermione.'

Food shortages were becoming a problem. Producing enough vegetables to feed nearly a hundred people was a priority. The first three Land Girls had been supplemented by two more and although the work was hard, they bloomed in the unaccustomed country air. Wearing baggy dungarees and Wellington boots, hair scraped back from their rosy-cheeked young faces, they pushed wheelbarrows full of compost or stones and spent back-breaking hours digging and planting for victory. They developed huge appetites as a result. Even Cowley the gardener, much as he resented the loss of his rose beds, gave them grudging praise, unable to resist adding, 'If they plant more than they eat it'll be a ruddy miracle!'

The stable yard saw an influx of chickens and empty stables filled with home-made rabbit hutches. The population of Chantry – human and animal – was greater than at any time since Jack Staunton had bought it fifty years ago. Hermione presided over this ragtag and bobtail of humanity, most of them young, inexperienced and much in need of supervision. For almost the first time in her life she was neither lonely nor bored and for the very first time in her life she felt needed. She, who until now had always been an outsider, was part of something – the war effort, the

185

hospital, a team of people. Despite her exhaustion, she gloried in that.

In the heightened atmosphere of war and the novelty of the surroundings, several romances were struck up. Land Girls competed with nurses for the attentions of the doctors and – in some cases – the recovering patients. Hermione had to dismiss two young auxiliaries who were found kissing the convalescents they should have been wheeling round the gardens in the soft winter sunshine.

'But Com, it's good for their morale!' pleaded one buxom girl, and Hermione had to smile.

'It may be good for morale but it's very bad for discipline. Besides, he might have been married – did you stop to think of that?'

'He's not,' the culprit said sulkily.

'How can you be sure?'

'He told me.'

'Joan, he wasn't going to *admit* to having a wife and three children, was he? But he has.'

'I don't care,' the girl muttered.

'*I* care. You're dismissed. Go and pack. Brymer is going to Sherborne at twelve, as it happens. He'll give you and Rosemary a lift. Here's a travel voucher for London – there should be a train at about two thirty, if it's on time. Count yourself lucky you don't have to walk to the station. It's fourteen miles,' Hermione said crisply.

The girl left the room and muttered to her waiting friend, 'Sour old spinster!'

Nicholas, overhearing, caught her by the arm and spun her round.

'Mind your tongue!' he said with unexpected ferocity. The girl blushed and burst into tears.

'Next!' ordered Nicholas.

He had been her assistant for several months before Hermione could bring herself to ask why he had registered as a conscientious objector. One evening, after a difficult day in which she had twice seen him insulted by patients (for Nicholas never hid the reason for his civilian clothes, but admitted openly and in their own contemptuous jargon to being a conchie) she raised the subject.

'It has nothing to do with the last war,' he told her. 'I was eleven when that ended and longing for my chance to have a go at the Hun. After that I went into reverse and started to train as a priest, but it wasn't God either who made me a CO. The Bible's pretty bloodthirsty in any case. I think the real reason is that my older brother and our dog were run over by a car one afternoon. We had gone out bicycling. I must have been twelve or thirteen, and Kit was sixteen at the time. It happened in a flash – one minute he was pedalling like billy-o a few yards up ahead with Gully loping alongside and the next minute they were sprawled on the ground bleeding. As it turned out Kit wasn't too badly hurt, though he still walks with a dot-and-carry-one, but poor old Gully lay in the ditch howling, his back legs shattered, eyes fixed on me in agony. The next car that came along, the driver stopped, took out a pistol and shot him. Kindest thing, he said. God! How I missed that dog! Made me see how vulnerable and how precious life is.'

A young doctor had come in as Nicholas was speaking. He sat down quietly and listened.

'And so, partly because – yes, I do object on grounds of conscience – but mainly, in the end, because of my *dog*, I could never deliberately take a life. It may not sound a very good reason but it's the truth, though I dressed it up a bit for the tribunal. Of course I hate Hitler and his creed as much as anyone . . . but those German lads I'm supposed to kill: how do I know they don't hate it as well? Dr Mason, I know you don't agree. You probably despise me.'

'I don't despise anyone's principles,' Mason told him, 'but I despise the self-importance that puts *your conscience* above the safety of our country.'

'Nicholas is doing war work, too . . .' Hermione interrupted.

'And how many *women* applied for his job?' the doctor asked.

'It's OK, Com,' Nicholas said. 'Dr Mason has to put those smashed-up bodies back together again. I wouldn't expect him to agree with me. Look, time I turned in. 'Night all.'

187

He was hardly out of the room before Mason was asking her to authorize one or two single rooms for patients whose nightmares were keeping others awake.

'. . . the dressing-rooms, for instance – they'd be just the right size.'

She never raised the topic with Nicholas again.

One of the first people to die was Mrs Brookes. She was almost seventy-five and had been at Chantry throughout Hermione's childhood. Her death had been hastened by the stress and hard work of the last year and yet she had been happy. Hermione sat by her bedside holding her hand, then made her way down to the kitchen to tell the servants. Ada Rawlinson had entered service aged fourteen, when Hermione was five; she had been trained by Mrs Brookes and worked under her ever since.

Ada said, 'She packed a lovely parcel, Mrs Brookes! No one had her touch with sealing wax – nor beeswax polish either. I learned everything from her. I don't know how I'll manage with her gone.'

'You'll manage,' Hermione said. 'You've got to. You're the housekeeper now.'

Occasionally a patient died, which upset everybody. The men were at Chantry to convalesce, on the assumption that they would get better and return to their units. Some died unexpectedly, as though unable to face the thought of war – or home. For several days after a wife or girlfriend had sent bad news they were especially vulnerable and Hermione learned to keep an eye out for signs of distress.

'They take it very hard, Com,' the matron confirmed. 'I could strangle some of those silly women out there – why don't they *think* before stepping out with some other chap? Makes you want to wring their necks!'

When this happened, Hermione would unobtrusively arrange for the man to get a fresh boiled egg at breakfast, or be the first to read the latest issue of *Men Only* or *Picture Post*. At times all she could do was put a jam-jar of meadow flowers on his bedside table – but she always tried to do something. She knew how rejection felt.

Sometimes Hannah or Rachel would be rejected by a patient they were attending. 'Bloody Jerry!' he might say, hearing them speak for the first time. Rachel would roll him briskly back into the centre of the bed she was helping to make and say, 'Yes, I am a Jerry. A *Jewish* Jerry. And you fight Hitler for the Jews. For other reasons too, of course, but Hitler is also *my* enemy.'

'Sorry. Not myself at all just now,' the man might say apologetically; or at worst, 'Funf has spoken!' echoing the ITMA catchphrase that united everyone in laughter and ridicule. Rachel learned to cope with hostility but Hannah would burst into tears and flee. If by chance she found Hermione alone she would bury her head against her shoulder, repeating under her breath in a desperate litany of need, '*Mutti, Mutti, oh meine Mutti, wo bist Du, Mutti?*'

Where are you, where are you, where are you?

Unlike the last war, Hermione didn't have to worry about anyone dying. Sandy was probably doing something useful in the War Office. She was concerned about Reggie, the carefree Spitfire pilot, and always checked the casualty lists for family surnames ... Shepherd, Campbell-Leith, Conynghame-Jervis. If she came across one she would despatch a note to the young man's mother or grandmother, Aunts Kitty or Sibby, but she couldn't honestly say that she grieved. She deplored the loss of young lives, knowing from bitter experience that not just their lives would be lost; girls would stay unmarried and babies unborn because of those early deaths.

Hermione had started to think that the real war could not touch Dorset, only its after-effects; that she herself was inviolate, hearing only the sounds of a distant battle in a faraway place. Yet paradoxically, the transformation of Chantry into a working hospital proved to be an excellent thing, shaking the domestic staff out of their set ways; testing her own mettle and proving it sound. For the first time in her life she learned the meaning of hard work (for although she had been diligent at the Slade, it had been pure pleasure). She rose early, kept appointments punctually and maintained a delicate equilibrium among the forty-odd people working under her. She came to feel she deserved the title of Commandant. Pride comes before a fall.

She had seen many casualties, wounded men who bore the devastating scars of violent action, but never action itself. There had been dogfights overhead and when they happened people would rush to the windows or out of the front door to watch anxiously as the little black insects in the sky circled and buzzed one another angrily. She knew there were men in these aeroplanes who might kill each other; but it was hard to connect the bodies lying upstairs in iron beds with those irritable insects and their miniature aerial squabbles.

RAF Warmwell, a Spitfire fighter station with more than sixty aircraft, was not far away. Her nurses often met the air crews at local dances; one or two had rashly got engaged. 'No time to waste, Com!' they'd say, flashing a ring. They were gay and optimistic, the young flyers debonair, making the most of their heroic status. Hermione envied their lack of inhibition. War had freed them from the stifling protocol of introduction, formal engagement and wedding ceremony. People met, promised to marry, and did so at hectic speed, not giving a fig for the old ways. Trousseau, bottom drawer, bridesmaids' pearls – all became secondary to the overriding biological urgency: reproduce, reproduce, for tomorrow we die!

By October 1940 the Battle of Britain was almost over. Hermione was at her desk – her father's desk – one morning, compiling a list of much-needed supplies. She turned to look out of the window, then at the sky, and high up and far away spotted a small aircraft in trouble. It started eddying clumsily, awkwardly downwards, spiralling like a sycamore seed, smoke pouring from one side, and she saw that it had one broken wing. As she watched, the plane began to disintegrate. It was too high for her to see what happened to the crew but moments later a tiny figure, followed, as though towing it behind him, by an unopened, tightly furled parachute, began to tumble downwards at terrifying speed. Hermione found herself inhaling huge draughts of air, gasping and choking uncontrollably. At a thousand feet the parachute's lofty crescents swelled and inflated, its fall became leisurely. Hermione's heart was pounding so hard that she could hear as well as feel it. She got up and hurried to the front door where a semicircle of other watchers stood, drawn like magnets by the drama above their tilted heads.

In swooping, almost skating curves the parachute descended, heading directly for the sweep of gravel before Chantry's main doorway. Everyone else seemed oddly controlled; only she was making animal noises of panic and terror. Her gorge rose, she wanted to be sick, she wanted to release her bowels in a stinking flood. She tried to run from the imminent crash, to hide herself, but although her legs trembled violently her feet did not move. When the man was only feet above her head, a voice beside her said, as if soothing a frightened horse, 'It's *all* right, Com. *There* there. *Come* with me. *All* right.' A firm hand grasped her arm and steered her indoors. She turned her head as the doll-like figure hit the ground and collapsed face downwards, all breath knocked out of his body. She heard feet scraping on gravel as everyone rushed towards the fallen man.

'Nicholas, I'm so ashamed. I am so desperately ashamed. I shall never be able to face people again.'

'Yes you will. You weren't frightened for yourself but for him, poor chap. Nothing wrong with that.'

'I had no control – no dignity. I behaved like a fool.'

'Com, lie down on the sofa. Shall I call Rawlinson to bring you a hot cup of tea?'

Hermione gave a hysterical giggle. 'A hot cup of tea? Oh Nicholas: such a cliché!'

'Not at all. It'll restore you.'

'Could you, if you can find her, ask Rachel to bring it?'

'*Rachel?*'

'Yes, Rachel. I'd rather face her than . . .'

'Okey-doke. Now, stay there and don't move. Be back in a tick to tell you what's going on outside.'

As the door closed behind him, Hermione began to weep.

This episode proved that her skin was thinner than it appeared. She would never have guessed it, but her behaviour made her more, not less, respected than before. Automatons have no problem with control. It is the weak, the terrified, the fragile who deserve praise. As to the young airman – he lived, and flew again, and survived that as well.

One evening, touring the wards – she no longer thought of them as bedrooms – after a new intake of patients, she found herself looking into a face that seemed familiar, though from a very long time ago. The man was asleep, his bandaged arms extended stiffly in front of him on the coverlet. His features were dark and frowning and he looked as though he had suffered a good deal. She unhooked the notes from the end of his bed and checked his name. It was Brymer, W. Brymer.

Billy Brymer! thought Hermione, in shock. She looked around for Nicholas ... not there. He must be in the corridor. Billy Brymer! I never thought to see him in my life again. The smell of the Guy Fawkes bonfire came back to her, and the sour reek from the phosphorescent gleam of urine trickling down a channel in the stone floor of the stables. She felt the hay stalks scratching her bare thighs and heard Billy's harsh throaty breathing. He was breathing harshly now. She shut her eyes and clung to the rail at the end of his bed. When she opened them, Billy Brymer was looking directly at her.

'Hello, Billy,' she said steadily. 'You must have only just arrived. Does your father know you're here? I'll tell him first thing in the morning. Go back to sleep now.'

She smiled at him and walked away from his bed and out of the ward.

CHAPTER THIRTEEN

'TANTE 'MIONE,' RACHEL SAID ONE EVENING, 'I AM WORRIED about Hannah. She is *pining*, I think that's your word. She has lost four kilos weight.'

'What is that in pounds and ounces?'

'Eight, nine pounds maybe.'

'Shall I arrange for her to see one of the doctors?'

'Yes, if you like. I will try and make her do it. But the problem is her mind, no, her *heart*. She pines for Mutti.'

'And you, Rachel?'

'I miss my parents too and think, will we look again into each other's faces? All our family were close – my aunts and uncles, my cousins, Oma and Opa – that is, my grandparents – saw each other not just on Fridays. But Hannah *needs* Mutti's love. She cannot bear this long parting.'

'*I* love her,' Hermione said unexpectedly, 'I love you *both*.'

'Yes, and we love you.'

She means: but it is not the same, thought Hermione. *Nothing* can replace a mother's love.

It was true that she loved both girls. By spring 1941 Rachel and Hannah had been at Chantry for more than two years and had come to seem almost like daughters. She had taken their education in hand, and a retired schoolmaster from the village came in every morning to give them three hours of lessons. In the afternoons they studied for two further hours on their own. Rachel's violin lessons had not been so easy to arrange; Grade Eight teachers were not two a penny. Yet in the end she managed that, too, although it meant that Rachel had to travel to Salisbury once a week, and Hermione worried about the soldiers and airmen she would encounter and whether a young woman was safe, travelling alone. She quickly learned that it was not her youth or her sex that put her at risk, but the fact that she was German. Rachel came home tight-lipped more than once, having suffered insults and jeering. She learned to say absolutely nothing and not to read German books in public.

Hermione had begun to make tentative plans for their future after the war, since she was not optimistic about the Rosenbaum family's chances of being reunited. She was on the point of applying to have the two girls naturalized as British citizens with a view to adopting them eventually, in case their parents should not survive the war, when an order arrived: Rachel Rosenbaum aged nineteen, Hannah Rosenbaum aged sixteen, both of Berlin, Germany, temporarily resident in the county of Dorset, were required to go immediately to the Isle of Man internment camp for aliens. Failure to comply could result in imprisonment for persons harbouring them.

The girls were so distraught that Hermione used a precious travel voucher to travel to London on an endlessly stopping train. In the aliens' section of the Home Office she confronted the official who had signed the order and pleaded to be allowed to keep them at Chantry.

'I personally will take full responsibility for both girls. I guarantee that they are not working for the enemy. They are more opposed to Hitler and his Nazi murderers than even you or me.'

'If you say so, Miss Staunton.'

'Besides, even if they *were* Nazi sympathizers – which is absurd – how could they possibly make contact? By posting a letter to Herr Hitler, Berlin?'

'There are short-wave wirelesses, Miss Staunton. There are codes in which apparently harmless letters or postcards may be written.'

Ironically, the little man sported a toothbrush moustache which, although ginger-grey, was otherwise exactly like Hitler's.

'But it's cuckoo – I'm sorry, Major Woodward – I don't mean to cast doubts on your decision-making process, but Hannah and her sister Rachel are young *girls*. They're still practically children.'

'If memory serves me correctly,' he murmured, 'they are nineteen and sixteen years old. Hardly *children*.'

She ignored this. 'They have no idea of their family's whereabouts. Their parents have disappeared without trace and they are frantic with worry. It is impossible that they would do anything to help their . . . tormentors.' She tried to be reasonable, logical, calm. 'Major Woodward, the Rosenbaum girls have lived under my roof for two years. What secrets can they possibly have that might interest the enemy?'

'Your whereabouts,' he said implacably, and his mouth shut like a steel trap.

'*My* whereabouts?'

'Oh come now, Miss Staunton, not your *personal* whereabouts: those, I agree, would be of little interest to the enemy . . .'

Hermione thought, he is being deliberately rude. I do not have to tolerate this. She gave him a basilisk stare and prepared to pull on her gloves.

'I understand that you run a convalescent hospital for seventy wounded servicemen,' he said, trying to recover the upper hand. '*Its* whereabouts, as a target for bombs, would be of considerable interest to the enemy. Given your responsibilities I am surprised you should think it worth taking a day off to plead for a couple of *Germans*.'

'I am against injustice anywhere. I am against the irrational persecution of the innocent – and I *know*, Major, as I suspect you do, that these girls are innocent. I am against ill-treating people because of their race. Those beliefs are keystones of that British way of life which our forces are fighting to protect. Goodbye.'

She left him seated at his desk riffling importantly through his papers and knew she had wasted her time. The whole interview had lasted less than ten minutes.

It was more than two and a half hours before the Sherborne train was due to leave. Hermione wondered whether to attempt to reason with one of Woodward's superiors but she had already learned that authority always joins forces to stand firm against outsiders. She walked out of the building in what her mother would have called 'a seething bate' and decided to use the time to look at the house in Eaton Square. She hailed a taxi. The London streets were largely free of debris but the gaps in familiar squares and crescents shocked her terribly. All decorum was gone. Bombed houses stood like women half-undressed, exposing their bedroom secrets – flowered pink wallpaper on the first floor, a broken lavatory dangling from its useless plumbing, furniture akimbo, fireplaces spilling with ash and clinker. The state of some surviving houses showed how random a blast could be. Some were cut clean in two; one side a heap of rubble and glass shards, the other open like a doll's house to passers-by. A dressing table on the very edge of the precipice displayed a flowered china dish flanked by two papier-mâché boxes. Their contents – Kirbigrips? a buttonhook? – were also, no doubt, intact. But what of the owner: unbuttoned, dishevelled, distressed, or dead?

Once the streets around Belgravia would have been full of uniformed servants or delivery boys. Now the uniforms were those of servicemen – not just British, but American, Canadian and various Ruritanian-style officers in tightly belted jackets and slim trousers. It was the London of the newsreels – busy, preoccupied, yet somehow thinner, greyer and tireder than the propaganda would have people believe.

The taxi stopped outside her house. It was intact but no longer pristine; the shutters tightly closed (for blackout purposes, though there was no one indoors to turn lights on when darkness fell); the window-boxes empty and bedraggled, brass guard rail and door-knocker unpolished, the steps unswept. She got out and stood on the pavement looking up at it.

'Looks like they've gone away,' said her taxi-driver. 'Lotta people round 'ere have scarpered.'

'Yes,' said Hermione, 'it does rather. Could you take me to Paddington?'

She was much too early, but the trains were always crowded and it would be good to secure a seat. She drank a cup of tea and watched people parting or being reunited at the platform barriers, observing their shyness and confusion, the women dolled up in perfume and their best clothes, men in uniform with freshly shaved faces. As the moment for departure or reunion approached, shyness would melt into tears or rapture and they would cling to each other regardless of who might be looking. I've never had that, she thought. They must have had their quarrels and infidelities and disappointments, but these couples have something that I don't. I shall never greet anyone like that, or say goodbye with such anguish; there isn't even anyone I desperately miss. Except for Sandy, except for Sandy, *except for Sandy*.

Hannah and Rachel spent their last evening at Chantry alone with Hermione in the blue parlour. They listened to Beethoven on gramophone records, the two girls shortening some clothes she had given them, but when the last notes of the last quartet had faded and the needle had scratched, clicked and ground to a halt, she could find no words to comfort them.

'Chantry has been our home and you have been like a mother to us,' said Hannah finally. 'Now you too we have to lose.'

'Hannah my dear, you are not *losing* me. We have to separate for a while – as families must in wartime. Chantry will always be your home and you can always come back here. I *promise*. Now, it is late and you have a tiring day tomorrow. Time to turn in. Rachel will come up in a moment. A kiss before you go?'

The girl crossed the room but before Hermione could get up from her chair she was on her knees, her head in Hermione's lap.

'No, no, no . . .' Hermione murmured. 'There there, don't worry, night-night, good girl.' She stroked the glossy dark hair and soothed her like a child. After a while Hannah controlled her sobs. They both stood up and Hermione touched her wet cheeks and embraced her, moved by the smell of her skin, her soft pliable body.

When Hannah had gone she said to Rachel, 'Will she be all right?'

'I don't know. She is very fragile – *sehr empfindlich* – you know, sensible.'

'Sensitive?'

'Yes, that. Of course I will try to protect her, I promised Mutti, but I cannot be with her every minute. Oh, dear *dear* Tante 'Mione . . .! You have given us so much.' They hugged each other and Rachel said, 'Who knows if we will ever be back? Who knows if I shall again see you? We *have* been happy here – and I never thought happy was possible, after I left Germany!'

'Happ*iness*. Certainly you will be back. I have promised. Anyway, I hear the Isle of Man has an orchestra. It sounds quite civilized!'

'That is what they said about the *Konzentrationslager* for Jews. But you have been a refuge to us and from the bottom of my heart I thank you.' Comically, touchingly, she dropped a little curtsey, like a well-brought-up child. They embraced each other tightly. Her footsteps receded along the corridor and up the uncarpeted stairs.

On her evening rounds Hermione steeled herself to stop beside Billy Brymer for exactly the same amount of time as anyone else. She did not speak to him every day – she could not possibly speak to every patient every day – but once or twice a week she would slow down and ask, 'How are you getting on, Billy? What luck that you were sent here!'

'It worn't luck,' he told her. 'I put in a special request. To be near me dad.' *And you*, his eyes said.

Perhaps he thought Betty might somehow have made her way back to Chantry, Hermione thought. Did he hope to find her again, just as she dreamed of being reunited with Sandy?

Most patients stayed six weeks, eight at most, and then moved on – either for intensive physiotherapy or back to their units. Billy did not leave; he hardly left his bed and would not be coaxed into a wheelchair to be taken out in the grounds.

'If you'd like to have a look at your old haunts,' she suggested carefully, 'I could arrange for you to go down to the servants' hall . . .?'

'No, thank you, Commandant,' he said mechanically.

Eventually she asked the doctor in charge, 'What's wrong with him? He's not malingering, is he?'

'Brymer? Don't think so. Not the type. His spirit's gone. Physically he's on the mend but his heart isn't in it. Some get like that – lose the desire to live. If he were an animal he'd crawl away and die. We've been easy on him so far, but if he doesn't make an effort soon . . .'

'Has he had any visitors – apart from his father?'

'No, Com,' interjected the matron. 'No letters either.'

'No wife? Any children?'

'Wife, no; children, who knows?' She pulled a face as though to signal, *men!*

Word must have got back to Billy that she had been enquiring about him, for a few days later he requested a private meeting. Two nurses escorted him as he tottered down to her study. She told them to wait outside and motioned Billy to a chair. He looked like a rag doll, a bloodless version of his old self. His eyes were deeply ringed with grey, blue veins ran along the sides of his arms and legs, his body and expression lacked all animation.

'Well now, Billy,' she said, 'you can speak quite freely. This conversation is private and will not be noted or repeated. What did you want to see me about?'

She thought he would ask about Betty, or perhaps attempt some explanation or apology for the rape. His feet in their checked felt slippers shuffled against each other, rubbing his ankles. His fingers twisted in his lap. A clean disinfected smell drifted over the desk. She remembered the acrid, fierce smell of lust and sweat long ago.

'Billy?' she repeated sharply. The telephone beside her rang but she ignored it. She put her elbows on the desk and leaned towards him. '*Billy?*'

The telephone continued. They both counted the rings. Fourteen, before it stopped. At last he raised his eyes and looked at her.

'Ye're my last chance,' he said. 'If ye say no I've nothin' to live for. That night in the stables – did ye 'ave a baby from me? Give it away, OK, but did ye 'ave my son?'

She might have expected to feel anger but a great wave of pity poured through her. Glory, marching, valour, terror, pain, death or triumph – for what? The future. Without a family, what was the point of war? The genes are everything, transmitting what the forefathers have bequeathed. Her failure to become pregnant meant Billy's future would die with him. He had no child to inherit the bloodline that stretched from the Middle Ages, from the pagan Britons, right back to Neanderthal man, carrying with it traces of the grunting, horse-riding, raping and pillaging men who had preceded him and culminating in his primordial rage that Bonfire Night. Suppose she said, yes, she'd gone away (and it was true, she had gone to the villa with her mother that spring; the timing would have been convincing) and borne his son, and it had been adopted. That assurance of posterity might heal whatever had cracked in his stubborn brutish yeoman heart. For a moment she was tempted to lie, if a lie could keep him alive. He stared at her with a madman's hope. When she was eighteen, twenty-three years ago, her virginity had been ripped from her when she was still so innocent she hardly knew it was there to be taken. He had shown her no mercy, *then*.

'No, Billy,' she said calmly. 'I did not conceive.'

His eyes dropped and he struggled to get up.

'Wait a minute. You must have had other . . . encounters . . . with women. There could still be children somewhere. Have you never married? When the war is over you can still meet a girl, become a father.'

He did not answer, but leaned his shrunken hands heavily on the arms of the chair and rose trembling to his feet.

'I'll leave ye in peace, then,' he said.

She came round from behind the desk and helped him to the door. The two nurses gossiping in the corridor hurried towards Billy and led him away.

He died within the week. 'DUO' was listed against his name – death of unknown origin. A discreet enquiry followed regarding patients' unauthorized access to medication but its findings were equivocal and no further measures were taken. Elias Brymer and

Hermione buried Billy in the village churchyard. Ada Rawlinson came to the funeral, and Ellen, who wept for her Josh, wherever he was. The choir sang, '*He who would valiant be . . .*' Hermione felt neither bitterness nor grief.

The war marched on, the shortages grew worse. By 1943 shops no longer offered paper bags; stockings were rare as gold dust and women painted their legs, sometimes with gravy browning. Tobacconists rationed civilians to five cigarettes a week (plenty available on the black market, though, at 5s 6d a packet) and sometimes refused altogether to sell them to women. Wine – when it could be found – was exorbitantly priced, beer was disgusting and even Chantry's wine cellar, after four years of Hermione's hospitality, was down to the last few magnums of champagne. These she was keeping for the day peace was declared. Fabric shortages made it hard for people to renew their worn-out clothes, even if they had the coupons. Old blankets were cut up to make coats; torn and faded curtains re-used – after the fashion of *Gone with the Wind* – to make dresses and blouses. Hermione regretted having given away, or thrown out, so many of her mother's clothes after her death. One morning, seeing a Land Girl wearing a skirt made from an artfully dyed sack, she took Phyllis and Ada Rawlinson up to the attic to look for the trunks in which some of Phoebe's old evening dresses had been stored. They opened up the lid of one, folded back the top layer of crackling tissue paper and gasped. Until that moment Hermione had not realized how unaccustomed she was to brilliant colours. Yards of apricot chiffon, emerald green silk and crimson taffeta were revealed, glowing and pristine.

'Oh Miss Hermione . . .' Rawlinson breathed. 'It's like a king's ransom!'

On the last day of 1943 they had a party in the great hall. There was no wine left to speak of, certainly not enough to supply a hundred people, but a posse of men had obtained some barrels of beer to help the celebrations along. Hermione did not enquire how this miracle had been achieved. The fire was lit and everyone stood round singing, watched from the minstrels' gallery by patients unable to leave their wheelchairs. '*You are my sunshine . . .*' they bawled, red-faced from the heat and reflections from the dancing flames; '*You'll never know, dear, how much I love you!*' and the inevitable finale, '*We'll meet again . . .*' Each young woman had received three yards of fabric as her Christmas present from the Com and many had already made them up into skirts, blouses or short frocks. The rainbow colours of her mother's social past swung and glittered round the fire. The radiogram was brought out, along with a pile of records in brown paper sleeves and soon Glenn Miller's orchestra filled the hall with its syncopated rhythm. Doctors danced with Land Girls; Ridley was seized by one young nurse and the vigorously protesting Cowley by another. Old Elias Brymer approached Hermione with a stiff, embarrassed bow but she motioned him to sit beside her.

'I daren't dance with you, Mr Brymer – it's years since I did. I'd disgrace us both!'

'Probably just as well, Miss Hermione – me being every day of seventy-six now, hard to believe but it's true.'

Drink had gone to his head and loosened his formal demeanour. Sober, he could never have spoken so intimately to her, but now he said, 'You was ever so good to my boy, Billy. He wanted me to give ye a last message before he died but he couldn't get his tongue round the words. Just kept saying, *Did she . . . did Miss Hermione . . . did she ever . . . ?* so I dunno what his meaning was. But he thought the world of you, that I do know.'

Billy's father, this decent old man, had known nothing about the rape. From the back seat of the car she had watched his hair turn from brown to grey to white. A life spent driving in silence. No wonder his son had wanted to punish her parents for being arbitrarily set above them, for having ostentatious wealth where they had nothing, for exacting deference without ever looking him in the face or granting him an identity other than that of under-groom, for taking from him the one person who promised him respect as a man. Her mother had dismissed Betty without a second thought; Billy's beloved to whom she gave a housemaid's name – Mildred. Yet Billy must have been ashamed. He had run away and never come back, until now. When old Brymer died, the line would die too. Who would preserve their memory, apart from a few ageing servants and Hermione herself. Had I wanted revenge, she thought, I could hardly have wished for a better one. But I do not.

'Whatever happened to *Betty*?' she asked. 'I seem to remember they were fond of each other, her and your Billy.'

'I dunno, Miss 'Mione,' Elias Brymer mumbled.

She realized that he was hardly able to hold himself together. She caught Ridley's eye and beckoned him over.

'Mr Brymer's ready to turn in,' she said.

The records played on, the dancing grew slower. Shining heads bobbed and swayed under the huge hammerbeam roof that soared into the darkness. The dying fire on its bed of molten ash burnished the dancers with a layer of gold and golden tears were reflected in girls' eyes.

'Time for Auld Lang Syne,' Nicholas murmured into Hermione's ear. She had wondered if he might ask her to dance but he had danced with no one. She glanced at her watch: five minutes to midnight.

'I'm not going to make a speech . . .' she said, after clapping her hands for silence, and they cheered affectionately, *Good old Com!* 'I just want to thank you for all your hard work in the last year and to wish everybody health, happiness and, please God, *peace* in 1944! Happy New Year!'

They linked arms, they swayed, they sang, they kissed, and in the mêlée Nicholas slipped his hand under her elbow and they withdrew quietly to the haven of the blue parlour, having first shooed out a red-faced couple. Hermione subsided into her usual chair.

'Ooof! That went off all right I think, don't you, Nick?'

'With a swing, old bean, with a swing!'

'What *does* lie in wait for us next year, I wonder? Is it too soon to hope that the worst is over?'

'Don't tempt fate, Hermione . . .'

She smiled at him. She had never felt so close to a man before. Sometimes she wondered if this relaxed affection meant she was in love with him – for that matter, perhaps they were both in love, postponing acknowledgement until the war was over. Nicholas's neat, quick body, his finely carved head and green eyes were certainly pleasing. He was watching her with his usual half-humorous expression. The clock struck fastidiously and they counted each chime in silence. At the twelfth she said, 'Dear Nicholas – here's to 1944. *Happy* New Year.'

He leaned across, lifted her hand to his lips and kissed it with mock gallantry. 'Happy New Year, Hermione.'

A few days later she received a letter postmarked Isle of Man. She opened it with the deepest foreboding.

Dear Tante Meini,

I write with much sorrow to tell you that my beloved sister Hannah Rosenbaum killed herself on the last day of the old year. She left a letter in which she wrote that she could not go on. I am sorry, I tried so hard to watch her but she locked herself in the toilet. You will understand that I cannot say more. She loved you, and I too, your affectionate

Rachel Rosenbaum.

P.S. Do not try to get me out of here, it is useless.

In a passion of anger and remorse, Hermione got Nicholas to type a copy of this letter and send it to Major Woodward at the Aliens Office. But she did not ask for Rachel's release.

CHAPTER FOURTEEN

BY THE SUMMER OF 1944 THE TIDE WAS TURNING. FROM Stalingrad to Rome the Germans were in retreat all over Europe, looting and shooting as they went. Humiliation made them vicious and they took revenge on the peasants through whose villages and farms they passed on their return to the stricken Fatherland, just as a few years earlier they had commandeered and plundered great houses and palaces in the days when triumph had seemed certain. In June, after months of secrecy, weeks of rumours, days of suspense, watching the weather, watching the moon, the clouds, the tides, came D-Day. The rescue of Europe had begun.

At first the invasion made no difference to Chantry. The five thousand Allied dead were dead; the 23,000 wounded were still someone else's problem. Doctors and nurses came and went, the leavers promising never to forget the times they had shared, the newcomers soon taking their place, closing the gaps. A new wave of medical staff from hospitals in the shattered cities arrived to deal with the expected convalescents from the Normandy beaches, and stared in astonishment at the healthy country bloom of Dorset people, whose sturdy limbs and tanned faces were almost shocking to drab and weary town dwellers.

'Don't you know there's a war on?' exclaimed one such nurse, as though the phrase were freshly minted. 'To look at you one would think you were on holiday!'

It was clear by now that the war was as good as won; but how long before Germany admitted defeat? Paris was triumphantly recaptured yet V-bombs still droned over London before cutting out, falling silently and killing with robotic randomness. Word of this came to Chantry as if from a distant planet. A sort of halcyon calm descended. The sun shone, the hedgerows bloomed with crimson hawthorn berries and brilliant black sprigs of elderberry. Hermione was bewildered by her own conflicting emotions. She felt the satisfaction of a job begun in ignorance and now performed with a calm authority that still surprised her. She knew she was respected and, by some of the men restored to health by Chantry's benevolent regime, even loved. They promised to bring their wives and children, girlfriends and mothers to visit her 'when this infernal war's over'. They wrote to her from their units, wistfully recalling the peace and pampering they had enjoyed.

What would she do once the war ended – revert to being a rich lonely spinster, head of the Staunton Trading Company? And what about Nicholas: did their future lie together? They made a formidably efficient team and had become, for all working purposes, one and indivisible. Hermione was aware that people speculated about the precise nature of their bond – but without a shred of evidence, no sign of a touch or tender glance, speculation withered. Sometimes after a disturbing dream she would be convinced that they were in love but her wealth prevented him from declaring his feelings. Yet she knew, really, that her affection for Nick was little more than an impulse towards the safe conformity of marriage. Those feelings were lukewarm compared to her passion for Sandy.

One glorious evening in late September, sunset flamed across the sky in streamers of crimson and gold. Supper had been followed by a companionable hour together listening to the wireless, ending with the nine o'clock news.

Hermione exclaimed, 'Oh, what a shame . . . Heath Robinson has died. You know – the man who drew the Professor

Branestawm books, the ones with the mad inventions. Machines for peeling apples and walking dogs at the same time . . . yes you do, come on, Nick, you *must* know. He had a killing sense of humour.'

But Nicholas said, 'Com, I need to talk to you.'

'Good-oh.'

'No, seriously.'

'Oh, help! Not bad news, I hope?'

'I don't know whether you're going to think so. Can we shut the door?'

He crossed the room and closed the door firmly, a signal that the privacy of the blue parlour was, for the moment, sacrosanct.

'I should like to tender my notice. This letter puts it in writing . . .' He withdrew an envelope from his inside pocket and handed it to her. She took it, staring at her name. The clock ticked delicately in the silence.

'Nick, I'm flabbergasted. I don't know what to say! You're *leaving? Why?'*

'First, I have been here four and a half years – long enough. Second, I have decided to re-enter the Church. But there is a third, personal reason which has brought the others to a head.'

Another pause. Hermione had learned to let people take their time. She did not speak.

'I have fallen in love.'

As he said it she knew – because her heart did not leap, her pulse thud, her cheeks flame – that Nicholas Hobson was not in love with her and that she did not mind.

'Who is she? Are you getting married? Oh Nick – I had no *idea!'*

'Dear Hermione. It's not what you assume, old thing. Gosh, this is difficult. I'd better start with the Church and work up to it.'

She smiled her wide, generous smile and sat back, arranging her skirt and smoothing it over her knees like a child preparing to be told a story. 'Go on then.'

'I told you I was ordained when I was twenty-four and spent five years in a slum parish in Manchester? I lost my faith because I could no longer believe that I was working with God against the squalor and misery I saw every day. The final straw came when I had to bury two-year-old twins who had died of smallpox. The two babies were put into one coffin, to save money. You may or may not know but it's the ultimate pride of the poor to give their last penny for a proper send-off. In this case, their last penny only stretched to one coffin. For them, it was a humiliation. After the service the family trailed along to the churchyard led by me in my nice clean surplice and I thought this is a *charade*. At least a doctor relieves pain. All I had to offer was holy words and empty hopes.

'I went to my parish priest who sent me to the bishop, and I asked him to release me from my vows. The bishop was a wise old bird. He said, *Go away for a year or two; do something else. I think you'll be back.* He covered up for me by telling the authorities I'd had a nervous breakdown.'

'But you hadn't?'

'No. I was exhausted and disillusioned but there was nothing wrong with my head. I was accepted by Bart's – St Bartholomew's Hospital in London – and started to train as a medical student. Then came the war.'

'And now you want to go back into the Church?'

'I feel guilty for having had such an easy time . . .' She tried to interrupt, but he stopped her. 'I'm not saying we haven't worked hard, Hermione, but *everyone*'s worked hard, not many in such glorious surroundings. I've had a cushy number. I've begun to hanker for the rough end of life, the broken people at the bottom who are mean and drunk and inarticulate and struggling to survive on *nothing*. That's where I belong. Or so my blasted conscience tells me.'

'So you lost your faith when you were surrounded by squalor and found it again once you were living in comfort. Why should your conscience have anything to do with it? It sounds like self-hatred to me. Any reason for that?'

He stared at her. 'That's very astute of you, old thing. Self-indulgence, more like. I don't pretend to be a saint. I may spend my life ricocheting between my ideals of poverty and my need for middle-class comforts. It's hard to leave all this behind . . .' He indicated the softly lit room. 'No time for books and Beethoven in a slum.'

There was a knock on the door. A young doctor put his head round it, looked at the two of them, sensed the atmosphere and withdrew. Hermione got up quickly and called after him, 'Can it wait till first thing in the morning, Dr MacIntyre? I'll be in my office by eight as usual . . . Okey-doke. Good night.' She sat down again.

'And the *third* reason?' she said.

'And the third reason . . .' he repeated heavily. 'Hermione – you've given *me* a refuge here; just as much as the chaps in the wards. But I can't escape one fact. I am a homosexual. What other people call a pansy or a queer or a faggot. Oh, and plenty of worse names, too.'

'*You*, Nick? Like *Oscar Wilde*? I can hardly believe it!'

'It is true. So you see, no wedding bells for me, no happy ending. No plucky young vicar's wife. Instead, not self-hatred, I hope, but secrecy, guilt, fear of blackmail and in the end, *always* disappointment. I am what I am. For ever and ever, amen. I can't escape it. *Now* you know the truth: I am a conchie and a queer. But although I haven't admitted it before, I hope I never . . . misled you.'

She wanted to say, who are you in love with? A half-formed image of Nicholas embracing another man flashed across her mind and she blushed as though he could read her thoughts. Looking at him with new understanding she said, '*Now* it all makes sense. Of course you never misled me. We have been – *are* – very fond of each other and *didn't* we make a great team?'

'Hermione, you're *wonderful!*' he said with relief. 'I dreaded having to tell you. Yes, we've been a tremendous team! Now look, I would like if possible to leave at the end of October. That should give you plenty of time to find a replacement. Not that you need one – you could run this show single-handed. In any case, pretty soon there won't be a show to run. The war will be over and you can have your house back.'

'Can we leave it till the morning?' she asked. 'I'm suddenly dog-tired.'

'Me too.'

Who is it? she wanted to ask. *Who is it?*

'Good night, dear old thing,' Nicholas said. 'And thank you.'
Warmly, chastely, they hugged each other and parted.

Auschwitz, Dresden, Berlin – Buchenwald, Belsen – the names
that tolled from the wireless and newsreels told a story of horror,
as an exhausted world gathered its forces for one final push.
Germany surrendered; the war was over. Hitler dead, Mussolini
dead – names that once would have been greeted with vigorous
booing now merited hardly more than a sullen 'Serve him bloody
well right!' or 'Good riddance to bad rubbish!' Suicide, assassin-
ation, murder and death – death was everywhere. Death by
starvation, death from cold, death from weakness and despair.
Civilians dead, women and children dead; Jews dead, homosexuals
dead, gypsies dead, the mentally and physically feeble dead; spies,
traitors and criminals condemned to die. How could Europe
recover from so many deaths?

Chantry began to empty. First to leave were the patients . . . not,
this time, back to their units but home to their families. One by
one, with dwindling farewells, the medical staff resumed 'normal'
life. There was little for Hermione to do except supervise the
gradual dismantling of the hospital, the dispersal of its staff and
the adding and subtracting of patients and resources. The tally
was respectable enough, if she had been looking for praise.
Between March 1940 and October 1945, Chantry Convalescent
Hospital had taken in 1,612 patients, cared for by a shifting staff of
37 doctors and 92 nurses, to say nothing of Red Cross helpers,
auxiliaries, kitchen staff, cleaners from the village, Land Girls and
gardeners. Fifty-one people had died, including Mrs Brookes
and – in the last days of the war – Elias Brymer. There had been
two suicides, one a nurse crossed in love (she had taken a fistful of
sleeping pills and obviously expected to be found in time, poor
child); the other an airman whose legs had been amputated. There
had been Billy. And, of course, Hannah Rosenbaum, who had
killed herself rather than face a life without her mother.

Far from being jubilant once the war had ended and everyone
was gone, Hermione sank into dark despair. She missed the pur-
posefulness of shared effort, of knowing herself needed.

Florabelle had taught her people's cruel derision in the face of physical deformity. Thanks to Rachel and Hannah she now understood anti-Semitism. Thanks to Nicholas she understood prejudice. All four people closest to her would have been sent to the death camps had they been in Germany. The litany of might-have-beens dragged her down in a horror of humanity. She looked back incredulously at the person she had been when the war began: that guileless, ignorant, blinkered self. Well, now she had grown up.

I will take things step by step, Hermione told herself. First, I shall find Rachel Rosenbaum and bring her back to live with me. I can help *one* person. One at a time.

PART FOUR

Home Art
Gone

1947–1972

CHAPTER FIFTEEN

14 April 1972

HERMIONE SOLD THE EATON SQUARE HOUSE SOON AFTER THE WAR. It seemed absurd to occupy five grand floors on her own and in the post-war mood of austerity she could not justify the staff needed to run it. Even so, she left with some regret. Her father had bought the house in the 1880s and it was imbued with his vigorous and benign spirit. But it was also, and more recently, imbued with the restless spirit of her mother. It was purchased at the asking price by a man describing himself as a company director, who sold it a decade later for three times what he had paid. On the strength of this he wound up his dubious companies and began to call himself a property developer, one of the first of the breed.

Her new London house, although a third the size of the Belgravia one, was not small. It stood in a row of elegant Georgian houses on a quiet, graceful street overlooking Chelsea Hospital. Its proportions (the drawing room, for instance, was twenty-eight rather than forty-eight feet long) enabled Hermione to dispose of the Eaton Square furniture that her mother had bought in the late Twenties, when Phoebe had had little to do except spend money as her acolytes suggested. The flimsy, modish pieces had dated; Syrie Maugham's reputation was in eclipse and the prices they fetched at auction were

215

sometimes lower than those Phoebe had paid. On the other hand the pictures bought in the Twenties had risen in value. These she did not sell. One loss was compensated for by an even greater gain. Hermione ordered some furniture and a selection of the pictures she had hidden from her mother to be brought up from Chantry to fill the gaps, and gradually the new house began to feel like home.

Phyllis, her personal maid, had left after the war to train as a nurse and been replaced by Ethel, the former housemaid whose fiancé, Josh, missing for so long, was finally presumed dead. Unlike her mother, Hermione did not need a maid to dress her hair and coddle her face; merely someone to get her clothes out, put them away, press and mend them. Ethel could do all this and she was loyal and devoted.

Early in 1947 – pitting her obstinate determination against the silent inertia of those in charge of records at the former internment camp on the Isle of Man – Hermione finally tracked down Rachel Rosenbaum. She found her in a girls' boarding school in Yorkshire, teaching French, German and music to dull and hostile pupils. Hermione had already tried various organizations representing musicians, music teachers, governesses and nurses in training. Boarding schools had been her last hope. The headmistress was persuaded to let Rachel go with the help of a generous donation to the school's playing field fund. Hermione, as she had promised six years earlier, brought her home to Chantry.

Rachel spent a weekend exploring the house, learning its new proportions – now that the hospital beds and equipment had gone – and choosing a bedroom for herself. On the Sunday evening she and Hermione sat together in the blue parlour.

'I can hardly believe it,' Rachel said. 'It is *all still here*.'

'My dear, not everything changes. Some things remain. This house. Me . . .'

'I feel my sister's presence everywhere. At times I can almost *see* her.'

'I know,' Hermione soothed. She too had caught glimpses of Sandy everywhere for months after he had gone.

'Perhaps for a while you would be better off in London. Tomorrow we'll look at the house I've bought. You'll like it. It's in Chelsea.'

Rachel was now a tough and battle-scarred young woman of twenty-five. Her diary, a series of cheap exercise books, was filled with black drawings, underlinings and crossings-out. It gradually became the orderly record of a peaceful life. Tante 'Mione had kept her word.

'Why didn't you contact *me*?' Hermione asked. 'You knew where *I* was!'

'I couldn't be sure that you would still want me,' Rachel had replied, 'and if you hadn't – I could not have borne it. If you had said, I know I promised but . . . things are different now. You might have been . . . anything, married, injured, dead. I *had* to let you find me. It is better to have hope than no hope.'

Hermione understood. She too preferred to wait for Sandy rather than approach him – which would have been far easier than tracking down Rachel – only to find he was . . . what were Rachel's words? . . . 'married, injured, dead'.

Hermione suggested that she might revert to the previous plan of adopting her but, without the imperative of escaping internment, Rachel felt this would be disloyal to her mother, who, along with her father, grandparents and her entire cousinage, had vanished in the violent events of the war. They had left no date or grave on which she could mourn and no message that might have enabled her to wrest some comfort, hope or sense from the waste of their lives. The dead send no messages. Hermione wondered if Rachel's refusal to be adopted was a sign of remorse at being the only one alive.

'It's not that!' said Rachel vehemently. 'It is because I *know* that the blood relationship is sacred. Somewhere I have a real mother and father – even if they are dead and buried. I know it seems impossible that they will ever come and claim me but, forgive me, dear Tante 'Mione, you can't replace them. You mustn't try and make yourself into what you are not. And, if there were no other reason against it, there would still be this: you are not Jewish.'

The sole survivor of the once-numerous Rosenbaums of Theresienstrasse could not be daughter to anyone else . . . not even the sole survivor of the Stauntons of Oldham.

*

217

Once Hermione had accepted this, she and Rachel became very close. Their relationship fulfilled the need they both felt for the daily small change of news, jokes and praise or sympathy. Hermione had always craved intimacy. Her next problem was to find something that Rachel could *do*. Rachel solved it by enrolling for a two-year course at the Royal College of Music. In theory, she was qualifying to be a violin teacher. In fact she was rediscovering her talent, self-respect and ability to live among other people in freedom, after six years of confinement.

Hermione began to play a more forceful part in the Staunton Trading Company. Under her shrewd eye and helped by her innate caution (she would have nothing to do with the groundnuts scheme, for example) the firm prospered. Her father had arranged things so that the company ran smoothly without any intervention from her; although if she chose to take an interest, her authority over its affairs was almost unlimited. In the post-war years it was hard for an importer of basic materials like iron, steel, and wool *not* to make money. Only the fur-importing side of the business operated at a loss. Hermione closed it down and with it, the trading outposts in Alberta and Saskatchewan and the Toronto office. She reckoned it would be a long time before the years of austerity were over and women – or their menfolk – could afford to buy furs again.

Before deciding where to invest and where to retrench, Hermione needed to visit the company offices and meet the ageing staff in London, Liverpool and Glasgow. She arranged these visits in the intervals between Rachel's college terms so as to have a companion, a second opinion. She needed someone with whom to unravel the diary of the day's events and fathom the probity of the dark-suited men who thought they ran Staunton Trading. She had increasing confidence in Rachel, whose sceptical intelligence she respected and even deferred to. Rachel could always tell who was trustworthy and who was lying, who was clever and being held back; and which of the pompous men who tried to flatter or patronize her were overdue for retirement.

Hermione's business acumen was based on common-sense principles. If something was explained to her that she could not

218

understand, she would not proceed, no matter how hard the accountants tried to persuade her. As well as a good brain and a gift for rapid mental arithmetic, she possessed what her father would have called 'horse sense'. Add up columns of figures yourself, do not take it for granted that other people have got them right. Check whether the smallest units are correct; the assumption will be that you have certainly checked the largest ones. Never be blinded by jargon or generalizations. Most forward projections are likely to be exaggerated; halve them if you want to be realistic. Above all, do not spend – reinvest! These were the rules laid down by her father when she was a solemn and attentive sixteen-year-old, and they served her well. One final precept he had also taught her: give to charity, but silently.

Many people in Rachel's situation would have urged Hermione to donate to the charities caring for Europe's millions of refugees and homeless people, but Rachel did not. She had seen too many of the unscrupulous exploiting the credulous.

'They need houses, schools and medicine, like everyone else!' she said. 'If you give money to refugee charities they remain forever refugees. Endow scholarships so that schools and hospitals educate and train their brightest children. Give to the Red Cross or the Quakers – they are the only ones you can trust.'

'And orchestras, Rachel?' Hermione teased gently.

'If they want music let them buy a gramophone,' Rachel replied, unsmiling.

Over the next few years Hermione gave away tens of thousands of pounds, founding scholarships, buying equipment and easing access for brilliant but underprivileged children to the best schools and medical training. These gifts never bore her own name but were known simply as the Rachel Foundation.

When the course at the Royal College ended, Hermione worried that Rachel might feel trapped again. She would soon be thirty years old; she must crave a separate existence and she ought to earn her keep. Rachel in turn knew, of course, that Hermione was rich – but her parents had been rich too, in Berlin before the war, and much good it had done them. Work, not money, conferred status and dignity. Paradoxically, her former fellow-internees from the Isle of Man led her to it. She started in a small way by helping some of the musicians she had known in the camp to make contact with one another and find engagements – at worst, as pianists in hotels and department stores, tinkling banal favourites; at best, giving solo performances in modest venues such as Conway Hall. She was persuasive, shrewd and hard-working.

Within two years she had set up the Rosenbaum Music Agency, operating out of a small office near Oxford Circus. Five years later, in 1957, she left Hermione's hospitable roof to marry one of her clients. Rachel was thirty-five and Benjamin, a cellist – more teacher than player – a decade older. It was not a love match but they liked each other, had plenty to talk about, and shared similar histories. Four years later, to her astonishment, Rachel became pregnant. She did not tell her husband at first, being convinced that the child would be miscarried or deformed, but the genes triumphed and she bore a daughter, a perfectly beautiful child with dark hair and serious eyes under a crumpled forehead. Rachel looked into the infant face and saw the features of her mother. Rather than burden this post-war, Sixties infant with a legacy of tragedy by calling her Leah or Hannah, or Rebekah after Benjamin's long-dead mother, she named the baby Judith.

In the same way as Hermione had tracked down Rachel, she could have found Sandy if she had been determined to do so. Even if Ellismuir Castle, the family home in Scotland, had been sold – like so many houses after the war – there were only a few careers for men like him: politics, law, the City, the diplomatic service or medicine (Sandy, she felt sure, would not have gone into the Church), all of which published directories listing the names or members. Yet beyond checking *The Times* every day, Hermione kept her distance. The deaths of his father Sir Donald and, in due course, his mother Violet were announced, but the name of Sandy Gordon-Lockhart was not to be found. He was two years older than Hermione and, having survived two wars, had every chance of reaching a ripe old age. She hugged her memories and waited.

*

220

Once Rachel had left to get married, her contact with Hermione inevitably diminished. Rachel and Benjamin often invited Hermione to join them for the ritual Friday evening meal or Sunday lunch, although after the birth of Judith these invitations became fewer. Hermione was once again without a close companion. Ethel unpacked the contents of her mind and – all too often – her dreams to Hermione every morning, her words clambering round and round her tongue like a mouse on a treadwheel. Hermione would have trusted Ethel Goodbody with her mother's best diamond tiara, or her life; but she could not discuss serious matters with her, neither the affairs of Staunton Trading nor the events she read about in the newspapers. If she were to ask Ethel what she thought of the tribes of young people, beatniks and hippies, revolutionaries or peaceniks, who wandered through London's parks and streets like colourful gypsies, she could predict Ethel's response: 'No better than they ought to be!' Ethel would have said. She was getting on and Hermione – herself sixty – needed someone younger, someone who could explain the galloping changes of the Sixties and the new world they ushered in.

She had resumed her friendship with Pixie and her husband Randall after the war and remained a devoted godmother to their daughter Madeleine: now grown-up, married and the mother of a baby boy. Hermione spent many evenings in the cheerful Bohemian atmosphere of the Finch house in Flask Walk, meeting 'arty types' of all ages – painters, critics, the occasional architect or designer. They had embraced the Sixties with enthusiasm, smoking pot and experimenting with LSD or the I-Ching; inveighing against the police, the Wilson government and the Establishment. The women wore long skirts, brightly coloured, droopy shirts with big felt hats, trailing scarves and dangling earrings; the men defended their quite untenable views on art, religion and drugs with a fervour and conviction that would have been unthinkable in the boardroom of Staunton Trading. All this astonished and intrigued Hermione, who understood for the first time how much the world had changed since her days at the Slade, forty years ago. They also seemed to carry on affairs with cheerful abandon, although most of them were married and well into middle age.

221

''Mione, don't look so shocked!' said Pixie, after Hermione had come into the kitchen in search of a cold drink and found her friend in the arms of someone else's husband. She and the man were quite casual about it. They stood, arms linked, smiling together at her scandalized face, making no attempt to pretend.

'I'm sorry,' Hermione said stonily. 'I'd better leave you to it.'

Pixie broke away. 'Brian, shoo . . .' she said to the man, and he slipped out of the door. She poured Hermione a glass of water and perched on the kitchen table.

'I've been wanting to ask you for ages, and this is as good a time as any. 'Mione, my dear, what do *you* do for . . . you know, all that? Oh hell, *sex*, I mean?'

'I don't do anything,' Hermione said stiffly. 'Does one have to?'

'It's not obligatory, no. But most people do *something*. Even at our age.'

'Well, I don't.'

'But you must have in the past?'

'I'm not a virgin, if that's what you mean.'

Pixie laughed. 'Well *that*'s a relief! I always thought you had a Great Love hidden away somewhere.'

'In a way, yes, I suppose so.'

'You wouldn't care to tell me about him? It *is* a *him*, is it?'

'Pixie, dear, it was a very long time ago and I've never really talked about it. But yes, it *is* a him. And not at the Slade. *Nor –*' she added emphatically, '*–* was it *Shebeare*.'

'Poor old thing. What happened? Was it in the war? Don't say he was killed?'

'No, nothing like that . . .' And Hermione might have gone on to tell the story of her childhood love but just then Randall came roaring into the kitchen with a tray of empty glasses and over-flowing ashtrays and said, 'Come on, girls, no slacking, more supplies for the troops!'

Hermione made a light grimace of regret at Pixie. *Seven for a secret never to be told.* She went in search of a shy young man who seemed to be the only other person present not intoxicated by drugs, alcohol or sexual adventure. Hadn't Randall said he designed something or other for Heal's?

A less hectic and hedonistic view of the Sixties was provided by Nicholas Hobson. After working for more than a decade in the slums of Liverpool, he was now the vicar of a London parish just south of the river. He had mellowed into a calmer acceptance of his faith and of the squalor and ignorance around him.

'All I hope for is to lift a corner of the darkness smothering one or two people,' he said. 'I find nowadays that I've lost my rage – but the awful black misery and gloom has gone, too. If I can be like an aspirin to people, making their lives more bearable – even for the rest of *that* morning or afternoon – I'll settle for that. I've stopped fighting God, the world, myself.'

His resignation saddened her. 'Oh Nick,' she said, 'you're better than aspirin!'

The brief respites she gave him at Chantry, never more than twenty-four hours at a time, kept their friendship stoked. She never asked whether he had any other relationship. Once or twice, when Rachel happened to be there at the same time with her beautiful black-eyed child, they would reminisce about the war. The little girl listened to stories of a time she could not begin to imagine.

More and more, as Hermione grew older, her thoughts returned to her childhood. She thought not only about Sandy but also about Miss Protheroe – her timid, incompetent governess: what could have induced her mother to employ such a woman? She thought about Nanny Rideout, dismissed and sent away from the house that for twenty years had been her only world. She could not remember Nanny ever going 'home' – yet she must have had a family, parents, previous employers? Nanny had been entirely devoted to her and Richard, to making a comfortable and secure world for them. Perhaps she had been trying to make up for her mother's cool neglect. Hermione seldom allowed herself to think about Florabelle, poor dwarf; poor, despised, rejected dwarf, contemptuously thrown out by her mother, whose only creed was that of beauty.

She rarely went into her old nursery and usually preferred

visiting children to sleep somewhere else. One Sunday afternoon, however, she made her way up the top flight of stairs and along creaking floorboards whose creaks had never changed in sixty years. She wandered along the nursery floor, opening every door and looking into the deserted bedrooms that had once been occupied by Nanny and the nursery maids. She breathed the dust motes that danced in the air of the room where she and Florabelle had slept. Hermione shivered. 'Someone must have walked across your grave!' Nanny would have said. The furniture had been put back after the war. It was all white, with mottoes traced in capital letters across drawers and table tops. WASTE NOT, WANT NOT was inscribed between the china knobs of the top drawer and DO AS YOU WOULD BE DONE BY on the one beneath, with big round Os circling the knobs. A Japanese screen stood in the corner where it had always stood, its faded lime-green silk embroidered with birds and butterflies and bamboo. Moth-eaten rag rugs were scattered over the wooden floor. Madeleine's little boys, Julian and Toby, as well as Rachel's Judith, should have the run of these rooms from now on, Hermione decided. She walked down three flights of stairs with the heavy tread of someone large, tired and old. In the drawing room, she rang for tea.

When it arrived, pretty Spode china on an inlaid tray, she said to the housekeeper: 'Rawlinson, you might remember – *do* you remember, years ago, I brought a girl from the village back here?'

'Yes, Miss Hermione, indeed I do. A few years after I came. That would have been the dwarf. I can't remember what she was called.'

'Florabelle,' said Hermione, 'her name was Florabelle.'

'That's it, yes, Florabelle! Goodness, it must be fifty years since I thought of her! Doesn't time fly? Whatever happened to her? Did you ever find out?'

'My mother sent her back home. She was Mrs Pinchbeck's child.'

'Mrs *Pinchbeck*! Glory be, there's another name from the past. Enjoy your tea, Miss Hermione.'

*

By the time Hermione was in her late sixties she had just two cousins remaining of her own generation. One was sickly and querulous and never left Scotland; the other was Henrietta Birmingham, known in the family as Hetty. The friendship between these two imposing female cousins had begun at her mother's funeral. Recently, Hetty had written to ask whether Hermione would care to invest in the expansion of a girls' boarding school she had bought in Sussex, called Raeburn after one of the Campbell-Leith family houses. Hermione had agreed, and also offered to endow three scholarships anonymously for 'needy girls from abroad, having non-British nationality and refugee status'. This, to Henrietta, somewhat eccentric condition had been balanced by the offer of a gift so generous that she had willingly agreed. Once it was secured, she suggested that a meeting was long overdue.

Henrietta came to the house in Chelsea, every inch the headmistress, dressed in charcoal grey, hatted and gloved, punctual to the minute. Her husband had died years ago; her only son James was doing 'frightfully well' in Hong Kong – yes, married; no children yet, alas.

Hermione said, with careful ambiguity, 'You must miss him terribly.'

'I *do* miss James, yes,' said Henrietta – and did not elaborate. Confidences came slowly to their generation. One did not pour one's heart out, even to a first cousin. Over tea she talked about her school, Hermione talked about Staunton Trading, they discussed a recent autobiography that they both happened to have read – safe topics that circled the personal but never intruded.

'My *dear*, what a shame we never became friends when we were children!' Hetty said when they parted.

'I'm afraid it was probably my *mother*'s fault,' Hermione sighed.

'Ah yes, the beautiful and wayward Aunt Phibby. She was a mythical figure to us as children, and infinitely mysterious and desirable as a result!'

'Mama was certainly that . . .'

'One always longed to know the real story.'

'Yes, we must compare notes. Some other time . . .'

*

By now the family tree had multiplied into the third and fourth generation. The aunts and uncles had kept their distance in the days when she was young and longed to meet them. The older she became, the more their descendants longed to meet her. No twig or branch of the Campbell-Leiths was unmoved by the fact that Hermione Staunton controlled a huge fortune and each member of the family could think of several good reasons why he, she, or their children should inherit it. Prejudice against money that had originated 'in trade' dissolved at the prospect of being willed it, for curiously, those who have not had to work to get rich often feel superior to those who have – when surely it ought to be the other way round?

Many of these relatives came regularly to visit her and Hermione welcomed people who invited themselves to stay. They would come down for Sunday lunch, sometimes the whole week-end; praising the flower and vegetable garden, the fruit from the orchard and greenhouses, the cook's 'good plain cooking' and the housekeeper's Constance Spry flower arrangements. Some-times they would be faintly put out to find another couple there too, having planned an unobtrusive campaign of persuasion for that weekend. At Christmas the older ones came in pairs or with their families, admiring the tall pine the gardener had selected that year, whose resinous smell pervaded the great hall throughout the twelve days. They thanked her – not without an inward twinge of disappointment – for the sensible and modest presents she gave and went away hoping that further credit had been added to their bank of goodwill. They did not understand that she was kind but not extravagant, or that it is more usual and much easier for people to be extravagant but not kind.

Hermione would have been surprised and hurt had she known that some of her relatives called her 'Hermeanie'. Stories were exchanged about her parsimony. 'She always asks us, "How many sprouts can you eat?" so as not to have any left over – is she the same with you?' Yet it was rare for any of them to ask *her* for the weekend, or even dinner. Those who brought a couple of bottles of wine as a gift did not find them on the table at meals. Hermione didn't offer wine. She herself had never liked alcohol and had not bothered to replenish the cellar after the war. There was water to drink with lunch and dinner, apple juice for the older children, Ribena for the little ones, and coffee or tea otherwise. Horlicks at bedtime, and Bovril for anybody who didn't feel well. Wine, in her opinion, was what men drank in their City restaurants or London clubs. That was where it belonged.

It was a heavy burden, trying to dispose of money in the best and most useful way. Her fortune and her shares grew and grew, until Hermione felt like the sorcerer's apprentice, trying to bring it under control. The point of money was not to spend it but to husband it towards a greater good. Plenty of people thought that meant *their* good and she got dozens of begging letters. If the letter was from an individual she occasionally sent a £10 note wrapped inside a plain sheet of paper, to deter them from asking again. If they were from charities she might send a £50 note. The charities bothered her most. The writers of their appeals sounded like good people, and so desperate. There were children starving all over the world, children as young as five years old working in factories; tribes being driven from their ancestral territories, people starving, dying of thirst, dying of illness everywhere. She felt for all of them, sent off some money, knew it made no difference. She was tempted to pick just one cause, almost at random, and leave everything to that. Immediately she would think of all the other needy causes that would go without. She reeled from the choices, the unthinkable, insoluble problem of where to leave her father's legacy so that it would be wisely and compassionately spent and not squandered. Time was passing, time was passing, she was getting old and nothing had been decided.

CHAPTER SIXTEEN

15–16 April 1972

BEAUTIFUL CHILDREN OFTEN GROW UP TO BE PERFECTLY ordinary-looking adults. Pretty girls can lose their looks very suddenly and by their mid-thirties already begin to 'run to seed', as the unkind phrase has it. Fat scowling teenagers are transformed by falling in love or losing weight; slender young women start having babies and regular meals and their bodies thicken. Faces change throughout people's lives and occasionally the best stage is the last. Hermione, who had been a gauche adolescent with that awkward stoop of a tall girl trying in vain to conceal her height, grew into a bulky young woman with few redeeming facial features. In middle age – as Nicholas Hobson had remarked – she became a handsome woman. In her sixties, most unexpectedly, she blossomed and by the time she reached her seventieth birthday she had turned into rather a beautiful old lady. Her hair, untouched by dye or perm, waved softly round her face and shone like silver. Her skin was smooth and fine and relatively unlined. Her blue eyes retained their guileless expression and her manner was, finally, assured as well as benevolent. She would have been amazed had anyone told her so – and no one did – but as she entered old age, Hermione was better-looking than at any time since her childhood.

For her seventieth birthday her relatives had got together under the supervision of Vivian, Lord Blythgowrie – at forty, very conscious of his role as head of the family – to organize what the younger ones called 'the big birthday bash'. Invitations had been sent out to the entire Campbell-Leith clan, most of whom were only too glad to accept. Only the senile or those who lived a very long way away indeed sent their regrets. Since it had not been kept secret from her, Hermione had provided a list of her friends and they were duly invited as well. In addition to this party, another was planned in her honour at the City headquarters of Staunton Trading – a glass of champagne with the more senior employees, followed by lunch with the board of directors and a presentation (a pair of engraved silver candlesticks, to add to the de Lamerie pair she already possessed). Finally, two weekends later, there was to be a fête at Chantry, complete with apple-bobbing, maypole dancing, sack races and all the trappings of a traditional country fête, at which another presentation was planned. This had been organized by the châtelaine of Somerhayes, Hermione's neighbour, with the enthusiastic co-operation of the vicar, who had hoped that a contribution to the organ fund would be thought a suitable way to mark Miss Staunton's seven decades.

The first party, for family and close friends, took place in a large private room at the Ritz. Hermione sat self-consciously enthroned on a low dais, her brown lizard handbag placed squarely at her feet. It contained a comb, a handkerchief, a penny in case she needed one for the ladies', a five- and a ten-pence piece in case she needed to telephone (hard to imagine why but as well to be prepared), an enamel compact and a £20 note for any other emergency. In front of her, holding glasses of rather good wine, jostling and chattering, was the first assortment of guests, the family tree made flesh. All the tribal surnames were represented. Campbell-Leiths were out in force, Shepherds flocked, and Bridgewaters, and Conynghame-Jervises, as well as a former Malling-Smith. Considering that they were celebrating a woman whose parents had been ostracized by their parents and grandparents, it was a remarkable turnout. Beside her on the dais sat Rachel's daughter

Judith, now twelve, wearing a dress that Hermione had bought at Liberty. Judith had picked it herself, rejecting the childish smocked, sprigged and puff-sleeved dresses that Hermione had held up to her, choosing instead a velvet creation that mixed shimmering golds and greens and ruby reds to startling effect. Hermione was wearing her favourite dress, dark green shot silk with mink-trimmed collar and cuffs, an old one from Hartnell. It suited her and she felt comfortable in it. She had not worn make-up since her debutante days but tonight she had put lipstick on, to mark the occasion. She crossed her hands in her lap with apparent docility while Vivian told her what to do. It had been her idea to have Judith on the dais with her – 'so I won't be bored if nobody comes and talks to me!' – but the move was interpreted by several guests as a sign that she had selected the child as her heir. This was not the case. Although her lawyers dropped repeated hints, Hermione had not yet made a will.

After an hour most of the relatives had arrived, shed their coats, powdered their noses, adjusted their jewellery and were sizing one another up like racegoers looking over bloodstock. As everyone knew and hardly anyone admitted, they had come to this well-groomed, high-stepping parade in pursuit of a prize they all coveted. They followed with interest the ebb and flow of Staunton Trading shares, read the annual report, noted how great was Hermione's personal holding and wondered if she was included under directors' emoluments. None knew exactly how much money she had to leave but no one's guess started below ten million pounds – a gross underestimate of the true figure, quite apart from the house in London, the house in the country, the deserted and almost forgotten villa in the South of France and all furniture, works of art and household effects thereto pertaining. Had they known about the Picassos and the Matisses they would have been more avid still; but no one except Ethel entered Hermione's bedroom and as far as Ethel was concerned, they were just some rather rude pictures that had always hung there.

'We don't know her *well*, of course – we do *try* and see her every couple of years but Scotland's a long way to come and you know, when one *is* in London there's such a *lot* to catch up with. Still, we make the effort – what about you?'

'David *adores* Hermione so we probably see her—'

'Once a year—' Elizabeth Bridgewater's husband interjected.

'Oh *no*. Heavens, surely, David, it *must* be more than that! I'd say at *least* twice.'

Once a year. Douglas's wife Una filed away this information. She said, 'Now that she's getting older one likes to keep an eye, don't you think?'

'Oh yes. Though isn't she looking *well*?'

'*Frightfully* well.'

In snatches of chat and gossip around the room the odds, the actuarial tables of inheritance, were calculated. Will it be soon? Will it be you? Will it, oh best of all, be me?

By now Hermione had a dozen relatives in the youngest generation, their ages ranging from thirtyish to tennish, and another dozen or so cousins once removed, most of them further removed by marriage. On her father's side, the Staunton side, there was nobody. Hermione was the sole remaining branch, the only legitimate Staunton. She wished for the thousandth time that Richard were alive to share the burden and lighten her load.

Cousins Anne Bridgewater and Hermione Kerr leaned forward, air-kissed each other's cheeks and stood back. Young Hermione, already twice-married Hermione, was showing off her excellent legs in a very short skirt.

'Hermi-*one*! My dear, you're *much* braver than me!' Anne, her spinster cousin who was nearly twenty years older, had opted for a more decorous length. 'People don't *go* much for mini-skirts in Suffolk, I'm afraid!' she explained, with a little laugh. Then, looking around, 'Have you brought the dear *boys*?'

'No – *bit* young, I thought. Jus' is fourteen but Richard's only twelve.'

'I expect you're right. What a turnout! She must be thrilled.'

'*Thrilled*. Oh Anne: have you seen the *Australians*?'

'I have . . . and do you know, I have the most dreadful feeling they're my *cousins*. By marriage, anyway. What's the woman called

– *Kytie?* She *claims* to be a Bridgewater and if it's true – which I suppose it must be or Vivian would never have asked her – that she's poor Peter's widow then she *is*. And those children . . . Joe and Rettie!'

'Poor old you, how awful.' Tactfully, young Hermione changed the subject.

In ones and twos, various friends and relations approached the dais on which she sat, almost as though paying homage. The dais had *not* been a good idea, Hermione decided. They would smile nervously at her, ingratiatingly at Judith, murmur a platitude and back away. Most people left a brightly wrapped package on the table beside her, adding some deprecating remark ('Just a token . . .', 'I'm sure you've got it already'), occasionally barbed ('*So* hard to know what to *give* you, cousin Hermione'). Judging by their shape, many of these packages contained books. One or two, stronger-smelling, contained soap: Penhaligon's, for this special occasion, rather than the usual Yardley's. The donors were not to know that every Christmas Hermione asked the chauffeur to deliver a dozen gift packs of scented soap to the nearest hospital. Hermione had used Pears ever since she was a child, in the days when Nanny said she was preparing to be a beautiful lady. She looked at the young girls who surged amid a sea of relatives, noisy, uninhibited, laughing with their mouths open, tossing their silken sheets of hair. They were as free and fluid as mermaids, and like mermaids, weighed down by their feet, which clattered and tottered noisily on platform heels more than an inch thick. Their shoes, unless they were patent leather, looked scuffed and dull. How odd, she reflected; when I was a girl, people had their shoes cleaned every day and their hair washed once a fortnight. Now it's the other way round.

'Doesn't she look wonderful? Amazing lady! We really *ought* to see more of her.'

'I know – if only she came to London more often. Dorset's such a long *way* . . .'

'Do you go down for many weekends?'

'I wouldn't say *many*, but from time to time one feels one *should* make the effort . . . she's so *lonely*,' said Geraldine Blythgowrie. 'Vivian sees her on business quite a lot and I try to send her up-cheering letters. She *adores* the twins, of course.'

'I don't believe it! *Dolly!!*'

'Pixie? Pixie *Renfrew*?'

'*Finch*, Pixie Finch: now and getting on for fifty years – though it's been touch and go at times, I can tell you! How absolutely amazing to see you. *You* must be Hermione's surprise. She told me she had a surprise and silly old me, I thought she meant a present. Oh Dolly, how *are* you? What are you *doing*?'

'Pixie, you haven't changed a *bit*. Look, you even still wear Bohemian clothes. You always wore Bohemian clothes. You could walk into the Slade now and no one would look twice. Oh crikey, do you remember the *click*?'

Joyously the two old ladies threw their arms round each other and laughed. Words poured out. Their eyes sparkled, they grew red-faced with excitement. The old are so square, thought a watching teenager. Pixie introduced her husband Randall, who paused briefly before muttering, 'Girl talk. Leave you to it.'

'Dolly, did you ever hear what happened to *Victoria*?'

'She's retired now. Lives in a cottage in Essex. With a younger woman.'

'I don't believe it . . . Victoria, a lesbian?'

'Of course. Didn't you know? Always was. Why, does it matter?'

'Well, no, but . . . oh *Dolly*, it's so good to see you! My dear, you'll never guess what *Shebeare*'s up to these days – *you* remember him? Gerald Shebeare?'

'Nope. Name doesn't ring a bell.'

'It must do.' Pixie lowered her voice. 'Hermione had a bit of a *thing* about him. I thought it probably best not to mention that I was still in touch, so he isn't here.'

On such occasions the 'family face' is made manifest. Despite every variation of age and sex, the Blythgowrie features shone through. The lucky ones had inherited the dazzling dark eyes of the eighteenth-century laundress who had bequeathed them to Phoebe. The unlucky, like Hermione, got the long, almost Hapsburg chin and giraffe limbs that looked all right on men but were a sad disadvantage to the women in whom that particular gene had dominated. In the current generation, it seemed to be recessive. The room was full of pretty young things in tiny garments, since fashion dictated that skirts should be as short as possible. They would catch sight of one another, shrug, grimace, and compare notes on men and clothes.

'Fiona! Fab dress! Biba?'

'Nope, Jane & Jane. Done your stuff with the rich great-aunt?'

'Yeah. Went up to her and said, give us your money.'

'*So-phie!*'

'Well, isn't that what all this is about?'

'One isn't meant to *say* so. *Love* the platforms!'

'Oh good. I can't *walk* of course.'

'Who shall I escort over to you then? *Him?*'

'Yuck, no.'

It would have been ingenuous of Fiona to admit that she rather enjoyed visiting Hermione – her second cousin once removed – because nothing at Chantry ever changed. The box in which the laundry was delivered stood waiting on the same spot in the stone-flagged corridor outside the kitchen; the biscuit tin was on the same shelf in the pantry; the envelopes in the same place in the desk, next to the embossed postcards. It was reassuring to find a world that always stayed exactly the same.

The well-mannered looked around the room for those with no one to talk to.

'I'm Anne Bridgewater – how do you do?'

'Anne – Cousin Rosamund's daughter?'

'Gracious, what a memory! Yes, that's right. I'm sorry – I know your *face*, of course, but . . .'

'I used to be Rachel Rosenbaum.'

'That's *right*! So you *did*! Who are you now and what are you doing?'

'I run a music agency.'

'How *interesting* . . .'

'With my husband.'

'You're *married*? How *nice*.'

'This is my husband, Benjamin Steinhaus. Up there with Hermione is our daughter, Judith.'

'A *music* agency, you said. Well, well, well.'

Henrietta Birmingham, resplendent in a pearl-grey two-piece in which she looked exactly like the late Queen Mary, waited until most people had had a word with her cousin Hermione and then crossed the room to speak to her.

'My dear Hermione. You do look well. What a splendid occasion.'

'Henrietta – so good of you to come. Are James and Juniper here too?'

'No, the children are still in Hong Kong, alas. James was very tempted.'

'Have you talked to Katie Bridgewater, who married Sibby's grandson Peter, *you* know, the poor chap who went off to Australia for some reason . . . it was never *absolutely* clear? She's here I believe, with two rather large children – what are they called: Joseph and Raimonda? So original . . .'

'How clever of you to remember their names. They fly out of my head like *doves*.'

'I know, Hetty, maddening. It happens to me as well, but they come back to the doo-cot in the end, don't you find?'

'Not *always*,' said Henrietta Birmingham, and the two silver-haired old ladies laughed at the inconveniences of age and decline.

Lady Blythgowrie circled the room anxiously, knowing that her husband Vivian expected her to act as hostess. She sensed him watching her out of the corner of his eye. He expected her to look like a matriarch in the making and she didn't feel like one.

'Mary, dear! Reggie! How *are* you?'

'*Hello*, Geraldine. We're fine, as usual. Where are the girls? Have you brought them?'

'Bit *young*, we thought. Only *eight*.'

'Doesn't seem to have stopped most people. Bloody place is pullulating with children,' said Reggie Conyghame-Jervis, and he made an abrupt movement with his foot as though kicking out at a flock of chickens.

Mary apologized for him. 'Reggie, *do* stop it! I'm sorry, Geraldine, dear – isn't he dreadful? Hang on, I think someone's about to make a speech.'

'My *husband*, I'm afraid,' said Lady Blythgowrie.

'Blast!' muttered Reggie under his breath. 'Just when I've spotted Myrtle and Boyo.'

'You'll have a chance to talk to him *after* the speech,' said Mary. 'Now *hush*.'

Reggie growled, but inaudibly.

'We're all here this evening to celebrate,' Vivian Blythgowrie began. 'We are here to celebrate the seventieth birthday of a most remarkable lady. Hermione Staunton has shone in our lives like a strong and steady light. The light of example, dignity, duty and –' he looked irritably at a pair of giggling teenagers, '– *exquisite* manners. At a time when, so often, these virtues no longer . . .'

Hermione, conscious that those who were not looking at Vivian were probably looking at her, gazed at the ceiling. A wide glittering chandelier hung suspended from a heavy brass chain, its polished facets gleaming. Not an old one, she thought: you can tell. This new crystal has a strange yellow shine to it. Old crystal is blue-grey. Though the one in the attic was always blurred with dust. I used to suck the corner of my skirt and polish a facet and hold it up to the skylight.

'*How thy beauty shineth amid the stars,*' he had said, '*oh eternal Queen!*'

No one else has ever thought me beautiful. I wish Sandy were here and then everybody else could go away and I wouldn't mind a bit. Oh dear, how ungrateful.

Vivian chuntered on in the measured tone he used for making a speech at the annual general meeting of an old-established company or charity, the sort of speech he was most often called upon to deliver. The women listened with docile, sycophantic smiles, the men thought about other things; usually money or girls. Funny how they all flashed their legs but tits were banned. Always one or t'other, never both. Waiters circulated with silver trays bearing tall glasses of champagne.

'Krug, d'ye think?' whispered Jack Bridgewater.

'Not a hope. Bolly if you're *lucky*,' muttered his first cousin once removed. They sniggered.

Vivian Blythgowrie neared the end of his peroration.

'And so I would ask you one and all to raise your glasses in hearty congratulations to Hermione . . .'

'*Hermione!*' they murmured raggedly, sipping in unison. (It was in fact Moët.)

The younger relatives, more used to twenty-first birthday parties whose subject was made to endure the ritual humiliation of stumbling through a speech, began to call out, 'Speech! Speech! Speech!'

Hermione smiled and stood up.

'It is frightfully nice to see you all here this evening,' she said. 'Lots of people have come down from Scotland. Others from Suffolk and Yorkshire and Worcestershire. All to wish me a happy birthday. I'm very pleased to see so many members of the family all together in one place. It normally only happens at weddings; or –' a tiny, perfectly timed pause '– funerals.' There were one or two embarrassed sniggers, quickly suppressed.

'Since I do not seem likely to die for a good while yet – my doctor says I am in excellent health . . .' (Good for her, thought Rachel; she's teasing them. *She* knows their expectations.) '. . . I am glad to be able to enjoy you all while still very much alive. I don't *feel* seventy a bit. And now I must thank Vivian, my grand-nephew, and his wife Geraldine for having organized this wonderful party. It's been a great treat. Vivian tells me there is a buffet so I'll stop talking and let you help yourselves. Once again, thank you all very much for coming and for that exciting heap of presents. I hope you don't mind if I open them later. And now let's start to enjoy that delicious-looking supper.'

She sat down amid emphatic – over-emphatic – cheers. A group tried to start up '*For she's a jolly good fellow*' but, lacking encouragement, tailed off. People began to move towards long tables laden with gleaming, multi-coloured platters of food. The hum of conversation rose to a roar.

'. . . complete waste of time, all this sucking up. She'll end up giving it to Battersea bloody Dogs' Home if you ask me . . . They always *do*,' one young man complained gloomily, his mouth full of brown bread and smoked salmon. 'Oops! Sorry, vicar!' He paused to remove a shard of lemon lodged between his strong white teeth.

'Not at all,' said Nicholas Hobson. 'I find this so-called *finger food* tricky too.'

'Didn' mean that,' mumbled Bill Shepherd. 'Swearing, I meant.'

'My dear chap, I have worked in one of Liverpool's toughest inner-city parishes. The word *bloody* is not likely to send me running for cover.'

'How do you know Great-aunt Hermione, if you work in Liverpool?'

'I don't any longer. I met her during the war, when she ran Chantry as a hospital.'

'Which war?'

'Don't tell me I look *that* old? The last war, 1939–45. You *have* heard of it?'

''Course,' said the young man sulkily as Nicholas moved on, thus forfeiting his only chance to gain some insight into his great-aunt, a portion of whose money he vainly hoped might find its way into his needy bank balance.

'Hermione Malling-*Smith*!' said Henrietta. 'How *very* nice to see you.'

'Mrs Birmingham. Gosh, heavens, it's nearly twenty years since I left Raeburn but seeing you *still* makes me think help, what've I done *wrong*?'

'I remember you very well, my dear – and didn't someone tell me you were *married*? Is your husband here?'

'No, I'm afraid not: neither him nor – oh dear – the next.' She laughed and went on confidentially, 'I'm *between* husbands at the moment.' Henrietta was too deaf to catch whispers and, as the deaf do, had to make a guess at the last remark. Something about a husband?

'You must introduce him,' she said graciously. Young Hermione, once the adored heroine of Raeburn School, thought good Lord, *that*'s very broad-minded of her and went off to look for her current lover. She eventually found him with Reggie, engrossed in comparing the merits of the mini-skirted young legs around them.

'*Naughty* boys!' she said, noticing with irritation that Roderick Campbell-Leith's young wife Gaye was wearing an even shorter skirt than her own.

By quarter to eleven the line of guests waiting to peck Cousin Hermione's unscented cheek and congratulate her yet again had dwindled. Vivian Blythgowrie had booked the room until eleven, hoping that no one would stay as late as midnight, especially with the trains all over the place because of a work-to-rule.

'For God's sake make people get a move on,' he told his wife peremptorily and Geraldine started to go round the room harrying one group and then another.

'I'm afraid Vivian *rather* feels it's time we should start to . . .'

'Geraldine! I was just telling David's son how *very* much . . .' people would say; or, 'Wonderful party! Hermione is obviously having a *whale* of a time, bless her!'

In the end Vivian summoned the microphone and a flunkey to switch it on. The sound system growled several times and then his booming voice came through: 'Hermione would like me to thank you all very much for coming and now she is about to leave.'

She took the hint, rose to her feet, accepted Vivian's stiff-necked public embrace and let him escort her through the crowd of relatives, some of whom mimicked little claps, to the side entrance where her car was waiting – the big green Rolls bought after the Coronation nearly twenty years ago. It was the pride and joy of Hamilton, her chauffeur. He was holding a magnificent sable stole that had once belonged to Phoebe. Vivian took it from him and draped it solicitously round Hermione's shoulders. Just as she stooped to get into the back of her car, he said, 'We must have a *talk* soon, Cousin

Hermione. Sort things out. Check that your *papers* are in order.'

She looked back at him. 'Do you think so, Vivian dear? Well never mind – perhaps we will. Thank you again for a *lovely* party. So *kind* of everyone. Hamilton . . .'

The chauffeur closed the door with a thunk and as the car moved away Hermione sat back with a small sigh. Hamilton, oblique but curious, said solicitously, 'Madam must be tired.'

'I *am* tired. I had planned to spend the weekend in London but I think I'll go to Chantry tomorrow, after all. I shall leave at about four so as to avoid the traffic and arrive in good time for dinner.'

'Certainly, madam.'

Vivian was left standing on the Arlington Street pavement watching the dark green Rolls glide away and wishing he had been more insistent. He was after all her main trustee: it was his *business* to check on her investments, keep an eye on the finances. Hermione must realize that she was responsible for millions of pounds yet she made him feel as though he were being vulgarly intrusive, rather than properly conscientious. He turned to the doorman.

'Call my car!' he ordered brusquely.

Hermione's presents accompanied her to Chantry next day and she spent more than an hour on Sunday morning opening them. They were much what she had expected: soap, toilet water, an unimaginative choice of books (*Dorset Churches*, or *English Cathedrals*, or *Scottish Castles*) apart from a very pretty opal brooch from Reggie and Mary, which surprised her. Vivian and Geraldine had given her a conical silver candle-snuffer. She checked the maker's mark: yes, Paul de Lamerie. Well, that was generous, although the symbolism was perhaps unfortunate.

She spent the rest of the morning writing thank you letters and was well under way when the telephone on the desk shrilled. Hermione lifted the receiver and smiled.

'Henrietta: the very person! I was just about to write and thank you for that subscription to the London Library. Frightfully imaginative and *most* generous. I shall use it a lot. What did you think of the party? Went off smoothly, I thought.'

They compared notes for a while on the fitness and coherence of their older relations ('*Did* you see Myrtle and Boyo? Weren't they priceless!') and the manners, dress and language of the younger ones. They compared notes on the trio of Australians, Katie Bridgewater and her offspring, who had moved like a battering ram through the crowd.

'They did seem to enjoy their *food* . . .' Hermione observed.

Henrietta smiled to herself on the other end of the telephone. It was unnecessary to criticize outright when so much could be achieved by inflection. 'I wonder how Vivian tracked *them* down?' she agreed.

Then Hermione asked, 'That young woman you introduced me to . . . Hermione somebody? Is she *named* after me?'

'She is, yes. She used to be a Malling-Smith. Doesn't that make her a cousin twice removed? Whose is the Malling-Smith branch? Kitty's, that's it, of course – young Hermione is *Evadne*'s daughter. I'm afraid she *is* known as Young Hermione.'

'I'd better not ask what they call *me*. Should I know her? She doesn't ring a bell.'

'I had her at Raeburn for a few years. Not *over*-endowed with brains – two or three O Levels and then off to be a deb – but always very nice-looking. She caused havoc among some of my staff.'

'I can imagine. She couldn't have been more charming – *most* insistent that I should take tea with her. No mention of a husband, although I gathered she has two young boys. Don't you find that people of her generation all talk about their lives in this up-to-date psychological fashion; they never ask themselves simply, is it right or wrong? Will it cause pain, or not?'

'One married for life, in *our* day.' Henrietta paused in brief contemplation of the late Mr Birmingham, adding, 'Did you arrange anything?'

'I didn't *rush* to consult my engagement diary. Now then, who else? Did you talk to Mary and Reggie? Poor old boy, he has gone to seed rather . . .'

'Reggie's a scamp; always was. Another charmer – it must run in the family – but not quite the glamour-boy he used to be. I think Vivian rather resents having to prop him up.'

'Perhaps Mary does, too. *She* seems a dear.'

'Oh definitely. Now Hetty, before you go, tell me what you make of Vivian?'

'He did his stuff.'

'He did. But he's becoming frightfully pompous, I thought. Much too soon. Plenty of time to be pompous later on. He can't be older than thirty-five, *half* my age. I didn't care for the way he patronized me.'

'Yes, my dear, that must be quite a novel experience for you! But Vivian must be a good ten years older than thirty-five? Forty at least.'

'Can it be *possible*? Everyone looks young to me nowadays. Sure sign of old age.'

The two women laughed and said an affectionate telephonic goodbye.

In the afternoon Hermione went for a drive. She asked Hamilton to leave her at the village church – 'I'll make my own way back, it will do me good. I don't take nearly enough exercise.' She wanted to stand alone, in silence, before the memorials to her father and her brother Richard. She had lived fifty years longer than her brother; ten years longer than her mother; and her father had died at seventy-five. It was hard not to think about death when one reached three-score years and ten.

The church was empty except for a couple of visitors shuffling round, guidebook in hand. She stood in front of her father's austere black granite tablet: JACK STAUNTON 1844–1919 'FOR THIS RELIEF MUCH THANKS' and heard the other pair whispering about the marble effigy of her brother. She waited for them to move on. Their footsteps clattered on the tiled floor; there was a smaller clatter of coins in the alms box; then she was by herself. What did the inscription mean? Could it refer to her mother? The quotation came from *Hamlet* and ended, *'Tis bitter cold, And I am sick at heart*, but that wasn't much help.

At that moment, as though in a vision, Hermione – never a religious woman – heard a voice speaking with calm authority. It said, *'This is my beloved son, in whom I am well pleased.'* She had

242

gone to church every Sunday throughout her childhood and the words of the Bible and morning service were incised in her memory like the villagers' names on tombstones in the churchyard or the Latin engraved on marble flagstones along the aisle. Faintly, like the retreating ghost of Hamlet's father, she heard again the sonorous voice: '*This is my beloved son, in whom I am well pleased.*' She accepted it quite calmly. It was not an illusion, but not a visitation, either. The voice was the product of her imagination, yet also a real voice. Did it mean that *God* was pleased with her brother? – she could not believe that, having been a religious sceptic for sixty years. Perhaps it was her father's voice she heard in her head? It did not speak in his tones, nor with his beloved northern accent but perhaps it was a message meaning that he had been pleased with his son – and with her, too. She had certainly been his beloved daughter. Mystified and confused but also obscurely comforted, she left the church and walked home through the golden glory of an April day like those she and Sandy had taken for granted when they were children.

CHAPTER SEVENTEEN

15–16 April 1972

SIR ALEXANDER GORDON-LOCKHART PERCHED UNCOMFORTABLY IN the front seat of his grandson's red Mini as it jounced along the new motorway at a speed for which it had never been designed. A dark green Rolls passed them, sedate and majestic at ninety miles an hour.

'Look at that!' exclaimed young Andrew. 'Lovely old car!'

'Silver Wraith. Used to have one of those in Turkey, not long after the war, when I was British minister there,' said his grandfather. 'Sole purpose was to impress the natives – *and* it did.'

'Betchalife!' responded Andrew.

It was the day after Hermione's seventieth party, but Sandy had long ago forgotten the date of her birthday and had not been aware of the party. The Mini had been young Andrew's coming-of-age present from himself and Chloë the previous year. To show his gratitude, Andrew was devoting a rare free weekend to taking his grandfather to visit childhood haunts. Despite the generation gap, the two had always been close. Sandy had hoped the lad might follow him into the diplomatic service, but Andrew's bent was for physics and chemistry and he was now a medical student at the Middlesex Hospital in London, working to the point of exhaustion by day and smoking pot to relax by night.

An hour later they were negotiating the winding Dorset lanes, still rather too fast.

'By Jove yes, I'm beginning to recognize this!' Sandy exclaimed. 'They've widened the road since my day and the new estate on the edge of the village is an eyesore but – yes, I'm sure I remember. In a moment we come to a copse on the left and then one turned left and just after that our drive veered off to the right.'

They approached a clump of mature trees.

'Could be here,' said Andrew, 'if that counts as a copse.'

'Now carry on for a bit here – whoa, not far – stop! Yes, there it is. Oh dear. One's heart does rather *sink* at the sight of a board saying Otterbourne Court Hotel.'

Andrew swung the Mini into the long drive, passing sedately under the double row of chestnuts that bordered it, culminating in a gravelled sweep before the front door of a mullioned grey stone Victorian house. A notice on one side indicated GUESTS' PARKING. A youth with rolled-up shirt-sleeves emerged.

''Afternoon, sir. Are you staying in the hotel? Take your bags?'

Sandy Gordon-Lockhart stood in the entrance hall gazing at the panelled walls and plasterwork ceiling that had sheltered his earliest years. Here, where the reception desk stood; here, where the side table was scattered with leaflets advertising local sights worth seeing; here, where a notice on one door announced GUESTS' DRAWING ROOM and on another SMALL DRAWING ROOM and on a third, OFFICE: PRIVATE; and down there, at the end of the corridor leading to DINING ROOM and BREAKFAST ROOM: GUESTS ONLY – these were the very rooms into which, as a small boy, he had been ushered to greet Mama, stand to attention in front of his untalkative papa, and shake hands with visitors. After that he and Hermione could escape and run upstairs to the . . . *Hermione!* Her flying figure rose before his eyes, making his head swim.

'Grandpa? You all right? Like to sit down for a tick?'

'What? – no thanks, I'm fine. Fine. Should we book in?'

'I've done all that. We're on the first floor, room numbers four and five. You're in Tulip and I'm Daffodil. Now then, rest before dinner? Long drive from London . . .'

'A Scotch would set me up.'

The shirt-sleeved lad picked up their bags as the two headed towards GUESTS' BAR.

It was a shock – more so than he had expected. The place had changed, become vulgar and impersonal, starting with the mock-Edwardian names for the bedrooms. Sandy happened to have been allocated the room that had once been his mother's, seventy years ago. Now its beribboned chintz wallpaper matched the curtains that matched the bedspread that toned with the bedside lights and blended with the apple-green carpet. In his parents' time it had been a jumble of colour and pattern with sagging, comfortable and well-polished furniture that signalled a lofty disregard for 'interior decoration'. Yet the view through the bedroom window looking down the drive had hardly changed and there were still green fields away to the right, dotted with placidly grazing cows.

Hermione! That had been the greatest shock, discovering how vividly the house conjured her up in his mind's eye. The long-limbed girl who had been his dearest childhood companion and, a few years later, the focus of his adolescent yearnings, had come to life in a flash. He saw again the glossy swing of her hair, tied back with a ribbon but forever getting into her eyes, and her brown hand brushing it back impatiently. Her legs, scratched and bruised from their adventures, in the long white socks and tan sandals she had worn through the hot summer days, strode as confidently through memory as they had run from him in his fantasies. He heard again her clear voice ringing in his ears: 'Major? Quick! Over here! Come and see what I've found!' Christ almighty, he thought – what is this Pandora's box I've opened?

The hotel served a good dinner and offered a decent wine-list. The apple crumble was a fair imitation of the ones he'd eaten at school and the cheeses were fresh. Young Andrew ate as though he hadn't seen food in weeks. Medicine was a hard grind, that was obvious.

'You plan to specialize in any particular area?' his grandfather asked.

246

'Bit early to decide. Not yet sure if I'll stay the course but if I do I thought perhaps the heart?'

'Yes, how is your heart? Nurses are supposed to be a happy hunting-ground, from all accounts.'

'Might be, if I had *time*. We work till we drop. Lucky if I get the chance to flirt for five minutes last thing in the evening, after the medicine trolley has been round.'

'Poor old chap! Sounds worse than being a duty clerk in the FO.'

'Much. Illegal immigrants doing sweated labour don't clock up the hours we do for the NHS. Meals? *Love?* Not a hope!'

'Any regrets?'

'Too early to tell. Your third year is hell anyway, the slave-labour stage. But it's *interesting*.'

'Suffering humanity exposed?'

Andrew looked up, surprised by his grandfather's perspicacity.

'*Yes*, as a matter of fact. You do get to see people in the raw – and their families, desperate for them to live or, just as often, desperate that they should die. The rich and powerful are in the same state of terror as everyone else, the only difference being, *they* have a private room. Illness is a great leveller. Yup: human nature *exposed* all right.'

'Have a glass of port? Or do you prefer brandy?'

'I'm good and pissed already.'

'I don't mind. Port may give you a headache, that's the only thing.'

'In that case I'll have brandy. Grandpa, you're indulging me.'

'Let's go through to the library . . . Waiter?'

On the other side of the next room a middle-aged couple sat listlessly turning the pages of old copies of *Country Life*. Both were smoking. The light from a side-table emphasized the folds of her chin and neck and made his bald patch shine. Sandy glanced at the shelves where his father's leather-covered volumes had once stood in rows of dark red, green and brown with gold-tooled titles. Now they held only cheap paperbacks, dog-eared magazines and some unfortunate china ornaments. Andrew made small-talk until the man opposite glanced up at his wife and said, 'I'm for beddy-byes! How about you?'

'Be up in a minute,' she said. 'Don't wait.'

She sighed as her husband left the room, her shoulders slumped. She turned a few pages, drained her coffee cup and murmuring, 'Good night,' she too went out.

Andrew and his grandfather sat in silence for a while, swirling the brandy in bulbous glasses, its aroma deadened by stale cigarette smoke. A black-coated figure walked briskly past the open door and Sandy summoned him.

'Take away the ashtrays, would you? Bring clean ones – and two more brandies.'

'Not for me,' Andrew protested.

'Keep me company. I'm feeling what my hero Duke Ellington would call blue.' Under his breath Sandy hummed the opening notes of 'Mood Indigo'.

'Old haunts? Tell me.'

'You wouldn't rather turn in?'

'At half past *nine*?'

There is a pause before the telling of a story; always has been, since the first tale-teller sat cross-legged under a tree at the end of the day; a pause while the speaker summons his thoughts, puts them in order and frames his first sentence. In that pause the listener focuses, prepares to be informed, amused, best of all, astonished. Andrew lit a cigarette (it was one he had already mixed with a small, an unusually small quantity of marijuana, for pleasure and relaxation and to help him sleep) and sat back. His grandfather's expression became abstracted as he let himself down step by step, descending the swaying rope ladder into memory.

'I was born in this house, probably in the very room I shall sleep in tonight. *Tulip*. It used to have pale green wallpaper with ivy trailing down it, and my mother's bed was covered with a Paisley-patterned bedspread, very light and soft. The curtains were red, with a dark green knotted fringe, like a lot of bell-ropes. There was a double door into the room, for some reason. I had to knock on the inner one and if she didn't reply I would go away. Her dressing table was covered with silver-framed photographs and a big three-tiered ivory and silver box with her jewellery in satin compartments. Pearls. Lots of pearl ropes. They smelled of her. I remember that.'

What *was* that smell? Soft, sweet, powdery, with a musky undertone of perspiration and a lingering overtone, very faint and only in winter, of smoke from the fire and the men's cigars. Sometimes as a little boy he had crept into her dressing room to bury his face in the garments that hung in pillowy ranks in the creaking wardrobe; or taken the soap out of the china dish beside her washing bowl to sniff it. Mama – ladies – mysterious women – laughing down at him, embracing him, pushing him away. The rope ladder swung beneath his feet.

'Anyway. My parents lived here till I was nearly thirteen and about to go up to Eton. I had a nanny and a tutor. I was tutored at home. When Grandpa Clan Lockhart died my father inherited the place in Scotland – Ellismuir. You know it. But I spent most of my boyhood under *this* roof.'

'Why have you never come back till now?'

'Mater was dead set against it. Not sure why. Of course the war broke out quite soon after we left – that by the way was the *First World War –*' (his grandson laughed) '– but once that was over it would have been natural for her to spend occasional weekends here. As far as I can gather she and my father were on perfectly good terms with the neighbours . . . no scandals like cheating at cards or shooting accidents – that wasn't Pater's style at all. Yet once they'd left, despite having lived here for a good fifteen years, she never returned. That – prohibition – *taboo*, almost, was so strong that I never came back either. While she was still alive I knew it would distress her and after her death it would have felt disloyal.'

Some skeleton lurking, his grandson wondered, and he prompted obliquely: 'I never met her, did I, but Dad says Great-grandmama Violet was what used to be called "a stunner".'

'Mater would have been horrified to hear herself described that way. "Stunner" was a word reserved for artists' models; lower-class girls one step up from tarts. If you mean she was lovely – yes, she was, in that voluptuous yet kittenish way the Edwardians found so attractive. But behind her soft manner she had a steely will . . . she was made of much sterner stuff than poor old Pater, which must be why it has taken me sixty years to go against her wishes.'

'Why *now*?'

Sandy Gordon-Lockhart whirled the brandy round the glass, inhaled its potent scent and drank. *Why* now? Because it had been suggested that he might write his autobiography – *In Foreign Parts: A Diplomatic Life*, by Sir Alexander Gordon-Lockhart GCMG – and dedicate it to Chloë. She deserved it, after all these years, but if that were the plan he'd better get a move on or she wouldn't be alive to see it. Was he here to recapture the blue remembered hills of childhood? That too. Or because, given Chloë's state of health, poor old girl, he was kept on a short leash by her querulous needs and young Andrew had provided a copper-bottomed excuse to get away for a whole weekend? Yes, that as well. But the secret motive was the quest for Hermione – H. Minor as he had called her for some forgotten reason. She was the real magnet and the real reason behind his mother's prohibition, although their childhood friendship had been entirely innocent. He had never touched her, though he had *looked* at her once. Just once. With no clothes on. Long white body, brown arms and legs and a fine line between them, unblurred by hair or modesty. He had so often summoned that image, it had almost been obliterated. But that was all . . . one look, no more.

Andrew drew deeply on his secret hash cigarette and waited with the forbearance of the mildly stoned, for whom time passes very, very slowly.

'Old age, one,' his grandfather continued eventually. 'It changes all sorts of things. You know time is running out and if you don't do the things you mean to do *now* you may never get the chance. Memory, two. I find myself harking back to my childhood with absolute clarity; just as I can remember sunbathing on the beach at Beirut with Chloë in 1928, the year we were posted there, the year before your father was born – was *she* a honey in her bathing costume! I remember all that far more vividly than the villa we rented last year in Cyprus. But three, most important: sentiment. Nostalgia. A sort of yearning for all that energy I had as a boy.'

'What do you feel sentimental *about*, Grandpa?'

'Usual sorts of things. Childish things. The secret places where I used to hide and play make-believe games. The animals – I had a pony and a dog of my own called Bobby who followed us everywhere.' (Silently, Andrew noted the 'us'.) 'Books – especially H. Rider Haggard's African tales – I liked adventure stories best. Games on rainy days. Games like L'Attaque and Ludo and Nine Men's Morris kept me quiet for hours.'

'You were an only child. Who did you play games *with*?'

Sandy looked up at his grandson and almost imperceptibly, his face closed.

'There was a boy nearby called Richard. Dick Staunton. He was a bit older than me, but he'd indulge me sometimes. Got himself killed in the war, poor fellow.'

How can I explain to this straightforward young man, my grandson, the beguilement and magic of my childhood – that *I was in love with a nine-year-old girl*? He'd laugh – anyone would laugh – *children* don't fall in love.

'I feel sentimental for that red-haired chap (hence "Sandy" – not that you'd know it these days) who was having the most enormously good time. Life was so full of zip, such *fun*. A diplomatic career has much to recommend it but *fun* isn't high on the list. So, if you ask why I've come back, I suppose that's the reason. To look for the little boy who was once me.'

His grandfather looked, just for an instant, like a man stepping back from a cliff edge, relief and anti-climax mirrored in his expression.

'I'm boring you, old chap . . .'

'Grandpa, you know perfectly well you aren't boring me.'

'Well, I'm hogging the conversation instead of allowing myself to be led docilely to bed like a child.'

Andrew laughed. 'The idea that *anyone*, let alone me, could lead you like a docile child is absurd, as you know very well. However, it is *my* bedtime. I'm tired.' He stretched languorously, arms thrown wide as a stag's antlers, then clapped his hand over a yawn. 'If you'll excuse me, Grandpa, I'll say good night. Thank you for an excellent dinner. Breakfast at nine?'

'Nine it is. Sleep well, old man.'

Here in this very room they had sat, the two of them, heads bent over *Jock of the Bushveld* and *King Solomon's Mines*, while she wove around him the spell of first love. How did she do it, that innocent girl? She was wound round his heart like a spider's web, with invisible gossamer threads. He had been Leo Vincey and she was Ayesha, the goddess of infinite power and mysterious beauty.

'*Whence comest thou, oh bold traveller, intruding upon my kingdom, yeah, even into my very temple?*' she would demand, head flung back imperiously.

'*To pay thee homage, oh great Queen, and learn thy timeless secrets!*' he had to reply.

Ever-inventive, Hermione would answer, '*Tell me, pale young foreigner with copper hair from distant lands, how cam'st thou here? Are all men in thy country as noble of countenance as thou art?*'

Even then, as a child, hers had not been the gestures of a little girl, nor his responses those of a little boy.

His companion who climbed and dared and fell and did not cry. By the power of childhood and memory she had stayed with him all his life. He had come back in search of her – but now he was here, did he dare to look? Hermione, his first love . . . there was an oath they swore . . . something they'd found in Kipling, that's it! *We be of one blood, Thou and I.* Sandy Gordon-Lockhart heaved himself out of his armchair and stomped upstairs to the room called Tulip.

Next morning Andrew and his grandfather met over Sunday breakfast, identically dressed in tweed jackets and checked shirts, except that Andrew sported jeans and red Hush Puppies while his grandfather wore cords and rubber-soled walking boots. They ate heartily, breakfast being the meal that the English do best.

'Any particular plans for today?' Andrew asked.

'Houses, gardens or a look at the sea . . . what do you think? There are some marvellous National Trust properties round here if you care for that sort of thing.'

'Long as there's a decent pub not too far away . . .'

'Beaminster's known for good food. How about having a dekko at Mapperton? Lovely old house.'

'Bonzo!'

Sandy raised an eyebrow. 'My patience, as every Arab knows, is considerable but I draw the line at "bonzo".'

'Testing, testing . . .'

He placed both hands on his knees, the 'frog position' he used to signal the end of meetings. It worked on grandsons, too.

Andrew rose to his feet with a grin: 'A shit, a shower and a shave, as we used to say in the sixth form. Twenty minutes? Meet you by the front door at ten?'

Sandy shook his head despairingly. 'Lamentable. *Lamentable.* The end of civilization as we know it.'

Together they walked out of the breakfast room, leaving the glum married couple (who had not, after all, made love on their thirty-fifth wedding anniversary) to contemplate cold toast.

The Dorset woods were carpeted with anemones and the first bluebells were just beginning to appear, a miraculous powdery blue with curly florets of diminishing size, like trumpet notes shimmering down the scale. Grandfather and grandson chatted over their pub lunch with relaxed camaraderie – Andrew talking about his future, Sandy about his past. Twice that day the Mini passed the gates of Chantry and twice Sandy Gordon-Lockhart looked the other way so as not to see a sign advertising its metamorphosis into hotel, school, hospital or industrial training centre. Had he dropped in at the village church – as he had half a mind to do, until the desire for a zizz overcame him – he could hardly have missed seeing a notice pinned up in the porch that said, FÊTE IN HONOUR OF THE 70TH BIRTHDAY OF MISS STAUNTON OF CHANTRY! It did not cross his mind that after sixty years, Chantry might be unchanged and Hermione still living there.

Back at the hotel, Sandy lay in a hot bath, a glass of whisky perched on the soap rack that bridged the water. ' "The *Lord's* my *shep*herd, I'll not want . . ." ' he sang, letting the hot tap run, ' ". . . He makes me down to lie . . ." ' A vigorous knocking on the wall signalled that he could be heard. Untroubled, he sang on: ' "In paa-stures green . . ." ' He drained the whisky and stood up, water sluicing his body.

Naked, she had let him look at her, sixty years ago. Her body had been long and white, her childish ribs showing under the translucent skin. Her stomach had curved gently down towards the cleft between her legs. Sandy Gordon-Lockhart looked at his slowly rising erection. No wonder I've had a lifelong penchant for slight, boyish women, he thought. One true love and every other a wraith, a pale shadow of her. When I met Chloë she epitomized the Twenties ideal: flat-chested, narrow-hipped, with bony shoulders and delicate little arms. We were pretty wild in the Twenties but of the many girls I'd danced with, none was so perfectly androgynous as Chloë. Love by association. I'd never seen anyone who looked so much like a captivating ten-year-old. It's why I married her – that and, if I'm honest, because the fact that she was the ambassador's daughter could do my career nothing but good. She was a virtuous girl, guarding her virginity even after we were engaged. Those clinging tube dresses left little to the imagination and I had a pretty good idea of her body long before I finally saw her, naked and suddenly shy, on our wedding night.

His erection had subsided. Sandy got out of the bath, put on a clean shirt, a different jacket, rubbed a corner of the bedspread across the toecaps of his shoes and went downstairs to join his grandson.

In the bar before dinner Andrew asked, 'Do you want me to make enquiries about that house . . . what was it called: Chantry? The people here are bound to know if it's still in private hands.'

'*No!*' said Sandy, in alarm. 'No, don't do that. It's not important. The great thing is to have had a snoop round – and spent a bit of time with you, old boy.'

Over dinner Andrew questioned his grandfather with a tactful mixture of deference and genuine curiosity. Listening fondly, he thought: he's led such a rich life and yet in a way very uncomplicated. Entirely devoted to three things: career; hobbies (jazz and amateur archaeology); wife and children – probably in that order. Dad always said Grandpa was the most single-minded person he'd ever met. 'Once he set his hand to something he'd never turn back.' Wonder if I'll be like that?

'Are you going to stick at medicine?' Sandy was asking his grandson, and Andrew, who until that moment had not been entirely sure, answered with sudden resolution, '*Yes!*'

Later, in his pyjamas and ready for bed, Sandy drew back the curtains in his room. It felt increasingly like Tulip, £45 a night incl. breakfast, and less and less like Mama's bedroom. He looked over the dark silhouetted trees towards Chantry, three miles away. A casual enquiry, he thought: 'That place next door – who owns it now? Don't suppose it's a private house any longer?' The hotelier, delighted to show off his local knowledge, would certainly tell me – but do I want to hear? At best she's still there, married to a beefy countryman or some pompous ass who'll have retired after being a judge or something in the City. At worst, all trace of her has been obliterated, just as my parents and my boyhood have almost been wiped out here. She must be nearly seventy by now, an old woman. Dowager, matriarch, pensioner. She must be grey-haired, like me. I cannot imagine H. Minor *old*.

Mater intervened too late. The pattern was set. I was lucky to meet Chloë. The galumphing girls that Betjeman adored were never my style. God, how well I understand Nabokov and Balthus, their obsession with the pubescent girl-child. Tomboy, virgin, hoyden, sylph. Her flat chest and tiny rose-tipped buds; the pale cloven mound. My nut-brown maid with conker-coloured hair, my sexless girl.

PART FIVE

Furious Winter's Rages

July 1973 – April 1974

CHAPTER EIGHTEEN

July 1973

IN THE CAR ON THE WAY TO DORSET, ELIZABETH BRIDGEWATER addressed her husband, David.

'If it were a title, you'd want to inherit it. It's *obvious* you're the person who ought to get the house and everything. Even if it doesn't make much difference to *us*, think of our sons: Guy – Jack – *their* families to come. Oh David, imagine having our *grand-children* here! You've got to tackle her. Find out. God knows, we put up with the boredom of visiting her often enough . . . you're *entitled* to it!'

'What about Blythgowrie? Anyway I can't possibly "tackle her", as you put it. Don't be absurd, Liz.'

'*You're* being absurd! It's perfectly simple. You say, "When you are *no more*, I want you to know that I . . . if I, you know . . . well, I would keep the house just as it is now." '

'What's wrong with "dead"?'

'For heaven's *sake*, David. You have to be more tactful than that!'

'So you want me to tell her that when she's dead we would like, as you put it, "to inherit her house and everything". I am to ask for three houses and twenty million pounds *tactfully*?'

'*Yes*, dammit! Now we're almost there, let me look at you. Your hair's standing on end, which is clever of it considering how little there is left. Have you got a comb? Here, I'll do it. Keep driving.'

'Ouch!' David said.

She patted the shoulders of his jacket, then took out her compact and painted a sharp red mouth over her own fading, puckered lips.

'That'll have to do,' she said. 'Here's the turning. Now remember – I'll make myself scarce – say, on Sunday after church. I'll pretend I want to stroll round the garden by myself. Are you listening, David?'

'Yes,' he said wearily.

Chantry smelled of wood and dust, polish and smoke, mothballs, fresh flowers and, in winter, of a distant home-made soup. Hermione smelled, if at all, of lavender – Yardley's Old English Lavender. More often the bottle stood neglected on a shelf in her bathroom cupboard, alongside one of Syrup of Figs, another (same colour, opposite effect) of Dr Collis Browne's Chlorodyne, as well as TCP, corn plasters and a thermometer. This was the sum total of her medicines, for at seventy-one she was still a healthy woman in possession of all her senses. She put it down to gardening. Now that Cowley had retired and his 'lads' were married men working in market gardens or nurseries, she and a man from the village coped with the garden between them. Hamilton cut the grass, riding on top of a dark green mowing machine that looked like a mongrel pup of the Rolls. Hermione usually gardened in her raincoat because it had deep capacious pockets. She had bought a new one just before the Coronation, in case it rained. Long earth-coloured streaks led into each pocket and a dark hyphen at the back of the collar marked the position of the inside loop. Most of Hermione's clothes were old because good things never wear out. Her shoes were handmade by Lobb's and would have cost several hundred pounds to replace, but she did not expect to buy another pair. She still had a pair of walking shoes dating back to her twenties, with laces that wound round brass eyelets and criss-crossed her instep. They had moulded themselves so comfortably to the shape and flexibility of her feet that the leather was like an extra skin. When they needed resoling she posted them back to Lobb's.

Nowadays Hermione's household had shrunk to three people; Rosa the latest cook/housekeeper, Hamilton the all-purpose chauffeur/handyman, and Felicia, her new maid from the Philippines, a convent-educated girl with a rare smile and a curious sing-song accent. She had been twenty-two when she escaped the political persecutors who murdered her father in front of his family. It took Hermione a year to process the girl's papers through uncaring officials in two countries but she had persisted. Now Felicia was safe, her love and loyalty absolute. Ethel Goodbody, who had retired after more than forty-five years in service, shared a small cottage on the estate with Ada Rawlinson, who was eighty. Hermione sometimes took tea with them. The remaining domestic staff had been replaced by a rota of good women from the village. They did not scrub as hard or polish as well as their predecessors but modern cleaning materials were more potent than hand-mixed pastes and oils, so the end result was much the same. Everyone had Sundays off. Hermione believed Sunday should be a day of rest and was quite prepared to eat cold food once a week in support of this belief. One must show consideration towards servants if one expects to keep them, and she disliked change.

Also on their way down to Chantry, neither set of travellers expecting to encounter the other, were Hermione's great-nephew Roderick – Vivian Blythgowrie's younger brother – his wife Gaye and their five-year-old daughter.

'You look wonderful, darling!' Roderick said fondly to Gaye. 'That dress suits you.'

'Make the most of it while it lasts. Soon be in maternity clothes.'

From the back seat of the car came Henrietta's alert, piping voice. 'What's maternity mean, Mummy?'

'Little pitchers have big ears,' her father reproved.

'Shush, sweetie, let Mummy and Daddy talk for a minute.

261

Roderick, are you going to tell Hermione about –' she pointed at her stomach – 'Herbert?'

'I think so, yes, making a point of the fact that she's the first to know. He'll be the youngest member of the family. Thought I'd ask her to be a sort of honorary granny since he won't have a real one.'

'What if Herbert's a she? *Sherbert?*'

'Well, that might make a difference – not to *me*, of course,' Roderick added hastily, 'but I daresay Hermione's a bit old-fashioned about male heirs.'

'No reason to be – she's a female one herself. Anyhow, fingers crossed.'

Roderick and Gaye Campbell-Leith arrived just in time for lunch, some twenty minutes after David and Elizabeth. The door was opened by Rosa. 'You'll find her in the drawing room. You know the way,' she said, and to Henrietta, 'My goodness, you've shot up!'

She led them across the hall, followed by Roderick's upright, manly stride and Gaye holding Henrietta's hand.

'Here they are, at last,' Rosa announced. 'Don't expect lunch before half past one. I'm having one of my *days* . . .' She stomped away muttering to herself, '*Six* for lunch . . . She'll want to ask the vicar next.'

'Great-aunt Hermione, how are you?' Roderick took her out-stretched hand and bent to kiss her cheek. 'You look *splendid!*' Straightening up, he greeted his fellow guests.

'David! Elizabeth! Lovely to see you both! You know *Gaye* of course but have you met our sproglet? This is Henrietta.'

A *girl*, Elizabeth registered. There'll be another child on the way soon, then. He'll want a boy in case his brother dies. Vivian's only got girls so far. David had better get a move on if he's going to talk Hermione round to our sons. No time to lose.

'What a *dear* little girl!' she said, beaming at their daughter. 'I *do* like little girls! Shall I call you Henny-Penny?'

'*Mummy* calls me Henny,' the child answered with a long, dis-concerting stare.

*

262

Over lunch Hermione said, 'By the way, the Australians are coming to stay. Heavens no, not this weekend! Katie Bridgewater wrote to ask if they might. Peter was a boy last time I saw him.'

Mama's funeral. Sibby's daughter and her family had turned up; the only people from that branch to bother. Had Peter been the thin-faced, hunched, miserable-looking one or was that his brother – now plump, balding, tucking into lunch?

'It's almost fifteen years since his accident,' David said. 'I flew over. He'd made no provision whatsoever for his family. Terrible mess. Poor old Peter.'

'They were a ghastly trio,' Gaye said. 'Why on earth are they coming all this way again?'

'Something to do with the children's education, perhaps? Anyway, I've written back saying they're welcome to come for a weekend.'

Gaye smiled radiantly. 'You *are* kind!' she told Hermione.

Dreadful, common people, thought Elizabeth Bridgewater; she's mad to let them visit. They'll be stone broke, thought her husband David, with a flicker of guilt.

'Watch out, is my feeling,' he said. 'That woman is a nasty piece of work.'

After lunch (shepherd's pie, marrow and runner beans from the garden; blackberry crumble, likewise, custard made with powder, not eggs) Hermione asked Gaye, 'Does Henrietta have a rest after meals?'

'Not usually,' Gaye said. 'But she's quite good at amusing herself – aren't you, darling? Give her a couple of books to look at or a drawing pad and crayons and she'll be fine.'

'I'm five now and I can *read* nearly, Aunt Mynie,' said Henrietta.

'*I* wouldn't mind a lie-down,' Gaye went on; and Elizabeth thought, ha! Pregnant already?

Seizing her opportunity she said heartily, '*What* a good idea! London is *so* tiring! Hermione dear, would you like us to take you out for a *drive* – it's such a beautiful afternoon – or a walk through the grounds – and while *Gaye* relaxes, it might be fun for Henny if *Roderick* showed her the nursery?'

'I could do with a swim,' Roderick said. 'I'll take Little Miss Fish here – anyone else care for the idea? Aunt Hermione, is there anywhere to swim?'

The stream, Hermione thought, the secret, magic stream where I rinsed out my clothes and fell asleep on the grass afterwards. The memory of that afternoon was a blaze of light. She and Sandy had looked at each other for the first and only time, the sun outlining their bodies. Her skin shone, her taut young limbs did whatever she asked of them and the world swung in a golden arc.

'There *is* a wonderful little stream, just across the meadow behind the house. It's about a twenty-minute walk. Would you risk that with a child? It isn't very deep.'

'If you say it's all right . . .' Roderick said, and glancing at his wife, 'I'll keep a very close eye.'

Henny started jumping up and down. 'I'm going to swim,' she said gleefully, '*I'm* going to *swi-im*!'

'I'll get her changed into her swimsuit,' Gaye said, rising to her feet. 'She can wear her dress over it while you walk there and back.'

'Great-aunt Hermione,' Elizabeth was saying solicitously, 'can I fetch you anything? A straw hat? Sun umbrella?'

'Do you know, I think if you wouldn't mind I'll lie down too,' Hermione said. 'You're very kind – but it *is* hot. After that I must do a bit of weeding and dead-head the roses. You two go and have your drive.'

Blast! thought Elizabeth. *Damn and bloody blast it!*

'We'd love to have you with us,' she said, 'unless you'd *really* rather not . . .'

'*Really*. Thank you, Elizabeth dear. Now Roderick, to get to the stream . . . if you go out through the French windows that lead from the study, on to the terrace, down the steps to the lawn and head up towards the left-hand wall of the kitchen garden . . .'

That evening, as Roderick and Gaye changed for dinner with the exhausted Henny asleep in the cot in a corner of their bedroom,

Gaye said, 'Your great-aunt's like a dinosaur – and like all dinosaurs, fascinating. Darling, do you suppose she can ever have been in *love?*'

Roderick said, 'Bound to have. She must have been in her twenties during the 1920s. Those post-World War One years were pretty wild.'

'Then *why* did she never marry?'

'My grandfather, her uncle Iain, said her mother was an unscrupulous man-eater who pinched her daughter's boyfriends. But that's old family gossip. I've really no idea.'

'Poor Hermione. I think she's a sweetie. I was watching while Henny told her that embarrassing story about the old witch with a big gloomy house, quite obviously based on her, and I don't think it crossed her mind. She's a complete innocent.'

'Possibly. But she's a very *rich* innocent and I'm not sure the rich can ever really be innocent. Innocents don't hang on to their money. They either chuck it about or get fleeced. Hurry up, darling . . . if we're going to tell her about Herbert without the other two there we ought to go down now.'

Gaye said, 'I'm just fixing my earrings – you go on ahead.'

Finding Hermione alone in the drawing room, Roderick sat down on the nearest sofa. He leaned forward, elbows on his knees, looked intently at his great-aunt and drew a deep breath.

'Aunt Hermione, *news!* You're the very first person to hear. We've only just got the results. Gaye's expecting our second child! Of course it would be *nice* if it were a boy, if only because we've got a girl already, but a son and heir would somehow complete the family.'

'How exciting!' Hermione said. 'Congratulations! When is the baby due?'

'Oh, not till February. Ages yet.'

Damn, thought Roderick, I wish I hadn't got to hurry this but if David and that wretched wife of his come down I simply can't say it. Gaye entered, sat on the sofa beside him and smiled rosily at Hermione.

'*So,*' he went on, 'we'd like to ask you a favour. You don't have to answer straight away; you'll probably want to mull it over. The thing is, Herbert – that's what we call the sprog, the unborn baby – Herbert won't have a granny. As you know, my parents are dead, alas, and Gaye's mother died two years ago; so this poor little scrap will only have one grandparent, Gaye's father. We talked it over and wondered if you would agree to be a sort of *honorary* grand-mother?'

'Roderick, dear, it's good of you to ask and I *am* honoured. But you're forgetting. I'm seventy-one, you know. I couldn't be a grandmama, not even a stand-in, for very long.'

'Nonsense!' said Roderick. 'You're in splendid health, we can see that for ourselves.'

Gaye put in, 'It's true, Aunt Hermione, you're amazing . . .'

'No reason why you shouldn't live easily another dozen or fifteen years. Plenty of time for grandmotherhood.'

'What would it entail?' Hermione asked. 'I have rather too many responsibilities already.'

'Oh, no responsibilities! Just pleasure!' Roderick said.

Gaye rescued him, knowing this was not what he meant at all. 'We hoped you might do what all grannies do – give a sense of the continuity between the generations,' she said smoothly. 'Take this afternoon, when we got those Edwardian books down from the nursery—'

'Schoolroom.'

'—schoolroom, to read to Henny. She'll *remember* that; and it makes a bond that goes back seventy years. I think those sort of things matter a lot, especially since she has so few older people to link up with.'

Footsteps could be heard clattering on the flagged stone floor of the great hall. Roderick knew it was twenty yards long. Time for a few more sentences.

'Don't forget, they'll both have plenty of godparents,' he said swiftly. 'But we'd like you to be their *granny*. To him – well, *it* for the time being – and young Henrietta.'

Hermione paused. 'I'm not sure how being a stand-in grand-mama would be any different from being an actual great-great-aunt.'

'It *sounds* nicer!' Gaye smiled. 'Please?'

266

'I'll think about it. May I let you know?'

'Of course,' said Gaye.

'Take your time,' said Roderick. 'Ah, Elizabeth – David! How nice!'

The dinner gong boomed as the clock struck eight.

'Shall we go through?' Hermione invited and David made a little play of offering her a gallant arm.

Goodness, thought Elizabeth as they ate cold salmon and mayonnaise, followed by lamb chops with mint, followed by bread and butter pudding and cheese – goodness, how difficult it is to eat a meal and make conversation without *wine* to ease the proceedings! But she tried valiantly, talking first about Wimbledon and then, realizing that Hermione never watched television, switching adroitly to their forthcoming holiday with the boys, which would include a visit to her unmarried sister-in-law Anne Bridgewater in Southwold. Before she could say – as her husband knew she invariably did say – 'Poor Anne, what a lonely life she must lead. Such a *shame* she never married!' he lobbed the conversational ball across the table to Roderick, who rallied deftly with news of their forthcoming trip to Gowrie Castle, where they always spent August with his brother Vivian. Cue for Gaye to recall how well Vivian had organized Hermione's birthday celebrations – mutual smiles and anecdotes across the table from Elizabeth and Gaye – and all the time Hermione sat at the head of the table thinking, they're perfectly intelligent people: why are they so *dull*? If my friends were here – Rachel and Benjamin, or Nicholas, or Pixie Finch and her husband, or even my cousin Henrietta – they'd be bored to tears. Yet I have to put up with this vapid great-aunt conversation. Why do they treat me as though I'm senile? Let me see if I can get them to talk about something more interesting.

'Has anyone been to the Hayward Gallery lately?' she enquired. 'A wonderful new exhibition has just opened.' She waited to see how they would respond.

'Really, how *fascinating*,' said Elizabeth; and turning to her husband: 'David darling – why haven't we *been*?' She turned vivaciously to Hermione. 'We'll go next week and report back, shall we?'

Hermione thought, all right: four out of ten for trying. She looked at Gaye.

'That's the Van Gogh, isn't it?' said Gaye. 'We certainly *intend* to go. I think it's so important for children to see great works of art.'

All right, at least she knew whose paintings are being shown. Six out of ten.

'I'm just too busy to get to exhibitions – one is conscious of missing a lot,' said Roderick, and David nodded manly agreement.

No marks to either of you.

'I saw it last week,' Hermione said.

Rosa brought in a silver-lidded barrel of Jacob's biscuits and a chunk of Cheddar.

'Coffee?' she asked grumpily, taking five cheese plates from the sideboard and placing one in front of each.

'Oh no, Rosa, it's getting late!' Hermione said. 'If we need coffee, we'll make ourselves some Nescafé.'

'Thank you, madam,' Rosa said. 'I'll start the dishwasher. There's cold bits in the larder for lunch tomorrow. The summer pudding's under a weight on the top shelf. Plenty of custard left in the old silver bowl. The skin needs stirring in.'

'That sounds fine. You go off now, Rosa. It's nearly ten o'clock.'

'The dinner was delicious!' said Elizabeth and there was a rumble of supportive murmurs.

'Good night, madam,' said Rosa dismissively.

If any of her four guests had known about Hermione's years at the Slade and had coaxed her into looking out some of her own drawings, the fortune they were trying to secure for themselves and their children might have come their way in the end. They knew the maker and date of her silver and the porcelain dinner service from which they had just eaten, and knew who had painted the ancestor portraits as well as the names of the ancestors, yet Hermione herself was somehow less noteworthy. They were really more interested in the cutlery.

Why, Hermione asked herself later, lying in bed while Felicia fussed around out of sight – *why* don't they tell me about the new world, their world; its manners, marriages, modes of living? Why does no one ever make me laugh? Why don't they ask me proper questions, instead of endless mush and gush? Is it because I'm old, or unmarried – or because they're all terrified of putting a foot wrong in case I cut them out of my non-existent will?

Across the corridor, as soon as David and Elizabeth were alone, to her surprise and delight he revealed a bottle of Scotch, one of gin, and one of tonic water in his overnight case. She crept down to the pantry to look for a lemon, bumping into Felicia on her way back as she emerged from Hermione's bedroom with an armful of discarded clothes.

'I wanted a glass of lemonade,' Elizabeth enunciated clearly, and mimed squeezing a lemon.

Felicia nodded vigorously and made a face to indicate sourness. 'Very good, madam,' she said. 'God bless you and keep you in your sleep.'

Elizabeth and David almost got the giggles when she described this episode. How long is it, she thought, since we laughed like this? We ought to do it more often. It's wonderful. They swigged their drinks out of toothmugs like schoolchildren at a midnight feast, which sent them both to bed in a good temper. They kissed each other good night (a rare event) before switching off their bedside lights. Elizabeth lay open-eyed in the darkness, trying to work out when they had last made love: was it ten years ago? No, be fair, must be less than that. They'd made an effort on their twentieth wedding anniversary, though it hadn't been a great success, but not since then. So: not for the last five years. David lay beside her wondering whether, if he touched her breast, he could get, and keep, an erection. Neither moved. Both slept soundly.

At the far end of the corridor, Hermione was conjuring up the delicious memory of Henrietta's warm childish body. Hardly anyone ever touched her any more. Physical contact was confined to the occasional handshake, her relatives pecked the air beside one or both cheeks, but that was all. The sensations when Henny nestled against her or threw a soft arm around her neck and whispered hotly in her ear, were utterly delightful. The child did seem genuinely to like her. I *will* be an honorary grandma, she decided, whatever that means. And if the next child is a boy they might agree to call him Richard.

Roderick and Gaye were woken early next morning by their daughter, who had climbed out of the cot to make her way as usual into her parents' bed. They both groaned as she burrowed in beside them, giggling.

'You sleep on, darling,' Gaye said, stroking the back of her hand against her husband's jaw. 'I'll take Henny down for an early breakfast.'

'No, I'll come with you,' he answered.

Gaye thought, how odd that Hermione has never known this marital shorthand, where meaning is all in the inflexion and what counts is whether the words are accompanied by a touch, a stroke, a kiss, or eye contact. What I said just then meant, I would like you to have the luxury of a lie-in but I don't want to face Hermione alone; and Roderick understood that perfectly.

'Mummy says I've got to call you Granny,' Henrietta stated later that morning. 'Why must I? I thought my granny was dead and gone to heaven.'

Hermione was nonplussed. 'Don't you want to call me Granny?'

'I liked you being Gate Gate Aunt 'Mione,' Henny said, adding kindly, 'but I don't mind *very* much.'

'Your mama thought you might want another sort of granny . . .' Hermione stopped. It felt wrong to try to tell the child that a grandmother could be conjured out of the air. 'I am *really* your great-great-aunt,' she said. 'If you like it better, we'll leave it that way.'

'I do like it better actually,' Henrietta said.

'Very well, that's settled.'

Roderick and Gaye avoided each other's eyes.

'We're off to church,' he said. 'Will you come with us? Are you a regular attender?'

'No,' said Hermione. 'I'll stay here.'

July sunshine blazed down on Chantry's spacious lawns, filtering through the trees and gilding each leaf and petal silver and gold. The grass was springy and warm underfoot. Elizabeth wandered round in a dream of anticipation. Some of these old roses are finished, she was thinking; no point in pruning them any more, they'll have to go. I'll put in some nice English ones from David Austin. But the basic layout mustn't be changed. Some of the trees have got too high; best to cut them down and plant saplings to replace them. Plant a tree for your grandchildren to see. I'll need an extra gardener; Hamilton's overdue for retirement. There are some very good homes for them. Hope Hermione has made provision for the domestics. He might even find another job. Not *that* old. Had it easy far too long.

Her reverie was interrupted by a deep summons from David. 'Li-iz! Hell-oo-oo!' He was waving at her from the top of the flight of steps leading to the terrace at the back of the house. 'Lu-unch!' he shouted. Elizabeth read his body language at once. Nothing definite had been said. He would have waved more energetically, grinned across the distance that separated them, even executed a rudimentary caper, instead of that awkward circus seal balance. Blast! she thought. Blast and damnation, why is he so feeble? I told him what to say, spent the weekend buttering up old Meany, gave him the opportunity to say it in peace – what *more* am I supposed to do?

'Coming!' she shouted crossly and set out over the grass for a cold, alcohol-free lunch. I'll make him leave the minute we've finished eating, she thought; bugger the washing up! At least we'll avoid the traffic going back into London.

By half-past three the guests had gone and Hermione was standing in the kitchen in front of an enamel bowl of hot soapy water. It took her an hour and a half to wash and dry the luncheon things. From the pile on the table behind her she took one plate at a time, dunked it, scrubbed it vigorously on both sides, rinsed it under running water and propped it in the wooden plate-rack on her right. Then she reached for the next. She could have put them in the dishwasher but why waste electricity and besides, she was glad of a manual task. It helped her to think.

David seemed a sweet-natured man, modest, and wearing pretty well for his age. Furthermore he was a lawyer. She had wondered in the course of the weekend if he were the right person to take over after her death. He had been coming to the house for years, cherished and understood it, knew every creak and cranny. But he was very, what was the expression, hen-pecked. Elizabeth seemed so *cross* all the time. Besides, David was dangerously overweight and a lot of people got heart attacks these days. As far as she could remember, she didn't much care for their sons, Jack and the other one whose name she'd forgotten. Not that she knew them very well. Modern young men looked so *odd*, with their long hair and gaily coloured clothing. It was hard to tell who were the good ones.

For a moment she had allowed herself to believe that she could be a grandmother; not of course, a real grandmother but an adequate substitute for poor Roderick's parents, both of whom had died while he was still at school. The little girl's clear-eyed objection had put paid to that idea. You cannot lie to children. Yet leaving her money to two innocents and letting their generation deal with the problems of her possessions had seemed the perfect solution.

CHAPTER NINETEEN

April 1974

KATIE BRIDGEWATER, THE SOURCE OF MUCH SPECULATION AND disapproval at Hermione's birthday party two years earlier, was on her way to Dorset with her children, Joe and his younger sister Raimonda (nicknamed Rattie because she had always been skinny). Mother and son had taken it in turns to drive the hired Triumph Herald through the unfamiliar English countryside. After planning and saving for nearly two years, they were on the last leg of their journey from Australia to visit their remote but extremely rich second or third great-cousin by marriage. From the back seat Rattie had been giving a running commentary on the landscape.

'Sheep, Mum, look! Scrawny little buggers. Gotta be fifty in that field – guess that's what they call a sheep farm over here!'

'Keep your mouth shut, Rattie, I'm trying to think,' said her brother.

'That'll be the day,' his mother muttered. 'Now you listen to me, Joe: I don't want no complicated plans. I don't want no violence. All I want is a sight of her will. Plus' – she giggled – 'maybe a dimond tarara an' couple pretty rings.'

Her daughter spoke up: 'An' what if she's got dogs everywhere, and her stuff's locked away in a safe, and there's a bloke seven foot tall looking out for her?'

'Then if her will doesn't see us right we pick up what we can carry and leave. Not forgetting to thank her politely. You two gotta mind your manners, OK?'

Her warning was unnecessary. The great house overawed all three of them. They entered its curved and pillared stone porch as decorously as if it had been a bank or a church. They were greeted by Rosa.

'Miss Staunton's in the drawing room. She's expecting you.' Rosa lowered her voice. 'To tell you the truth she's not feeling too well. I thought she might cancel when Mrs Rachel had to cry off but she said you'd come a long way. Anyhow she didn't know where to get hold of you.'

Rosa led them through the hammerbeamed hall towards the blue parlour. Joe followed, wide-eyed. *Big* money, he was thinking; real big money! Whole place is straight out of a film.

Hermione levered herself out of her chair, grasped her stick and walked towards them with a welcoming smile and out-stretched hand. Their large brown hands enclosed her frail white one and Joe thought, this old biddy can't hardly lift a hairbrush. A scene was unreeling in his head . . . *night, darkness, music starts to go boom-boom, masked figure creeps into dimly lit room, hump in the bed sits up* . . .

'*Joe!*' his mother said. 'Say "how d'ye do".'

'How good of you to come!' Hermione said when she had eased herself carefully back into the chair. 'I expect you'd all like some tea after your long drive?'

Over rattling tea-cups, Hermione talked about Peter, Katie's husband.

'He was my aunt Sibby's eldest grandson, you know.'

She can't possibly remember him, Katie thought; Pete wasn't even twenty when he scarpered to Australia. She risked em-broidering their tale. Pete's squalid death became an act of heroism; he had died saving a small child from – from – a drunken trucker swerving along the road. Katie, his grieving widow, was left to bring up Raimonda, only four when her dad passed away, and Joe who had been six. The smallholding in Queensland became a prosperous sheep-station; their wood and corrugated iron house became one of the finest homesteads in that part of the state; while Joe found himself enrolled as a student at the University of Queensland.

'How interesting,' said Hermione dutifully. 'What are you studying?'

Joe glanced at his mother.

'Agricultural management,' Katie improvised.

'And Raimonda? What are your plans when you leave school?'

'Rattie's – Raimonda's going to be a dental hygienist,' said her mother.

'My word!' murmured Hermione. It is difficult to respond with enthusiasm when you hardly know the person concerned, or even what the proposed subject entails. 'A dental hygienist, how tremendously interesting! Peter *would* have been proud.'

When Rosa had gathered up the tea things in a tiny quartet of tinkling and ringing, porcelain cups meeting saucers diminuendo and silver teaspoons trembling to a halt, Hermione suggested that the visitors might like to go upstairs and settle in before dinner. Their strident voices tired her and the effort of making conversation, when each remark dropped like a stone at their feet, was exhausting. Her words – which to any well-brought-up English person would have meant, 'Now I need a break so could you all please leave me alone for half an hour?' – fell on deaf ears.

'Oh, we brought nothing much. Just a wash bag and my curlers,' Katie said with a laugh.

'Perhaps you'd care for a tour of the house?' Hermione offered, on the falling inflection she used for a question expecting the answer No.

'That'd be real great,' said Katie politely, 'wouldn't it, kids?'

'I'll take you round,' Hermione said. If only Rachel and Judith hadn't postponed their visit at the last moment. If only the dear girl's audition had not been changed to Monday. If only she could have practised on *my* piano. I do so wish Rachel were here. Without her, this weekend is going to be rather a trial.

275

However many rooms she missed out, it was impossible to walk round Chantry in less than forty minutes, so it was six o'clock by the time Hermione reached the sanctuary of her bedroom and her legs were heavy with tiredness.

'I don't know what's the matter with me,' she said, as Felicia knelt to unlace her shoes. 'I never used to need a rest in the afternoons but suddenly I'm good for nothing unless I manage at least half an hour on my bed.'

Felicia pointed overhead towards the Australians' bedrooms one floor above and made a mildly disapproving face.

'Not behave nice like other people in family . . .'

'I daresay. But they *are* family, you can tell. The girl has classic Campbell-Leith features and she's got the laundress's eyes – she was a famous family beauty. No, it's up to me to make them feel at home. Or at any rate, comfortable. It's Friday evening – they'll be gone by Sunday lunchtime. I've told them it's Rosa's day off.'

Felicia placed a footstool beside the high bed and positioned her hand and shoulder for Hermione to lean on, noting the deep sigh and evident effort needed to reach the haven of the cool pillow. Hermione closed her eyes and listened to the familiar rustle of garments being dropped into the linen basket or hung up in her dressing room. 'Dear Felicia . . .' she murmured gratefully. Felicia thought, madam is too good for her own good!

When the dinner-gong boomed, Joe levered himself off his bed, put his Barbarella comic on the bedside table and rummaged for a clean T-shirt. He rejected one that said: SHEEP FARMERS DO IT WITH BOOTS ON (on the back it said THE SHEEP WEAR THE BOOTS) and chose another slogan proclaiming I'M FROM QUEENSLAND – YOU HAVE BEEN WARNED. He tucked the T-shirt into his jeans to signify that this was posh, tightened his belt buckle, added a brown suede waistcoat and swaggered towards the long mirror. As an afterthought, he washed his hands in the corner basin and smeared them, still damp, over his hair. He peered into the mirror over the basin, frowned at himself under beetling brows and thought: more like Warren Beatty than Steve

McQueen. *No girl was safe once she had glimpsed his dark, brooding good looks* . . . His mother banged on the door.

'What'yer doing in there, son? Tying a bow tie?'

He tiptoed across the room and flung the door open, startling her. 'Very funny.'

Katie lowered her voice. 'I don't want either of you drinking too much tonight. OK, Joe? Rattie? Lay off the beer. Or whatever she offers.'

'OK,' they agreed.

They ate in the small dining room with Katie and Rattie on either side of Hermione, Joe opposite. Conversation was a struggle. Hermione would have liked them to tell her about their estate, the sort of crops they grew, how many staff it took to run it and did they get around it on horseback, but Katie shied away from details.

'You know we have just elected a new government?' Hermione tried.

'What do you think of that Patty Hearst, then? Robbing banks!' Katie ventured.

'You got any beer?' Joe asked.

Hermione said, 'I'm afraid not. There may be some fruit juice in the kitchen. Shall I ask Rosa?'

'Water'll do,' Joe muttered.

'Who's your favourite singer?' Rattie asked and Hermione turned to her gratefully.

'I find Maria Callas's voice *quite wonderful*,' she said.

Dinner, coffee and Bendick's Bitter Mints were concluded by half-past nine. At ten o'clock Hermione said, 'Well, time for me to turn in. Do stay down here by the fire if you'd like to . . .'

'No, no,' Katie assured her. 'Bedtime, eh guys?'

They waited until midnight, hearing various distant and ill-coordinated chimes. Joe put down his comic, Rattie pulled on a pair of gloves and Katie scratched lightly with her fingernails on both their doors. They all stood in the long, dimly lit corridor listening keenly. The old house creaked and groaned and a brisk wind rattled the trees but otherwise it was perfectly silent.

277

'She went to bed two hours ago,' Joe whispered hoarsely. 'Dead as a doornail by now.'

'Wish she was!' answered Raimonda, and Katie put a hand across her daughter's mouth to stifle her nervous giggle.

'Where we going?'

'Study,' said Katie firmly. 'If we're properly looked after in her will we'll play fair and wait our turn like the rest. By the look of her it won't be long.'

The three crept down two flights of stairs and along the corridors in a parody of caution and silence. Nothing stirred.

'She's crazy not to keep a dog,' Rattie whispered to her brother. 'A dog'd be a real bugger right now.' One of the stair treads creaked loudly. Rattie jumped and felt her heart pound frantically. Joe uttered a short bark of laughter, instantly muffled.

Step by step they descended and found their way to the study, inhaling the smells of leather and velvet. Joe switched on the torch and its beam fell upon the globe that stood on the desk. Rattie spun it on its axis.

'Hey, Mum, look, we've come all this way,' she said in a normal voice.

'Ssshh!' hissed her mother, rapidly opening and shutting drawers. Joe moved round to stand above her directing the light over her shoulder.

'Can't be nothing there or she'd have locked 'em,' Rattie said.

'No harm in having a look . . . *hey*, kids, look what *I* got!' Katie held aloft a long brown envelope marked, in Hermione's handwriting, *My Will*. 'Treasure trove!'

'Lock the door,' said Joe hoarsely. 'Lock the door and let's have a read of it.'

'No,' Katie said. 'Much better take it upstairs 'n' read it in the comfort of our own room. Then we'll decide what to do, 'n' Rats can put it back.'

They made their way stealthily back up the stairs, past family portraits that watched them through painted eyes, plump white hands resting on feathery dresses; past the seventeenth-century oak chest that stood on the first-floor landing, the sixteenth-century Dutch tallboy of blackened wood, marvellously carved and embellished, that stood where it had always stood by the turn in the stairs, past the Edwardian pen and ink sporting sketches, to the safety of Katie's room. They angled the two bedside lights on to the typed pages spread across the counterpane and craned over the Last Will and Testament of Hermione Charlotte Maria Staunton.

Katie read in a hoarse whisper, racing through the legal preliminaries. Eventually she reached the list of bequests. It was short, simple and unsatisfactory. '£250,000 to my beloved friend, Rachel née Rosenbaum Steinhaus and the same sum of money to her daughter, Judith Steinhaus'; a number of other bequests to people whose names were unfamiliar and then the crucial paragraph: '£50,000 each to all first cousins descended from my mother's family; £10,000 each to their children, theirs to dispose as they wish upon or after their twenty-first birthday; £1,000 to every great-niece or -nephew and to any great-great-nieces and nephews; and £500 to every other Campbell-Leith descendant no matter how remote, their legitimacy being properly verified.' There was a list of personal bequests: £2,500 to each of her staff, regardless of their length of service, 'if they are still in my employ at the time of my death'. This meant, Katie registered, that her children got less than Hermione's servants. Five thousand pounds to the local church 'for the restoration of the fabric of the reredos' and another £5,000 'for the perpetual care and maintenance of the memorials to my beloved father Sir Jack Staunton and my brother Richard Staunton'. Odds and ends to various schools, charities, good causes. The most significant paragraph read: 'The remainder of my goods and chattels, including all property, furniture, works of art, jewellery, silver, and all monies, shares, trust funds and other financial holdings owned by me, subject to payment of the usual duties, taxes etc. as may be in force at the time; it having first been diligently ascertained by exhaustive enquiries that there are no descendants whatsoever, legitimate or not, on my father's side extant, everything of which I die possessed shall pass directly to the oldest male heir in my mother's family, the Campbell-Leiths of Gowrie Castle in Peebleshire . . .'

The last of the eight pages was signed and dated October 1973.

'And so on and so on blah blah blah,' Katie concluded. 'Witnesses, names and numbers, thank you very much Miss Staunton our fees will be a million pounds, and let's stick a postage stamp on. Sod the tight-arsed lot of them!'

'What do we get, Mum?'

'Nothing, good as nothing,' she said, feeling the righteous anger bubble in her chest and rise up through her throat. She wanted to scream, shout, hit someone, weep. All that way, all that money saved, a thousand dollars borrowed from the bank on top, kow-towing and lying to the bank manager – and for what? Nothing. 'Not enough to cover the bloody air fare. Bloody Qantas.'

'Who gets it?'

'That pompous fart in his penguin suit. Stood up and spouted at her party. Bloke with a girl's name, forget what it was.'

'What we gonna do?'

'Take what's owing to us. Rattie, take this downstairs, quiet as you can, tippy-toes, put it back. Second drawer from the bottom, left-hand side. Ought to keep it locked. Serves her bloody right. While you do that, me 'n' Joe will have a little *think*.'

The clock struck one, the mouse crept down. In her bedroom directly beneath theirs, Felicia lay uneasily awake. She had felt the vibrations of feet passing along the corridor and, a quarter of an hour later, coming back; and now the floor vibrated again with a volley of sinister tiny creaks. What were they up to, these uncouth strangers? She crossed herself. Mary mother of Jesus keep me and all good people the world over safe this night from the evil that besets us Amen.

Ten minutes later they assembled in Katie's room. Their mother lowered her voice.

'Now here's what I reckon. You've seen the will, nothing there for us, not what's worth the trip anyhow. But your dad was a real close relation and you've got rights. You're family, same as the rest, why should you lose out? Plenty of stuff here – she won't even miss it! Me an' Joe will go downstairs and pick up a few odds 'n' ends. Joey – go get something to wrap 'em up in. No point smash-ing the stuff.'

'What about me, Mum?' Rattie asked indignantly.

'You gotta stand guard. Listen. Look. There's others in the house aren't as old, don't sleep so sound. Anything moves, you come 'n' warn us. There's a safe in her study. Probably written down the number of the combination and stuffed it in her desk, daft old galah. But it might be wired up to a burglar alarm – the police – don't wanna take no unnecessary risks, right?'

'Right, Mum,' they both said.

'Lovely. Now, guys, if anyone disturbs you, say you was looking for the toilet. And remember . . . *no violence*. We ain't criminals, we're just taking what's owing. OK – good luck, everyone. One last thing – you two had a piss? Right – let's go.'

Rattie waited until she guessed her mother and brother had reached the ground floor before setting out herself. Stand guard, my foot! She was quieter and cleverer than either of them. She'd do a little scouting on her own. Probably not touch nothing, just snoop around. For the thrill of it. She crept down the stairs keeping close to the wall where the treads were least liable to creak. On the main corridor she counted the doors before stopping outside Hermione's room. Nothing stirred. She grasped the door-handle and lifting it upwards slightly (an old trick) turned it and pushed the heavy oak door open. A thin shaft of light from between the curtains showed the outline of a high bed, from which she could hear the sound of stertorous breathing. She closed the door gently behind her, stood still and counted to fifty. The breathing did not falter.

Downstairs in the study Joe and his mother slid drawers open and shut. Papers, papers, old envelopes, more papers. They found nothing more interesting than an envelope filled with twenty-pound notes. Katie stuffed it inside her pants, where its faint scratchiness added a note of irritation to the tension of the night. Joe turned the handle of the safe just in case it had been left unlocked. *Moving like a cat, the tall black-clad figure crossed the room with practised grace, his eyes easily piercing the darkness. Music here goes boom-a-boom-a, all scary. An owl screeched outside the window: hoo-hoooo!*

'Nothing here, Mum,' said Joe. 'Safe's locked.'

Katie switched on the green-shaded lamp that stood on Hermione's desk and he jumped at the explosion of light piercing the darkness.

'You crazy or what?' he hissed. 'Someone'll see.'

'Gotta look for the combination!'

She riffled frantically through the drawers but failed to find the code. It did not occur to her to try the date of Hermione's birth.

'OK, Joey boy, on we go!'

She switched off the desk-lamp and they made their soft-footed way towards the drawing room.

Rattie crossed Hermione's bedroom to the chest of drawers that had belonged to Sir Jack Staunton. A square leather box stood on top. She took it down. Inside she could feel some rings, a creamy pearl necklace and a set of drop earrings. Small beer, but she scooped them up and stuffed them into her pocket, ignoring two large crystal drops. Gently she replaced the box thinking, this is *easy*. The throaty intake and exhalations of breath from the bed continued. Rattie's eyes had adjusted to the darkness and she could see quite clearly. How could the old bat hang those pictures of big naked broads up there for anyone to see? At least Joe did his wanker mags in private. C'mon, Rats, *concentrate*. Drawers next. The top one was full of soft silky garments and her probing fingers met nothing solid. In a corner of the second drawer, however, they encountered a long felt pouch. Its weight in her hand was satisfying; its crescent shape promising. She took it out and slid the drawer shut. As she did so the alarm system emitted a piercing and repeated whistle. Hermione sat up in bed.

'What's the matter? Felicia? Who is it?'

Momentarily, Rattie panicked. 'Shut up, you silly old bag!' she spat. 'Fucking *shut up*!'

Hermione screamed, her mouth open wide, tongue gleaming in the faint light, screamed again. Rattie grabbed the pouch, banged a hand against her pocket to make sure the other things were firmly in place and raced out. Hermione dimly saw a swift figure cross her room and heard the door wrenched open. The figure disappeared into the corridor. Behind her the silence closed down.

The sudden intrusion and wickedness by someone who was hardly more than a child was extraordinarily shocking. Hermione's body struggled to muster its aged defences. Her heart raced. Her breath came in gasps. Her mind tried to anticipate the next blow. Would the girl fetch her brother to gag her, tie her up, probably hit her if she tried to resist? She would be helpless against his youth and strength. They had been her guests, she had made them welcome in her house – had they intended to steal from her all along? To kill her? She must alert someone before they came back. Hermione staggered out of bed, heart thumping like a drum-roll, and on trembling legs crossed the room to the chest of drawers. Without disabling the alarm, she slid the second drawer open and shut three times, hoping it would set off a repeated alarm down at the police station. The whistle shrieked like lightning through her tranquil bedroom. Clumsily, she struggled back to bed and slumped against the pillows breathing hard, eyes wide and staring, teeth chattering, listening for the stealthy footsteps of a man who might kill her.

Joe and his mother were in the blue parlour wrapping a third group of Meissen figures in one of Joe's T-shirts when they heard the scream from upstairs. They stood like pillars of salt, their eyes locking through the darkness.
'*What* the *fuck?*' said Joe.
'*Don't move!*' hissed Katie. 'Stay where you are. Listen . . .'
They listened. A troubling interval of silence; then feet racing lightly along the corridor and up the stairs. Silence. Then the distant alarm shrieked three times. Silence.
'Now!'
They sprinted up the stairs two at a time, Joe clasping the bulging T-shirt against his chest. Katie flung open the door to Rattie's room. Her daughter's eyes were wide and her face blanched but in her upraised hand she held a tall diamond tiara. Joe thought, man oh man, just like the Statue of Liberty!
Rattie held out the tiara to her mother, unable to suppress a wild

giggle. 'See, Mum: got what you ordered!'

Katie said, 'Right – chuck the stuff into your bags – Joey, start the car – *hurry!*'

Drums thundered to his running footsteps as he swung round the banister and raced for the car . . . With a powerful vroom-vroom it sliced through the gravel . . . the girl, blond hair flying, tits jumping up and down, vaulted over its open side . . . the car slewed round as Bonnie and Clyde roared into the night.

Clothes and comics were stuffed into a couple of backpacks, the Meissen figures shoved into one corner. A shepherdess's hand broke off; a violin from another group had already cracked. The two women hurried down the stairs for the last time, past the portrait's dark eyes – so like Rattie's – towards the waiting car.

When the sound of their footsteps had died away, Hermione waited for five minutes, then levered herself with infinite exhaustion and will-power off her bed. My world is ending, she thought. Her heart was pattering a long ominous riff, like drums at the circus before the entry of the lion-tamer, spangled and glorious in red, flanked by his roaring lions. She crept along the corridor, one shoulder against the wall, pausing at every step, towards the adjoining room. She leaned over the narrow iron bed, twitched the bedcovers and stroked Felicia's face. The girl lay rigid, eyes wide and pupils fixed, paralysed with terror. Screams – people moving secretly at night – running feet. The figures from her nightmare were back. She had beseeched God and Hermione to keep her safe but nobody could protect her from the horror which blocked her way and would not let her move. It was pitiless.

'Felicia . . .' Hermione moaned with a final effort. 'Oh Felicia, you must *help me* . . .'

PART SIX

Quiet Consummation Have

April–November 1974

CHAPTER TWENTY

WITH HERMIONE SLUMPED ON THE FLOOR BESIDE HER BED, FELICIA was galvanized at last. She woke Rosa, who dialled for an ambulance. It arrived in less than twenty minutes. The ambulance men were kind and competent. One listened to Hermione's heart and pronounced her alive. Her inert body was manoeuvred on to a stretcher and, balancing it skilfully between them, they negotiated the stairs, crossed the great hall without glancing to either side and slid the stretcher gently into the back of the waiting vehicle. It was dark, no stars, drizzling lightly. The Bridgewaters had vanished into the night.

Felicia had tried to insist on travelling in the ambulance but Rosa managed to dissuade her by pointing out that she could be of little help to Hermione.

'She's her maid cum companion,' Rosa explained to the ambulance man, 'but she's very nervy. She'll not be much use at a time like this.'

Felicia was uttering impassioned prayers and tender cooing sounds which meant: I'm sorry I didn't protect you! I knew they were villains! I should have warned you! Forgive me . . . don't die. I beg you not to *die*.

Moved by her anguish, one of the men said reassuringly before closing the doors, 'I don't think she'll die, lovey. Sooner we get 'er to hospital, the better. You relax now. She's in good hands, don't you worry. She'll live.'

His comforting words were heard at some deep level by Hermione, spiralling between shock and safety, reality and dream. She reacted as she had always done: not by letting go, but by holding on. Instead of surrendering to the tug and pull of the waves through whose swell she was floating tranquilly towards death; instead of allowing herself the luxury of drifting easily into the distance, Hermione rallied. With a huge effort, she summoned the last of her will-power to battle against the deceptively sluggish current. Had she been drowning, this would have been the moment when she kicked out, gulped air and headed for the shore. I am going to live, she resolved. *I am going to live!*

As the ambulance negotiated the winding country roads as fast as the law permitted, its driver heard the blaring of a police siren speeding rather faster from somewhere nearby.

'Cor blimey,' he muttered to his colleague in the front seat, 'no incidents for a week and suddenly two come along at once!'

His mate nodded. 'Never rains but it pours,' he agreed.

The district general hospital stabilized Hermione's condition, kept her in intensive care for two days and then, lacking the expertise and equipment to keep her alive should she suffer a second crisis, sent her by ambulance to London. Hermione was awake and conscious when she arrived at the Middlesex Hospital.

The nurse on reception, looking at her notes, said cheerfully, 'Happy birthday, dear!'

'Wha'?' Hermione asked indistinctly, having not fully recovered control over her tongue.

'It says here, d.o.b. 14 April 1902. Today's the fourteenth of April. Many happy returns!' *She'll be lucky*, thought the perky little blonde; looks in a bad way. Still, she's had her three-score and ten. The formalities of booking in a new patient completed, a porter was directed to take her to the intensive care beds on the fifth floor.

'ICU – then she'll go on to Sharp's ward.'

Hermione, exhausted by the transfer, had her eyes closed when the young house doctor came to have a look at her. She felt a nurse's cool fingers on her pulse and heard them talking above her head.

'I'll confirm with the prof,' said a young male voice, 'but my guess is she may have to spend several more days in intensive care.' As they moved out of earshot he added, 'I don't like the look of her. Colour's wrong and her heartbeat's all over the place. Monitor and let me know.'

'Right,' the young woman replied.

Hermione tried to say, next time her pulse and temperature were checked, 'Every time I start to fall asleep someone comes and wakes me up again . . . do, please, just leave me in peace, would you?' but although her lips moved slightly, only an indistinct murmur emerged.

Modern medicine performs miracles every day on old and young, rich and poor alike. In the battle for Hermione's life, one side possessed the latest and most costly machinery; green zigzags, keenly scrutinized; a battery of pills and stimulants to regulate the heartbeat and thin the blood; a network of fine plastic lines inserted into veins providing nourishment and sustenance, over-seen and controlled by an orderly bustle of nurses and junior doctors. They checked Hermione's eyes, lips, skin colour, chest, heart rate, systole and diastole, food intake, out-take, liquid ingested and excreted, themselves in turn supervised by the mighty god, her consultant. Ranged against them was the insistent pull of old age, a heart shocked beyond its normal ability to recover, a body that had dragged itself through life unaided and unaccompanied and lacking the one beloved face to beckon it back. In this battle, modern medicine won the first round, at least.

A week later, Hermione woke up, fully alert for the first time, to find a young doctor standing beside her scanning her most recent notes. His eyes met hers and registered a keen intelligence.

'Ah, good,' he said. 'You're looking a lot better today. I'm Dr Gordon-Lockhart and you must be Miss Hermione Staunton?'

There was a pause; such a long pause that he wondered whether her ears or her speech or, worst of all, her mind had been affected.

At last she said slowly, 'Yes. How do you do?'

'How do you do? Do you know what day of the week it is?'

'I'm afraid not.'

'Do you know what month it is?'

'April – I hope. I came here on April the fourteenth,' she said, speaking slowly but making perfect sense.

'Do you know what year it is?'

'1974.' (*Theventhy*-four, she enunciated with difficulty.)

'Excellent. Now for the jackpot – who's the present Prime Minister?'

'Harold Wilson.'

'Very good indeed. Nothing wrong with the brainbox.'

Hermione peered at his name-badge and having verified that it bore the name he had just spoken, said, 'Now may I ask you a question?' (*Quethun.*)

'Fire away.'

'Is Gordon your Christian name?'

'No, though lots of people call me Gordon, or Dr Lockhart. My Christian name is Andrew. My surname is Gordon-Lockhart. Double-barrelled. It *is* a bit confusing.'

'Oh.'

There was a long pause, during which Hermione breathed deeply and waited until her heartbeat had slowed. Trained to patience, even when most impatient, especially towards those recently snatched from the jaws of death, Andrew Gordon-Lockhart stood beside the bed smiling down at her. She tucked her hand under the bedclothes in case he tested her all-too-rapid pulse. Be still, my beating heart! She looked steadily up at him and thought, My whole life has been moving towards this moment.

'I used to know a Gordon-Lockhart. *Sandy* Gordon-Lockhart.'

'Same name as my grandfather,' he said.

'In Dorset. When we were children.'

'In that case it *was* my grandfather. What a coincidence. Now, I just want to run through your vital signs before the consultant starts his round. Any questions are for him to answer, really, not me. I'm just the junior house doctor. Galley-slave.'

Next time he stopped beside her bed to make conversation and verify that Hermione was compos mentis and not imagining things – so many female patients fantasized about their doctors – Andrew Gordon-Lockhart said: 'Quite a coincidence – you and Grandpa knowing one another! When was it again?'

'A very long time ago. We were both children. He lived in a house called –' her tongue stumbled thickly over its pronunciation and she tried again: '*Otterbourne* Court. We were neighbours.'

Seems sane enough, Andrew concluded. Otterbourne was the name of their fake-posh hotel. Department of funny coincidence. Light-headed with tiredness, he resisted the urge to do a John Cleese department of funny walks imitation.

'I don't suppose he realizes you're here?'

'No.'

He thought for a moment. Don't want to pre-empt Grandpa; ought to ask him first – but he's spent a lot of time recently in search of his childhood, probably as a way of occupying himself since Granny died, and here, undoubtedly, was someone who'd been part of it.

'Would you like me to tell him? He lives in Scotland nowadays, but I have an idea he's in London at the moment. Could you cope with a visit?'

Hermione had spent more than sixty years waiting for her true love to return. She had never made any move towards him. She could have found him, had she set her mind to it, but she had chosen not to search. The small boy she had first known, even the twelve-year-old she had last seen, could bear no resemblance whatever to the grown man he had become, let alone the old man he must now be. Suppose he were pompous and overbearing like Vivian Blythgowrie? Suppose he were bent, arthritic, blind? It wouldn't *matter*, she thought fiercely; and besides, if that were so his grandson would scarcely have suggested a meeting. What if he were married, and brought his wife? No, that she could not bear.

'No hurry, Miss Staunton. Think about it, and let me know next time I see you. Today's Friday. I'm taking a few days off after Sunday . . . final exams coming up; need a bit of time to cram. Could you let me know by Sunday, do you think? He'll probably head back to Scotland next week.'

'Yes of course.' Better make sure. 'Is his wife in London too?'

'My grandmother died – let me think, eighteen months, coming up for two years ago now.'

'Oh, I didn't know. I am sorry.'

'Yes, she was a dear. Well, Miss Staunton, I'll leave you in peace. Try and get some sleep.'

Sandy! Suddenly he had materialized, stepping out from behind the black magician's curtain, smiling and bowing – look, it was an illusion all along! I was always there, you just couldn't see me! Yet while invisible to her he had lived a whole life – married, become a father and now grandfather of this competent young doctor who possessed the power to reunite her with her one true love. Hermione felt her heart thunder so hard in her breast that she looked down at her nightdress, expecting to see it rise and fall to that hectic motion. I must slow it down, she thought; this is bad for me. I may still die and so *much* is about to happen.

Hermione thought about many things besides Sandy. During the long white hours in bed, while her body and mind gradually recovered their powers and her heart pumped laboriously, she thought about the three Bridgewaters, her assailants. They had fled to Australia, presumably, with her mother's tiara – not that she cared about *that*. She supposed they were wicked. Although coarse and grasping, they had not seemed wicked. The word wickedness was too easily bandied about; flung at people who were chiefly callous, thoughtless, harassed, ignorant. The men who had shot Felicia's father and raped his wife and daughters – *they* were wicked. Not those three. After Peter's death, they must have struggled to keep going, never knowing the ease of having *enough*. The family had ridiculed their manners and their appetite at her birthday party, yet they *were* Bridgewaters and judging by her looks, the girl more Campbell-Leith than any of them. How glibly the rich condemn people who lead lives of quiet desperation. She thought about Billy Brymer. He had humiliated her, raped her and burdened her with a lifelong secret but suppose she *had* borne his child? If it had been a son, that boy would now be sole inheritor of Chantry . . . a fine revenge for Billy and Elias Brymer, Dorset born and bred for generations, and for all the anonymous men and women who had served her parents and herself. Was it wicked of Billy to want to redress that balance? I don't *know*, she thought wearily. I am nearly at the end of my life and I still don't know.

She used to believe that her mother was wicked. Phoebe had deliberately set out to crush Hermione's self-respect. She had belittled her talent as an artist and reduced her to a mawkish painter of pet animals. She had sent Florabelle back to the squalor and misery from which Hermione had rescued her. She had nipped any tentative friendships in the bud, unless they involved good-looking young men of her own social standing, in which case – as with Gerald Shebeare – she had annexed them. Yet Hermione had never understood why Phoebe had shunned, or been shunned by, her family – the 'Scots pines' whose children and grand-children, nephews and nieces and remotest descendants crowded around her now when she no longer needed them. Her sickroom was crammed with blowzy bouquets and fulsome get-well cards. It would have been crammed with the senders had her consultant not banned all visitors.

Hermione's seventy-two years had been sheltered by money and although she had worked hard she knew nothing at first hand of the rough and tumble of the world. She had read about it, seen it on television and heard its consequences discussed in the board-room. She was well informed and far from naive. But only during the war, when she had been 'the Com', had she lived an ordinary life and worked among ordinary people. Those, she realized wist-fully, had been her best and most fulfilling years. Five out of seventy-two! Not much to boast about.

Plenty of people might have thought the Staunton Trading Company worth boasting about, and she knew without conceit that she had made a decent job of it. Since the war she had gradually assumed more authority. The bulky, dark-suited men who sat behind leather-covered desks guarded by a flurry of telephones and secretaries took it for granted that *they* ran it, but it was her watchful eye that forced them to adhere to her father's guiding rules. Sir Jack had embodied a philanthropic approach to business that, nowadays, was considered outdated and almost absurd . . . the notion that it was possible to treat employees and customers alike with fairness and courtesy, to look after their interests and still make money.

Hermione suspected that his principles would be jettisoned as soon as she was gone. Without her, the STC – as people called it sloppily, though she herself never did – would soon be riven by union disputes and boardroom struggles. She could not bear to think of it losing its good name. The Staunton Trading Company had been a by-word for probity. *Probity* was not Vivian's cup of tea at all. He paid lip-service while she was alive and he still felt the need to curry favour. Once she was dead, the old ways would be abandoned. He might call the company after his side of the family: not Blythgowrie – heavens, no, they wouldn't pollute the noble house by associating it with *commerce* – but Jervis, perhaps, and her father's honourable name would not even survive as the S in STC. The last reminder of the Stauntons would have vanished, with no one to defend the vigorous roots of which she herself was now the only branch.

And Sandy. Her eyes drooped. Has been married. Is now a widower. May have several children. Good-looking boy, the grandson. No resemblance though. I am tired, she told herself. I will have a little rest and then think about Sandy.

News had spread fast through the family network; the news that Hermione had had a heart attack; was in intensive care; might die, was bound to die, would soon die; had or had not made a will. The one thing everybody agreed upon was that she had no obvious heir. Vivian Blythgowrie, by common consent, was the most probable – but did Hermione *like* him? Besides, he had no son. She might give everything away to her favourite charity. What the hell was that? Perhaps the money would go to some musical foundation – that Jewish woman, Rachel Rosenbaum: what's her name nowadays? No one could remember, so Rachel was left in peace. To dogs or cats or horses? But Hermione had never seemed particularly fond of animals. Where then? To whom? To you but not to me?

All this pent-up speculation had to go somewhere and much of it was dissipated on the telephone. People would ring each other up – concerned at first ('Is there any more news? Have you been to see her yet? No, me neither – they're not letting anyone near her, apparently. Sounds pretty serious.') then shrewd and bargaining. The conversation usually began with an attempt at subtlety.

'Wasn't it *dreadful* about the theft? Poor Hermione!'

'Awful, yes. Did they ever catch the Australians?'

'Looks as though they slipped the country before anyone realized what had happened. Luckily they were interrupted and not much is missing. Apart from the Staunton tiara.'

'That alone must be worth a quarter of a million. Appalling. Police doing anything?'

'She never wore it. *Such* a waste. Phoebe had some amazing stuff.'

'Gigolos probably nicked it.'

'Darling, *hush!*' Stifled laughter. Serious again.

'Felicia might know about the jewellery.'

'Oh, *Felicia*! She's hopeless! I gather she didn't even wake *up*.'

Then, slyly, 'Did Hermione ever drop any hints? About – you know – I mean –?'

'Good heavens no. Talk about *money*? Not a hope.'

Vivian Blythgowrie was by now sufficiently confident to buy a small flat for his mistress, in which she was installed with grateful squeals and big hugs for her kind protector. He kept the title deeds in his own name and the telephone number ex-directory.

The get-well cards continued to pile up in Hermione's pristine small room. Roderick Campbell-Leith telephoned, his authority penetrating the cocoon that the hospital had thrown around her.

'Aunt Hermione? Roderick here! No, don't worry, I can hear you perfectly. Look here, what's all this about a *heart attack*?'

'Only a very minor one,' Hermione assured him.

'Are you being well cared for? Who's your consultant? Would you like me to make enquiries about the best man in the field? Second opinion? What about coming to us to convalesce? Henny often asks about you and of course you haven't even *met* the new one yet, little Maria. Yes, gorgeous baby. Gaye's fine.'

Pause to signal change of gear. New, more sombre voice.

'I take it everything's being properly taken care of in your absence? Arthur Jenkins doing his stuff and all that?'

People always seem to imagine that if women are large they must be insensitive, thought Hermione – I wonder why, since the exact opposite is true?

She stopped giving vague replies and said firmly, 'I made my will some time ago, Roderick dear. Everything's in perfect order.'

'Aunt Hermione, I didn't mean *that*.'

Damn, he thought; damn and blast! He wound down the conversation with fervent expressions of sympathy and concern and signed off with the assurance that Gaye sent lots of love.

Hermione knew she was only toying with the idea of not seeing Sandy. She was prolonging the delightful period of anticipation, knowing that it might end in bitter disappointment. Not that she could possibly be disappointed in him . . . old, grey, bent, gaga; fat, bald, forgetful, querulous – it made no difference how he looked or behaved, he was her only love. Would he remember their childhood nicknames for each other? Would he remember the dandelion clocks they blew, or the afternoon with the cow-pats? Would he remember the chandelier in the attic? Ayesha, Leo Vincey, his dog . . . what was the name of his dog? Help, she thought, my mind must have been affected – I've forgotten the name of his dog! Billy? – no, idiot, not *Billy* – Bob? – that's it, Bob. She could remember the dog, paws propped at the foot of a tree, whining at the pair of them twenty feet aloft, and how Sandy had looked down and called out: 'Bobby!' That's it, *Bobby*!

His dog was called Bobby, of course! Dear old Bobby.

Would he remember anything, or – like her – everything?

Next day when Dr Gordon-Lockhart came to see her, she said, 'Yes is the answer to your question. *Yes.* If your grandfather is still in London, and *if* he'd like to see me – yes, it would be lovely to meet again.'

'Good. Any particular day suit you?'

'Since all my visitors are being kept at bay – *thank* you for that – it doesn't make any difference. Whenever is best for him.'

'Bonzo!'

'I beg your pardon?'

'Sorry. I mean, *good.*'

Hermione laughed and her young doctor said, 'Excellent sign, the patient's first laugh.'

Sandy Gordon-Lockhart was not immediately convinced that he wanted to see Hermione. Memories of her were bound up with memories of his own childhood, the feeling of himself as a boy – young, free and easy, no aches and pains, senses acute, no need for hearing aid or reading glasses, body unblemished by decline, mind unaware of what the future would hold and untroubled by any doubts. He had lived and revelled in the present. As an adult, the memory of Hermione had provided a haven whenever he was bored, frustrated or oppressed. When Chloë bewailed the lack of congenial company 'in this god-forsaken outpost of civilization' or some numskull of a junior abased himself for making a mistake, or an insincere foreign diplomat professed admiration for the British way of life – 'Your national sport the *cricket*! This sums up British character, the cricket!' – at such times Sandy would retreat to the green summer landscape where he and Hermione had leaped and climbed and crawled and balanced and run and rolled and all but flown through long afternoons, testing their strength and daring. Outwardly the supportive husband or judicious envoy, creasing his brow in apparent concentration, he would re-enter the body of a lithe brown boy to play with Hermione in the woods and ponds of their secret places. She had inhabited his dreams and enlivened his fantasies. She had been the longed-for, the archetypal female, her body smooth and fluent, wishes always parallel to his own, eyes bright, hair uncoiling, nymph to his shepherd, dryad to his Actaeon. Despite his marriage – and he had been *fond* of Chloë – and although he had occasionally trifled, briefly, unimportantly, with discreet young women, Hermione had been his only love.

Yet he had not been a bad husband. Those were Chloë's last words to him – still grudging, even on her deathbed – 'You haven't been a bad husband, Sandy.' There was no answer to that, even if she had lived to hear it, so he had folded her small cold hands inside his own, bent his head over their twenty fingers and closed his eyes. With these fingers I thee stroked, he thought; with those fingers thou me touched. Our withered grey hands gave each other pleasure when they were smooth and we were young. How often, as I bounced above you, I stared into your closed eyes, wanting to bore into your brain and discover your true thoughts. *Did* I ever please you or did you just endure me, doing your wifely duty?

Chloë had not spoken again. She died five minutes later, after a short choking struggle. *Cheyne-Stoking*, they had called those desperate last breaths: ironic, since she'd been a chain-smoker all her life. In the guilty, frozen hours after she had stopped breathing he consoled himself with the reflection that theirs had been a marriage achieved and completed, without scandal or shame and with no more than the usual share of melodrama or reproach. It had lasted forty-five years and after the first two he had ceased to love her in any active sense. He hadn't been a bad husband – she was right – though probably what she meant was that he hadn't been a good one. Having penetrated her body, he had tried her mind and found it empty. She retained her sexual desirability, he could tolerate living beside her, preserve the formalities, be pleasant and attentive and, in the final months and weeks of her illness, genuinely dutiful. H. Minor had always been the time-bomb that could destroy his marriage and probably his career as well, were it ever to be detonated. But she had not made contact and he could not.

His grandson shattered this equanimity when he rang with the news that an old lady, claiming to have known him as a boy, had been admitted to his ward. She was very ill, Andrew warned him over the phone; one heart attack already, another on the cards; could die any time. Name was *Staunton* – ring any bells? – Miss Hermione Staunton.

'Has she *asked* to see me?'

'Not exactly. I was the one who suggested you might like to and she thought about it for a few days and then sort of . . . acquiesced. She didn't push it. Like, I think you could say no and she wouldn't be offended.'

'No chap hovering?' Husband; son; male of other description?

'Her notes say she's never been married. No children either. Plenty of relatives waiting to rush in . . .'

Where angels fear to tread, Sandy thought.

'Can I let you know? Take a bit of thinking about. Helluva long time ago – water under the bridge – all the clichés. Let me mull it over. Don't say anything yet.'

Well, so now she had returned. Couple of years younger than himself so she must be over seventy. He'd heard about poor old Dick – gone in the first war – and her parents must have died long ago. She'd never married. That was odd – or maybe not odd. Women of her generation often didn't. Devoted themselves to good works, became headmistresses or in this case ran her father's business? Staunton Trading – a huge company – little Hermione Staunton must be pretty well off by now. Presumably she'd inherited the lot. No wonder the relatives were gathering, perched in the surrounding trees, watching, preening, biding their time.

That realization decided him. Hermione needed protecting. He rang the hospital and asked for the ward; waited while an overworked switchboard operator tried intermittently to connect him to its one busy line; asked a nurse to page Andrew and finally heard his grandson's crisp, harassed voice.

'Gordon-Lockhart.'

'Hello, old man. Grandpa here. Won't keep you. Your patient – Miss Staunton – course I'll pay her a visit. What are the hours?'

'For you, Grandpa, any time. The prof's given her permission to start having visitors from tomorrow. She mustn't get agitated.'

'Righty-ho then. Tomorrow. Around eleven. You going to be within reach?'

'I'll try and stick around. Depends.'

'Good-oh. Tell her for me, will you? See you tomorrow.'

The deed was done. Now he must plan his strategy. Best rule when meeting strangers was: try and talk to them in their own language. Disarms them. Makes you seem on their side and gets them on to yours. But he and Hermione weren't strangers – and their only shared language was the secret web of nicknames and make-believe they had woven around each other. He had been H. Major and she H. Minor. They had acted out *King Solomon's Mines* on sunny days and played board games when it was wet, ensconced in her nursery or his, alone except for hovering nannies. If that was their common language then that was the one he must use. The vocabulary of 'Sorry to hear you haven't been well' and 'How are you feeling now?' or 'Very good to see you again' would blow away the magic and it might never be recaptured.

Sandy entered Hermione's room with a jaunty step, went over to her bed, pulled up a plastic-covered armchair and sat down. She had braced herself to offer condolences on the death of his wife – it was quite recent, after all – but without preliminaries he said, 'Now I'm going to give you a test, like Penelope did Ulysses when he came back after twenty years. To prove that you are who you say you are.'

She blinked. Strong, dazzling.

'What if I fail?'

'You won't.'

She shook her head to clear her vision – not vigorously, like a child, but like the old person she was, just a barely perceptible movement.

'Well then, I shall test you too.'

'All right.'

'You go first.'

Sandy asked, 'What secret name did I have for you?'

Hermione, instantly: 'H. Minor. And yours?'

'H. Major. Easy. Your go.'

'What did I take you up to the top of the house to see?'

'The chandelier in the attic.'

'Right. Now your turn.'

'What was the name of our companion and what was it?'

'Bobby. A dog. Golden retriever.'

'Labrador; otherwise right.'

'Have I proved myself enough?' she asked.

'I'd say so, yes . . . what about me?'

You are you, only you, never anybody else.

'Oh yes, Major – yes, you have. It's you all right. And I am me.'

Andrew, lingering nearby in case of trouble, entered Hermione's room.

'It's *her*, Andrew!' his grandfather said. 'It really is Hermione . . . after *how* many years?'

'Sixty . . .' she supplied. 'Nearly sixty-two. We haven't seen each other since September 1912.'

'Good grief, really? More than sixty years!'

'Major, what *was* Penelope's question?' Hermione asked.

'Ignorant as ever! That infernal governess – never taught you a damned thing – what was she called? That I *have* forgotten.'

'Miss Protheroe.'

'That's the one. Go on, Andrew, you tell her: how did Penelope recognize Ulysses?'

'I've no idea,' Andrew said, grinning.

'Hopeless. Both hopeless. Only *he* knew that their bed was built round the trunk of an olive tree! *That*'s how she could be sure he wasn't an impostor.'

'OK. So it's her?' Andrew asked.

'She knows all our private nicknames, and the name of my dog.'

'Bobby,' said Hermione, and in her bubbling voice it sounded more like Halleluia.

Sandy smiled radiantly into her pale but ecstatic face.

'That's it. Bobby. Dear old Bobby. He was a lovely dog.

Remember how he used to rush ahead and then come back and bounce round us?'

'Of course,' she said; and once more the image of long-dead Bobby, eyes bright, tail wagging, circled them both before dashing off again to nose joyously through the undergrowth.

CHAPTER TWENTY-ONE

SANDY GORDON-LOCKHART HAD ALWAYS THOUGHT HE LIKED ONLY small, slender women yet, even flat on her back in bed and diminished by illness, it was obvious that Hermione had grown up to be immensely large. Of course, it couldn't matter less. The only thing that mattered was that he had found her again and by some miracle she was *still her*. Hermione, he thought incredulously, is what she always was, my magnet and anchor, my nut-brown girl. Blood raced like molten gold round his body, rejuvenating him, filling him with energy and eagerness. He felt, preposterously, as if in this state he could read without glasses, hear with the sharpness of youth, shin up trees again. The retired diplomat was a disguise that he could cast off, like a snake's skin, to reveal the tawny-haired, firm-limbed boy within. She has brought me back to life and metamorphosed me into Sandy, he marvelled. How her gaze pierced me! How she scrutinized my face! Our eyes clung to each other, verifying the past. I am certain she loves me too.

He began to make plans.

That evening he wrote her a letter, the latest in a long line of letters but the first she would receive. As he sat in the dark red study of his London flat, a room lined with boxes of documents, books, and the papers he had intended to sort, label and store, the walls receded as though a stage had revolved. He became one among several score of boys in black suits, sitting in Lower School after breakfast on Sunday, the time designated for 'writing home'. His pen was not a gold-tipped Parker but a tapering wooden pen-holder with a scratchy nib slotted into one end, needing to be dipped into an inkwell every couple of lines. His handwriting became larger and rounder; a schoolboy's careful script.

Dear Minor,
It was topping to see you today – hang on, I'm getting confused! Start again. *My dear Hermione*, I was so glad to see you this morning, thanks to the miraculous intervention of my grandson. We have everything to discuss and discover. As soon as you are pronounced fit to travel I should like to whisk you up to Scotland, to Ellismuir, and ensconce you in the second-best bedroom – reputed to have sheltered Mary Queen of Scots on her flight from . . . no, I jest. Ellismuir isn't nearly old enough for that. But it is comfortable and can be made warm, if warmth is what you need, and there is plenty of room for you and in all likelihood a couple of nurses as well. We shall restore you to health and then see what is to become of us.
I am so glad to have found you, I can't put it into words.

He paused, unsure how to end, and simply wrote, *Love, H. Major.*

Two days later, returning to the hospital to discuss plans in detail, he found her room thronged with people. She was propped up on pillows, combed into neatness. Catching sight of him over their heads, she signalled silent appeal. Andrew was nowhere to be seen. Sandy checked his stride and went in search of the nearest authority figure. In his most authoritative voice – the one that implied, you're the chap in charge, I'm your sort of chap, let's sort this out – he said: 'Miss Staunton – over there in a private room attached to Sharp's ward – is surrounded by visitors. She's just had a heart attack. I don't know who gave permission. Last week visitors were banned. Can someone clear her room?'

The consultant stopped a passing nurse and peered at her name badge.

'Be a good girl, Yvonne, get that mob out of the side-ward off Sharp's. Say they're disturbing your patient. Look, just *do* it.'

Yvonne was in her first year and not used to telling people what to do but her terror of the consultant was much greater. She swished in and routed the relatives. Sandy, hovering, overheard their comments as they trailed down the corridor. I was right, he thought: she *is* in need of care and protection. What a heartless bunch. Come, live with me and be my love.

Going into her room he said, 'H. Minor, high time you visited Scotland!'

'How can I? I'm stuck here. Did you see my visitors just now? They're beginning to get me down: I was really rather glad when they went.'

'You're not answering my question. When can we get you up to Scotland? They couldn't come near you there.'

'You mean, just disappear? Oh Major, what fun! But I'm supposed to be not very well . . .'

'We'll hire a nurse. An experienced, capable woman who knows about tickers.'

I know about hearts, she thought, gazing at him, and now that mine has found you again it beats like a metronome.

He sat down beside her bed and covered her blue-veined hands with his own.

'Did you get my letter?' he asked.

'What letter?'

'I wrote to you – oh, Monday.'

'They're hopeless with post here. Not yet. But look, Major, if I did come and stay could Felicia come too?'

'Who, or for that matter *what*, is Felicia, pray?'

'Felicia's a young woman, my sort of companion cum dresser, what Mama would have called a lady's maid. She's had an awful life, poor creature, and she's become rather dependent on me. She's also *most* efficient.'

'Then Felicia must come too. I'll arrange it. Let me check how soon you might be let out. Can you *write* – sign things – all that?'

'My handwriting's still pretty wobbly. Major, why did you never *write* to me in the old days? You *promised* . . .'

'*What?*'

'When you went away to school. I looked and looked for the post every morning. You never wrote once.'

'Minor, that's piffle. I never heard such utter tosh. I wrote all the time! *You* never answered.'

'I never had a single letter from you. I sent you *heaps*. I put them in the hall to be posted and they all went. In the end I gave up.'

'Someone must have swiped them. I wrote dozens of times, promise.'

'But why should anyone take our letters?'

'Haven't the foggiest. Probably your beastly mother.'

'Probably,' she agreed, thinking – so Mama was even jealous of *him*. We have layers to unravel yet. She met his eyes and they exchanged a complicated smile.

Sandy concluded, 'So I'll arrange for you to come, with a nurse or two and Felicia if you want her, to my house in Scotland. Ellismuir. What's your address?'

'Same as ever. Chantry Manor.'

'You're still at *Chantry*? Good grief! I was down in those parts not long ago – with young Andrew, as it happens – but it never occurred to me you might still be there. I thought they'd have turned it into a hotel or conference centre or something vile like that.'

'Well, they haven't. I still live there. It looks pretty much the same as when you knew it, except that I got rid of all my mother's gloomy Scottish furniture.'

'My house is *full* of gloomy Scottish furniture!'

'I don't mind,' she said radiantly. 'I shan't mind a bit.'

'Minor, we've got so much to talk about.'

'I know. A lifetime. Let's eat it slowly.'

A young nurse came in and smiled at the sight of two dear old crocks holding hands and looking at each other with dopey expressions.

'Sorry to interrupt you two love-birds,' she chirruped, 'but it's time to do Hermione's observations.'

'It's pronounced Her*mi*one. Like Persephone, not Creon,' Sandy told her sharply. 'Or if that's too much trouble you could try calling her "Miss Staunton". What are "observations"? Or rather, what are you observing?'

The nurse gaped at him. 'Sorry?' she said and then, recovering her small authority, 'I wonder if you'd mind waiting outside?' That usually did the trick. If not, you whipped out a bedpan. Nobody stayed for that.

'Come back . . .' said Hermione after his retreating figure.

'Of course.'

Before Hermione left the Middlesex Hospital, Sandy – with a word of endorsement from his grandson – arranged a private talk with her consultant.

'She's seventy-two years old,' Professor Eaton told him, 'and her basic health is good. She's not overweight, she has never smoked, she says she doesn't drink and she still takes a certain amount of exercise. Lungs are fine; limbs are fine, no sign of arthritis. Memory and concentration seem good. But that heart's always going to be a problem from now on. Being on the tall side and, to use a non-medical term, *statuesque*, Miss Staunton's blood has further to circulate so the heart has to pump harder. All's well till something like this happens, and then the weak points are exposed. On the one hand it could happen again at any time; on the other hand, well looked after and regularly monitored, she could – I'm only saying *could*, no guarantees in our business – she *could* live for another ten years. Perhaps even longer. You say you've known her all her life?'

'Ye-es . . .' Sandy prevaricated.

'What did her parents die of?'

'Mother: I don't know. Father: not sure either.'

'Any siblings?'

'One brother, died in the First World War.'

'Children?'

'None, as far as I know.'

As far as he knows, the consultant thought. What sort of lifetime friendship is this?

'I'm going to send her home with a strong recommendation that she should have a qualified nurse with her day and night – which means on twenty-four-hour shift, so you're going to be paying for three. It's a considerable outlay; but for peace of mind, at any rate for the first couple of months, it's either that or a convalescent home.'

'I was hoping she could come and convalesce with me.'

'Where?'

'Scotland. The Lowlands.'

'Sounds all right. Nice and quiet. Good air. Space in the house for three nurses? They'll expect a bedroom each.'

'Plenty of room.'

'Right. Good. Now then, the nurses will be in charge of all that side of things, but let me talk you through her medication . . .'

He decided they would travel up to Glasgow by rail, transferring to a little local train that went as far as Carstairs, to be collected from there by a driver in a Land-Rover. Hermione thought the train journey was luxury incarnate. They had a first-class compartment to themselves, requisitioned in advance by Sandy. She lay on a rigid stretcher placed across the seats by the window, Sandy next to her, facing the engine. Felicia was on the other side by her feet, back to the engine. Three cardiac nurses sat in the next compartment gossiping about famous patients they had cared for in the past, breaking off every now and again to sway in and check Hermione's indications. She had tried to protest, horrified at such extravagance.

'It'll cost a fortune,' she said, when Sandy explained the arrangements.

'Minor, you've *got* a fortune,' he told her.

'But it's a crime to waste it.'

'Listen to me: it isn't *waste*. Waste would be if we tried to make the journey as you suggest, crammed together in a narrow second-class compartment. Waste would be you inhaling cigarette smoke and God knows what muck, being maddened by other people's children. Waste would be spending hours on the motorway stuck in traffic jams – even Rollses are subject to traffic jams – and your having another crisis, when we've just met. Now that *would* be a waste.'

This is heaven, Hermione thought. He makes the decisions, overrules me, takes care of me, organizes everything. I have never been so happy in my life.

Ellismuir Castle, the ancestral home of the Gordon-Lockharts, was not at all as Hermione had imagined. Far from being castellated and turreted, brooding high above a sodden green and purple landscape, it was an austere, square house built of grey stone, with long thin windows and not a tower to be seen. Inside it was unexpectedly snug, with rooms of moderate rather than gigantic size and log fires in the drawing room, dining room and Hermione's bedroom. The furniture was Scottish, smoke-blackened chairs with unyielding backs that sometimes sprouted antlers but mostly it was a shapeless jumble of sagging, comfortable old armchairs over which were thrown tartan rugs interwoven with hair from generations of dogs. Their successors – a pair of aged, corpulent black Labradors – sprawled on them still, clambering down reluctantly in obedience to a staccato word from Sandy.

'Trout! *Down!* All our dogs have been named after fish,' he explained. 'In alphabetical order. My grandfather had Flounder and Gudgeon; these two are Sturgeon and Trout – though looking at them now, it ought to be Turgid and Stout.'

She laughed and he thought, oh good: I can trot out all my old jokes for her. Chloë got so sick of them.

Hermione asked, 'What about Bobby? He wasn't named after a fish.'

'Bobby was different. He was at Otterbourne, not here.'

Ranged around the stone-flagged entrance hall were three or four swarthy suits of armour. Soot-stained ancestors glowered from the walls. Family photographs were perched on every flat surface in the drawing room. Hermione recognized young Andrew – at prep school, by the look of it, winning something, just like Sandy whom she had watched winning the sack race all those years ago – and in another picture frame she also recognized Violet, Sandy's mama, a graceful, wasp-waisted figure in ruffled silk.

'Oh look! Your mother. I'd forgotten how beautiful she was.'

'She *was* beautiful. So, as I recall, was yours. But don't you sometimes feel that *all* Edwardian ladies were beautiful? Gauzy, willowy dresses, piled-up hair . . . hard not to be.'

'And there's your papa.' Hermione picked up another photograph and scrutinized it, looking intently from the picture to Sandy and back. 'You're not in the least like him.'

'I know. It's all from my mother's side. The dance of inheritance, becking and advancing – "Tarantella", by the way. Belloc. Do you still like poetry? Good. Chloë didn't care for it. Said she couldn't see the point. Be warned: I shall sit by your bed when you're trying to rest and insist on reading poetry out loud. Back to resemblances, real or imagined. The mysterious selection from the genetic sackful. It's all pretty random and sometimes makes no sense at all. You didn't spot me in young Andrew.'

'No – but I would now.'

She picked up a group photograph taken at some shooting party seven decades ago. In the centre sat the stout, pop-eyed figure of Edward VII, his mistress placed unashamedly beside him, then a line of royal hangers-on. On the King's other side sat her mother, his hostess for the weekend, and beside her his host, Sir Jack. Phoebe looked like a poisonous snake, glittering and treacherous, but her father stared confidently at the camera, not in the least overawed by his royal guest. Next to him was Violet and then her husband Donald, Sandy's father. Behind them stood a score of lesser gentry and at the back, the estate servants, among whom she thought she recognized the two Brymers. Hermione peered more closely at the picture, struck by a resemblance.

'My word! It's quite extraordinary but *do* you know – ?' and then stopped.

Sandy, bending down to fondle one of the dogs, looked up. 'Sorry, I didn't catch that. Shut up, Trout, silly old hound! What did you say?'

She shook her head. 'Doesn't matter. Nothing.'

He grinned at her. '*Maddening* Minor.'

It *is* possible, she thought, it is much more than remotely possible. The genes dancing? She looked at the photograph again. No, she told herself, two men of about the same age, height and build, both with wiry grey hair, prove nothing at all.

'I'm not in it,' she said. 'Too young, I suppose. But Richard is . . . oh *look*, Major – there! *You* remember my brother?'

'Course I do. Dick used to beat me at Nine Men's Morris and Ludo and he taught me the names of birds. He was wonderful at nature studies, all that sort of thing.'

He is the last person in the world, Hermione thought, who remembers my brother, and I have found him. He knows my past and he fills my present and as for the future: it can wait. I feel perfectly serene about the future, as long as I don't die yet.

'I'm so glad you remember him. He was such a sort of shining boy. But where are *you*?'

He almost pouted, his face once more that of a disappointed child. 'They said I was too young. It wasn't fair. *Dick* was allowed to go and he was only a year or two older than me.'

She laughed. 'Oh Major – you remember and you're *still* cross, after all this time! It was more than that, though – let me work it out – he was more like *four* years older. Heavens, if Richard were still alive he'd be nearly eighty. I can't imagine it.'

Hermione scrutinized her brother again. Dear old thing, you can see how proud he was at being allowed to join the grown-ups. She put the picture firmly back on the table.

More photographs, this time of obscure, long-dead rowing eights or cricket elevens, hung in the downstairs corridors along-side framed cartoons by Spy and Low, Fougasse, David Langdon and Osbert Lancaster. John Betjeman's poems sat on a footstool beside the lavatory, buried underneath copies of the *Countryman*.

He led her slowly upstairs ('Take the steps one by one') to see her bedroom. It had a mullioned window looking out across a valley and miles of hillside wreathed in misty heather. Another door opened into a bathroom.

'Oh good!' she said. 'My *own bathroom*! I needn't go out into the corridor!'

'Easily done. I had one door knocked through and bricked up another.'

The bedrooms on either side were occupied by her nurses. Felicia had been despatched to the room beyond them, at the end of the corridor. As soon as Sandy had gone, she came in to unpack Hermione's suitcase.

'Miss Hermione, I like your Sir Sandy, he is a very nice gentleman. Very kind, very good. But why *I* not in next room, like usual?' she asked.

'The nurses are next door and not you, Felicia, because that's what Sandy has decided. It's his house and he's in charge, so you and I are both going to have to do what he tells us. Which I find *quite wonderful.*'

Felicia subsided and Hermione thought, I shall have to handle her with great tact. It doesn't matter. Nothing matters. I love him, I always have and now I've found him.

Entering the drawing room before dinner, Hermione found Sandy in full tartan fig. She gasped at the splendour of him and he laughed.

'Don't admire me too much or it'll go to my head and I'll come down tomorrow in ambassadorial gear. I can, you know – knee-breeches, plumed hat, the lot! I'll never wear it again, of course – fit only for the dressing-up box – but Highland ceremonial is still called for a couple of times a year.'

She was thinking, he looks like the hereditary chief of the Clan Lockhart. He looks like a great man, an old man, and my dearest love. Her face grew sombre with the weight of her love.

Sandy, afraid that he had intimidated her, added smilingly, 'I'm not serious. I never dress for dinner. I just thought I would tonight, as a sort of sign of how – glad I am to have found you, and that you're alive, and here, and – oh Minor, I shall get all soppy in a minute. Stop me.'

He held out his arms. Shyly, awkwardly, she walked towards him. He wrapped his arms around her and held her. She was a few inches taller than he was but it didn't matter. It simply couldn't matter less.

A huge antlered chandelier hung in the dining room but that night the pair of them dined alone at a long table lit by silver candelabra. He presided at its head, Hermione on his right. The correct *placement* may be observed even when there are only two at dinner.

'I warn you,' Sandy said, 'I won't have Felicia eating with us. Definitely not in the evenings, anyhow.'

'Certainly not. But, you see, she's jealous of you,' Hermione explained. 'She's probably afraid you'll want me to dismiss her. It'll pass. Give her time.'

'How did you come by her?'

'It's quite a long story – do you really want to hear? Well then, I read about her in the literature from one of the charities I support. They tell these horror stories of people being persecuted and ill-treated and mostly one just feels so helpless. Her father was head of security in the Philippines. The whole family lived in a government compound. Felicia's got five sisters and two brothers. Anyway. He was shot dead one night by the rival faction for power and she and her sisters were all raped. I thought, I can't take them all – but I could shelter *one*. So I wrote to the charity and arranged it. Took ages. Officials are so obstructive. Even the Home Office.'

'My dear, tender-hearted Hermione: do you make a habit of rescuing girls in peril?'

'Occasionally, yes. Do you remember Florabelle?'

'Who?'

'Ah, I see you are an impostor after all. *Sir, sir, I must away . . . you have brought me here under false pretences.*'

'*Stay, I beg you, most noble Queen.* Say that name again?'

'Florabelle.'

'Wait . . . no, it's no good. Flora doesn't ring a bell. You'll have to explain.'

'You're right. You *didn't* meet her. I was testing. She was after you'd gone away. Florabelle was a dwarf I rescued just after you started school, when my parents went to India for three months. Richard was at school too so I was all by myself. I mean the servants were there but no one else. I had Nanny to look after me and Miss Protheroe was supposed to keep me occupied but you know how hopeless *she* was. I was lonely. I read a good deal and – wrote you lots of letters, which I gave Nanny to post – but anyway, never mind, that was the time when I got Florabelle to keep me company.'

'Poor Minor! Lonely Minor. Have a glass of this to cheer you up. It's rather good.'

'Oh I never drink wine. Water will do.'

'Water will do but wine – *good* wine – is a pleasure. Start with it half and half. I don't want to drink alone every night.'

He half-filled Hermione's glass with water, topping it up with a swirl of wine that curled into the glass like smoke, tingeing the water a grapey pink. She sipped and, although she did not care for its thin unaccustomed sourness, smiled.

'It's a pretty colour,' she said. 'And I daresay I shall get used to it.'

He stretched his hand across the polished surface of the table to hold hers and they looked at each other in the candlelight. Hermione thought, if I don't soon tell him how much I love him – that I've never loved anyone else – that I waited for him – if I can't speak the words soon my chest will burst open and my heart will fly out of its own accord.

'Your hand is trembling,' he said. 'You aren't cold?'

'*Oh foolish youth! Think'st thou that I, who have ruled for two thousand years, should feel an earthly chill or tremble at mortal touch?*'

He was spellbound. He gazed transfixed into her pale face and steady eyes. She holds my heart between her two hands, he thought; how soon can I say so and be sure that I won't let her down? They looked at each other. Love unspoken shimmered and danced between them, like the candle flames.

Sandy was the first to break the silence, afraid that the emotion was too great, the moment too soon, her strength not yet up to it.

'So you used to have a *dwarf*...' he began, just as the house-keeper entered to remove their plates.

'Excuse me, sir: will you have cheese or pudding?'

'I don't know. We might want *both*. Hermione?'

'Thank you, nothing for me.' Go away, leave us alone, don't break the spell.

'Nor for me either.' Go away, don't break the spell, leave us alone.

'Coffee's in the small drawing room, sir. Will you want anything else? Port?'

'No, thank you. Oh well, if I do I'll get it myself. That was a splendid dinner. Good night, Mrs Mackillop.'

She left the room, and Sandy took Hermione's hand again.

'What an extraordinary life you must have led. Tell me about this dwarf.'

Hermione told him the story of finding Florabelle and her being sent back again to the misery, ignorance and squalor of her village home, but her mind was beating its own rhythm beneath her words. He is holding my hand, she thought, and his hand feels warm, a bit heavy, rougher than mine. His fingernails are square. He used to bite his nails when he was a boy. No man has held my hand like this ever before in my life. I like the feeling. It is as though he were sheltering me; it makes me feel safe. Still talking, her eyes took in his face and hair, adjusting the reality of this old man against the memory of that small boy. The shape of his head had not changed; the hair was thinner now but still springy. His eyes were still blue; a paler, thinner blue than when he was young, the edges and whites of the eyes pinker than before. His nose was exactly the same: noses don't alter much. I remember (she thought) I used to draw it from memory. Because of that his face, the shape of his head, the curve of the bones are so deeply imprinted that I could never forget. And last of all, his mouth. Look how he purses it now, slightly, unconsciously, listening to me. His lips curve towards me, only fractionally, but it is as though . . .

'After that I saw her occasionally, from the car, when we were driving past, but I was never allowed to talk to her again,' she concluded.

'Minor, what an *appalling* story!' he said. 'I wonder what happened to her, poor dwarf?'

'She died in the flu epidemic. Nobody ever looked after her.'

'Except you.'

'Yes, except me. Just for a few weeks.'

Who looked after *you*? he asked himself. That mother of hers,

315

Phoebe – she was a bitch; Mama always said so, though not of course in those words. What did she call her? 'Odious female!' That's it – *odious female*. Phoebe may have been exquisitely beautiful but she liked tormenting people and didn't even spare her own daughter. Did she read our letters when she confiscated them? It's so long ago I can't remember what I wrote but it can only have been innocent make-believe. Or perhaps *not* so innocent. Look at us now: sixty years later and utterly absorbed in each other. Only now I am a man, not a child, and the fact that we are both old makes no difference – I want to make love to her. She must have had lovers. Perhaps she will tell me, some other time. I hope we still have plenty of time.

'Hermione,' he said, to capture her attention, 'you have been ill. You need lots of rest. I'm keeping you up.'

Oh, she thought, he isn't going to kiss me after all. For a moment it seemed as though he might.

'I daresay you're right,' she agreed, as they both rose from the table. Sandy went ahead towards the door, turning to smile at her as Hermione said, 'Thank you for a lovely evening, for having me here, making me so welcome. I can't tell you how wonderful it is. Oh, Major . . . look, please, could you possibly kiss me?'

He paused with his hand on the door-handle, turned round, took a step towards her, clasped her in his arms and for the first time since childhood, they kissed. Hermione was startled at first – it wasn't what she had expected, but then she had never known what to expect – but as the kiss lengthened she clung to him and felt a wave of heat rise up through her body that was novel and dizzying, potent, enjoyable, almost overwhelming. At last she stepped back.

'Goodness!' she exclaimed. 'So that's how it's done!'

'Do you remember how we kissed when we were children?'

'How could I forget? I've never kissed anyone since.'

It can't possibly be true, Sandy thought. Doesn't kiss, never drinks wine? She must be hiding something from me. Well, that makes two of us. He laughed as though at a shared secret, put his arm round her shoulders and guided her through the trophied hall and up the worn stone staircase towards her own bedroom. Outside her door he stepped back.

'Good night, Minor,' he said, just as a nurse emerged further along the corridor. 'Sleep well.'

Next morning the night nurse roused her at seven with mock-severe reproaches.

'Can't have you staying up so late again, Miss Staunton. I was beginning to think something must have happened. "She ought to be asleep," I said to myself last night. "Doesn't she realize she's been very ill?" It was *after eleven o'clock*, you know.'

So why do you come and disturb me now, Hermione thought, when I *was* asleep? The sooner I can get rid of them all the better; get rid of everyone, for that matter. I'm sick of people fussing over me. All I want is to be left alone with Sandy. He looks after me, really looks after me, not like people who are paid to. But she lay back docilely and closed her eyes until the tinkling of thermometer against glass and the twitching of sheets and blankets had stopped. She wanted to think about the evening; recapture the separate pleasures of being listened to, understood, cherished, held, kissed. Instead, she fell asleep again.

Two hours later Felicia came in to help her dress. She was soft-footed, competent, but her silence was odd. Usually Felicia liked to describe her dreams and prayers.

'What is it, Felicia dear?' Hermione asked. 'What's bothering you? Tell me.'

The girl demurred, turned her face away, smiled nervously, but eventually she said: 'Will he want me to go away? Can he dismiss me?'

Hermione felt a pang of remorse. I should have explained. No wonder she's bewildered.

'You called him a good man and he *is*. Of course he doesn't want you to go away. And even if he did, I would not agree. You are in my care now, do you still not believe that? You are *safe*.'

CHAPTER TWENTY-TWO

THE DAYS LENGTHENED; SPRING CAME TO SCOTLAND; THE HOT and radiant Scottish May. Hermione grew stronger. First one nurse left, then another, until only the nicest one remained in case of any emergency. Increasingly, Felicia spent time in the kitchen with the procession of village people who came to cook, clean, deliver milk or meat. She loved sitting round the table watching the slow talk, liking their ruddy faces and straightforward ways. They in turn seemed to accept her; they accepted her shyness and foreignness and did not cross-question her.

Hermione and Sandy got used to each other's company. Gradually, not hurrying, digressing to talk about other things, they unravelled the story of their separate lives, making their way through the lost years towards the present. He wanted to know about the Campbell-Leiths and she had to admit that she scarcely knew them herself.

'I've had very little contact with my mother's family. Tall as Scots pine, harsh and upright. This great dark-green forest of people. Like Burnham forest. It never did come to Dunsinane. Most people have a whole network of relatives but while Mama was alive I never met any of mine. After she died they came swarming out of the woodwork, of course, after her money. As for my father, he had nobody. It was as though he came from the darkness of Oldham and the darkness closed over again. That's how it seemed to me. I've no idea who his parents were or what happened to them. He had a sister who died quite young. That's all I know. I assume I haven't a Staunton relative in the world. Sometimes if I found myself in that area I would flick through the phone book but although there *are* a couple of Stauntons, I never rang. How many people can name their great-grandfather, after all? And I didn't want to tempt anyone to . . . exploit me.'

'Mm-hm.'

'My father must have been completely bereft when his sister – she was called Hester – died. It's the only plausible explanation for my parents' marriage . . . love and loneliness on his side . . . but on hers? She wasn't pregnant. Richard was born more than a year after their marriage. She didn't *have* to marry Papa, just because he asked. She was beautiful enough to have had anyone she wanted and I can't understand why she should have chosen to marry for money, when she was still so *young*. Eighteen.'

'Her family probably forced her into it,' he said, unsurprised. 'High-born beauty has always been exchanged for money – providing there's enough of it, and the one with money understands that the favour is being conferred on *him* and not the other way round.'

'Mama certainly drummed *that* into me. Making money is *bad*. But it never ceased to madden me that my mother's family combined this air of effortless superiority with being rapaciously greedy. They were quite unscrupulous about accepting Papa's money yet they treated him like dirt because he *worked*. They weren't too proud to take anything he offered, but too proud to be civil in return. Far too grand to talk to me – *or* her, poor Mama. They crushed her spirit, I think.'

'How?'

'By despising her. *Such* contempt, simply because she married "into *trade*". She was eighteen and my father was fifty. How much choice has an eighteen-year-old girl?'

When she told him about her time at the Slade and how her

mother had refused to allow her to develop an independent life as an artist, he seethed with belated fury.

'Why did she have it in for you? I shall *never* understand.'

'I think there were lots of straightforward reasons and some very deep and complicated ones. To pick one of the straightforward, for instance, it must have been a crushing disappointment when I turned out to be plain.'

'What nonsense, you were a ravishing child! I wish I had a photograph to prove it. I often wanted one but for some reason there weren't any. You had long arms and legs and hair that sort of dashed from side to side when you ran. Oh my darling, I remember your long brown legs so clearly! You weren't *plain.*'

Darling, she heard; he called me *darling.* Like trumpets sounding and horses prancing. She said, 'I had your legs off by heart, like the rest of you. I often drew you from memory. That's how I first discovered I had some talent. Mama didn't like that, either. I'm surprised she let me go to the Slade. It got me out of her way, that's the only reason I can think of. It was wonderful to find something other people actually thought I was good at.'

Sandy dug out a drawing book from the box of toys kept for visiting children. Handing her a pencil he demanded that she draw something.

'Show me. Anything. Just *draw.* Let me see.'

Shyly at first – it was years since she had attempted even a pencil sketch – Hermione began to draw. Sandy sat in a deep armchair, his limbs accommodated by its ancient curves, his legs crossed. The shape he makes is all ease and rounded lines, she thought; he folds himself into this familiar place and is enfolded by it. Nothing changes. The presiding sense here is of comfort and relaxation. Her eyes darted up and down from model to page and back, her hand gradually rediscovering its former facility. She had meant only to draw a quick outline, a sketch to show that she could get the proportions right and capture a rough likeness. Instead, she became absorbed by the old technical problems: how to catch the play of light and shade, the way his trousers fell in folds from the knee and the ovals of light that shone on his polished shoes.

He sat motionless, watching her concentrate. She was wearing a shapeless navy cardigan over a pale blue shirt, a brooch pinned at her neck. Her skirt was a headmistressy dark grey, her stockings opaque, her shoes old-fashioned, deeply creased across the instep. *My graceful girl has turned into an old lady*, he thought, *and I missed all the stages in between. Like those speeded-up films that show a rose unfolding, three days compressed into ten seconds, my Hermione has gone in a flash from childhood to old age. Yet she is still and utterly herself and I have never felt so tender towards anyone.*

The gong boomed for lunch, surprising them both. Sandy stretched, uncrossing his cramped legs.

'Oof!' he said. 'Stiff. Must be getting old. Let me see.'

He came over to where she sat and looked at the page.

'Stop. Don't tinker with it any more. It's finished. It's marvellous. Gosh, Minor, I had no idea you were so good! You've got me to a T.'

'I sometimes used to think I could be really good.'

'What do you mean, *could* be? You *are* really good.'

How can I explain? she thought. *He means, you can catch an adequate likeness. I mean, I might have been able to paint as well as Gwen John, if only I'd had the courage.* For the first time in decades she remembered her final painting at the Slade, the one Professor Tonks had admired, of the attentive small boy in grubby shorts and Aertex shirt who sat with his chin propped on his fists, elbows on knees, watching a scene of carnage. She remembered Tonks's question: *Have you the hunger?* No, as it turned out, she had not; money and her mother had killed the hunger.

'You flatter me, dear Sandy! But I told you – I developed the facility for catching your likeness, and I used to do it to – cheer myself up, I suppose. Not to let you vanish altogether.'

'Can you still? As a boy, I mean.'

'Ages since I tried.'

'Try now. Just quickly – lunch is waiting.'

She drew him in profile, a few rapid lines, a squiggle of curly hair, a clean young jaw, and dotted in a smile at the corner of his mouth. He watched in amazement.

'It's me! Me sixty years ago! Quite uncanny. Minor, you are *extraordinary*. What other hidden talents have you got? Come and tell me over lunch.'

A day or two later, Sandy took the car and came back with drawing materials for her: a large and a small pad of heavy, 180 or perhaps even 220 gram cartridge paper and several pencils of different hardness, from H3 to B2. The weight and texture of the paper was a joy, like old linen or calico, its colour the same bleached creamy white. The faintly uneven surface gripped her pencils so that they travelled resolutely and did not just slide across it. He had even bought a square India rubber with rounded corners, a faintly powdery, silky texture and a sweet clean smell. She had forgotten the pleasure of good materials, the way they focused her mind on the task. Eye to hand, *eyes*, Miss Staunton!

She had been shy at first, shy to let him see her work, shy almost to see it herself, being so long out of practice. Yet she was amazed at how quickly the facility and her powers of concentration returned. She started drawing every day – the dogs, him, the view through her window. Little by little her horizon widened. She grew bolder; started dispensing with the India rubber, then switched from pencil to using a pen. She sent off to Winsor and Newton for a set of watercolours. Soon she was producing large, bold paintings, their skies not timid but thunderous, hills not wishy-washy but great prehistoric lumps of rock, tinted fiery purple, magenta and blue as though they had just cooled. Sandy was proud of having devised such a rewarding way of forcing her to sit still and rest – for she was an energetic woman and immobility was hard for her. He praised her work lavishly and took away some sketches to be framed. He planned to hang them in the main downstairs corridor, removing the old London clubbish cartoons and setting spotlights in the ceiling to pick out Hermione's adventurous palette.

One mild afternoon when the sun shone and the spring leaves sparkled, Hermione slept for an hour and awoke feeling refreshed, thirsty for bracing draughts of air and the high horizon. Together they set off to walk, the dogs following at their heels.

'I think it's time to tell you about my wife,' he said after they had gone for a while in comfortable silence. 'My marriage. Do you want to hear?'

'I want to hear everything,' she answered. 'I didn't like to ask you about . . . Chloë . . . it didn't seem to be any of my business.'

'Tactful Minor. Are you *bursting* with curiosity?'

She thought, can I bear to listen while he tells me how he fell in love, how he proposed, about being married? I shall look attentive and if necessary turn my mind to other things.

They trudged steadily uphill, the dogs nosing ahead, running, coming back to check, just like Bobby in the old days. He matched his pace to hers, never letting her see how he moderated his strides, pausing every now and again to lean sideways against his stick so she could catch her breath.

'I came down from Oxford in the summer of 1922 and since I'd got a degree in modern languages and a great desire to travel, I did the obvious thing and joined the foreign service. It was all so easy in those days – one's parents or an uncle or, in my case, a godfather had "connections". You met him at his club for a chat with some senior figure, sat an exam – dead easy – and you were in. All changed now. They really put them through the mill, the graduate entrants, though I daresay connections still don't hurt. Goodness, how the world has changed! Not entirely for the worse.'

'Go on,' she said.

'I did a year in London learning the ropes, then was posted to Lisbon – they usually start you off somewhere dull and straightforward – and then a couple of years later to Paris.'

'What year was that?'

'Let me work it out . . . 1926, 7? Must have been.'

'Oh Major – when I left the Slade I desperately wanted to go to Paris. If I had it would have been the same year. We might have *met*! Only I couldn't go. Mama wouldn't allow it.'

'What a waste. Imagine you as a Bohemian young artist – your own studio – a sort of English Gertrude Stein.'

'Hardly . . .'

'Minor, what *fun* you would have had! *God*, how you must have resented her—'

'Go on about the embassy in Paris.'

'That was fun too, in quite a different way. The last gasp of the *ancien régime*. Still extremely formal. Wonderful parties. Men in white tie and decorations, the girls practically naked in skinny little frocks, bare shoulders, bare arms, short skirts – I *wish* I'd known you then.'

Wanting him to get to the point, meet Chloë, get it over, she said, 'Major, could we sit down for a bit?'

'Of course. Sorry. Am I tiring you? Actually there's a glorious view from over there, if you can manage another few yards – it's not far.'

They climbed a gentle incline and suddenly the ground fell away at their feet. Below and to their right a lochan glittered in the sun, deep dark blue, quite unexpected. Bracken fronds shone pale green against the heather. Distant hills glimmered purple, lilac and grey. He put down his stick and unfolded a mackintosh for her to sit on. The ground bounced beneath her, springy and resistant. She breathed deeply, air so pure you could smell it, ticklish heathery scents and a faint odour like some herb; thyme, maybe. Her feet rested on a little rock. The dogs had collapsed beside him, panting. She heard their breath, Huh, huh, huh.

Sandy settled himself and asked, 'Would you care for a swig of whisky?'

'I don't think so, thank you, no.'

He dug into the pocket of his jacket and brought out a silver flask; tipped it to his lips and swallowed. She watched the muscles in his throat, the line of his jaw sculpted into a clean curve by the jutting of his chin. She could hear the minute scratching of his jacket as he put it back and a different scratching as he extended his legs comfortably in the heather. Midges zoomed round her ears with their high tiny whine. The orchestra is striking up before the opera, she thought. Scraping of bows against instruments. Attentive audience. Suspense.

'Go on,' she said.

'Chloë Jourdain. Bit younger than me; the ambassador's

daughter. I can't say with hand on heart I was not influenced by that. At the same time she was exactly the boyish type I liked – which was *your* fault. The hours I spent dreaming about you during my hectic adolescence in an all-male environment . . . Whether or not I knew it at the time, those one or two summers when we ran wild—'

'Two.'

'Yes, I know – two summers – I was *in love* with you.' Air, sky, declaration, joy. 'Lots of people would say that's impossible; children can't fall in love. Love's about desire and sex and marriage and founding a family. I won't slight Chloë's memory by describing what I felt about her, and in any case I *did* love her – but Minor, you were my *passion*. Did you know that, at the time?'

There are so many questions to ask. *Why,* in that case, didn't you come looking for me? You were male, you were free, nobody could stop you – if I was your passion, as you were mine, why did you let me go? Weren't you ever curious? Lonely? Weren't you cut in half and aching, as I was? Instead of answering his question she asked, 'Did you ever know a man called Hamish Buchanan?'

'What's that got to do with . . . yes, of course I did. Jamie. Dead now. Sweet old boy. The family place is near here – well, near – forty or fifty miles. Why?'

'I met him once, at a deb dance. I used to sound out a lot of the men I danced with in case they'd known you. I wasn't even sure at first if you'd survived the war. Anyway. Hamish Buchanan said you were coming shooting with him and I asked him to—' Stop talking, she told herself. Let him go on. 'Sorry. I shouldn't interrupt.'

'Where was I?'

'You were saying, if it's not immodest to repeat it, that I was your passion.'

'You were. You are. Oh Minor, you must know I'm dying to make love to you?'

Long pause, partly terror. Fixedly, in a monotone, she said, not looking at him, 'Not here.'

'No, much too uncomfortable—'

'And a bit public . . .'

'*Public*, Minor? There's nobody for miles around. But there's something else we have to talk about first.'

'Now?'

'Later. Let me briefly finish telling you about Chloë.'

'It would help if you could kiss me . . .?'

She leaned her head sideways towards him, he leaned towards her, their faces turned and mouths met. Her face was warm from the spring sunshine, his lips tasted faintly of whisky, his mouth more so. She entered the cave of his kiss, still slightly shocked by its vastness when hitherto she had known nothing but chaste, closed lips against cheek. These kisses were like a yawn; a huge, liquid, hard and soft yawn, shockingly private. He moved away, and her eyes opened.

'Oh *Major*!' she said, breaking into a smile. 'Heavens, it does take some getting used to. I see now what they mean by *intimacy*. Kissing is very intimate, isn't it?'

'Minor, my dear, do I gather from what you're saying that you *really* haven't been kissed very often? Last time you said it I assumed you were just being discreet.'

'Never,' she said. 'Honestly – never before. Go on about Chloë.'

'*Never?*'

'That's part of my story. You tell yours first.'

He finished briskly, passing lightly over the engagement – the wedding ('I thought you might have spotted it in *The Times*. Or seen the pictures in the *Tatler*.' 'Mama read that, I didn't.') – and the early, young-married years so that Hermione need not hear about their happiness.

She listened, conscious – not envious – of what he and Chloë had shared. In 1928 he had been posted to Lebanon . . . Beirut, the Paris of the Middle East, so she had heard. As a good-looking young pair they would have been invited to exotic parties, in fancy dress perhaps; made expeditions to – was there desert in Lebanon? No, but ruins, surely? She banished speculation and watched the angle of his elbow, his chin leaning on his cupped hand, eyes alternately gazing across the view and turning to check her response. He was doing his best to be considerate.

Finally he concluded, 'In 1929 our first son came along, David,

326

young Andrew's father, and a few years later, another son, Murdoch. He was a bit of a scamp, Murdo. Still is. And that was all. No more children – which meant, no daughters. Most men think they'd like a daughter and I was no exception, but it didn't happen. In any case we were in Egypt by then. Not the best place in the world for women giving birth.'

She had no family history to offer in return. No falling in love – Shebeare was hardly even the stirring of the tiniest bud of love and Nicholas no more than a half-hearted attempt to make bricks out of straw.

'The people I've loved have mostly been *women*,' she said.

He looked at her in surprise. 'Minor! You're not trying to tell me . . .?'

'No no, I'm not. I've had a number of women friends and a few younger women of whom I've been enormously fond, Felicia being the most recent, but I've never fallen in love with them, or with a man, either. Nor any man ever in love with me.'

'*I am*,' he said, very seriously.

The dogs shuffled and scratched; one lifted his head to snap at a butterfly, missed. Sandy got to his feet and held out a hand to pull her up. She took it in both hers and in the second before he swung her upright, she declared for the first time in her life, 'And I love you.'

They walked carefully downhill, watching their feet for obstacles, being at an age when they couldn't risk letting themselves trip and fall. The silence was not strained. The day was ebbing already, the air cooling fast.

'That was *heavenly*,' she said when they reached the house.

'Good! Dinner at eight?'

Hermione climbed to her room, but Felicia was not in evidence. She had barely enough energy to untie her shoelaces before falling exhausted on the bed. As she closed her eyes and began the descent towards unconsciousness, she thought: what did he mean by *we have something to talk about first*?

That evening they dined not by candlelight but in the glow of the chandelier that made the silver and glasses sparkle with crystal brilliance. They ate artichokes doused in lemony butter followed by a lamb dish with an unexpected sweetness. With it he made her try a delicate white wine, undiluted.

'I like the wine,' she said. 'I like the lamb stew better. What is it?'

'Apricots,' he said. 'You make an ordinary lamb stew with garlic, onions, carrots and tomatoes but you *also* add a dozen dried apricots and a few spices like, oh, cardamon, saffron if you've got it, and put it in the oven to stew in its own juice.'

'Gracious!' she said. 'How clever of you to know all that. I can't cook in the least, I'm afraid.'

'Minor, you do have the *most* surprising gaps.'

'I know,' she said humbly. 'I regret it. I've had this very *odd* life. It's probably because of the money. It cuts one off from an awful lot of things.'

When Mrs Mackillop had brought in the cheese and retired for the evening he moved his chair towards her and leaned forward.

'I said there was something else . . .'

'Yes.' She felt her heartbeat accelerate but her voice was level, and her gaze.

'It's going to be a – God, I don't know – a revelation. Probably a shock. Let me lead up to it sideways. Crabwise. All right?'

She paused to steady her voice. 'All right,' and as she looked at him her inner voice pleaded, I trust you. Don't let anything go wrong now.

'When I went off to school you and I took it for granted that we would see each other again?'

'Soon. That Christmas.'

'But my Scottish grandfather died and we moved up here.'

'Nobody explained that to me in so many words at the time but I gathered eventually, yes.'

'When you grew up, though, you must have thought I – we –'

'Would meet, of course I did.'

'And when we didn't . . .?'

'I couldn't look for *you* because I was a girl, it would have been dreadfully forward. I *could* have tracked you down via *Burke's* or

Debrett or something but I had always been told that men made the running.'

'I wasn't *men* . . .'

'No. But *I* was "girls". It was also partly because of my mother. She made it hard for me ever to have *my* friends in the house, whether in London or Chantry.'

Bitch, thought Sandy.

'I never had a very high opinion of myself. If you had found me a let-down and been polite and distant and gone away, then I – oh Major?' – she threw her hands on the table, palms upwards, in a movement of passionate appeal, 'I couldn't have *borne* it!'

'My poor love. What a struggle you had. Let's go and sit next door while I explain why *I* didn't come and look for you.' He wanted her beside him for the next revelation, not across a table, no matter how close.

In the drawing room a log fire was flickering to an end. Warmth and light from the glowing embers reflected on the fur of the sleeping dogs, burnishing it bronze. Sandy led Hermione to a deep corner of the sofa and sat down next to her, throwing one arm along the back. He went on, 'So you waited for *me* to find *you*?'

'Yes.'

'And wondered why I never turned up?'

'Yes.'

'Listen. Give me your hand. I did plan to come and find you after Oxford. I hadn't thought very clearly what would happen next, beyond assuming we would still love each other and get married. When my Finals term ended I came home – here – to relax and wait for my results. Lot of walking, some fishing, the odd friend to stay. You know. Then the shooting season. But before that, around the end of August – this was 1922 so I was twenty-two – I announced to my parents that I was going to spend a few days with friends in London and while I was there I'd try and look you up.'

Hermione thought back. 1922, the year I was presented. That interminable summer of dances and strawberries and vapid young men.

'Go on,' she murmured.

'Mama said nothing at the time but later that day she sought me out and absolutely forbade it. When I insisted on being given a reason she said – oh Minor, oh Minor – she said, Jack Staunton had been her lover. For *years*. In the Dorset days, when they were neighbours. No one knew. And that I was your brother. *Am*.'

The last piece in the mosaic. The last chord in a quartet. The last clue that unlocks all others. Her body thrummed as though dozens of telephone wires were singing and vibrating through her veins. *We be of one blood, Thou and I* – the intuitive knowledge had always been there. *This is my beloved son, in whom I am well pleased.* The blood rushed to her face, suffusing it with a deep rosy blush, so that she looked revived and young. Sandy, the winner of the sack race, sharer of half her genes.

'*Say something!*' he pleaded.

'I always knew. Not consciously, but at some instinctive level I always knew.' She paused, suspended between past and present, re-adjusting both. Sandy, her brother. 'I mean, think back to our code-words, as children . . .'

'*We be of one blood, Thou and I.*'

'You see? So I am shocked, yes, in a way – goodness, I hardly know what to feel – not shocked *appalled* but shocked *amazed*. Poor Mama, I wonder if she knew. No, can't have done. But what about Papa . . . I wonder if *he* did? He must have guessed. But I'm not surprised. I'm relieved. It is the *one* good enough reason for you not to have tried to find me.'

They looked at each other with bewilderment and awe, with the ecstasy of children gazing down upon a miniature world from the high branches of a tree, the ecstasy of archangels soaring above their heads.

CHAPTER TWENTY-THREE

NEXT MORNING SHE WOKE TO FIND EVERYTHING BLANKETED IN fog. The view through her windows, when Felicia came to draw back the curtains at nine, was opaque. Hills, trees, lawn, sweep of drive leading to house – all whitewashed out.

'It's raining,' said Felicia unnecessarily.

'I can see it's raining. Doesn't look like lifting, either. Well, so it's to be a day indoors. Felicia, look at me –' she touched Felicia's arm to compel her attention. 'How are *you*? Are you managing all right? I know I've been neglecting you.'

'They're nice people,' Felicia said. 'Very kind. There is a man called Angus . . .'

Hermione made a questioning face (head sideways, eyebrows raised) and Felicia smiled shyly.

'Looks after dogs and cars. Mends things.'

'I know – the handyman?'

Felicia nodded. Angus was a thickset, laconic Scot who shared the companionship round the kitchen table. Solid, reliable, watchful. Weather-beaten face and hands; hands always busy fixing something. He had a room at one end of the corridor where the guns, gun books, fishing tackle and dogs were quartered. Nothing

331

had happened, but they were becoming aware of each other.

'I know the one you mean. Nice. Are you becoming –' Hermione smiled, '– *fond* of him?' She mimed hand on heart, deep sigh.

Felicia shook her head.

'Well, if you did I would be very glad.' Emphatic *glad*. 'I'd love you to find someone.' She put her arms round the young woman and hugged her. Felicia returned the hug. 'Oh *good*,' Hermione said. 'Now then: clothes for a day indoors please, Felicia dear. I may spend the morning sketching – though *not* outside. Is my bath ready?'

Sandy was affectionate but remote over breakfast. He ensconced himself behind *The Times* and although quick to spot when she needed more toast, coffee or marmalade, he seemed disinclined to talk. When breakfast was over he said, 'Minor, would you excuse me for a morning of letter-writing and admin? Might as well take advantage of the rain . . .'

'Of course,' she said. 'I ought to write some letters too.'

We are beginning to get used to each other, to talk like ordinary grown-ups, she thought; already we sound like a couple. How quickly our childhood language of games and fantasy has receded! It served a purpose – gave us names and voices with which to rediscover our past. And look what we have found.

Hermione commandeered writing paper and a table in the little sitting room. She spent ten minutes wondering what she could possibly say . . . *Dear Rachel, I seem to have found my brother . . . Dear Pixie, it turns out that all my life I have been in love with my brother?* Even the free-wheeling Pixie might be shocked at that. Instead she wrote a brisk letter to Vivian Blythgowrie thanking him for visiting her in hospital, and for the flowers. She added that her convalescence would soon end ('I am now back to normal and in fine fettle' – *that* would annoy him!) and once back in London, she would like to give him lunch and catch up on the affairs of Staunton Trading. Could he suggest a couple of convenient dates at the end of the month? She drafted letters to various bigwigs at Staunton Trading indicating that, being far from dead yet, she would be pleased to receive the most recent accounts and a summary of events since the beginning of April, sent to the London house. Once she had achieved the right note of authority she made handwritten fair copies. She did not put the Ellismuir address on any of these letters, but scribbled *Scotland, 24 June 1974*. She also wrote a warm note to Sandy's grandson, young Andrew, thanking him for his care of her and giving the good news about her convalescence, leaving it open for Sandy to read if he wanted to. She sent a note to Rosa at Chantry saying that she and Felicia 'and a guest' would probably be down soon. She informed the London housekeeper that she would be back 'by the end of this month, though probably not for very long', giving Sandy's address so she could forward any post. At last she sat back, gazed into the impenetrable greyness beyond the window and allowed herself to contemplate Sandy's revelation.

First of all, was it a revelation or had she – as she assured him – always known? Secondly, was it going to make any difference? Thirdly, would she tell anyone? The last question was the easiest: no. Sandy had evidently not done so and if he had kept it secret, she must do so, too. Had *Chloë* known? She doubted it. Had her – goodness, this was going to take some getting used to – had *their* father known? He must have done – must at least have begun to suspect. She thought back. There had been an occasion when she was about sixteen and had asked Papa if he knew what had happened to Sandy – meaning, in the war – when he had warned her off with unusual sharpness. And there was that phrase in his will about *legitimate* descendants. But this could have been designed to deter impostors.

She stood up, stretching to ease her cramped back, and looked round the room. On the mantelpiece were several photographs. The usual shooting line-ups; one of his father – well, of Sir Donald – in full Highland dress; another of Sandy and Chloë arriving at Buckingham Palace on some, presumably, official occasion; a picture of Sandy's mother at an Edwardian fancy dress party. Hermione took that one down and scrutinized it. The back was closed by flexible metal pins. One was loose. She fiddled with it and the back fell open. Behind the outer, posed photograph

333

– Violet as Cleopatra or perhaps Titania – was hidden another, a sepia snapshot of her father. Papa was sitting on a garden bench, legs crossed, smiling broadly at the person behind the camera, one hand extended as though inviting the photographer to sit beside him. Who else could it have been but Violet? Did he have a similar picture of her hidden somewhere – in his wallet or some secret drawer in his desk? Perhaps the bench held some special significance for them both. She took the photograph and studied the face of the father she had truly loved, who had been dead for nearly sixty years. On the back of the picture was written faintly in pencil, *To my Love, from her Love. OC 1912. OC* – Our Child? Or simply Otterbourne Court? Did Sandy know it was there? She turned the photograph over again, suddenly ashamed of intruding on that private long-ago love. They could not have known that Sandy would grow up to resemble his real father so closely. Now that he was seventy-four, a bit older than Papa when the photograph was taken, the likeness was unmistakable. But there was nobody – apart from the two of them – left to notice.

Would it make a difference? Violet had been telling the truth and Sandy was the son of her lover, not of her husband. She had told him to prevent him seeking out his half-sister – for fear of what? The Victorians abhorred relationships between cousins, let alone siblings, believing that if they were to marry it would lead to hereditary weakness, idiocy, lolling heads, shambling walk; or, if not that, moral turpitude, alcohol or drug addiction, family shame, the genes taking revenge – but none of that could make any difference now. She and Sandy were not idiots, not disgraceful, and well past the age for children. Hermione heard steps along the corridor and instantly felt guilty. He came in.

'Ah, there you are! What have you got there?'

She felt herself blanch, but it was too late to try and shove the picture back so she held it out to him: 'Sandy: have you seen this?'

He looked at it.

'Yes. I have. Mama showed it to me, as proof that she was in love with your – *my* real father – and he with her. She said he had kept its twin, a picture of her.'

'I'm sorry. I didn't mean to pry.'

'Don't apologize. I daresay I would have shown you anyway. Touching, isn't it? Now then, a drink before lunch?'

Lunch was spartan. Cold ham, cold bleeding beetroot, a plate of sweet home-grown tomatoes, a jug of crisp celery; bread, butter, cheese. A silver bowl piled high with golden apples. Water in a jug for her. A squat decanter of wine for him.

'Hope this is enough for you?' he said. 'Today's Mrs Mackillop's day for stocking up. She drives to the nearest supermarket and lays in stuff for a month.'

'And you normally go with her?'

'Doesn't matter a bit. More important to talk uninterrupted. One thing I didn't make clear last night is that I *loved* my father – my Gordon-Lockhart father, I mean. People thought him a bit spineless but he wasn't, though he could be comically absent-minded. He was sensitive, perceptive, with more than a touch of other-worldliness. Not a naturally gregarious man: no wonder, with his stutter. He liked music and poetry – *that* he instilled in me too. Yet he ran this place well, held it together through two wars and handed it over to me in good working order. Not easy for him, the least practical man in the world.'

'He died after the second, didn't he? – I remember seeing it in *The Times*. In all those years, nothing was ever said?'

'*Never*. I'm sure my mother never told him. That was the really civilized thing about our parents' generation – they knew when to keep their mouths shut. None of this self-indulgent confessing, *letting it all hang out*, as my grandchildren would say. The fact that all three of us happened to have red hair was an extra stroke of luck. Mama was fond of him, you know. She may have loved your – *our* – father but she was married to mine for over fifty years. They weren't unhappy together.'

'I'm glad about that, for your sake.'

So he hadn't been made miserable by those buried secrets. Were they the cause of her mother's spleen and venom? Had the punishment fallen upon her? These were questions to ask herself, Hermione thought; not Sandy. She changed the subject.

'Listen, Major, I want to ask you something.'

335

'Fire away.'

'You have been simply wonderful and being here has restored me. But I ought to get back to London – there are things I need to deal with – and I *would* like to spend part of the summer at Chantry. Can you get away, will you come with me?'

'My dear, my love – of course I'll come. I'm full of curiosity. Chantry – after all these years. I remember the nursery floor exactly.'

'It hasn't changed much.'

'Good! I have things to do in London too' (I must talk to David and, if I can find him, Murdo, he thought; tell them I am going to marry again) 'but after that, yes, spending some time in Dorset – goodness, what a prospect. Memories.' He shivered and drained his wine. 'Back to boyhood.'

Outside the rain fell steadily. No question of a walk. After lunch they separated and Hermione went up to her bedroom, intending to read or at least think. If Sandy was her brother, did it make a difference, since apparently no one else knew, or had guessed? But a difference to what? Marriage . . . money . . . she bobbed along on a current of hypotheses that she had not resolved when sleep swept her away. She woke up two hours later, and saw that an envelope had been pushed under her door. Levering herself stiffly off the bed, she picked it up. A firm hand; broad nib, black ink. 'Hermione – private'. She took it back to bed and slid her thumb under the flap.

My dearest Hermione, it began.

Not Minor then – this is serious.

It was hard for me to tell you – it must have been hard to hear. Please don't think it changes anything. Who can ever know the pressures that impel people into an affair? Jack Staunton was a remarkable character and what matters is that he and my mother took care to protect the innocent and make sure they didn't find out. By 'innocent' I mean my other father, and your mama, though one hardly thinks of her as innocent. And of course, the two of us. I ought to tell you that he left me some money.

So Papa *had* known! Violet must have contacted him, when the likeness made possibility a certainty. Had she contrived a last

336

meeting, perhaps several, between their leaving Otterbourne and Papa's death seven years later?

I didn't get it until after Papa died and I took over in 1946: presumably to spare him wondering why a long-ago neighbour should have left his son £100,000. It was a great help towards things like central heating, repairing the roof and school fees. I told Chloë it was a windfall. (She never knew, by the way.)

Good!

My darling, why am I writing this, when I could say it? Because of all those other letters I wrote and you didn't get. Because I think about you all the time even when you are just a few rooms away. Because you were brave and stoical last night, although I must have shocked you. Because the fact that we are related by blood as well as by everything else doesn't change a thing unless you feel it makes a difference. Because I love you – Because I want to marry you – and most of all, because I want you in my arms, in my bed. You don't have to answer – all my love, Sandy.

A love letter, my first-ever love letter! Oh Sandy, oh Major, oh tongues of men and angels.

That night they dined by candlelight again, with wine, Burgundy this time.

'Goodness,' she said, 'I think I must be getting the hang of this. It's really quite nice, isn't it?'

When they had eaten dinner he had a brandy, and then another, and suggested she went ahead of him to bed. He helped her to her feet and, body pressed hard against body, they kissed. It had been two months since she arrived. If they waited any longer it would only start to complicate matters, he thought.

She had dismissed Felicia and was reading by the light of her bedside lamp when he rapped at the door. It had to be him; Felicia's was a timid double knock. Yet Rattie's invasion of her bedroom was still so recent that apprehension flooded her veins, making her heartbeat quicken and panic leap into her throat. She called, '*Who is it?*'

'It's me. Can I come in?'

Could he come in? How many times had she imagined this moment. He was wearing an old tartan dressing gown. No pyjamas.

'Heavens, Major! You might have warned me,' she scolded clumsily.

'I didn't dare, in case I lost my nerve. I'll go if you want. Sorry. Just tell me what you're reading . . .'

'Poetry. I . . .'

Her voice trembled so much that she could not trust herself to finish the sentence. Her mouth was dry and her heart pounding. She held up the book and he crossed the carpet to stand beside her bed. Opening the book at random, he began to read, in a voice not much steadier than hers:

> *'My love is of a birth as rare*
> *As 'tis for object strange and high:*
> *It was begotten by despair*
> *Upon impossibility.'*

'Oh, wonderful!' she said. 'Wonderful – Donne, isn't it?'

'Marvell.'

'Yes – go on.'

> *'As lines, so loves oblique may well*
> *Themselves in every angle greet:*
> *But ours so truly parallel,*
> *Though infinite, can never meet.'*

He looked at her with eyes curved and wrinkled in a questioning smile.

'Shall we try and prove him wrong, Minor, at long last?'

'We can try. I may not be able to. I'm a bit scared – even though it's you.'

She held the bedclothes back with a wide gesture, displaying a white triangle of sheets. He undid his dressing gown cord, stood for an instant naked before her, the same beloved flesh and blood after sixty-two years, however changed by time. She turned

338

modestly to switch off the light as he slipped into bed beside her; then raising her arms above her head in the darkness she pulled up the nightdress and let it fall to the floor.

'Where are you?'

'Here.'

'Kiss me.'

They smiled as their lips encountered the planes of jaw and neck before locking mouth to mouth. Again the cavern gaped and out of the darkness came the minty flavour of toothpaste and the sweet moisture of tongues and Sandy thought, thank God for that, it's going to be all right! But she's nervous, poor Minor, and no wonder.

'Minor,' he said, stroking her gently under the tent of sheets, 'do you remember the day of the cow-pats?'

'When we both got all smelly and covered in muck. And that blissful cool stream. Trying to clean up so Nanny wouldn't be cross. *'Course* I remember.'

'Afterwards, drying in the sun, we looked at each other. How shy we were . . . I feel shy now, as well. Oh Minor, it's been so *long*!'

'Mmmm – oh goodness, Sandy, that feels nice. Let me just – shift a bit.'

As she moved he caught an innocent whiff of lavender water. Gently, unaware of what she was doing or why, she began to tremble.

'Not yet,' he said.

But she misunderstood and said, 'Nothing's wrong. I'm just getting comfortable.'

'Well done. Now we fit.'

'Oh Major, this is *heavenly* . . .'

'Gently. Very gently. Now give me your hand . . . you could try doing *that*.'

'Glory be! What a wonder this is.'

'Lie still or it might happen too fast.'

The darkness, when she opened her eyes, was not pitch-black at all. She could see his outline against the window. His shoulders above her made a rampart clad in warm flesh, his mouth grazing her skin was terrifying, thrilling, unimaginable. She shut her eyes again. Small uncontrollable sounds escaped her.

'Ssshhh . . . Relax. I'll look after you. My *love*.'

A pause, a quickening of breath, a moment on the cliff edge – what happens now? she thought. Then he rolled over on to his back and in the silence they both fell wordlessly asleep.

Ten minutes later she woke, damp and seeping. *A miracle*, Hermione said to herself. Now I must go to the bathroom. She slipped out of bed and tiptoed across the room. When she came back he sighed with pleasure and said, 'Oh my love . . . we did it! But then I'm afraid I fell asleep.'

'So did I. Isn't one supposed to?'

'*You* can. For some reason the man isn't meant to.'

'Well I don't mind. You go to sleep.'

'My darling.'

CHAPTER TWENTY-FOUR

Sandy met his elder son for lunch at a discreet French restaurant in Soho, one that he often patronized for its comfortably shabby atmosphere, good food and widely spaced tables. Andrew had forewarned his father that 'something was going on' and David was apprehensive.

'De Gaulle used to come here during the war, you know . . .' Sandy said, trying to make conversation in the awkward gap between the ordering and the arrival of their food. He would have liked another whisky.

'Pa, you've told me that dozens of times already. First time when you were on leave from God knows where – Bulgaria or something – and I was going back to prep school. "And the décor hasn't changed since . . ." Right?'

'Sorry, old boy. Getting forgetful in my old age.'

'Not just forgetful, I hear – positively impetuous.'

Irritated at having his disclosure forestalled, Sandy said firmly, 'I have known Hermione Staunton since I was a small boy. The word "impetuous" hardly seems appropriate.'

'But you left Dorset when you were what, ten? Twelve? I'd always understood that you grew up at Ellismuir.'

'By and large, yes. David, why don't I do the talking and you listen?'

'Very well.' His son folded his hands and sharpened his expression as though paying attention to an irresponsible and spendthrift client.

'Hermione and I were childhood friends. We share a lot of memories. We lost touch, I grew up, married your mother, and she and I were together for more than forty years. Nearly two years after her death and not through any positive volition on my part I came across Hermione again.'

'Andrew brought the two of you together.'

'Yes. Do you wish he hadn't?'

There was a pause while the waiter set their first course in front of them and poured the wine for Sandy to taste.

'Now this is a jolly good Burgundy so enjoy it,' he said.

'I can't help feeling it's a bit . . .'

'. . . disloyal to your mother?'

'Well, yes, that. And hasty. I mean, dammit, Pa, she only *died* eighteen months ago.'

'She died in December 1972, as I am not likely to forget. David, I refuse to be led into an argument. I was not expecting to remarry – though I *have* been lonely, which may not have occurred to you – and Hermione Staunton is probably the only woman in the world I would even contemplate marrying. But since we have been brought together again by what I regard as the miraculous intervention of young Andrew, I am telling – not asking – you, I *do* intend to marry her as soon as possible. I hoped you would come along to the Gloucester Road flat for a drink so that I could introduce you to her. And Murdo, if he's in London.'

'I haven't an idea where he is at the moment. I'm quite happy to meet this lady, Andrew says she's a sweetie – but he also says she's old, frail and very ill.'

Ill she may have been, Sandy thought, but her recovery seemed complete and her energy was amazing. He had been afraid of making love to her that first time for a number of reasons, not least that the physical effort might prove too much for her. They had made love half a dozen times since, with increasing wonder and success.

Sandy smiled to himself as he recalled moments whose ardour had astonished him – and would doubtless appal the disapproving middle-aged man who sat opposite him, slinging back Echezeaux as though it were common or garden plonk.

'*Has* been very ill. Until she was scared half to death by a burglar she had been in excellent health. Now restored. Nor could Hermione ever in her life have been described as "frail". But that's neither here nor there. The fact is, old boy, I'm not asking your permission to marry her; I am doing you the courtesy of saying it is my intention to do so. If I knew where the hell your brother is I would tell him as well, but it would probably involve sending runners with forked sticks to Timbuctoo. Now eat up your food, concentrate on your wine, and give me a chance to do the same.'

Could have been worse, he thought afterwards, as he sat waiting for Hermione on a bench outside the National Gallery. If David had reverted to sulky small boyhood – well, he too had become a boy again on meeting Hermione. Her disarming sweetness would soon win his son round. And his loyalty towards Chloë was commendable, he supposed. David had always been a cautious chap, fearful of change. That's what made him such a good insurance broker. A dark green Rolls halted beside him and Hermione was handed out.

'Collect us from here in an hour and a half, Hamilton,' she said. As the car glided away she turned to Sandy, 'My darling! Was your luncheon all right?'

'He was a bit cagey. But you'll win him round. Now then, take me to your pictures!'

They married a month later with only Andrew and Felicia for witnesses. 'Sir Alexander Gordon-Lockhart and Miss Hermione Staunton, quietly, at Chelsea Register Office' as the notice in *The Times* put it next day.

That evening they gave a champagne party at the Chelsea house for a score or so of friends and relations – many fewer than had milled around at the Ritz some two years ago. The marriage had come as a surprise to many of their guests. Rachel knew, of course, and so did Pixie and Randall. But Henrietta Birmingham had not been told ('Didn't want to set the family telephone wires humming,' Hermione explained) and nor, to his barely contained fury, had Vivian. The London property market was on the verge of collapse – he'd lose several thousand pounds on the flat and now he'd probably lose sexy little Sabrina as well. Might as well kiss goodbye to Chantry, too. Blast Hermione! Roderick and Gaye bore up bravely and decided the best tactic was to charm the old boy, who seemed a dear and had been a most distinguished diplomat in his time. Could have been worse. They mourned the loss of Chantry, which – surely? – they had almost secured for themselves and their daughters. *Why*, Sandy wondered, do people half one's age imagine that they alone hold the secrets of diplomacy and guile? This young Lamia coiling round him, dimpling and smiling so prettily: did she really think he'd never come across her kind before? He disengaged himself from Gaye and was accosted by Elizabeth Bridgewater.

'Mm, what gorgeous champagne! What *is* it?'

'Krug,' said Sandy. 'Glad you like it.'

'Is Krug one of the best?' she asked ingratiatingly.

'Medium-range,' he lied.

'*Jolly* nice though. Not bad at all. My husband always buys Sainsbury's own brand. I must tell him to try this. Now *do* tell me, Sir Alexander – oh, may I? how *nice* – Sandy then, I'm *dying* to know how you and Hermione *met*?'

Elizabeth, glad to have made a good impression, turned away to find Anne Bridgewater and pump her for information about the thieving Australians. All three seemed to have vanished without trace, which only went to prove the incompetence of the police and customs, since a large crescent-shaped object studded with more than four hundred diamonds could surely have been expected to show up on any airport's metal detector. (Their pursuers had forgotten the Australian passion for travel. Katie and her children, using some of the twenty-pound notes seized from Hermione's desk, had bought a camper van and travelled round southern Europe for several months before selling the Staunton tiara in Naples and hitching a lift the long way home on a cargo boat. None of them ever committed another crime. Rattie, her dental education amply paid for by the proceeds of the tiara, went on to become one of the country's leading orthodontists, practising under the name of 'Dr Raimonda Staunton'. Joe went on to direct spaghetti Westerns. The Staunton tiara went on to the head of a black-eyed Mafia bride.)

The last guest left just before midnight, when Sandy had held the last magnum of Krug upside down to prove that it was empty and the last angel on horseback had been retrieved from the last serving plate amid a carpet of wilting lettuce leaves.

'*Lovely* meeting you . . .' cooed the departing guests, full of champagne-induced goodwill. 'Marvellous to see you so *happy*, Hermione!'

Others, hoping to salvage something from this ill-timed liaison, declared, 'You must have dinner with us soon . . .'

'Yes, very soon,' said Sandy.

Rachel embraced them both lovingly.

'If only Hannah could have been here!' she said. 'She would have been happy for you. He's a lovely man, a *good* man!'

When they finally returned to the drawing room, young Andrew was waiting.

'Well done. Just want to do a quick check. Don't mind? I'm not staying.'

He rummaged in a briefcase, withdrew a stethoscope and pressure pump, and listened to her pulse, her heart, her breathing.

'Fine. All fine. Keep taking the tablets. And now, slipping off the mask of Cupid with some relief, I'm away – back to the hospital. Glad it went well. Congrats, both. 'Bye.'

They stood in the doorway watching the red Mini rattle away.

'He's a darling,' said Hermione.

'Best of the bunch,' agreed Sandy. 'Yours are a rum lot, aren't they?'

'I suppose they are, a bit. My great-nephew Vivian is really *frightful*.'

'Bloody good businessman though, I'd say.'

Now for my first act of wifely submission, she thought. A month ago I would have been tempted to point out that I am *also*, as he puts it, a bloody good business*woman*. Not even Sandy credits me with that.

'My beloved husband,' she answered, 'it's been a long day and I'm tired. Do you think we could have the post-mortem in the morning?'

Slowly, they climbed the stairs towards the marital bed.

They didn't even consider going on honeymoon. The very word seemed slightly ludicrous . . . moon, June, buffoon, honeymoon. Honeymoons were for shy young couples setting off with tin cans tied to the back of the car and a tissue-papered trousseau. Hermione and Sandy were impatient to get on with ordinary life. They had waited a long while for happiness and needed time to settle down to it, and each other.

Sometimes they reminisced about the long golden days when they had ranged the Dorset landscape under a high pale sky, untrammelled by stiff legs or bad backs, clothes or convention, tiredness or trepidation. It had been a perfect world.

'We had our paradise,' Hermione said. 'But did we know it at the time?'

'Part of the bliss was *not* knowing,' Sandy said. 'Thinking the whole of life would be that good.'

'And now it is. I never imagined I could be so sweetly happy. Every day is a gift.'

Gradually they worked out new pathways together, often by revisiting the old ones in the golden autumn landscape round Chantry and Otterbourne. Walking-sticks in hand, they trudged the lanes and drovers' paths between the hedgerows, pausing frequently so as not to tire Hermione. It would have been lovely to run uphill, climb trees, or roll through meadows but that energy belonged to the Major and Minor whom they didn't any longer need, blotted out – even surpassed – by their present selves.

Like detectives, they searched for clues to the missing years in between. Hermione dug out the visitors' albums that had been put away in the cupboard room beside the kitchen, the one called the honey pot, full of treasures that no one could bring themselves to discard. The books were bound in tooled leather. On the front in gold lettering was inscribed *Chantry Manor Visitors' Book* with dates: *1896–7, 1899* (a pregnant Violet), *1902* (a pregnant Phoebe), *1905* (Hermione made her first appearance, holding the hand of her nanny). Inside, on pages of thick grey cardboard edged in gold, visitors had signed their names, sometimes adding elaborate sketches or cartoons. Someone had stuck in the formally posed group photographs and amateur snapshots in sepia, dated and captioned them, often facetiously. The four people who featured most often were Jack and Phoebe, Violet and Donald. Through a magnifying glass Hermione and Sandy scrutinized their parents' faces searching for a complicit glance, the touch of a hand. Jack and Violet had been discreet; there was no trace of an illicit relationship, other than the frequent proximity of the two couples. But then, they had been nearest neighbours. Otterbourne was barely three miles away.

'How ever did they managed to carry on an affair? It isn't as though they can have spent the night in each other's houses. Living so close, no excuse for not going home.'

'Must have had trysting places in the park or the woods.'

'I'm surprised we never bumped into them!' Hermione smiled.

Sandy bent his head over the book again. 'I must say, darling, your mother was an absolute cracker!'

'I know . . .' Hermione said. Her head beside his, peering too, she went on, 'But doesn't she look sad – especially in the early ones? And *young*? Later on she just looks discontented.'

'Perhaps she knew?'

'I'm sure she didn't. Her pride wouldn't have stood for it.'

'Look at your – my – papa. Good God, in this picture he looks exactly like Murdo. You must meet Murdo, though it isn't easy: one never knows where to find him. He's a sort of Flying Dutchman; what they call a hippie nowadays, though he'll be forty this year. Might be anywhere . . . Kenya, Camberwell, California.'

'Do you suppose he's heard about us?'

'Can't imagine him reading *The Times*.'

'I'm curious to meet him. Specially if he looks like Papa. Oh Major – look – there's *you*!'

*

Hermione regretted having burned her mother's letters after her death. With Sandy's support she could have braced herself for any revelation. Besides, what could be left to learn? The catalogue of admirers, suitors, lovers, hangers-on, exploiters and ultimately gigolos was all too familiar. Phoebe's systematic campaign to deprive her of money, self-esteem or any control over her life had happened long ago. But one afternoon, taking down a book from the small boudoir next to her parents' bedroom (a bedroom she and Sandy had chosen not to use) she found two letters hidden between its pages. The first, in her mother's looping handwriting, was evidently a rough draft. It was written in pencil:

> June 1895
>
> My beloved,
> Misery compels me to break my word. I cannot remain silent. I must tell you that night and day I long for you, shut up in this prison with a man I can never love. My heart belongs to you and only you, for ever. I dream of you coming to my rescue, now that I do not even have our Child to console me. The Babe was lost – I suffered a miscarriage – I would *never* have let them take him from me. My husband does not reproach me. If he did I would refuse to speak to him. Oh adored and precious H, our Love is . . .

Hermione could not read further. The passion struggling to express itself in childish prose was pitiful. It revealed aspects of her mother – tenderness, pleading, despair – that she had never seen. The second letter, anonymous, undated, began:

> Dearest Little Girl,
> I received your letter and must rebuke you, as I once did in our pretty games, do you remember? I am vexed that you have broken our vow not to communicate. We are locked deep in one another's hearts for ever and a day but the World must never . . .

Again she could not go on. Should she show the letters to Sandy?

No, she decided. These old ashes should not be stirred up. Nor did she want to speculate that this was what had persuaded – compelled – Phoebe to marry her father, or guess at the duplicity involved. The four-square, shrewd yet emotional man posed next to his dazzling young wife in the earliest photographs could surely not have been tricked into an unwanted marriage, least of all by her mother's dour and disapproving family? She screwed up the letters and flushed them down the lavatory. Then she sat in the chair beside the window of the boudoir for a long time, staring out across the russet and gold autumn afternoon, past the copper beech towards the neatly trimmed maze. Here her mother must also have sat, like the Lady of Shalott, waiting for her Lancelot.

Hermione's thoughts ricocheted. This was a new explanation and surely the right one . . . a young girl seduced and abandoned by her lover, ostracized by her family, forced into an unwanted marriage. The sadness that veiled Phoebe's face in the photographs must have had its origins in that letter, with its hopeless plea for rescue. This would explain the thicket of dislike that had grown up between her parents, and between herself and her mother. Sleeping at its centre was the figure of a young girl, almost a child, cursed by her own flawless beauty. Understanding this, made generous by her present happiness, for the first time Hermione felt real sorrow over her mother's death. The old resentment had festered for nearly forty years until now – and now, at last, she was able to forgive. Poor Phoebe, desperate for youth even at sixty, waving from the sea to the laughing party on board, so close to the boat yet still not audible, bobbing, waving, shouting soundlessly . . .

Billy Brymer she had forgiven long ago, watching him die, knowing that he fell into a void leaving no posterity. She had been eighteen when he raped her. *Remember remember the Fifth of November* . . . not an easy date to forget, but a very long time ago. She had never talked to Sandy about that episode but one dank afternoon they were walking round the old stable yard discussing how some of the outbuildings might be turned into a weekend retreat for Andrew, perhaps Murdo as well. When it began to rain they sheltered in the garage workshop where the horses had once been stabled.

Hermione pointed to the hayloft and, trying not to put too much emphasis on the words, said, 'Up there's where Billy' – *raped? seduced?* – 'deflowered me.'

He stopped in his tracks and stared at her, shocked into abruptness. 'Billy who? What's this?'

'I ought to tell you just to get it out of the way, but I don't want you to be cross. It was such a long time ago. I can think of it quite calmly now – just as at last I can remember Richard without agony. I don't want to stir it up again. Billy Brymer – you know, used to be a groom – well, one Guy Fawkes night when I was eighteen, he tricked me into coming here with him and pushed me into the hay and . . .'

It was not so simple after all. She could not dismiss that violation. She felt tears rise to her eyes, a stifling, choking sensation in her throat. She controlled herself, turned and walked away, saying as casually as she could, 'That's it, really.'

Sandy did not follow.

'Hermione! Come here!'

She looked back. His face horror-struck, he stood rooted to the spot. She felt the welling ocean of tears she had never wept for the loss of innocence and trust, the end of dominion over her body, the beginning of disgust for her own flesh. If she released them now she would weep and weep and never stop – weep for the years of marriage she had never had, the children she had never borne, the beloved but in the end unsatisfactory substitutes with whom she had tried to compensate for having no flesh and blood progeny, no intimacy, no descendants, nobody. She would weep for Florabelle and Hannah, Billy and Betty and old Elias, the last of his line just as she was the last of hers. Except for Sandy, except for Sandy, *except for Sandy*. Through him and his sons the Staunton bloodline flowed on.

'There isn't any more to say.'

He took a few steps towards her and stopped, silenced by the weather pattern of emotions sweeping across her face.

'Hermione? Darling?'

'If you would just – *hug* me – I'll be all right. Shouldn't have said anything. There. Better now. Sorry.'

Why share what cannot be undone? Some things are best left unsaid, even to your nearest and dearest. Silence is so much harder than speech.

'All right now. Tea? And then the news? Come under the umbrella, then . . .'

Now she had a comforter, the only one she had ever wanted. Life had turned full circle and if only she had known this was how it would end, she could have borne the rest so much better. She took Sandy's arm, tucked herself under the umbrella against his warm side and with bent head watched her narrow feet avoiding the puddles and the flickering, bouncing raindrops. She knew Sandy wouldn't ask any more questions. As they entered the stone archway and eased off their galoshes on the boot-scraper by the front door he said, 'How about "Rhapsody in Blue"? Lot to be said for Gershwin . . .'

Hermione rang for Rosa and ordered tea and crumpets. Ten minutes later they were settled beside the fire in the drawing room with the gramophone playing, a cosy, baggy old pair in whom, to look at them, all passion was long spent.

'My poor love. All right now? This is better, isn't it? You looked shattered back there, for a moment. Mmm, scrumptious crumpets!'

She hated the music sliding about, its glib emotion and easy tricks, yet he was listening with real delight. Between men and women a chasm yawns, she thought; but at least we are shouting to each other across it, which is better than standing alone on the edge, peering down. All my life I have longed for a companion, a *husband* really. The man I have married is even closer than that – not only my lawful wedded husband but also my secret brother, my magnetic north. I have dragged this sad sack, my body, through seventy-two years and longed to join it to his. Now that I have done so – and in spite of the miracle of making love, which overwhelms and rejoices and tires me more or less equally – I find myself still alone. But not as lonely as my mother and father, living

351

side by side and hiding their secrets for twenty-five years; not alone like Florabelle, Rachel or Felicia; not forced by nature or fate to live a solitary life like Nicholas or Billy. I have come to understand families; the invisible ropes of blood that pulse like umbilical cords between us, whether we like it or not. In spite of everything I am alone. That is the human condition, inescapable; and judging from the small sinister quakes in my chest, before too long I shall die alone. In the meantime this warm familiar room and this beloved man are a haven of light in the darkness.

Seeing him looking at her, she smiled and stretched out her hand.

'More tea?'